THE WARRIOR WITCH

HAYDEN BLACK
AND THE
SALEM WITCH TRIALS

BOOK FIVE

B.C. TAYLOR

NOSLRAC PUBLISHING, LLC

Copyright Page

The Warrior Witch
Published by Noslrac Publishing, LLC

Cover designed by Alerim

ISBN 978-1-959090-31-1
Library of Congress Control Number: 2024905930
First Edition paperback 2024

Noslrac Publishing
authorBCtaylor@gmail.com
brooklynctaylor.com

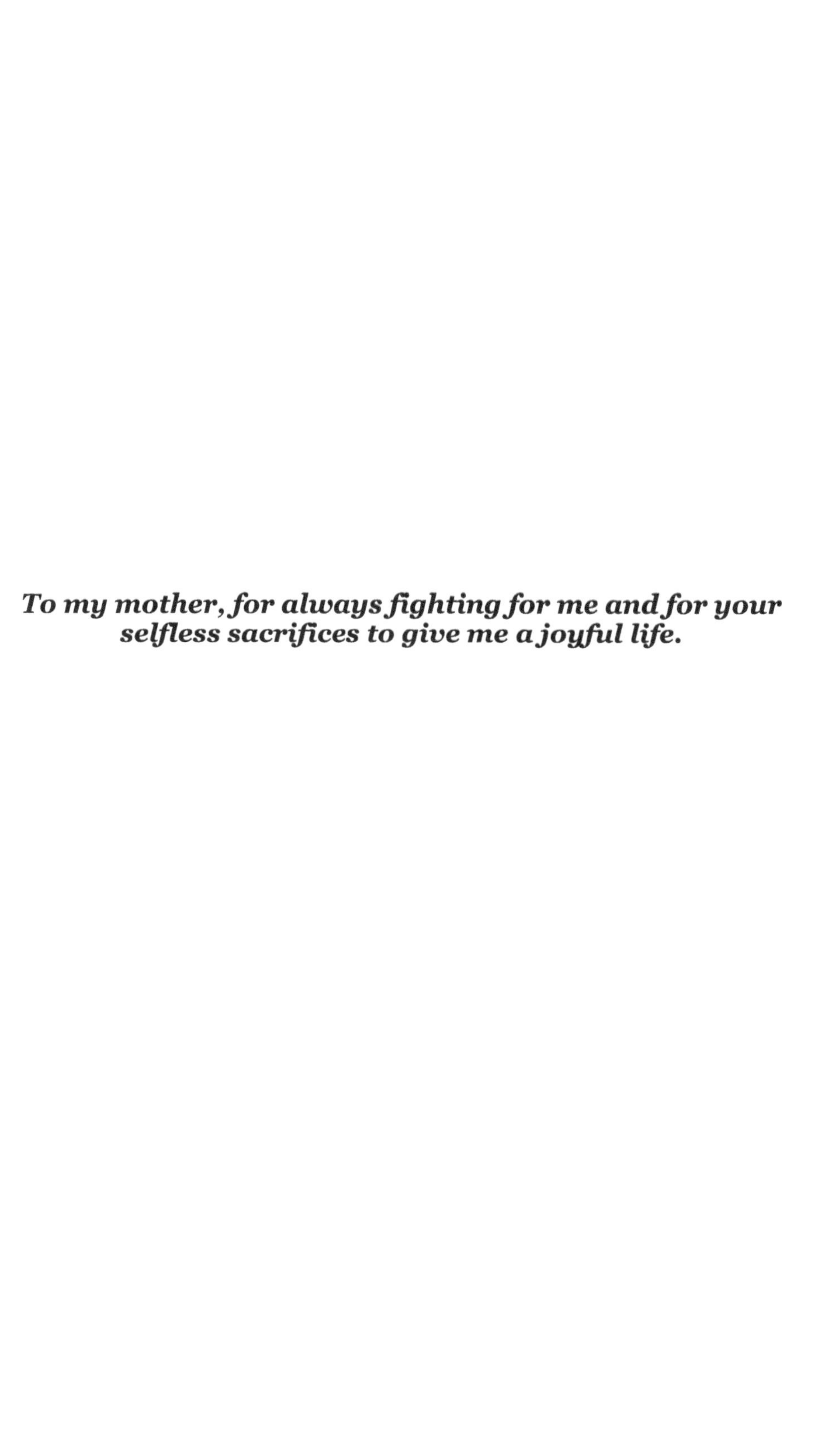

To my mother, for always fighting for me and for your selfless sacrifices to give me a joyful life.

Table of Contents

Reading Order

The Lost Witch

The Dark Mother

The Nephilim's Glory

The Earth's Curse

The Warrior Witch

The Salem Witch... Coming Oct. 2024

CHAPTER ONE

THERE ARE WEIRDER WAYS TO LEARN ABOUT DEATH

It was the wicked smile of doom as I stared into the eyes of Death herself.

I couldn't move fast enough, scrambling away from the personification of Death. Black lightning crackled to life, a bolt thicker than my leg shooting from my chest to blast Amara, my magic protecting me of its own accord.

But the lightning absorbed *into* her.

Gaping, I stood beside Jamie, reaching a hand to meet his open palm, our fingers intertwining.

How could we escape Death herself?

"Do not be afraid, Hayden." Amara's voice was a sickeningly melodious song rolling off her tongue, a deadly weapon to lull her victims into a false sense of security.

White holy flames sizzled from Jamie's hands in a torrent to attack Amara, but as the inferno reached her, the white flames swirled around her in an ineffectual blaze until they, too, were consumed.

A raging squall of wind tore through the sanctuary, but despite Apalla's power, the air parted around Amara. Even the beams of sunlight radiating from the Prophetess's hands seemed to soak into Death's body, like nothing from this worldly realm could harm her.

"We're all going to die," Kelsey said callously.

I shot her a glare. "Not helping, dude."

She shrugged. "Just calling it like I see it."

"You are not destined to die today," Amara declared, her spine straight as a rod as she slipped her hands into the black sleeves of her robes hanging off her arms.

"Gee, thanks, Death. That's really reassuring coming from you," I retorted sarcastically. "Because Death is so honest about when it's going to claim your soul."

"Yes, I am," Amara said without inflection. "Death has never hidden its truth from the world. It is unflinchingly honest, and mortals fear the painful truth, not a lie wrapped in a pretty façade. I have no reason to lie to you. If I wanted you to die, you would already be dead, and not even *you* can stop me."

She spoke about death with an ease that chilled my bones, and I had to forcibly stop myself from shivering. But a shudder ran through the others. Amara's words were unsettling to all us mortals, yet they rang eerily true.

"If you aren't here to kill us, then why are you here?" I questioned, letting black lightning spark at my fingertips.

Not that it would do anything against Amara, but having Spirit magic close made me feel braver. Because that's what the black lightning was—Spirit magic. I had always had access to it, but after passing my Earth Trial, it was so much *more*.

She cocked her head. "Is it not obvious?"

Everyone except Thea shook their heads. The Heart of Earth was the only one who seemed to know what was going on. Thanks for the warning, Thea.

"I am here to train you."

I blinked at her in surprise. "What?"

"Train her?" Jamie echoed from beside me, still gripping his flaming broadsword in one hand with mine clasped tightly in his other.

"You can't mean..." Apalla trailed off, her hazel eyes growing wide as she glanced between me and Amara. "Of course!"

"Wanna explain, Palla?" I asked, not taking my eyes off Death.

"Death was the first master of Spirit," Apalla said in awe. "You're going to train Hayden to harness the power of Spirit."

"What?" I asked, glancing at Apalla in shock. "What?" I repeated as I swiveled my head to stare at Amara, who simply nodded. "But how? Death is... well, dead. And Spirit... it's alive."

"As your friend said, Death was the first to master Spirit. Other than the Creator, of course. For Spirit can give life as surely as it can take it away. You must master life and death to truly master the element of Spirit. And who better to teach you than Death herself?"

Nausea rolled in my stomach, and Spirit stirred my soul. Amara spoke the truth.

"Why help me?" I demanded, keeping my guard up despite the whisper zinging through me that said I could trust Amara. But this knowing... it was disconcerting. I knew it was Spirit, but it was hard to trust what I was hearing.... Was I even hearing it correctly? "Isn't death aligned with Darkness?"

"That is not so," Amara said with a simple shake of her head. "Death is a neutral entity. I am not aligned with Lilith. Death cannot exist without life, but souls are eternal. When a mortal body perishes here on Earth, I usher the immortal soul to the Garden. I am neither good nor evil, light nor dark, but a certain truth.

"My very existence is a result of Lilith. For when she fell from Grace, I was created to end her, a task that has been impossible as the Mother of Demons is both immortal and invincible. But you... you, Hayden, will be the one to defeat her, and at last, I shall ferry her soul across the veil, wherever she is to end up. So, yes, I am here to help you because I will finally claim the first soul who has escaped me for eons."

The truth of her words rang through me like an echo in my soul as Spirit, the keeper of the secrets of the Universe, caressed my own spirit, speaking intimately the words told by the oracle long ago. After Harbor's sacrifice, I had thought the Oracle meant those words for the Nephilim, but as I stood face to face with Death, I realized the words were meant for me.

"Death is your gift," I murmured under my breath, my piercing blue gaze considering Amara in a new light.

Amara inclined her head in a nod of acknowledgement. "I look forward to helping you master the ultimate power of the Universe."

"Hayden," Jamie snapped my name as he ripped his hand from mine. "You can't seriously be considering this." He gestured at Amara, his royal blue eyes boring into me. "She's *Death*."

"What other choice do I have?" I quipped.

"You're welcoming Death to Asylum. I get that you're a demon and Darkness doesn't bother you like it does the rest of us, but Hayden, it's *Death*. She can kill us all."

"So can Lilith," I shot back. "At least Amara is on our side."

"Force her to leave Asylum. You have the power of *five* elements. You can fight her."

"Death doesn't *die*, Jamie," I argued. "What are we going to do? Kill her?" I said with an eye roll.

"Tell her that you don't want her help," he raged back at me with a fury like fire.

"No, James," I snapped, my voice layered with the voice of the angels, a tone that brooked no argument as I used his full name—a right only afforded to his mother and sister. "I will not turn away the only master who can teach me Spirit magic. Kova is *gone*," I emphasized. "Who else can teach me?"

"She has a point," Kelsey said, flicking her platinum blonde hair over her shoulder as she casually leaned a hip against the altar, as though Death in our midst didn't scare her in the slightest. Then again, Kelsey was the type of woman to look Death in the face and say, "No, not today," and survive the encounter.

"But is it wise?" Isleen questioned, earning muttered agreements from the Council adults gathered in the room.

"You could learn on your own," Amara offered, unfazed by the insults thrown about her as we debated right in front of her. She shrugged like it didn't matter either way. "Spirit knows all things, and with the power unlocked, it will speak knowledge to you."

"Then why come here at all?" Apalla asked with more curiosity than accusation in her tone.

"Because I can teach you faster," she stated factually. "Spirit is not hindered by Itself, but by the minds of the mortal it speaks to. Already, Hayden has questioned the words of wisdom from Spirit, and so, she shall always wonder if she hears correctly. The power of Spirit is so great, it will likely drive her mad before she can master the element."

My face paled three shades as the blood drained from my head. How did Kova not lose her mind when she was training for her Spirit Trial when she was Alice Parker, the Reigning Salem Witch?

"Alice did not have a teacher, but she had her mother, whose voice frequently guided Alice. Because of her intimate ties to Heaven and that she knew who her celestial parent was, Spirit did not overwhelm her. But the vast power of Spirit overwhelms mortals without heavenly knowledge in ways that you are not prepared for unless you master the element quickly."

Power sizzled over my skin like electricity, and I knew Amara was right. Spirit wasn't like the other elements. It was stronger, more potent, more powerful... just *more*.

"Thea?" I must have been crazy because I turned my back on Death to face the twelve-year-old child goddess. Twelve years old... the same age I was when Gabriel claimed me as the Salem Witch. The Heart of Earth's green eyes snapped to mine, glowing with the full power she wielded in stark contrast to their dimness before we traveled to Lilith's Island. "What do you think?"

The child goddess smiled knowingly. "I cannot make this decision for you, Hayden. But I advise you to listen to the voice of Spirit within you. It will not lead you astray."

"But how do I know if it's my voice or Spirit's?" I asked with a whine, the words sounding hoarse.

But all Thea offered was a smile.

Throwing my shoulders back, I shook out my jagged black locks as I met Amara's creepy red eyes. Trusting my intuition over the voices of advice pounding into me from all directions, I announced, "I will train Spirit magic with you."

Shouts rang out, echoing against the cathedral walls so I couldn't separate one voice from another. Not that it mattered, as everyone except Kelsey and Thea shouted absurdities at me, condemning my choice to accept Death.

Jamie's hands clamped around my deltoids, and he shook me, his voice cutting through the others' and silencing their objections. "Are you absolutely *insane*, Haywire? I know the pain you're going through. I know your grief, but are you seriously suicidal enough to welcome Death into your life?"

I rolled my eyes at the flaws in their logic. They wanted me to deny Amara's help, but without it, we would all be doomed to die at Lilith's hand.

"I'm not suicidal, Jamie," I snarled, ripping free of his grasp. "Just the opposite, actually, since I prefer to master Spirit than let the power drive me insane."

"Look at her, Hayden. How can you possibly trust something that looks like *that*?" Apalla berated. "Just her physical appearance is petrifying."

Gray light flashed as Amara shifted her appearance. The woman with porcelain skin and blood red eyes disappeared and a little girl with candy-apple red hair, jade green eyes, and deeply tanned skin stood in her place.

"Would you prefer I resume this appearance?"

"Nope."

"No."

"Definitely not."

"Seriously?" I asked the others. "What's wrong with this look?"

Apalla shivered. "It's *way* creepier when Death is a little girl."

"I'd rather see her true form, so I remember whom I'm dealing with," Jamie grumbled.

Amara shrugged her little shoulders, and gray light flashed again as she returned to her adult form. The only thing that remained the same about her appearance was the vibrant color of her red hair, and her facial features were the same, but aged to thirty-three.

"I didn't mind the human look," I mumbled under my breath, but didn't mention how unsettling I found Amara's adult form.

"You're seriously going to train with Death?" Apalla accused.

I opened my mouth to retort a savage reply but was cut off.

"Seriously, though, how many powerful witches can randomly appear in the woods? Like, please tell me this is the last one."

The room stared at Kelsey as she rolled her eyes. For as much as I disregarded the rules, Kelsey leaped over lines of etiquette, the consequences irrelevant, like they didn't apply to her. Or at the least, she wasn't afraid Death would smite her.

"What?" She shrugged, slapping her hands on her hips. "It's not like I'm wrong. First, Hayden shows up and is declared as the Salem Witch. Then the Heart of Earth, then Silas. And now, Death?" She flailed her arms at Amara, then waved a hand at me. "Common denominator—Hayden. It all started with you."

"Thanks, Kels," I replied drily. "That really makes me feel better."

"I'm just saying, I'm fine with Death, but I hope Amara is the last supernatural being to—"

Alarms blared as the Spellery bells rang.

Power zapped through my body in response, like Spirit was as alert as I was.

"Lilith," I growled. "She's at the wards."

"What?" Jamie's gaze snapped to mine as I tightened my grip on my weapons. "How do you know that?"

"I—" I began to respond, then faltered. With a shake of my head that sent my uneven hair flying, I said, "I don't know. I just do."

"Spirit speaks to you, always. Even when you are not aware of it."

I cast a wary glance at Amara, then nudged Jamie with my elbow, prompting him to grip my arm.

Red light flashed around us, and the sweet tang of smoke stung my nostrils as my filthy, blood-splattered combats slammed into the ground on the east side of Asylum.

The sight nearly brought me to my knees.

Demons swarmed inside Asylum, charging through a gaping hole in the wards. The wards were normally clear, allowing us to see outside to the Briar Woods surrounding the town. The magic was so potent, any witch could detect the wards with magic. But not anymore.

A sheet of smoke separated Asylum from the outside world, except for the massive hole ripped in the wards, a purple hue tingeing the edges as Lilith's magic held the wards agape for her demons to surge into our once protected town. Demons crashed into exhausted Knights, who had barely recovered from the battle waged at Lilith's Island.

How were we going to survive this?

How was Lilith doing this?

And then my eyes fell on the Dark Mother where she lounged on a throne of bones held aloft on a palatine carried by pit demons, her tattoo of a writhing snake biting into a golden apple on full display where it was inked on her chest.

On either side of her, four more pit demons carried a wooden cross in the shape of an X. To her left, my mother hung from the cross I had seen her nailed to earlier. But on the right... I nearly vomited at the sight of Kova's bloodied face, swollen and bruised past recognition.

I only knew it was her because of the fiery red hair. She hung limply from the cross, unconscious.

Lilith didn't just possess the power of the Mother and the Crone. She possessed the power of a fully realized Salem Witch.

"Oh, Kova." Apalla gasped from beside me. "No." She covered her mouth with a hand, choking back a sob.

An agony demon leaped at her. Jamie whipped his broadsword up and outward in an arc with frightening speed. His blade sank into the fleshiest part of the demon, black blood splattering. But agony demons' weak point were their eyes. That or beheading them were the only ways to kill the grotesque demons.

The agony demon howled and struck at him, backhanding Jamie so he flew to the side.

I reacted without thinking, whipping out with my air magic to catch him. A bolt of black lightning shot from my open palm, zapping the agony demon. Electricity sparked, and in a flash, the agony demon was dusted.

Lowering my sword, I gazed at my open palm as smoke drifted off the smooth, pale skin. Jamie reappeared at my side in a flash of red, staring at me with wide eyes.

Lifting Nightmare with a new determination, I fixed my penetrating gaze on Kova crucified to a cross alongside my mother.

Thrusting my foreboding black blade into the air as a warning to my enemies and a beacon of hope to my allies, I shouted the only thing I could think of to rally my troops.

"Arcana, attack!"

A roar resounded through Asylum as witches attacked with renewed purpose. My broken, sparse forces charged forward like a bull at a matador.

Chaos and thunder sounded as the tides of Light and Dark collided, and I was lost to the battle, stabbing and slashing and cutting and blocking and slaughtering enemy demons as I wielded sword and sorcery with unparalleled strength. Demons fell by the dozens to my hand and crumbled under the magic of my circle.

Knights fought with bitter resentment against the Darkness infiltrating our home. Purpose filled their hearts as they commanded their elements, our gifts from the Divine, against the dark magic of Lilith's army, even as droplets of red blood fanned through the air.

Witches slashed and hacked, spraying black blood on their clothes and skin as their sharpened blades pierced dark flesh.

But little by little, we yielded to Lilith's army as our Knights faltered under the unrelenting force of demons.

"Hayden," Apalla shouted, pointing at the Knights behind us. "We're falling back."

After barely surviving Lilith's Island, the witches of Asylum couldn't keep with the pace of this battle. And Lilith constantly had refreshed forces. Unlimited refreshed forces.

My circle and I were more than pulling our weight, protecting Knights wherever we could while constantly diving into the mass of demons standing between us and Kova.

But my circle couldn't be everywhere at once. We couldn't protect everyone, and if we didn't do something soon, everyone would be dead before I could free Kova. The only reason we weren't yet was because Spirit magic seemed to be protecting Kova's free will from Lilith's clutches.

"We need a plan," Jamie said, diving under the swing of a pit demon's club before sinking his blade into its abdomen.

I spun in a circle, blasting off shots of my four elements as I frantically wracked my brain for a plan. Any plan.

"I have an idea."

"Is it a good one?" Kelsey quipped.

"I have an idea."

"Haywire," Jamie growled, crossing his blade with another two pit demons.

"I know, I know," I shouted, yanking at my jagged hair with a hand. "I'm trying... but until we seal the wards, we're sitting ducks. And we can't hack our way through all the demons.... I have to get behind enemy lines."

Jamie spun to face me, a look of devastation painting his face. It was hopeless. And we both knew it. Jamie could spook us to the hole in the wards, and I could cast a ring of holy flames around us to protect us from the demons, but we didn't know how to seal the wards. And in the amount of time it would take us to repel Lilith, how many more Knights would fall?

The only solution was to fight.

Angel Boy and I shared a look. We would fight to the bitter end. Together.

Thea tugged on my jacket sleeve and pointed at the wards. "Hayden, look."

Something miraculous was happening.

Lilith's forces began to fall from the rear lines within the wards of Asylum. Her army stretched endlessly beyond the wards, but something attacked her army at the entrance, surrounding the immediate threat as the Knights pulled back under the onslaught of demons.

"Let me guess, you caused it, Haywire?"

I shot him a wicked grin. "As much as I want to take the credit for this, it isn't me, Angel Boy." My face twisted in confusion. So, who was doing this?

And then my magic sensed the presence of my loyal demons, revealing themselves at long last to the Dark Mother they had once served, openly defying her as they fought furiously for their freedom.

"For Asylum," roared the feral voice of a black panther. "Attack!" Jackal shouted as he led the charge of my demons against the brethren they once called brothers.

Lilith shot to her feet. Her dark purple eyes narrowed on my army of demons as her lips curved in a snarl. Her mouth opened, and Spirit crashed into me.

She was about to use the Voice of Command.

I had to stop her.

Five elements combined into a ball of white light in my palm, and I raised my hand. But I wasn't fast enough.

A serpentine smile twisted her red-painted lips.

My heart dropped into my stomach.

"Demons," Lilith shouted, the power of her Voice of Command rippling through Asylum, and I felt the magic of the demonic hierarchy rippling through my blood. "If you side with Hayden Black, stand down, and allow the demons loyal to Hell to *end you*, as you so deserve."

"No!" I screeched bloody murder.

Lilith had taken everything from me. I wouldn't allow her to take Jackal and my other demons from me.

I threw myself in front of Jackal as he froze in a crouch. Nightmare flashed through the air as I severed an agony demon's head from its shoulders. The white light I had summoned in my hands detonated like a bomb of heavenly magic.

Black lightning exploded from me like a thunderstorm ripping through the land. Magic unlike anything I had ever wielded before rippled outward to slam into my loyal demons. Spirit was death to a soulless being, but Spirit didn't kill my demons. It *protected* them.

Cages of black lightning crackled around my demons, not to confine them, but to save them from Lilith's demons. Helplessly frozen by Lilith's command, it was the only way they would survive this battle. I hadn't even known what I was doing when I unleashed the Spirit magic.

The fifth element just did it, like it had a consciousness of its own and knew what I wanted before I did.

Dark purple eyes flashed in the darkness as Lilith glared at me. Snapping her fingers, she called, "Elliot." Flourishing a hand at me, she growled, "Handle her."

Elliot stepped forward, the shadows peeling off him as he emerged from the lingering darkness just beyond the wards, his rapier blade in hand. Scowling, he started toward me, shoving and pushing demons out of his way until they noticed his charge and split in a wave to let him approach.

This wouldn't be much of a match.

Prowling forward with the predatorial intensity of a wild jungle cat, I met his first strike with my black Nightmare.

Elliot's thin rapier clashed against my blade with unexpected force. My teeth ground together as the force rattled my bones.

He was stronger. Stronger than he had been on Samhain. Where was he getting this extra power?

Even with his extraordinary strength, Elliot was a mediocre opponent at best. Underhanded, conniving, and a dirty fighter—yes. But a good fighter? No.

"The Dark Mother will defeat you," he insisted, and stabbed his rapier at my heart.

Instinctively, I parried as I used the elements to blast away the demons converging on the nearby Knights.

"And I cannot wait to watch her crucify you to a cross next to the others." He hissed venomously, like the lowlife scoundrel he was.

I smirked maniacally at the delusional demon-channeling witch. "And I cannot wait to use the full power of the Salem Witch to strip you of your powers, once and for all." Another strike of his rapier bounced off Nightmare as I met his attack with unfazed ease. "I can't decide who I'm going to end first—you or Lilith. I think I'll save you for last, so I can watch the fear in your eyes as you realize the might of the power I wield at the behest of the Creator. And once you are good and truly terrified of God and Goddess, only then will I destroy this dark power of yours and leave you with *nothing*."

"Over my dead body," Elliot growled.

I grinned wickedly. "Okay then."

Thrusting forward, I buried Nightmare into his gut, piercing through his soft, vulnerable flesh. Blood gushed from his wound, and my eyes widened in surprise. His blood wasn't dark maroon. It was black.

My eyes snapped up to meet his black orbs.

"Oof."

Dark magic blasted into me, and I tumbled heels over head through the air until my back smashed against a tree, and I crumpled to the ground.

Coughing, I forced myself to standing and held my hand open, summoning Nightmare to it. Ripping out of Elliot's abdomen, it cut a fresh wound through his side before sailing through the air to slam into my palm.

Jamie appeared at my side in a flash of red, Apalla clutching his hand.

"Are you okay?"

I nodded. "Elliot's blood is black." I met Jamie's wide royal blue eyes, then searched Apalla's hazel ones for answers. "How is that possible?"

Jamie's mouth dropped open, but no words came out.

"Blood has positive or negative energy because it carries the aura of the person," Apalla said. "That's why you bleed red, while Lil-Lilith bleeds black. It could be simply because he is aligned with the Mother of Demons."

I shook my head, turning to glare at Elliot as he retreated across the battlefield. "I don't think so. Remember Samhain? He's grown more powerful, and not by natural means. There's something satanic about him—like he's devolving into a demon."

The air grew taut at my words, as though the element itself were unsettled by the possibility.

"We can't do anything about it right now," Jamie said. "Let him retreat. The Knights need our help."

Together, we plunged into the chaos of battle.

Stabbing and slashing with Nightmare and my amulet athame, I gutted demon after demon in a relentless torrent of blades combined with elemental magic. The powers of air, fire, water, earth, and lightning mingled together, working together without my command as they fought on my behalf. I was a raging storm, untouchable by the demons that pursued me.

But some demons were smart and attacked my exhausted Knights, who were drained of their magic from the battle on Lilith's Island.

But I was faster and smarter and more powerful.

Wherever a demon attacked, my elemental storm met their blow, protecting the Knights so they could flee.

But it wasn't enough. For as much power as I wielded, plowing through battalions of demons, there was always another to take the last one's place. Lilith had an endless supply of pawns to throw at us. And while I could prevail, Asylum could not.

"Hayden," Jamie roared as he slashed through another two demons, severing their torsos from their legs. The demons fell to the ground in four pieces, decaying rapidly into dust. "We're being overwhelmed. Lilith is going to take Asylum."

My gaze scanned the battlefield, scrutinizing every detail of the war waging mercilessly around me. The Knights couldn't hold out much longer, and we had suffered too many wounds and casualties.... But without the wards, we were at the mercy of Lilith and her army.... As if she had any.

We needed to expel her from the wards. The wards Kova had created with her Nephilim and Salem Witch magics mixed with Olde Earth Magic from Apalla's tribe.

My eyes flicked to Apalla, then Jamie, then Thea.

A cunningly brilliant idea drifted through my mind, like Spirit spoke the answer directly to my soul.

"If you give me a minute, I think I can make this worse."

"Not the time, Haywire." Jamie grunted as he shoved his sword through the mouth of a charging hellhound.

"I was being serious, Angel Boy," I said as black lightning blasted from my hand, the Spirit magic more natural and intuitive than any of the elements I wielded before it. More natural than fire. A grin pulled at my lips as I curled my hand into a fist. "I meant I can make this worse *for Lilith*."

"Worse?" Apalla scoffed. "She's kicking out butts."

"For now."

"For now?" Kelsey shrieked the words back at me. "What do you mean for—"

Sucking in a breath, I summoned my air magic to boom out of me. "RETREAT. ASYLUM RETREAT."

Jamie looked at me, aghast. "Hayden, are you crazy? We can't yield to her."

"Trust me on this one, Angel Boy. Where there's a witch, there's a way." I winked a mischievous wink at him, hoping he got my message. "Fetch Ethan, would you? We need a complete circle."

He disappeared in a flash of red light.

"Thea, you know Olde Earth Magic, right? You transferred the knowledge to this mortal body?" I asked as she directed a beam of green light from her staff to blast a horde of demons charging for a legion of Knights.

"Yes." She didn't miss a beat as her freshly renewed power slammed into a row of slate-covered brimstone demons.

"Get ready. Apalla—get that gold and pink magic ready. I need a celestial touch from you, Jamie, and Thea."

Red light flashed as Jamie materialized in front of me... without Ethan.

"Where is—"

Jamie shook his head. "Ethan's tapped out. All the healers are. They've drained themselves mending the injuries from the battles. Any healer still standing is out here"—he gestured to the battle raging around us—"preventing casualties."

"I need a water elemental, Jamie," I yelled. "I can't do this without a full circle."

"There isn't one, Hayden," he snapped back. "The only one I can think of is Naida, and—"

"Absolutely not."

"Exactly, so what do you want me to do about it?"

A current from the Universe flowed unhindered around me, tapping me on the shoulder. It was as if time slowed as Spirit imparted Its knowledge, and I turned, my jagged hair fanning out around me, my eyes landing on a dark-haired girl fighting with sword and sorcery on the battlefield below us.

My hand shot out, wrapping around Jamie's forearm. Wordlessly, I raised my longsword to point at the girl fighting furiously against the dark forces surrounding her. Jamie followed my line of sight, then freed himself from my grasp and disappeared in a flash of light. I watched as he re-materialized next to the girl, stabbed the demon bearing down on her, then wrapped an arm around her and spooked to my side.

"Dani Sanchez." I scanned her from head to toe, searching for injuries, but all I found was black blood and dust.

Wide-eyed and breathless from exhilaration, she glanced between me and Jamie, confusion etched across her features.

"I need a water elemental," I explained. "You're up, kid."

Her lips parted slightly as her eyes widened further. "I-I... you want me?" she asked incredulously.

"You're filling in for Ethan," I said, sheathing my athame.

"What is it we're doing, exactly?" Apalla asked, launching another volley of scarily precise arrows at Lilith's demons.

"When Kova founded Asylum, she combined her Nephilim magic with the Olde Earth Magic of your tribe. We have Olde Earth Magic"—I pointed a finger at the Heart of Earth, then at Jamie—"we have a Nephilim, a witch descended from the Winnebago Tribe"—I gestured at Apalla, then at myself—"and a Salem Witch. Dani completes the circle with her water magic."

"You want to recreate her spell," Kelsey said, her voice slightly breathless. "Can you do that?"

"Not exactly. We're going to re-create the spell to seal the hole in the wards and revoke Kova's access by basing the wards on our magic instead of hers. Even with the power of the Salem Witch, Lilith can't penetrate our magic."

"Why not free Kova?" Dani asked.

Regret lanced through me as I shared a look with my circle. I wanted to save Kova and my mom more than anything. Spirit filled me, pouring into me constantly and reviving the magic within my body. But my circle... they were exhausted. It would take more than a few hours for them to regain their full powers, and as worn down as we looked, I knew we felt even worse.

One advantage we had was that Lilith hadn't crossed to this side of the wards yet. If we sealed them now, she was still outside the boundaries of Asylum.

"Because if we fight Lilith like this, we will lose," I told her honestly. "But casting a circle... it gives us a fighting chance to save Asylum so we can live to save Kova another day."

Dani pursed her lips and begrudgingly agreed. "What's the spell?"

"Palla?" I asked.

Her eyes flashed gold on command as she searched her visions for a suitable spell. "Got it."

"Kelsey, can you—?"

Before I finished speaking, Kelsey opened a channel of communication, telepathically transferring the spell in Apalla's mind to mine.

"Let's do this."

I sheathed Nightmare and cast a circle of holy flames around us.

I call upon the element of air,
Here and now, I cast this spell,
Bind the wards and seal them well,
With breeze from Heaven to blow away Hell.

Air blasted in a raging squall, the wind tinged with Apalla's pink magic as it seeped into the wards. Sunlight glimmered as her Daughter of Apollo powers fueled the magic. The edges of the hole in the wards shrank as the first of the five elements worked its magic.

I call upon the element of fire,
Here and now, I cast this spell,
Bind the wards and seal them well,
With flames from Heaven to burn away Hell.

Forked tongues of white fire sparked as Jamie unleashed his element, pushing his holy power to merge with Apalla's air and sink into the wards, closing the hole further as the elements heightened one another.

I call upon the element of water,
Here and now, I cast this spell,
Bind the wards and seal them well,
With rains from Heaven to wash away Hell.

Horizontal rain pummeled against the wards, each drop sinking into Kova's magic and expanding the wards to shrink the hole. Water magic exponentially increased the power of the first two elements, each building off the last as a circle grew greater than the sum of its parts.

I call upon the element of earth,
Here and now, I cast this spell,
Bind the wards and seal them well,
With vines from Heaven to prune away Hell.

Vines writhed and flowers bloomed and plants protruded from the soil, releasing spores. Pollen floated through the air with leaves and flower petals to press against the wards, sealing them further.

One last push, and our combined elemental, celestial, and Salem Witch magic would seal the wards.

I call upon the element of Spirit,
Here and now, I cast this spell,
Bind the wards and seal them well,
With Soul from Heaven to overpower Hell.

Thunder cracked in the sky as black lightning charged the air with electricity. Static shock zapped the wards as the white light of Spirit merged with the other four elements to seal the hole. As the wards slammed shut, dusting demons as the protective magic closed on their bodies and cut them in half, a sonic wave of power blasted outward, sweeping through our circle to crash into demons with unrelenting force.

Lilith screamed an infernal shriek from the other side of the wards as she pounded her fists against the hard wall of the elements.

"Hayden," Apalla called, "the demons." She gestured to the Knights and witches fighting bitterly against the dark beings still within the wards. On the defense, our military didn't counter a single blow and barely blocked the attacks from fangs and claws.

"Apalla, Thea—cover the Knights while they flee. Dani—get out of here."

"But I can—"

"Now," I commanded, the fierceness of my tone brooking no argument.

Apalla dove into the crowd of demons, sunlight blasting them as she cleared a path with Thea right behind her, using her staff to wield her green magic.

Dani chased after them, using her water like a whip.

Offering my hand to Jamie, I said, "Spook me to the center of those demons."

Jamie spooked us into the chaos—the center of Lilith's demons inside the wards.

"Get outta here, Angel Boy."

"But Hayden—"

"I don't want to accidentally fry you to a crisp, Jamie. And I don't trust myself yet since I just unlocked the full extent of my Spirit powers."

Eyes widening, Jamie gulped, then nodded before disappearing in a flash of red.

A wicked grin danced across my face as I cracked my knuckles, summoning my magic to the surface to dance over my skin. Black lightning ricocheted out of me, shooting in every direction, leaping from demon to demon, eliciting agonized shriek after shriek before dusting the demons into oblivion.

As the lightning drained the power from my body—this terrible, mighty power—Spirit just as quickly refilled the sea of energy swimming in my belly.

The lightning zapped and crackled through the air, and before the sparks could cease, Spirit shot more lightning from my body. Power ripped out of me in a final explosion of white light and black lightning that flickered through the night sky with a resounding clap of thunder.

Silence blanketed the world.

All that remained was ash floating on the wind.

Then the pounding of Lilith's fists against the barrier of the wards like a petulant child beating their hands against the ground in a temper tantrum.

With deadly calm, a killer calm, I spun on my heel, opened my hand and thrust it forward. A bolt of lightning exploded from my palm with such force, a current of air whooshed through my jagged hair as the bolt cut through the dark night, streaking as it shattered into Lilith.

The Mother of Demons flew backward with such power, she crashed into a tree, felling it, and kept flying, hitting tree after tree until she finally hit the ground.

Convulsing on the forest floor, her body smoked from the sting of my lightning, but I couldn't find it within me to feel sorry, except for the pain I caused the trees.

"Hayden," Thea admonished from afar.

"Sorry, Thea," I shouted the apology.

Lilith wouldn't be rising anytime soon, and my wards locked her out of Asylum. Her demon army that made it inside was destroyed, but my people were exhausted.

"Go home, everyone," I commanded. "We are safe now." My eyes met Apalla's as my circle rejoined me. Gold flashed through her hazel eyes, and she nodded in confirmation.

Knowing Asylum was safe, I felt exhaustion begin to claim me. All I wanted to do was go home and sit in the comfort of my dog—

My heart nearly stopped. Tears pooled in my eyes, but I couldn't cry. Not yet. Not as Jamie took my hand and spooked us to the cathedral to reconvene with the Athenian Council.

Amara stood still as a statue. During the battle, Amara hadn't moved a muscle, which just made her creepier.

"Well done, Hayden." Amara inclined her head as she slipped her hands out of her open-armed robes and spread her arms. "You wield the magic of Spirit naturally for having just unlocked the power. Our training will be fruitful these next seven months."

"Uh, thanks," I responded wearily.

Brain fog crept in as my eyelids grew heavy. Despite the regenerating power of Spirit, I was ready to crash, and it had nothing to do with the physical toll of fighting, but the emotional.

The double doors to the cathedral crashed open, and Isleen, followed by Kane and an escort of Knights, stormed up the aisle to where I stood. Cold determination shone in her pale eyes.

"Ah, crap," I groaned. "What did I do wrong this time?"

Jamie snorted next to me.

Apalla's eyes flashed gold, and an amused smile tugged at her lips.

"It takes a special kind of idiot to pull off what you just did," Isleen lectured. Grabbing me by the shoulder, she pulled me into a tight embrace. "Thank Goddess that you're as shrewd and cunning as your mother. We might have a shot at winning this war, despite Lilith's advantages."

"Thanks." I grinned sheepishly. With hunched shoulders and a broken spirit, I spun on my heel, dried dirt crunching off the treads of my combat boots as I turned to leave.

The threat was terminated. Lilith couldn't penetrate the wards, and I was done. Done with the Council, done with my friends, done with... just done.

"Hayden, we need to talk about—"

"No," I interrupted her, swiping a hand through the air. "No, Isleen." My shoulders slumped as the weight of the last two battles weighed on me. "I made my decision about Amara, and I'm sticking with it. There's nothing left to discuss. I want to go home," I finished, half pleading, half demanding.

"Despite your status as the Reigning Salem Witch, we do not consider this to be a reasonable request.... Permitting Death to live within these wards... it's beyond foolish. It's—"

I detonated like a bomb. "Does the end of humanity sound like a better option to you, Isleen?" I whirled around to face her daughter. "You can see the future. Tell me, Apalla, what does it look like if I reject Amara's help?"

Golden light flashed in her hazel eyes, and a mask of horror claimed her face.

"That's what I thought," I growled, turning back to Isleen and the rest of the Council. "Kova survived Spirit alone because she is *Nephilim*. I don't have that advantage. In fact, I'm the exact opposite. A demon princess with the power of Spirit." I laughed humorlessly, the noise hoarse as it croaked from my throat. "And if I don't learn to control the power soon, I'll descend into a mad, raving lunatic. Unless the future says differently?" I demanded of Apalla. "How long until that happens?"

Her face fell as she cast her eyes away. "Three weeks."

"Ha," I laughed a cold laugh, casting Isleen a reproachful glare that she didn't deserve, but my nerves were shot. My emotions were shot. My body was alive, but mentally, I was holding on by a dangerously frayed string. "Three weeks until I lose my mind. Three weeks compared to the seven months I thought I would have to master the fifth and final element. By the time my seventeenth birthday comes around, it won't matter if Amara isn't here because I will have lost my mind."

"Hayden, there has to be another way."

"There isn't," I snapped. "Amara is staying, whether you like it or not, or I'm leaving with her."

I repressed a shudder at the connotation of my words. The thought of leaving with Death wasn't particularly enticing.

"If it helps," the cold voice of Death drawled, "when I am not training Hayden, I can leave Asylum and return to the celestial realms." She shrugged. "Although, I always have a presence in Asylum, as I do in the rest of the world. You cannot repel my existence from here."

"That's not terrifying at all," I muttered. "But it proves my point. We can't stop Death, so we may as well welcome her to our side."

"Hayden, stop and think about the consequences of Death—"

"I have!" I roared, the elements layering my voice to a threatening tone. "I hate Death more than any of you right now." Amara didn't flinch at my accusatory glare. "It took Dad and Salem. Death claimed Harbor." My bottom lip quivered as I fought to control my emotions. "I've lost so much to Death already. I'm not scared of meeting her face to face. I'm scared to lose more by not fighting *with* Death instead of *against* it. If one of you has a better idea, I'm all ears." I gestured around the room for one of them to supply an idea. "Anyone? Any ideas on how I can master Spirit without losing my mind? No one?" I scowled. "Didn't think so."

"Just because we do not see another solution does not mean this is the only option, nor the best," Isleen fired back. "Think about the people's reaction to—"

"If I may," Thea interrupted in a totally un-Thea like fashion. "Amara and I have known one another since her creation."

We stared at her with wide eyes, but the child-goddess merely shrugged.

"The Earth is ancient. Far more ancient than the human souls Amara ferries across the veil to the Garden. Amara does not have the authority to steal a life without permission from the Creator's plan. Her powers are simply to transition souls from one world to the next. Her presence here need not be advertised, as it would disrupt the peace of the town. However, it is not a concern for the safety of mortal lives."

Silence blanketed the cathedral.

"I will return when Hayden is ready to train," Amara announced with an air of finality as she shifted into her original form of the little girl with candy-apple red hair and jade green eyes.

In the blink of an eye, she disappeared. There was no flash of light. She didn't spook.... She was just gone.

A shiver raced down my spine as I thought about Death's presence in the air around us. She may have been out of sight, but that did not mean she was not present.

"Then it's decided." I motioned at the spot Amara had disappeared from. "Amara leaves when she's not training me. Nobody outside this room has to know about my new master. And Death will not steal the lives of our people."

Isleen and the others opened their mouths to balk at the authoritativeness of my tone, but I raised a flat palm. "If you fight me on this, the town will perish. I will descend into madness, and no one will be able to stop Lilith from taking the Maiden's power from Thea," I warned. "Amara already lives among us. I think it is wise not to enrage the personification of Death. Now, I want to go home. Don't try to stop me."

Spinning on my heel, I strode toward the heavy double doors of the cathedral propped open with a stone. Surprisingly, Isleen and the Council didn't argue. I wasn't sure what convinced them, but I didn't care as Jamie caught up with me, matching his stride to mine.

Leaving the Council and my other friends at the cathedral, I trudged home.

Even with Jamie's company, it was the loneliest walk of my life. He insisted on walking me to my house, and Thea spooked, so I knew she was waiting for me there, but even with all the company in the world,

I would feel cold and numb like I did now, and it had nothing to do with the frigid January air, especially since I wore my charmed leather jacket. No amount of magic could expel the chill of despair from my bones.

Silence stretched between us.

It wasn't uncomfortable, but it wasn't comfortable either.

Jamie understood the suffering that came from losing family because he had lost Harbor, his twin, his other half. But me... I had lost the only family I had ever known—my familiar and my father, whom I had just gotten back after years of separation. And now my mother was crucified to a cross with Kova was alongside her.

Lost to my thoughts, I barely registered walking past the wrought iron gate at the front of my house, but my mind snapped back to reality as I stepped into the warmth of my Asylum home. Operating on autopilot, I let Jamie steer me to the fireplace for its eternally burning flames to warm me.

But even the silver flames of Heaven and Hell couldn't drive away the numbness.

Dad... Salem... Kova...

Gone. All of them gone.

And all I had was seven months to get myself together and pass my final Trial so I could end Lilith for eternity. *If* I could bring myself to kill her.

I am with you. When all seems lost, I will bring you victory. You are never alone, Hayden.

"Do you want something to eat? Waffles or one of those disgusting microwave burritos you love so much?" Jamie asked with the hint of a smile.

"No," I answered hollowly. I knew he was trying to make me feel better, but nothing could mend my broken heart. At least, not right now. I needed to grieve. To wallow. Because tomorrow I had to wake up and train with Death so I could save the people that needed saving. "I want to go to sleep." I didn't meet Jamie's eye, instead staring at the flames. "Go home, James. Go check on your mom and aunt and Harlan."

He didn't move from my side. Not a muscle twitched.

"Jamie, I'm serious. I'm ready to crash. I need a shower and sleep. And you need the same. Go home. I'll see you tomorrow."

Jamie regarded me skeptically, then grabbed me by the shoulder and pulled my body into his. His hand slipped up to my head as his other landed on my hip, and he pulled me into him to press a kiss to my forehead.

"Thank Goddess you're alive," he whispered, then let me go.

Some of the cold numbness thawed, and the anvil crushing my chest lightened a fraction.

With one last reluctant glance, Jamie squeezed my elbow, then left the house to return to his own.

And as the front door shut behind him, I collapsed into a heap on the rug in front of the fireplace, using the power of the elements to muffle my sobs so Thea wouldn't hear.

CHAPTER TWO

THE ORIGINAL MASTER

The air under the covers was sweltering, unbearable for any mortal other than me. My body boiled as emotions raged within me, but I refused to emerge from the bed.

Three days had passed since my Earth Trial. Three days that I hadn't left the house. Three days that I spent grieving my loss.

I had promised my father I wouldn't wallow. That I would rise again stronger than before, but when I returned home... to the home I had shared with them both, especially my familiar... the grief was overwhelming, and I spiraled into a pit of despair and anguish.

Sweat beaded on my forehead from the heat and humidity shimmering in the air under the layers of blankets, the unbearable temperatures summoned by fire and water. Air swirled above my blankets, leaving me untouched, but craving nearness to its beloved witch as I cried into my pillow. I felt rather than saw the plants on my windowsill grow rapidly, extending from their pots as elongated vines and branches and stems for the flowers and leaves and petals to poke through the edges of the blankets to comfort me with their pastel colors and soothing scents.

And lightning... black lightning filled the air with its humming electricity, sparks zapping from my body to the outlets and lights and anything that used its power. My entire house had probably short circuited by now, but I didn't care.

I let the storm rage around me.

And I knew it wasn't just around me, but an overwhelming storm had brewed in the sky above Asylum. Wind raged against buildings, screaming and howling as thunder clapped in a deafening "BOOM", and water rained down in sheets, drenching the town as lightning cut through the sky and struck the shaking ground.

Thea counteracted the quaking of the earth, stilling the ground as my powers worked of their own accord.

Hot energy crackled through my body, and for the first time since discovering I was a witch, my magic raged out of my control.

I had felt anger before, blood boiling from the heat of my rage that lashed out with magic, but this... I reached for my hold over the elements, grabbing the leash that held the power swirling in my stomach, but it was gone, replaced by more power, more energy, more magic. There was nothing to grab hold of. Just raw magic bottled inside me, the power accumulating like pressure in a shaken soda bottle after dropping a mento inside.

I was about to explode.

"Hayden," Angel Boy's familiar voice screamed my name, but it was faint, like his voice was ripped away by the wind. "Hayden, you have to stop. Call in your powers or the whole town will be destroyed!"

His voice was hoarse, like he had been screaming for twelve hours straight at a concert. *That* was the overwhelming power of the elements raging between us to muffle his words.

My muscles twitched in response. I tried to pull back the covers to unveil my sweat-soaked body, but every movement lit up my nerves like a live wire, electricity zapping me with agonizing pain as though it hated the movement.

Because it did.... The lightning... it wanted to be released and without a ground, my body was an overloaded wire, burning like a resistor.

Sunlight burst to life in the room, bright enough to shine through the four blankets piled on top of me, and I tried again to move my arm, crying out in agony as I pushed the covers off my torso, but they stayed covering my legs.

An unrelenting tornado spun around my bedroom, pushing my circle away from me. Apalla gripped the edge of my bedroom door, holding on for dear life as it flapped in the wind, her feet lifting off the floor as she turned horizontal. Her powers of air were inconsequential against the elemental storm, and the best she could do was shelter herself against the wind.

Jamie lay flat against the floorboards, his fingers digging into the shaggy rug stretching from under my bed. As he raised a hand to crawl forward, the force of the wind caught his palm and nearly ripped him off the floor. The only reason he didn't go airborne was because Apalla shot a blast of air at him, pushing him to the ground. Jamie's face smacked the floor, and he released a painful grunt, followed by a groaned, "Thanks."

Thea's small body remained unfazed because of the protective orb of green magic encircling her, but she stood on the opposite side of the room from Apalla and Jame and every time she tried to extend her magic to them, my elements cut it down.

"Hayden," Thea's melodious voice called. "Hayden, please, cease this magic."

I opened my mouth to tell her I wanted to, that my magic was controlling me, not the other way around, but electricity reacted to the movement and zapped my jaw closed, nearly taking off my tongue.

"She's nonresponsive," Jamie called to the others. "We have to do something. It's like she's unconscious and the elements are controlling her."

Thank goodness he understood what was happening.

"Form the circle," he shouted, his voice dull against the wind.

"And how are we supposed to do that? We don't have a water elemental," Apalla called back, and I could see her shake her head. "Ethan isn't here, and I doubt either of you can spook back with him."

"And we don't know if a circle will work," Thea added.

"We have to try something."

"No," Death's voice cut through the room. And then the blood red eyes of Death incarnate stared into mine with an intensity that could break bone. Amara's cold, bloodless hands gripped my bare forearms. "I will."

Her pointed nails dug into my flesh hard enough to draw blood, but as our skin made contact, I felt the magic of Spirit course through her. Her crimson eyes flashed jade green as the leash on my powers returned, but not to my control.

Amara held my powers in her hands, a guide rather than an owner, and I wondered if this was how it felt to be channeled? But I sensed Amara's intent, and it was not malicious or greedy. She did not seek to claim my powers as her own—she had more than enough—but she would control my magic with hers as my will power failed me.

But she could not dilute the power in my veins, and the power did not want to stay bottled inside of me, but craved release.

Black lightning ricocheted through me.

My bones rattled as the power detonated, jarring my soul within my body. A bolt of lightning thicker than an oak tree blasted out of my chest and through the roof into the sky above.

Gawking, I stared at the sky through the gaping hole in my ceiling. Half the roof was blown off my room. How big was that lightning strike?

But my magic... control of my magic had returned. My body hummed with power, like it would overload with energy again, but for now, my magic would heed my call.

Swallowing roughly, I forced myself to push aside my grief for the time being, and thrusting a hand into the air, I called back my elements and diffused the tempest raging above the town.

Air, fire, water, earth, and Spirit rushed into my open palm, greeting me like a long-lost friend, as though they had missed my magical presence when I let them roam free.

"What on earth was *that*?" Jamie roared at Amara, shoving his nose in her face as he got perilously close to Death.

"*That* is the power of the Salem Witch," Amara said forcefully, her red eyes staring at Jamie unflinchingly. "A mortal body can contain only so much power, but Hayden is no mere mortal. There is a reason she is the most powerful Salem Witch in history and why the Creator chose her soul to live within her body. As part demon, Hayden's body is robust enough to channel such power."

"Like Kova," I said as understanding dawned on me. "She is Nephilim. Before me, she was the strongest Salem Witch in history because her body is part angel."

"Precisely," Amara agreed. "While it is not always true that a Nephilim Salem Witch is stronger than one who possesses only witch genetics, the Creator chooses the soul and the body for the right mission, and both yours and Alice's require your powers to be stronger than Salem Witches in history's past. Except for Eve, of course."

Amara smiled a knowing smile, like she was sharing an inside joke only she understood. It was the creepiest smile ever, with those scarlet eyes and teeth filed to points.

Jamie and Apalla shuffled their feet uneasily, glancing away from the disconcerting personification of Death. Princess of Hell or not, it was creepy enough to make *me* uncomfortable.

"Why did my powers rage out of my control?" I asked, wanting to change the subject so Amara's smile would fade.

"Because you have not used your powers."

"What?" I blinked at her. "That was never a problem before."

"Before, you did not possess the power of Spirit, which amplifies and exponentially multiplies the power of the other elements, making them more concentrated. Your magic is *beyond* what it was, Hayden. You can no longer go days without using your magic, otherwise it, combined with your emotions, will bottle up inside you until your mortal vessel can no longer contain the power, and it will unleash itself in an uncontrollable explosion, much like what just occurred. But, if you discharge magic on a consistent basis, it will not accumulate inside you, and you can control how, when, and what amount of the elements will release from your body."

"So, basically, I have to train with magic daily, or I'll destroy Asylum with an elemental bomb?"

"Precisely."

"And the storm was because of *me*?" I asked with wide eyes, staring through the hole in my ceiling at the blue clear sky above. "*I* did all that?"

"Making a mess of things as usual, Haywire," Jamie said with a lazy smirk and a wink.

By the Creator, my insides melted at that wink, and my cheeks heated as my mind flashed back to my first kiss with him. My only kiss with him.

Ugh. Hayden, focus.

"Uh, ahem," I coughed, clearing my throat as I tore my gaze away from Angel Boy, my face flushed. "How do I make sure it doesn't happen again? How does Kova keep her power contained? I never even sensed it."

"Alice is a Resurrected Nephilim. Because she died in her Trials and chose to return to the mortal realm, her powers are near limitless," Thea explained, leaning against her staff. "The true power of the Divine Spirit flows through her at all times, and she has complete control. As an immortal, her body can contain the power. It is a gift bestowed only on those who are selfless enough to return as immortals to finish their sacred duty."

"As for you," Amara began, surveying me from head to toe where I sat on my bed. "You cannot control the power completely as you have not passed your final Trial. Until then, you must discharge your powers regularly to prevent the element from accumulating until the magic explodes out of your control. Such is the magnitude of the Spirit."

I stared at my hands in fear and awe. This power could destroy if I allowed it.... Incomparably great power that I could control... I hoped.

How much was the power of Spirit?

Infinite, an ethereal, eternal voice whispered in my mind, almost with reverence.

"Infinite," I muttered under my breath as I observed the black lightning crackling over my hands, turning them over to stare at my palms.

Power coursed through my soul, and I shuddered at the thought of this power in the wrong hands. And not for the first time in my life was I afraid of myself and the magic I wielded.

Then it is a virtuous thing that I chose the soul I did to burden with the task of the Salem Witch. You are the right soul, Hayden, even when you feel unworthy. Especially when you feel unworthy. If you doubt yourself, then have faith in Me. The voice of the Creator rang through my head clear as day, drowning out the world around me as my circle and Amara conversed. It was a voice that was immeasurably ancient and forever young. *You will not possess the full powers of*

Spirit until you pass your final Trial. Only then will your soul become the blessed vessel to channel My power. Until then, know that I am with you, know that I think about you, know that I fight for you.

I have called you by name and will be your refuge for all your life, for I have noble plans for you, my child. Air blows, fire glows, water flows, earth grows, but Spirit... Spirit knows, and it knows all things, for it is the keeper of the mysteries of the Universe. Embrace your power, Hayden. Do not fear the gifts I have granted you.

My hands curled into fists.

I had spent too much time wasting away in my bedroom, moping and wallowing in my misery. No longer.

The world needed me. Asylum needed me. My friends needed me. But most of all, I needed me. I needed to fight for what I had left and to reclaim what I had lost. And I couldn't do that if I spiraled into a pit of darkness and depression.

Throwing back the covers, I leaped from my bed, startling Amara and my circle. Well, maybe not Amara. It was hard to tell with those creepy red eyes and emotionless expression. Did she emote? I wasn't sure. It was as though she was mortal, or has been, but immortality had stolen the vulnerable humanity that might have existed.

Standing barefoot on my rug, wearing nothing but black sweats and a ratty black sweatshirt, I clenched my hands. Balls of silver flames burst to life around my curled fists. Wind howled in the air above our heads and the earth quaked beneath our feet as thunder rumbled and rain fell from the sky at my command.

"You said I needed to master Spirit before I lose my mind, right?" I asked Amara. When she nodded, I raised a burning fist. "And I have more magic than I know what to do with, but if I don't use it, it will explode." I stared at the hole in my roof. "That's nothing compared to the magic I feel inside. With Spirit..." My eyes met those of each member of my circle, and then Amara's unsettling blood red ones. "With Spirit, I can win this war, even with Lilith channeling my mom and Kova."

An unsettling grin spread across Amara's face, revealing those lethally sharpened teeth. "You shall make the Darkness tremble."

Maddox drooled as he stared at Apalla, who plucked her bow string, eliciting a chirruping twang that resounded through the Spellery's student lounge. Her eyes flashed with golden light.

We sat around a table. Me, my circle, the elemental Majors and Minors, and some of our more trusted friends from the Spellery—Maddox Fenske, Terren Reed, Tyler Burns, Damien and Dani, and Kelsey.

Not to mention my loyal demons. Jackal perched on my shoulder in his black cat form, his tail flicking back and forth behind us, and Buddy snoozed peacefully on the rug in front of the burning fireplace. Hyde—another one of my loyal morphers—perched on the ledge outside the window in his preferred hawk form.

"Mom suspects, but she's intentionally not asking. You know how she is about the rules." Apalla rolled her hazel eyes as she flicked golden hair over her shoulder.

Isleen had always been a stickler for the law.

"By not asking, she has plausible deniability," Jamie agreed. "She's turning a blind eye, so she isn't morally torn between adhering to the law and doing what she knows is best for Asylum."

The Athenian Council was ridiculously slow at enacting war preparations. It took eons to approve any little action, and Naida wasn't helping with her constant rebukes in Council meetings. Meetings I had to waste my time attending on the regular.

Instead, we took matters into our own hands. And by "we", I meant my circle and our fellow Spellery students.

Which was why we convened in the student lounge, discussing war strategies. Ty Burns had been especially helpful at modifying the Fire Tower's forge since his dad was the Forge Master. Like mounting cauldrons to the windows to hold molten metal. Fire elementals would melt the metal, and earth witches could use the liquid to attack demons. Despite their fire resistance, demons weren't immune to molten metal.

Terren Reed, while a Spellery graduate, was a public figure to the St. Salem witches. He commanded a certain kind of authority and served as the general for earth witches with the help of Fawn Gardener, the current Earth Major.

Actually, most of my friends had graduated from the Spellery. Except for Dani Sanchez and the other Majors and Minors, I was the youngest of the group. Damien and Apalla would be replaced soon since they no longer qualified for the Spring Equinox Major Tournament. Not that we were having it this year, given the tumultuousness of the times.

"What modifications do we still need to make to the forge?" Jamie asked Tyler.

Jamie, as my head general of the entire Spellery, led these meetings so my mental energy could focus on brainstorming battle strategy and figuring out where in the unseen realms Amara had disappeared to.

She hadn't materialized in the physical realm since I blasted a hole in my roof two weeks ago. The only reason I hadn't exploded from the overpouring of Spirit in my body was because I released a massive bolt of lightning every day from the top of the observation deck of the Divination Tower.

Which I would have to do again in the next hour. The power was building inside my core. It didn't help that I tuned out Ty's answer about the forge, letting my mind wander to the modifications I wanted done to the Spellery pool and healing tower.

We needed to transfer the healers from the hospital to the school's infirmary. Them and all their equipment. Without alerting the Council to our movements. They wouldn't do anything without a formal meeting to discuss the legality of the project, then a formal document with all seven approvals had to be drafted, which was a bit of a problem considering Lilith held Kova prisoner.

And I still had no idea how to save her.

Electricity zapped through me at the thought. Spirit hated abandoning Kova as much as I did. But there was nothing I could do. We weren't ready to face Lilith. The attack right after returning from her island had proved as much.

"Hayden," Kelsey's voice cut through the chatter at the table. Every eye turned to me as I met Kelsey's gaze. "Go discharge." She jerked her chin at the door of the student lounge. "We will handle things here."

My gaze cut to Jamie's royal blue one. Nodding, he nudged me in the ribs with his elbow. "Go," he urged. "You need to focus on mastering Spirit. The rest of us can handle this."

Half-heartedly, I rose from the table and trudged out of the lounge and into the empty fourth floor corridor. Most of the students were in class, and those with free periods were training in the combat or magic rooms. Nobody, not even the kids, took this war lightly. Asylum knew the stakes and the direness of our situation. Without Kova... I shuddered to think about the carnage that would be inflicted on our beloved town without her here to fight for us... not to mention Lilith's supercharged powers gained by channeling the Resigned Salem Witch.

Starting toward the east, I wound through the hallways toward the Divination tower so I could take the stairs directly inside the tower instead of navigating Kova's ridiculous magical staircases that would spit you out on some random floor. One stairwell on this level took you to the ground level if you tried to go *up*. It was absurd. Now that I knew she was Alice Parker, I needed to have a word with her about her architecture skills.

Cool, fresh air blew over me, tousling my hair as nature welcomed me into its wintery realm. Snow piled on the guard rail encircling the tower. As the sun melted the snow, the frigid temperatures froze the water into icicles that stretched down the sides of the walls like long, skeletal fingers.

Silence surrounded me, nothing but the howling of the wind and the light thuds of my footfalls landing against the wooden floorboards to accompany me as I walked to the western point of the observation deck and stared at the town bustling with life fourteen stories below.

The town I loved so much. The town that had become my home these last four years. The town that I would protect with my life.

Spirit tickled the back of my neck, and I whirled around to meet the blood red gaze of Death.

"Hello, Hayden." Amara grinned her petrifying smile that bared her filed teeth. "Are you ready to begin your training?"

"Where have you been?" I snapped, not diluting my fury at the imposing celestial. "It's been *weeks* since my magic exploded, and you were the one who said Spirit would drive me insane if I didn't master the fifth element."

"You have not been alone until now, so I did not come to you so as to not unsettle the others."

I blinked at her as I reflected on the last two weeks. She was right. I hadn't been alone except to sleep. My every waking hour was spent with the Council or at the Spellery to make battle plans or to train with the other students.

"Fair enough," I grumbled. Waving a hand, I gestured at her. "So, you're committed to this form?"

Amara cocked her head. Charcoal gray light haloed around her, and Death morphed into her original form, the form I had met her in—a girl no more than twelve years old, with candy-apple red hair and glittering jade green eyes.

"Do you prefer this form?" Amara asked with a hint of amusement.

I nodded.

"Hmmm," Amara hummed in her throat. "Your friends seem perturbed by the innocence of this appearance, but you are not." It wasn't a question.

I shrugged. "It feels more... natural."

"Ah," Amara sighed, a knowing smile twisting her pale lips. "Shall we begin?"

Black lightning crackled to life at my fingertips in response to her question. I hadn't even called it yet.

And that lack of control scared me. I had to trust Spirit to control itself. It would listen to me, but unlike the other elements, it could and *would* act of its own accord.

"Lightning is like you, Hayden. If gone unchecked, uncontrolled, it can destroy."

I gulped, fear widening my eyes as I stared at Amara.

"But," she emphasized the word. "It only seeks to destroy what is bad and give life to what is good. That does not mean it will not listen to you. It is eager to fulfill its duty. It will protect you of its own accord, but it *wants* you to enact your will in alignment with its own to destroy what is tainted and dark in this world."

"So, if I use Spirit on a demon..."

"Spirit would obliterate the demon instantly. The touch of such purity is certain doom to a creature of darkness."

"But I can wield Spirit even though I'm a demon."

"Spirit is the magic of a *soul.* And you are a soul, Hayden, in a mortal body. Spirit manifests itself as lightning, as a physical entity, but it is far more than a mere tangible element. It is the giver of life. *Neshama*—the human soul—is the creation that instilled free will in mortals. *Neshama* is an act of creation—a divine act of *tsimtsum.*"

"What's that?" I asked. "What is that word you just said?"

"*Tsimtsum,*" Amara repeated in her disturbingly melodious voice, and the word seemed to sing through my body, mind, and soul.

As though Amara knew exactly what I was feeling, she said, "The response you are experiencing to the word comes from the power of the Spirit within you. *Tsimtsum* is a spiritual contraction by which the Creator removes part of Its infinite unity. The more complex act of *tsimtsum* is, the greater the corresponding potential for imperfection."

"That's why evil exists in the world," I spoke softly, understanding how free will created opportunity for evil.

Amara nodded solemnly. "When the infinite Spirit, which is whole, withdraws, then evil—the lack of perfection—is created."

Spirit was part of me... a piece of my soul alive in the world.

I could *feel* it as surely as I could feel the wind rushing over my skin.

"How does it work?" I asked, raising my hand to stare at the electricity sparking around my fingers. "It's not like the other elements. When I use my magic, energy drains from inside me. But with Spirit, if I don't discharge the lightning, it's overwhelming, all-consuming. Even when I release the power, I feel like I'm overflowing. Like it recharges itself."

"Because Spirit is more than a mere element. It is an entity of its own. The cost of power for the elements is energy. There is a finite amount. Spirit is not like that. The more of yourself that you give, the more it gives back. The cost of Spirit is *you.*"

Fear should have pierced my heart. I should have trembled from the weight of Amara's proclamation. It should have terrified me that I would have to give myself to the unknown to wield such incredible power.

But it didn't.

Nothing ever felt so natural, so destined.

"The Divine never takes without gifting to you what is destined for your soul. They act for your highest good, even if you don't understand it. Whatever you sacrifice to Spirit will always be given back to you."

And I believed her.

For some unfathomable reason, I trusted Death.

"Now, call upon the fifth and greatest element, Hayden, and give yourself to it, so it may transform you into the ultimate master," Death spoke with such conviction, the assuredness was odd coming from someone so youthful in appearance, and I wondered if that was how others saw me when I was twelve and a fresh witch.

Closing my eyes, I inhaled a deep, calming breath and tunneled into my gut, where my power swirled with a bright, glowing light that could not be extinguished by even the darkest, vilest beast.

And I found that sliver of silver light, buried deep, deep below all the temporary, trivial power. The elements were the building blocks of life... the basic pillars of magic... but this sliver of light, no matter how small it seemed, held the power of the Universe within it. It was divine and pure and heavenly.

It was my *soul.*

The link to my loving Creator, who crafted me so carefully, with love and intent, who chose *me*. And as I touched the sliver of silver light, I felt unconditional love, so great and vast and infinite that I knew nothing could ever compare. I was called, chosen. And as I poured my love back into the silver light, there was an explosion of pure power unlike anything I had witnessed in the mortal world.

Nothing could compare to the Creator's power. The ultimate power of *Spirit.*

Energy rippled through me, alive underneath my skin, like it was its own entity—part of me yet separate at the same time. Spirit writhed and conducted through me, singing through every muscle and nerve and vein, but it wasn't uncomfortable. It felt like everything was within me. Like the entire Universe was contained within this power.

It was everything and nothing. Hot and cold. Light and dark.

Dead. And alive.

My piercing blue eyes flared open.

Black lightning crackled around me in a cage. Wind howled, fire burned, water flowed, and earth rumbled in response to the sheer power encircling me like the brightest halo of the most brilliant angel. Night had fallen—how long had my eyes been closed?—and I was a silver beacon of light atop the highest point in the town. Black lightning shot outward, into the sky above, where a storm of elements brewed at my command.

It was exhilarating beyond description. I had never felt such purity, such undiluted goodness. And it existed within me. It *lived* within me.

And it was mine to command as the ultimate weapon in the war I would wage against the Darkness.

The elements ceased as I called the power back to me. The black lightning zapped toward me, harmlessly absorbing into my palms as I held them open to welcome the element.

Silence rang in my ears as I raised my head to meet Amara's gaze.

"Excellent, Hayden. Excellent." Amara grinned, those jade green eyes shining with pride and conviction. Conviction that I would win this war and end Lilith's reign of terror. For eternity. "You will master Spirit faster than any Salem Witch, and you will claim ultimate victory over the Darkness for eternity."

"Again," Amara barked.

"Relax, Amara," Jamie called from where he leaned against the brick wall encompassing my backyard. "Hayden killed and resurrected the tree a thousand times. She's nearly perfect at it."

"And she will do it a thousand more times until she *is* perfect at it, boy," Amara retorted without inflection. Her monotonous nature was all the more terrifying since the woman dressed in enough black to rival my wardrobe.

I summoned black lightning to my palms, letting it crackle and hiss as it zapped over my skin, moving from my core to my hands like a current of energy.

Months had passed since Amara arrived in Asylum, and we had trained harder than all my previous years combined. Amara was more ruthless than Kova at magic training. And rightfully so. With only a few full moons remaining until my seventeenth birthday, every second counted. I would master Spirit if it killed me... because if I didn't, then my deadline became literal.

We woke at the break of dawn to practice with the elements one by one until I reached Spirit, and I spent the rest of my day wielding the frightening black lightning.

It was the worst seven months of my life between the grueling, unceasing pace of my training and the bitter grief that plagued me... but the pain lessened little by little. And Amara's instruction expedited my learning tremendously.

Whether it was Amara, or the element itself, Spirit came easier than the other four elements—even fire, which I considered my element if I hadn't been chosen as the Salem Witch.

Spirit's essence was rejuvenating unlike anything I had experienced before.... Just as Amara had said. The more I practiced with it, the more I wanted to use Spirit, even if I simply called the element to keep me company. It was like sitting with an old friend in comfortable silence, and part of me wondered if that was how daughters felt when they hugged their mothers. A feeling I hoped to experience for myself.

Spirit filled my chest, bringing a different kind of warmth than the heat from the blazing sun above. Love built in my heart, and energy coursed through my veins. Power rushed through my muscles like a coursing river, and magic beyond any power in the Universe infused every cell of my being, as if the element touched my very soul, because that is exactly what it did.

Bringing my palms together, the Spirit in each hand connected to form a closed loop with my body, and with it, sent a bolt of electricity jolting through me. The electricity wasn't painful or shocking but refreshing. Like more than my body was affected by my use of the fifth element.

The more I worked with Spirit, the more I understood why not every witch could wield it—it was dangerously intoxicating, powerful beyond belief, and the most intense feeling of love I had ever felt. The power and feeling of wielding it... it was indescribable.

My vision latched onto the dead tree. Blocking out everything else, I extended my magical senses toward the tree in a desperate effort to connect with its essence. The tree had been dying since before I moved into my house, but every day, I harnessed the powers of Spirit to pour new life into the tree. Spirit manifested as lightning for the Salem Witch, and as such, Spirit could both take life and return it.

My black lightning was capable of such a feat, but I had yet to prove it. I had yet to master the skill of resurrection, but I wielded lightning with unparalleled prowess in a fight. I had always been good at combat, even without magic. Like I was born to fight. A skill I had inherited from my biological sire.

As I readied to release the power resting between my palms, a new thought surfaced in my mind. Closing my eyes, I called upon my earth magic, beckoning the power to help me. Without moving a muscle, I let my earth magic stretch beneath me to explore the ground. It rushed out, sweeping over anything and everything on or within the soil. My magic connected with the tree, gliding over its outer bark and rushing up the roots like water sucked up by the plant to burrow to the center of the tree where its spirit resided.

The tree's essence was faint, a lilac light barely shining against the darkness of death clawing at it. My magic touched it the same way a mother's hands would gently cup their child's cheek.

As I connected with the tree's spirit, I thrust my hands outward and directed Spirit into the tree. Black lightning burst from my hands, striking the tree, and earth magic sang back to me, vibrating with the currents of Spirit rushing through every cell of the tree's being.

A gasp came from behind me, but I didn't bother to look at my friends as I focused on the tree, its life force, and the power I poured into it. The light at its roots—the pleasant purple light that was once so small—grew and grew until it pressed against the bark exterior of the tree, eager to grow and expand. The light flowed to the roots, relishing the cool soil that fed it nutrients. Spirit flowed to the branches, causing leaves and blossoms to bloom, ready to soak in the warmth of the sun overhead.

The tree felt alive, a stark contrast to the dull energy before. I withdrew my magic, allowing earth and Spirit to return to me. Groggily, my eyes fluttered open. In place of the broken tree dying in my backyard stood a magnificent wisteria tree with green leaves and purple blossoms. The trunk now twisted and curled in on itself, but while it would be wrong on another tree, it seemed fitting for the unique tree glowing with life again.

As fast as the energy drained from my body, Spirit resurrected the power within me.

"Very good, Hayden," Amara crooned in her eerily melodious voice from where she stood with Thea and Apalla at the edge of the yard.

Ethan was missing because he was coordinating the healers at the hospital and stocking the Spellery with supplies on top of training more students to field dress wounds and magically heal simple injuries so the more experienced healers could use their magic to address fatal wounds.

I stared at my hands as black lightning zapped between my fingers. "It's strange—I'm tired but energized at the same time."

"That is so," Amara confirmed, sweeping her hands to the sides like a preacher at the altar. "Spirit allows you to take life as well as give it. It is a paradox, one that requires balance between two equal but opposite forces. As you use this magic, the contrasting feeling will lessen until it feels as natural as breathing."

I didn't bother to mention that it already felt natural, like it was the purpose of my soul.

"Remember, Hayden, you were born the Salem Witch. Our Creator molded your body with the intention of you wielding Spirit. Trust your soul. It remembers how to use the magic—your body must catch up."

Apalla's golden wand buzzed. Muttering under her breath, she twirled the wand to open the message. Golden words made of light poured out of the wand, and with a sigh, Apalla swiped a hand through the air, dispelling the wand message.

Her hazel eyes met mine. "Mom needs us at the Parthenon to meet with the Athenian Council."

"War preparations?"

"War preparations."

"Ugh," I groaned, scrubbing my face with my hands. "Send her a message to stall her—we need to hit the Spellery first to review the defenses with Kelsey. Apalla—head to the Council and sit in on their conversation while Jamie and I take the Spellery. Amara—"

"I will return tomorrow morning for training, Hayden. See to the defenses against Lilith's impending attack and meet with the Council."

"For a second there, I was excited I wouldn't have to train, but I take it back. I'd rather train."

Jamie chuckled. He knew it wasn't about training because he felt the same way—we didn't want to deal with the Council.

Isleen and the others were trying to be helpful, but the political red tape and constant deviation from actual war preparations to discussions about Regalia Kensington and the Supreme Council were more of a hindrance than a help. The most fruitful actions were the tasks I entrusted to Kelsey to handle under the table.

Since she technically wasn't part of my circle, Kelsey wasn't under the Athenian Council's watchful eye overseeing the Spellery's defenses. Well, except Kane, but when he walked in on us setting up crucibles of molten metal in the forge, he turned on his heel and walked out without a word.

Kane was a military man, and he understood that we added more to the war efforts in a single day than the Council could in an entire week, especially when it took them a month to approve my defense plans. Well, the defense plans that I proposed to them, which didn't include all my other brilliant ideas that they were none the wiser to. Hence, the need for Kelsey and the other St. Salem's students.

"Before you leave, Amara, I have some things to discuss with you." Thea placed her palm against the wisteria tree.

My narrowed eyes darted between the child goddess and celestial. "Why?" I drew out the word.

"Death and the Earth have long been friends," Amara smiled at me. It was meant to be pleasant, but when Death smiles at you with blood red eyes and teeth filed to fangs, it's more traumatizing than pleasant.

Amara shifted from the towering, intimidating woman into the appearance of a young girl with candy-apple red hair and jade green eyes.

Apalla glanced away as Jamie shuddered beside me. Only Thea and I were unperturbed by Amara's shift in appearance. It was unsettling... like a creepy doll in a horror movie that looked innocent, but terrifying power lurked beneath the surface. But I was a demon. *I* was the most intimidating being in Asylum, and even Death did not scare me. Not after training with her for months on end.

"Shall we?" Jamie offered his palm to me.

Red light enveloped us as my hand slipped into his calloused palm, and smoke stung my nostrils as nausea rolled in my stomach.

My combat boots slammed into the grassy field outside the Spellery's Healing Tower on the west side of the castle.

Jamie shielded his eyes from the sun as he squinted at the Healing Tower. "Is that a cannon?"

"Uhhh, maybe?" I smirked at Harbor's ingenious invention.

"What do you mean by 'maybe'?" Jamie asked suspiciously.

I waggled my eyebrows at him.

"She said 'maybe' because she doesn't know we *finally* finished installing it," Kelsey drawled in her snooty voice as she sauntered to us, flanked by Damien and Ethan.

Basically, I had authorized all my friends to oversee the battlements and prepare the Spellery as our base of war operations. The Council assumed the Parthenon would be our base, and I let them think that so my friends and I could equip the Spellery while their gaze was trained on the Parthenon, but I knew better.

Because I knew Kova better. Isleen and the others had known Kova for longer, but I knew her soul. Not only was Kova my mentor, my friend, and the stepmother I didn't know I had, but she raised me for all these years, and she was the Salem Witch, which bonded us in an inexpressible way.

Kova had built St. Salem's Spellery to be a school, yes. A place for witches to learn and practice and hone their craft, but there was a reason she built it as a castle in the exact center of Asylum.... For the same reason she stashed a Terracotta Army and the bones of her fallen witches in the catacombs in the tunnel under my house and the Spellery.

All of it was a cunningly crafted plan for the next Salem War, because Spirit whispered things to her, just as it whispered secrets to me. Knowledge we could not know otherwise. But that was our gift.

"Haywire, why do you have a cannon?"

CHAPTER THREE

SKELETONS IN THE CLOSET

"Haywire, why do you have a cannon?" Jamie asked, scrunching his eyebrows together. "Cannon balls aren't exactly the best weapon against an army of *demons*."

I shared a conspiratorial smile with Kelsey.

"Because it's not just any cannon," Damien said, tilting his head back to stare at the multiple cannons protruding from the castle walls.

Jamie's eyes narrowed to slits. "I'm going to hate this, aren't I?"

"It was your sister's idea." My smirk widened at the stunned expression on his face. "It's a *water* cannon. I found the schematics sketched in her grimoire." I held up my charm bracelet and pointed to the blue conch shell pendant.

Jamie whipped around to look at the cannons mounted to the Spellery tower.

"It's hooked directly to the pipeline connecting to the well that provides water to the entire school," Ethan explained. "So, water elementals can blast demons."

"Be careful to not blast *us*," sounded a semi-bored drawl.

Jackal's tail curled around my calf as the black panther rubbed against my leg, nuzzling his wet nose against me. Leaning over, I stroked the velvety fur on his head, eliciting a deep, satisfied purr from him.

"Don't worry, *pet*," Kelsey sneered. "It's not holy water."

Jackal hissed at her.

Kelsey and Jackal actually adored one another—this was just playful banter—their bond having formed and strengthened during hours of mind control training. After my Earth Trial, I stopped training with Kelsey, but my loyal demons did not. After Lilith breached the wards, my demons adamantly committed themselves to Kelsey's training.... Because she might be the only witch other than me and my circle who could save my demons from being slaughtered by Lilith's Voice of Command.

A smile split Jamie's face as his gaze shifted from Harbor's invention to my face. "Thank you," he said softly, bumping his elbow into my side. "She would love this."

"I know I'm the demon, but Harbor had a certain wickedness about her that made it so much more fun when we were together." Sighing, I crossed my arms over my chest as I glanced at the tower. "I miss her and her crazy ideas."

Jamie snorted. "And what about your crazy ideas?" He raised a skeptical eyebrow.

"Possibly worse because she's not here to help me, but probably better because she's not here to stop me."

Smiling, Jamie rubbed a hand over his face, then massaged his jaw. "Come on, Haywire," he said, tossing his arm around my leather-jacket clad shoulders. "Let's check on the rest of the castle."

Angel Boy fell into step beside me as we strode through the massive doors of the Spellery and into the entrance hall.

"Any idea how to counteract the Voice of Command so your demons can fight?" Jamie asked, glancing at Jackal prowling behind us. At some point, Buddy teleported to join us and lumbered beside the black panther.

I smiled at my beloved demons, the first two to pledge themselves to me, and sighed. "Not even a hunch. Not like witches knew about the Voice of Command until Jackal told me about it."

"Which means they can't fight with us in the Salem War," Kelsey said, scrunching her nose as her brow furrowed.

"Which might not be the worst thing," Damien said. "Ninety-nine percent of Asylum isn't happy about the demons' presence inside the wards after the First Eve's attack in January." At the menacing growl coming from Jackal, Damien threw his hands in the air in surrender, adding, "Not me."

Like Damien had said, I relocated my army of seventeen thousand demons inside the wards after Lilith's attack. I couldn't risk her slaughtering them unarmed and vulnerable outside the wards.

"I didn't think they would be, but Jackal, Buddy, and the others are loyal to me. They are *my* demons, and they are fighting for their freedom as much as we are. If the witches don't trust the demons, that's one thing, but they need to trust me as their leader. If they have a problem with the demons, they can bring it to me. Got it?"

"Got it." Everyone nodded their agreement. My immediate circle and friends didn't fear my demons, but I understood the unease fostering between witches and demons, and the last few months had been filled with my circle and Kelsey chasing fires and reprimanding both sides.

"Great. Fill me in—how are preparations progressing?"

Kelsey jumped into explanation, detailing the changes taking place inside the Spellery. The entire school was outfitted for attack, the classrooms converted to rooms filled with cots for the Knights and citizens of Asylum and stocked with weapons and potion bombs and extra supplies.

With any luck, only the Knights would have to fight, but a sickening feeling in my gut said we would be relying too much on our civilian army. The good news—almost every adult in Asylum volunteered in some way or another, even if it was to watch the young children when the battle began. I allowed the Athenian Council to manage that much, so I could focus on the more vital war efforts.

The hospital was being packed and relocated to the Spellery. The infirmary at the school was huge, but it didn't compare to the space of the hospital, and arguments had erupted between Knights and healers. Especially since the Council hadn't sanctioned the move. Yet. Healers wanted to stay in the infirmary with their extensive resources, but Knights agreed that we needed to move the equipment per our military strategy.

Kelsey and Ethan quelled the resistance by explaining it was impossible to protect both the school and the hospital, and the Spellery was our source of operations, and in its entirety, the castle provided more space and protection. The hospital wasn't a fortress. Kova built the castle for this exact purpose—to protect Asylum should the need arise. Plus, how were we supposed to get the injured to the hospital if we had to retreat to the school? We had to be prepared to retreat to a single, centralized location.

Little fires ignited everywhere in the midst of our war efforts, but Kelsey was on top of things, even if she was snippy. But that could just be part of her snobby charm.

"Uh, Kelsey?" I interrupted her as she read a list of my ideas off a notepad and specified which were completed and what was left to do on the incomplete tasks. "What's with the army of teenagers headed this way?" I gestured to the mass of Spellery students marching intently toward us.

"Uh oh." Kelsey glanced over her shoulder, then rolled her eyes. "I was going to tell you, but it slipped my mind."

"Tell me what?" I narrowed my eyes at her.

"They want to fight," announced Tyler Burns, the boy who took me on my first date a couple years ago after the State Grimoire Games. He was a fire elemental and a nice guy, but it never went anywhere thanks to my duties as the Salem Witch. At least, that's what I told him. But he knew it was more than that.... He knew it wasn't personal, because he saw the feelings that were there before I was willing to admit them. Him and the rest of the Spellery. Thankfully, my first kiss with Jamie was not advertised to all of St. Salem's, even though Kelsey knew about it. Perks of being friends with the former witch of terror.

Standing next to Tyler, Dani Sanchez led the group of witches, most of whom appeared to be fifteen or sixteen, but many younger witches accompanied them, to my displeasure.

"And like I said a million times before—NO," Kelsey emphasized the last word with her classic sass and hair flip.

Nausea slammed into my gut, and I hated the words Spirit whispered in my mind.

As Dani and the other witches opened their mouths to argue, I raised a flat palm and bellowed loud enough for them to hear, "Hold up a second. How old are all of you?"

Tyler shrugged. "Majority of them are sixteen, the rest a fifteen, with a handful of younger witches."

"And you expect me to let you fight in a war against the Mother of Demons?" I asked, my expression incredulous. "Are you nuts?"

"Asylum is our home, too," Dani argued savagely. "As much as it is yours, and the Spellery is our school. If anything, it belongs to us more than you, considering you haven't attended for the last two semesters."

"Hey now," I whined, frowning at her. "Not like I didn't want to."

"We get it," Tyler added. "You're the Salem Witch. You had other things to do, but this is our town. It's the only home most of us have ever known. We want to protect it."

"And you were younger than we are now when you were claimed as the Salem Witch."

"Yes, but you're forgetting one crucial fact—I have the power of *all* five elements. You have *one*."

"You didn't possess all the elements when you fought Elliot in your Air Trial," Dani shot back.

I seethed. How dare she come at me with her logic?

Carefully, I considered the group of teenagers, my penetrating gaze making them shift in uncomfortable silence as I processed their request.

With a sigh and a shake of my head, I announced, "Fine."

A cheer rang out from the group.

"Haywire, have you completely lost it?"

"A long time ago, Angel Boy." I raised my voice, silencing them, "*But* only the sixteen-year-olds are allowed to fight. If you're fourteen—absolutely not. You can either help in the infirmary or the weapons room, but you do not leave this fortress. Fifteen-year-olds—same goes for you. You do not leave the Spellery under any circumstances, but you can fight from the school by manning the equipment on the walls.

"Fire witches—shoot your flames through the windows. Air elementals—use your magic and bows from a distance. Water witches,"—I jabbed a thumb over my shoulder at the Healing Tower—"you have a water cannon. Use it. Earth elementals—throw rocks at them, but don't hit our people. If you can stay on the ground floor and use your powers from afar, do it, but by no means are you to exit the castle. Am I understood?"

Excited energy seemed to zap through the air as my jittering classmates nodded their heads fervently and shouted triumphant cheers as they ran off to tell their friends.

Gazing at the sky, I let out a heavy sigh. "Please don't let me regret this," I prayed under my breath.

"I have to say," Kelsey drawled, watching our fellow Spellery students disperse, "I'm surprised you caved so easily."

"I have to say—I'm surprised you think the idea hasn't crossed my mind," I said grimly, the words ash in my mouth.

"You knew the students would ask to fight?" Jamie's hand wrapped around his broadsword hilt, his knuckles white.

My brow furrowed as I admitted the dark truth. "No. I was afraid I would have to ask them to fight before they've reached adulthood."

"You think the war will be that bad?" Damien asked, his quiet voice trembling with trepidation.

"It will be," Jackal answered. "How many of your witches have seen a demon?"

"All of us have seen a demon." Kelsey gestured to Jackal.

The black cat rolled his eyes. "Yes, because they've seen us. But how many have faced an enemy? Fought one? Killed one?"

"Maybe half the adults in town," Jamie estimated.

"Exactly," Jackal drawled in his pretentious tone. "And those demons were nothing more than pawns compared to the army the Mother of Demons will unleash on us."

"What do you mean?" Kelsey demanded.

"The worst Asylum has seen is probably a pit demon?"

I shrugged. He wasn't wrong. Most Asylumnites had seen demons, but pit demons were nothing compared to the horrors Jamie and I had witnessed in the last few years.

"Pit demons are large, but they're fools. Moronic guard dogs of the underworld. The Morningstar keeps them is because they obey orders without the need for the Voice of Command. Albeit, not well, and nothing too sophisticated, but they do listen. That is *nothing*," he emphasized the word. "Compared to what lurks the Dark Mother's army. You'll need every sword if you have any hope of surviving."

Kelsey paled until her face held a greenish tint. "I'm going to go throw up now."

"I will do whatever it takes to save them," I said, a shadow darkening my face.

"Haywire," Jamie growled, pulling on my elbow to spin me around to face him, our noses nearly touching. "What does that mean?"

"It means I will do whatever it takes to save the world." I took half a step back and pressed a single hand to his cheek as I softened my tone. "This is *my* war, Jamie. I've lost too many people I love—my mom, my dad, Salem, Kova, *your sister*." I emphasized the last words, knowing it was the only thing that would get through to my stubborn-headed Angel Boy. "Harbor sacrificed her life so I could save the world. I refuse to let her death be in vain, Angel Boy. So, please, don't ask me to stay out of the line of fire. She didn't, and neither will I. I'm more powerful now. More capable. And with the power of Spirit, I *will* win. Nobody else will die for me. Nobody."

"Fine," Jamie grumbled. "I... It's just..." He blew out a haggard breath. "I worry about you, Haywire. I don't like you putting yourself in any more danger than you're already in. I lost Harbor. I can't lose you, too."

"But Angel Boy, it's my job." Gingerly, I placed a hand on his cheek. "I've been in danger since the day I arrived in Asylum. I can't quit just because I'm scared."

He touched his forehead to mine, his thumbs rubbing my jaw. "I know you can't stop being the Salem Witch, but that doesn't mean you have to recklessly throw yourself in harm's way to protect everyone."

"It's my duty, Jamie. You said it yourself—lives will be lost in this war. But I was blessed with incredible power for a reason, and I will use it to save every life I can. And since when am I reckless?" I asked with a sassy smirk.

Jamie released an exasperated sigh mixed with a strangled laugh, then pulled back to stare into my eyes with his royal blues. "I know you're right, but that doesn't mean I have to like it. I can't help but want to protect you." Profound emotion passed between us, and I struggled to hold his gaze. "I can't lose you, Haywire."

"And I want to protect everyone. Including *you*. We can't keep each other out of the line of fire, but I'll watch your back if you watch mine?"

"I suppose that is the best I could hope for," he grumbled, his knuckles cracking from how hard he squeezed his fists.

"Deal. Now, let's move before Isleen sends someone to hunt us down."

He chuckled, rubbing a hand along my back, then offered it to me. "I wouldn't put it past her."

My hand slipped into his rough, calloused palm, and something about the contact made me feel safe.

Red light flashed as my body was sucked into the tube and I hurtled through time and space to be spit out at our destination. Smoke stung my nostrils as I blinked at my surroundings.

The Parthenon swarmed with witches rushing to assist with various war preparations, and in the midst of it all, my golden-haired best friend awaited me in the lobby, her nose shoved in a book. She probably saw us coming before we spooked.

"Whatcha reading?" I asked, bumping my shoulder into hers.

"Advanced Channeling Using the Dark Arts," she responded, not taking her eyes off the page.

"Whoa, Apalla. Heavy topic," Jamie said, peering over her shoulder to read the page.

"Dark topic for dark times," I muttered as I peaked at the book.

The massive, leather-bound tome must have weighed a hefty bit. I wondered how Apalla's arms didn't hurt from holding the old book. Or how the book didn't disintegrate in her hands, the leather was so dry and cracked.

"Where'd you get the book, Palla?" I asked, glancing at the cover. "This wasn't in the stack we piled in the library last night."

"Because I found it in the cathedral. In Lilith's old office. I thought maybe she hid important books somewhere special, so I used my Prophetess gifts to find this book and others." With a sigh, Apalla pulled the book away from her face and closed it. "Before you ask, no, I haven't found anything useful. Not yet, anyway."

"Anything of interest?"

"Tons. But nothing that will significantly help us with this war. It's mostly what we already know about Adam's and Lilith's story. Ancient myths and legends put into writing."

"Why not destroy these?" Jamie asked, gingerly taking the book from Apalla's hands to study it. "If it were me, I'd burn the books instead of going to the effort of hiding them."

"Because she relishes the immortalization of her story on paper," I replied, a shadow darkening my face. I knew Lilith, and I knew her twisted mind. "But Apalla, why can't you use your True Sight to see how I can kill Lilith? Or free Mom and Kova?"

"It doesn't work like that." She shook her head in dismay, but golden light flashed through her eyes. Tucking the book under her arm, Apalla rose from the bench she had been sitting on. "Come on. The Council is on the brink of another argument."

Jamie and I followed her through the labyrinth of corridors to the Council's private chambers, our feet navigating the twisting path by muscle memory as we conversed.

"You know my powers don't work that way, Hayden. I see what *might* happen. Not a guarantee. But the future isn't always decided yet, and despite my powers"—and Apalla's powers were mighty—"I can't see any potential outcomes for any of our current problems."

"Which means there are more decisions in my future." I repressed a groan. After the last few months—after the past four Trials—I was decisioned out.

Jamie opened the door to the Council's private chambers that served partly as a meeting space and partly as a break room with a cozy couch and a roaring fireplace lit all year round. Knowing what I did now, I knew those were Kova's flames burning indefinitely.

Apalla followed my lead as I strode through the door and took my designated seat at the head of the oak table opposite of Isleen, the High Priestess, and Apalla sat to my left as Jamie slid into the seat on my right. Where he always belonged.

"Hayden, Jamie," Isleen greeted us, but there was an exasperation to her tone that told me I wasn't going to like what she had to say next. "Thank you for joining us. We have a bit of a situation. With the Supreme Council."

Jamie and I froze in our seats as Apalla grimaced, her eyes flashing gold.

"What kind of situation?" I inquired, not moving a muscle in my body except those needed to talk, motionless as a statue. A deadly kind of motionless as my heart dropped in my chest.

"The Supreme Council is refusing to send their military to Asylum to fight against Lilith in the Salem War."

"Shocker." I rolled my eyes and leaned back in my chair. "We knew this from our..." I selected my word carefully, "negotiations when they were in Asylum before my Earth Trial."

Zola rasped out a cough. "Negotiations in which you banished the Supreme Council from Asylum?"

I grimaced at the memory as a flush stained my cheeks. "Admittedly, not my finest hour."

"And now Asylum is paying the consequences," Isleen reprimanded.

Shame coursed through me. I had known this would come back to bite me in the butt, but Asylum shouldn't suffer because of me. But I should have known better. Regalia was as ruthless as Lilith. She would punish Asylum, let people die, if it meant balancing the scales between her and me. And there was plenty she wanted revenge for... starting with my little case of hidden identity at the State Grimoire Games, then me pulling status as the Reigning Salem Witch at the Regional Grimoire Games, and then my threats at the National Grimoire Games... and finishing with their banishment from my town.

My bad.

But I couldn't take it back now.

"It's in the past," I said, ignoring the lump of regret settling in my chest like a weighted stone. "We need to focus on the resources we have and plan our attack and defense strategies."

"It's not in the past, because it's impacting those resources you're talking about," Dante said, his ember eyes glowing.

Disappointment slammed into me. I knew the Council wasn't happy with me, and I understood why, but I couldn't fix things with Regalia. She wasn't exactly the forgiving type. She would make me suffer even if I groveled.

"What about our sister witching communities?" Jamie asked, glancing between Isleen and Kane. "My mom is an ambassador. She personally delivered your message."

"None have answered the call," Isleen spoke softly with remorse-filled eyes.

I shared a bewildered look with Jamie and Apalla.

"What do you mean?" I braced my hands on the table as my stomach flipped from the intuition twisting my insides. "I thought we used Kova's name to call on them?"

"We did, but the witching world doesn't know Kova's true identity as Alice Parker," Zola explained. "And I will not betray my ancestor's wish to remain anonymous, in case she is freed to live her immortal life."

"Then what about my name? They won't answer the call of the Salem Witch?" I asked, almost frantically.

Isleen shook her head, her blonde hair shaking with it. "They're all too afraid to face Lilith. Even if that weren't the case, Regalia issued a declaration. Any witching community who assisted us in our war efforts will be tried with treason."

My mouth dropped open in stunned disgust.

But Isleen didn't stop there. "And she has summoned every able Knight from every community in the world, like she had said she would when we met in December."

Apalla buried her face in her hands, and Jamie scrubbed a hand over his face as I stared at Isleen with wide eyes.

"And it gets worse."

"How could it possibly get worse?" Jamie demanded.

"They're demanding we send our Knights to Jerusalem."

The Athenian Council shouted and screamed in a chaotic concert of hoarse voices. We had been arguing for hours. It started as a debate but quickly heated to hotter than a forge fire.

Nobody wanted to support the Supreme Council, but it wasn't a simple yes or no decision. It was a political minefield. And Regalia knew exactly what position she trapped Isleen and the others in. If they didn't heed Regalia's command, it would be treason, giving the Supreme Council license to seize the town. But if we sent our troops, Asylum would be slaughtered. There was the option I had suggested, which was to evacuate Asylum and let me face Lilith one-on-one, to which everyone vehemently disagreed, especially Angel Boy.

"Hayden, are you absolutely certain the First Eve will not attack the Supreme Council instead of Asylum? They're the head of every government in the witching world. Take them out, and we fall into chaos," Dante explained.

"No, that's not Lilith's goal." I shook my head at their naivety. "She doesn't care about overthrowing the Supreme Council. If she did, they'd be destroyed already."

Naida snorted at my comment. She had stayed suspiciously quiet during the shouting matches. Oh, she had shouted plenty, but something lacked in her snooty motivation. Like she didn't care very much—just wanted to stoke the flames.

"Then perhaps we should send our Knights to Jerusalem," Professor Periwinkle suggested. "And send the Salem Witch with. If the First Eve will attack wherever you are, Hayden, then let us send you to where the most warriors are stationed."

"One problem." I frowned. "Jerusalem doesn't have wards, and right now, Asylum's wards are the only thing keeping Lilith and her *millions* of demons from slaughtering us. Her forces are overwhelming. If we fight without protection, she will kill everyone before I can get close enough to fight her."

"Why doesn't she command her demons to raze the other witching communities to stop them from helping us?"

"Because the Supreme Council has done a wonderful job of dividing the witching world for Lilith. Which is another reason she won't take them out—she knows they're more of a pain for me than they are for her."

"But overthrow them, and she controls the entire witching world. She could control us through Regalia."

"That's not entirely true," Jamie countered. "Even if she destroyed the Council or if Regalia was compromised, her position and political power would be nullified, and Hayden would become our Commander-in-Chief. Lilith knows Hayden would raise an army, but with the Council intact and refusing to fight, Lilith has a stronger foothold."

"Lilith won't attack the Council because she can't be in two places at once, and Asylum is far more important to her," Apalla chimed in, supporting my claims further as her hazel eyes flashed with golden light. "It's been decided," she announced, her tone grim. "And I don't think she cares if we know."

"What I want to know," drawled the nasally brittle voice of a water witch I knew and loathed. It was a voice I hadn't heard since the Grimoire Games nearly two years ago.... "Is why this Lilith chick cares so much about Asylum?"

A heartbeat of silence fell on the room as I shared a startled look with Jamie and Apalla.

What was she doing here?

Whirling around, I pinned Mareena Bishop with my piercing blue eyes.

"What's so special about Asylum?" Mareena demanded again.

I shared a glance with Apalla and Jamie, communicating in the silence, but Mareena's eyes traced everything, bouncing between my face and my friends'.

What is your cousin doing here? Isleen asked Jamie as she telepathically linked our minds.

Jamie scoffed in our heads. *How should I know? I haven't seen her since...* Jamie trailed off, leaving awkward silence ringing in our heads.

But Apalla's eyes flashed. *She's here of her own volition. She wants answers.* Apalla licked her lips. *I don't think it's nefarious, but she won't leave without an answer about Lilith.*

"Well?" Mareena asked with all the snobbery one person could possibly exude.

Inhaling a heavy breath through my nose, I shared one last look with my friends as we reached a consensus through our telepathic channel.

"It's not about Asylum," I admitted. "It's about the witches in Asylum."

Mareena's eyes narrowed as she hiked out a hip. "Explain."

I bristled. Who was she to come into my war room and demand answers? But as Jamie stepped closer to me, his smoky warmth seeped into my skin, and the tension released from my shoulders.

Snorting out a breath, I rolled my shoulders like a bull before it charged. But I would leash myself.

Do we want her to know the full truth? Isleen asked skeptically.

I don't see the harm in telling her, Apalla answered. *We didn't hide the truth from the Asylum witches or any other witching community.*

We just didn't advertise it, Jamie agreed.

Nausea rolled in my stomach, and Spirit whispered its awesome guidance.

"Lilith is after the Power of Three," I blurted, trusting the intuition slamming into my stomach.

My friends and the Council stared at me with wide eyes, surprised I blatantly told Mareena the truth. The full truth. Or maybe the surprise was more from how nicely I said it.

"And how does the Mother of Demons acquire the Divine's Power of Three?" Mareena raised a skeptical eyebrow. "And how does Asylum fit into all this?"

"When my mom, Leyla Nightfall, was born as a demoness with a soul, Lilith transitioned from Maiden to Mother. So, when Leyla birthed me, a second demoness with a soul—"

"Lilith became the Crone, Leyla's the Mother, and you're the Maiden. Yah, yah, I get that." The blonde water witch rolled her eyes as she slapped her hands on her hips. "Still doesn't explain how a demon can gain the Goddess's power."

"It's not Goddess's power, per se," Apalla explained. "It's the Power of Three, which combines representations of the holy aspects of the Goddess to magnify powers to be greater than their sum."

"To what end?"

"With the Power of Three, Lilith will have enough magic to sever Earth's connection to Heaven, isolating mortals from the love of the Creator, and shroud the world in darkness."

Mareena's jaw dropped in a mix of shock and revulsion.

"And Lilith will become the supreme ruler over human- and witch-kind," I finished, staring Mareena unflinchingly in the eye.

"That's why she wants you," Mareena accused, pointing a slim finger at me. "Because you're the Maiden. But she needs all three aspects to form an unholy trinity, and right now, she only has the Crone."

I shook my head sadly, my black locks flying around my head like a dark halo. After Lilith's attack, Apalla used a spell to regrow my hair to its normal length instead of the jagged hair cut Lilith gave me on her island.

"Lilith channels Leyla," Jamie explained. "She has two-thirds of the power she needs."

"And she channels Alice Parker—the Salem Witch before Hayden—making her even more powerful," Apalla added as her eyes flashed as she used her True Sight to check in on Kova, like I had asked her to do periodically.

"So, Lilith will chase Hayden to wherever she goes?" Mareena concluded. "Why not move yourself? Duh?"

"It's not that easy." I breathed out a sigh, running a hand through my wild black locks. "I'm not the only means for her to gain the Maiden's powers."

"What is that supposed to mean?"

"Thea," my circle said together.

"The little girl with green eyes always hovering around you at the Grimoire Games?"

I nodded.

"What does Lilith want with a child?"

"She's the Heart of Earth."

Mareena's eyes widened as her body jerked, her spine erect. "But that means..."

"If Lilith can channel me or Thea, her power won't be limited to that of our powers combined. It completes an unholy trinity, power exponentially stronger than the summation of our powers, and the powers of the Salem Witch and the Heart of Earth will magnify the Power of Three. The Goddess blessed me with unbreakable free will, so Lilith can't gain my powers unless I willingly relinquish them to her. Thea does not have the same blessing," I lied smoothly.

Nobody, not even my circle, could know the truth.

"Lilith knows wherever Thea is, you are," Mareena pointed out. "That's why she's coming to Asylum. She doesn't care about the Supreme Council. They're nothing to her. But you... either you can provide the power of the Maiden, or you are the only thing standing between her and the Heart of Earth. She's coming here to kill you."

I nodded solemnly. "She nearly killed me in January."

"Then what's to stop her from killing you this time? And with everyone else?" Mareena shot back, throwing her arms wide.

"The power of Spirit." I tossed my head back with all the confidence of the Salem Witch, making my hair ripple on an unseen breeze. "I'm more powerful than before. Even with the power of the Mother and Crone and Alice Parker's elemental magic, Lilith and I are equally matched. But make no mistake, Lilith channels the power of one Nephilim Salem Witch. There's no telling how powerful she will become with the power of the Heart of Earth."

It was the most terrifying thought imaginable.

Apalla's eyes flashed, and Isleen's lips pursed. "Hayden, do you think..."

"Lilith will try to incapacitate me, steal Thea's powers, then torture my friends until I yield my powers to her to heighten her magic further?" I raised an inquisitive eyebrow at the shock expressions on my friends' and the Council's faces. None were as stunned as Mareena, whose jaw hung open wide enough to catch flies. "Yeah, I'm working on a solution."

Spirit whispered secrets through my mind... secrets and mysteries not to be shared aloud.

"So, if you die, the whole world falls to Darkness?" Mareena asked nonchalantly despite the morbid pile of smoking crap I dropped on the room.

"About sums it up." I shrugged a shoulder.

"And without the Supreme Council's resources, Asylum has dangerously low numbers of Knights. But you don't want to join them in Jerusalem because..."

"Because, without the wards, Lilith's army will annihilate us. Even if me and my circle are there to fight her. We can't protect everyone and fight her at the same time."

"Which is why you want to stay in Asylum. The wards give you an irreplicable advantage."

"Exactly," Isleen confirmed with a nod.

"Then we're in." Mareena straightened her spine, throwing her hair over her shoulder with all the snobbery in her body.

"We?" I asked, sharing a bewildered look with Jamie.

Mareena gestured to herself. "We as in Blairsville. We will fight with you."

My jaw dropped open.

"I'm sorry, what?" Apalla asked in shock. Mareena surprised the Prophetess. Was that possible?

"Try to keep up." The water witch rolled her eyes. "The Blairsville Knights will fight with you against Lilith."

"But why?" Jamie asked for me because my jaw was still on the ground.

"Uh, because I don't want the world to fall to Darkness. Duh." Mareena flipped her hair over her shoulder.

Scooping my jaw off the ground, I asked, "And why would the Blairsville Knights follow you?"

"Because they'll listen to my dad, and I'm going to tell him to help." She said it like it was obvious and I was a moron.

Isleen let out a light gasp between her open lips. "Of course. Blairsville's High Priestess passed away and Marinus"—Mareena's father, if I had to guess—"was elected High Priest last year."

"So, Marinus is willing to incur the wrath of Regalia Kensington and the Supreme Council by helping Asylum fight Lilith?" I asked Mareena, still flabbergasted at her willingness to help.

"Dad's not afraid of Regalia." She shrugged. "They used to date or something."

"Shocker there," I muttered under my breath, using the power of air so only Apalla and Jamie heard, earning stifled snickers from them.

"And Dad wants to be on the winning side. Like I told him, you"—she pointed a confident finger at my chest—"will be the one who wins. And if Regalia survives Lilith, she won't survive you. He sent me here to assess if your military intellect matches your renowned powers." She shrugged casually, like she couldn't care either way. "Turns out, you aren't as dumb as I expected."

"Gee, thanks," I deadpanned, then rolled my eyes.

"You're welcome," she said, ignoring the sarcasm. "Now, how are we going to get my Knights here?"

Sharing a look with my friends and Isleen, I smirked a wicked smirk. For once, I had a solution.

Thea and Silas were a powerful duo.

Green magic swirled in two portals as Thea used her vast Heart of Earth magic, and I slowly channeled the limitless power of Spirit into Silas to power his portal. Unlike before my Earth Trial, I could keep this up eternally, always refilling my power sources with the unbelievable vastness of Spirit.

So, why couldn't I spook? Or open a portal?

"Angels," I grumbled to myself.

"What was that?" Mareena asked from beside me.

"Nothing," I muttered. "How many more Knights?" I gestured to the steady stream of witches filtering in through the portals and entering Asylum through the archway of entwined twin white oaks.

"A third of the Blairsville Knights have passed through, but our citizens are coming, too. The adults will fight in exchange for keeping the kids safe."

"That's only a third?" My eyebrows raised into my hairline. Thousands had already entered Asylum. The Knights alone must have been a force of ten thousand, and with the adult citizens... we might stand a chance in this war.

Mareena shrugged, as if the sheer size of her force didn't impact her.

Drawing my silver wand from its hidden pocket in the sleeve of my leather jacket, I twirled the magical stick and muttered the spell to send a wand message.

Awaiting a response, I stood in comfortable silence with Mareena. She was still a snob, but she was a useful snob. Not even Apalla could have predicted this change of heart from the water elemental, but the Creator must have heard our prayers.

Pale yellow and red light flashed, and smoke stung my nostrils as Jamie spooked with Apalla and Isleen.

"What's the sitch?" Apalla asked.

Motioning to Mareena, I said, "Blairsville citizens are willing to fight with Asylum in exchange for protecting their youths."

"Where do we put them that will be safe?" Isleen asked, voicing the question that made me summon them.

I shared a look with Jamie, Apalla, and Thea. Silas's eyes remained closed as he maintained the portal, since his powers were limited compared to the Heart of Earth's.

"About that..." Apalla began.

Isleen raised a flat palm. "Let me guess. You've outfitted the Spellery to accommodate our forces." She looked directly at me.

I smirked deviously and waggled my eyebrows.

"Yeah, but the castle can only hold so many, and we need it as our base of military operations," Jamie said. "Hence the problem with housing civilians."

"What about the catacombs?" Thea asked, shifting her staff between hands as the emerald sparkled with her green earthy magic. "I can remove the Terracotta Army and station them around Asylum."

"Keep it as a back-up," I said. "But I don't want Lilith to know about my army of the dead—if I can figure out how to wake them—and keeping a bunch of kids in a tomb with skeletons probably classifies as childhood trauma."

"You have an army of the dead?" Mareena asked, raising an eyebrow.

"Army of corpses, skeleton army, whatever." I shrugged, my palms facing up.

"You just keep getting weirder and weirder."

Jamie snorted. "You have no idea."

"Hey, that's my line," I whined at him, but matched his charming smirk with a grin of my own, my cheeks heating at the prolonged eye contact.

Focus, Hayden.

"How about the Crystal Caverns?" Apalla asked. "Thea and Hayden could use their earth magic to clear tunnels under the cavern."

Spirit zapped through me, tugging at my stomach as intuition spoke to me.

"I don't think that's a good idea." Hiding underground seemed confining. Lilith could trap the citizens, and we would be useless to save them.

My eyes found Jamie's royal blue ones, and profound understanding passed between us as we spoke volumes with just a look.

I'm sorry, I said. *It's the only way.*

Running a hand through his golden locks, he dropped his head to stare at his feet, grappling with the grief of sacrificing the piece of him holding so desperately to the secret he shared with his deceased sister.

Lifting his head, his blue eyes met mine again.

"Hide them in the lagoon."

It was useless. Completely useless.

Apalla and I had scoured the library and the Advanced Annex with the help of Mrs. Wright, the Librarian. But there was nothing, and I mean absolutely nothing, about how to break Lilith's Voice of Command for my demons.

Or how to free my mom and Kova.

Every spare minute I wasn't training with Amara, I spent in the library with my nose shoved in a book. How did Apalla do this all the time? No wonder she was way smarter than me.

Apalla hadn't left in a week. Isleen and I brought her meals, but from the looks of her greasy golden locks and the bags under her eyes, she hadn't left the room to shower.

At least she was getting some sleep now, even if she was drooling on the book she used as a pillow.

Breathing out a huff, I returned to the book on my lap to rub my burning eyes. I had been reading nonstop for hours but found nothing.

Part of me wondered if mine and Apalla's efforts were fruitless or if, by some stroke of luck, we would stumble onto a revolutionary secret that might save us in this war.

Months had passed since my Earth Trial, and we had found absolutely nothing related to the Voice of Command or how to free a mortal from the Mother of Demon's control.

And I had a nagging feeling that both Kova and the Voice of Control would mean the difference in the number of lives lost in the Salem War to come.

CHAPTER FOUR

THE VOICE IN THE NIGHT

"Are you sure you want to attempt that?" Amara's flaming red eyes traced the black lightning zapping my skin. "Last time it blew up in your face."

Death and I had been awake for hours, practicing with the elements, especially the power of Spirit. After my success with using Spirit to resurrect the tree, Amara wanted me to kill the tree and resurrect it a million times.

I could do it in my sleep without looking. The power of Spirit was second nature. An entity of its own, Spirit often acted of its own volition.

But I wanted to try something different.

I shot her a reproachful glare. "'Blew up' is a harsh term for what happened," I grumbled as she perched on my brick fence.

"So, black lightning blasting from your chest to circle back, strike your heart, and knock you out cold was a pleasant sensation?" She raised a single skeptical eyebrow.

"Spectacular." I replied with an eye roll. "But I have to try again.... I need all my magical skills at my disposal when I face Lilith... and to pass my Spirit Trial."

Amara sighed. "I am not convinced this is the best way to accomplish your goals, but I relent. Knowing the fundamentals of spooking might enhance your understanding of Spirit."

I clapped my hands together. "Thank you, thank you, thank you."

"Dampen your excitement, child. I do not anticipate this being successful."

"If that type of optimism doesn't get a girl up for training in the morning, I don't know what does."

"The motivation to not die in the lethal Salem Witch Trials."

"Fair enough." I snorted and waved a hand at her. "Teach me your ways, oh, Master of Death."

"Close your eyes and summon the essence of Spirit. Do not manifest it outside your body, but allow its power to build within you, filling every nook and cranny and crevice and dark corner of your being. Let the essence of Spirit connect with your essence, the soul that is you. Remember, you do not have a soul. You *are* a soul, temporarily residing within a mortal body."

Death's melodic voice soothed my mind until my magical senses took control. As I did so, Spirit filled every particle of my being, filling me with light. If someone looked at me now, I was positive they would see a blazing ball of white light, my hair floating on the air like a dark halo.

"Good," Amara sang. "Good, just like that Hayden. Now visualize yourself somewhere that makes you feel warm and at home. A place you are comfortable in body, mind, and soul. Then simply will yourself, your true self, your soul, to be there. Then allow your soul to pull your body along, so when you open your eyes, you are in the place to wish to be."

Images of my house—the one in Asylum, not the one in Salem that Lilith destroyed last Samhain—filled my mind. I thought about my room, full of warmth and comfort. Memories of my father, freshly awoken, sitting on the couch in front of the living room fireplace or serving tea at our kitchen table or cooking in the kitchen I never used.... Memories flooded my mind. I thought of Salem, sleeping on piles of my dirty clothes. And I willed myself to stand in front of my bedroom fireplace with its mantle carved with ornate angels.

"Do you see it, Hayden?" I nodded, my eyes still closed. "Good, now let yourself have it. Allow yourself to go in the direction your soul pulls. Three... two... one."

Magic ruptured in my chest, ripping out of me in a powerful blast. Weightlessness surrounded me, like sleeping on a waterbed. And then my own lightning struck me in the chest. I flew backward and slammed into the ground, my spine bending around a rock. My eyes flew open as the air rushed from my lungs, and I struggled to breathe.

I tried to call upon my air magic, but a sharp shock zapped my body, electrocuting every cell, and my magic short circuited. I hadn't sucked in air after getting whiplash since I had mastered air magic, so I suffocated as I fought my muscles to work.

Air screamed into my lungs, burning my throat and nose, but I eagerly sucked in the blessed breath, swallowing deep lungfuls until my racing heart steadied its beating. Sucking in calming breath after calming breath, I pushed into a seated position with a groan.

"As I said... blew up in your face." Amara chuckled lightly, and it might have been the scariest sound I had ever heard.

With another groan, I flopped onto my back.

"Hayden, you cannot spook. You must make your peace with it."

"But you said Kova could spook by her Fire Trial." I threw my hands over my head, letting them smack against the ground. "I've mastered four elements. I should be able to spook."

"That was Alice. And you are you. You are not the same as your predecessors."

"Because she's Nephilim? Is that why she can spook and I can't?"

"Hayden, it is not our bloodlines that determine our powers, but rather the gifts bestowed upon us by the Creator. While we wield the same elements as other witches, we are blessed with unique and diverse gifts. While you cannot spook, Alice does not compare to your natural battle finesse."

"She excels plenty if you ask me," I grumbled.

"After three hundred years of training, yes, Alice is a skilled combatant, but after a short four years, you outmatch her. Do not diminish the consequence of your gifts, for they hold a heavy weight."

"I suppose you're right," I admitted begrudgingly. "But it doesn't seem like enough. Not when Lilith has my mom and Kova."

"If you insist on learning something new," Amara mused, "there is a spell I can teach you. It is called the Spell of Salem."

A shiver of power raced down my spine.

Rolling to my feet, I stared at her. The name alone... there was power in those words. And the Spell of Salem must be tied to the Salem Witch... the *original* Salem Witch, if I were to guess.

Death regarded me with her creepy red eyes, her fair features set in a serious expression. "I will teach you this spell, but before we begin, you must understand this is a hallowed, sacred spell. It is as ancient as the Salem Witch herself, and it is not a spell to be used carelessly."

"Hey, I can be serious," I protested.

"You have little to no restraint."

I pursed my lips as I glared at her. "I have restraint... I just don't always choose to practice it. Seriously, Amara, I've had to restrain myself a lot over the years."

"It is both sad and terrifying that *that* is you acting with restraint." Shaking her head, Amara sighed. "Nevertheless, I believe you demonstrate control when it comes to the seriousness of the stakes of this war, which is why I will teach you this fearsome spell." Slipping her hands into the arms of her black robes, she continued, "This spell cannot be used by a soul other than one who wields Spirit, but it has only been used once before it was lost to history."

"Only used once? That means..."

"Eve was the first and last Salem Witch to use this power. But without another Salem Witch for Eve to teach the spell to, the ancient knowledge died with her."

"Then how do you know it?"

"Did you not hear me? Eve *died*."

"Oh, um, right." A deep flush crept into my cheeks, and my face burned redder than a tomato. "If you've known about this spell since Eve died, then why haven't you used it, being a master of Spirit and all?"

"Ignoring that there has never been a need for me to use the spell, as the personification of Death, I am a neutral entity in the Universe. My purpose is to maintain balance between Light and Dark. If I used this spell, it could tip the scales one way or another and thrust the Universe into chaos. This is a spell to temporarily re-animate the dead, which opposes the very nature of my being, so I cannot use the Spell of Salem in this immortal life."

"Oh yeah, casually drop the bomb that this spell raises the dead. No biggie." I scoffed, then stared at her, my expression completely flabbergasted.

She frowned at me. "I was getting there."

Sometimes Death didn't get sarcasm.

"Never mind," I said, clamping my lips together to keep from laughing. "Please, continue."

"The Spell of Salem harnesses the power of Spirit to infuse inanimate objects with temporary life. These objects can then process thoughts and perform their own actions or be controlled by the spell caster, as long as they remain attached to their power source—Spirit. However, there are limitations to what objects you can use this spell on. You cannot spell a living being—human, demon, angel or otherwise."

"What about plants?" I thought of the wisteria tree in my backyard.

"Plants possess spirits of their own. This spell temporarily infuses Spirit into the object. If you tried this on something living, it either will not work or will cause harm to the being."

"Don't use it on any living thing. Got it." A thought nagged my brain. "What about an object that was alive once, but is now dead?"

Amara smirked at me in a totally unsettling, kinda creepy way. "Do you have anything particular in mind?"

"A skeleton."

"Eve used this spell to raise the bodies of her fallen comrades."

"Wait, what? I thought Eve was the first human."

"Ah, I forget how limited mortals' minds are."

"Hey," I whined in protest.

"The animals of earth by the Creator sided with Eve in her battle against Lilith. Most fell to Lilith's sword, but with this spell, Eve resurrected them, and their reanimated bodies fought alongside her one last time."

"That's heartbreaking."

Emotion clogged my throat as my thoughts flicked to my fallen familiar, who gave her life to protect me, to save me from Lilith. Months had passed, yet I felt like I didn't have the chance to properly mourn Salem and the life she had shared with me. Life these past months wasn't... it wasn't the same.

"This spell does not bring back the dead, Hayden. I trust you know nothing short of the Creator can return a soul to this Earth. Not even the Salem Witch."

"I know," I sniffed, wiping away the single tear rolling down my cheek. "I just miss her."

Amara placed a cold, pale hand on my shoulder. It was probably the only time she had tried to comfort someone, considering how awkward it was. But her actions were heartfelt.

"You will see your familiar again. You will see your father and other loved ones. Death is never really the end."

Sniffling, I swallowed my congestion and inhaled a slow, deep breath, like Harbor had taught me when she was my master of water. Acknowledging my grief, I accepted it, felt it in all its fullness, allowed my body to feel its physical effects, and then I released it, letting it wash from my body like a shower washing away dirt.

In place of my grief, fierce determination flooded my chest, determination to focus on the here and now so I could learn this spell and avenge my fallen family and friends.

Lilith wouldn't know what hit her.

"Teach me the spell, Death."

"To invoke the fifth element in this spell, repeat after me, 'Quintessence.'"

Straightening my spine, I threw my shoulders back. Reaching into my core, I called upon the power of Spirit, letting its warm glow infuse my entire body before reciting that single fateful word of the most powerful spell in history.

"Quintessence."

The word rolled off my tongue—the power charging the air with electricity in a concentrated shot of Spirit, stronger and more potent than any magic I had experienced before. The word itself was filled with the awe and power to overcome insurmountable trials.

As I uttered the Spell of Salem, I felt invincible, like nothing in this silly material world could harm me, and if it did, it didn't matter because my mortal body was temporal compared to the eternal nature of my soul.

The Spell of Salem was both mystifying and remarkable, and as I said the word aloud, a sense of serene joy and understanding filled me, yet the power of Spirit within me was exhilarating, intoxicating, and electrifying, enlivening the dead parts of my spirit and awakening my slumbering magic.

Closing my hand into a fist, I raised it to stare at the intense white light radiating off my skin like the halo of an angel. An aura of absolute purity as Quintessence imparted its knowledge. And I understood with absolute clarity how and when to cast the Spell of Salem.

For the first time since losing my dad and Salem, since Kova was imprisoned, I had the power to rescue her.

The fire in my fist burned brighter as my resolve solidified. "I'm coming for you, Kova. I promise."

"Hayden, you need to see this," Apalla called from her adjacent table in the library. Candlelight flickered in the braziers holding flames in the center of each table, adding to the minimal light of the library repelling the pitch darkness of midnight.

Students and professors had long since abandoned the Spellery library, every witch in Asylum too busy preparing for war to waste their time studying. But Apalla and I didn't waste a minute *not* studying, searching for the answers we so desperately needed.

Snapping my head up, I shot my gaze to her hands in which she held a thick leather-bound book with yellow, jagged edges.

The tome flew across the room on a gust of wind, so the spine slammed into my outstretched hand.

A faint smile flitted across my lips. With all the power of the Salem Witch, the novelty of magic was often lost. But sometimes the miracle of magic was found in small, subtle moments like this one.

The smile melted off my face. "This book is written in Enochian." My piercing blue gaze snapped up to meet Apalla's. I recognized the language from its lettering, which matched the inscription on my longsword.

"I can't read it, but—"

"But I can," I finished for her, marveling at the book.

"What is the title?" Apalla moved to stand behind me and peak over my shoulder, as if she could read the words by being near me.

"The Book of Raziel the Angel: The Tome of Secrets"

Power charged the air. Raw energy infusing every molecule of life as though the words I spoke were a real, living thing.

"Whoa, did you feel that?"

Staring wide-eyed at the tome, I silently nodded, afraid to speak. This was not a book to read aloud, for the words alone could create. After all, were words not spells? Were the power of words not why witches feared speaking Lilith's name aloud? Were words not used to bring to life all of creation? What I held in my hands was holy and precious and dangerous.

And in my soul, I knew it held the answers I sought.

The chair legs scraped against the polished wooden floor as I pulled it out from the table. Without taking my eyes off the book, I sat and opened the cover to the first page.

The ancient book was handwritten with ink and a quill, and when I touched a finger to the page, Spirit whispered that it was older than every other book in the world. It was the first of the written word. It was not of this earth but brought to Earth by this angel—who had written the script in Heaven—and given to Adam and Eve at the command of the Creator.

It all made sense now... archaeologists and historians called the written word the dawn of civilization and this book... this book was the first. Civilization dawned with Adam and Eve—Eve, who was the mother of humans and witches.

Raziel, the Angel of Secrets, also known as "Gallistur", is one of the ancient angels of old, who remains dutifully at the side of the Creator, recording his knowledge and mysteries and magic. His angelic name translates to "Creator is my mystery", a name befitting the angel tasked as the Keeper of Magic and the Angel of Mysteries of the Universe.

Having knowledge presented to him by the Creator, Raziel is responsible for recording the utterings and conversations of Heaven in his eternal book. It is through his understanding and interpretations of these discussions that he was commanded to inform the human and witch races of vital information, per the Creator's will.

Upon direction from the Creator, Raziel shared knowledge with Adam and Eve after they ate the fruit of the forbidden Tree of Knowledge of Good and Evil. Once they were tainted, Raziel was commanded to share with them the knowledge that would lead them home and closer to understanding their all-powerful Creator.

In generations past, Raziel was responsible for imbuing knowledge on Enoch, who later ascended to the young celestial named Metatron. Enoch's son, Noah, received wisdom from Raziel and used it to build the ark at the Creator's direction. And so on through the generations,

Raziel has impacted knowledge and wisdom on mortals at the Creator's behest.

I was completely engrossed in the book. Hours passed, but I didn't stir from my seat, keeping my eyes glued to the ancient text as I scrutinized every word for the information I sought. But as I read the book, my anxiety only heightened.

The writings were detailed about magic, planets and zodiac, and spiritual laws and the power of speech, thoughts, the energy and spellcasting power of words, and the integration of a person's soul within the confines of a mortal body in the physical world, but nothing to answer my desperate questions.

The further I read without answers, the more discouraged my heart grew. If this book couldn't tell me how to save everyone, then was there a way to save them?

Raziel, being the Angel of Secrets, can be called upon, like all angels.

Hold up. Angels could be called on? Why wasn't I calling Gabriel's butt down here? Angel Boy, get your dad on the angel phone.... I had a lot of questions for the Messenger Archangel.

Although, mortals should be aware of the displeasure they invoke on themselves by summoning a celestial being with whom they do not hold favor.

Ah, crap.

Raziel, despite his dealings with mortals throughout history, is known to be less inclined than other archangels to respond positively toward those who summon him. However, there are recordings of both humans and witches who have called upon him successfully and unsuccessfully, though the latter have suffered an unsavory punishment.

I didn't even want to know.

Be warned, those who summon this mighty angel, for if you incur his wrath, that day shall be your last. Pursue other avenues of knowledge first and only call upon Raziel in your darkest hour of need. For the risk is heavy and should be avoided at great cost.

But if all is lost, there exists a spell....

This was it. This is what I was looking for. It wasn't an answer to my questions, but it would lead me to the angel who held all the answers.

Raziel, I was coming for you.

Wind whistled as it blew through my hair, tousling the black locks.

Standing on the observation deck atop the Spellery's Air Tower, I tipped my head back to stare at the silver light of the half-moon.

Red light flashed in my peripheral as Jamie spooked to the top of the tower. Warmth seeped into my back as Angel Boy approached, his hot breath brushing the back of my neck as he stepped in closer.

His hands gripped my biceps, squeezing lightly.

"What are you doing?" he whispered into my ear.

Humming contentedly in my throat, I tore my gaze away from the moon as I turned to face my Angel Boy.

It was just me and him... the two of us while we waited for the rest of my circle.

The past few months... I couldn't remember the last time Jamie and I were alone together. If we were, we were training or planning battle tactics—like the water cannon.

Moonlight washed out Jamie's bond hair, making it appear more silver than his actual golden-bronze. His familiar smoky scent filled my nostrils, and I sighed, swaying into him.

The tension that wound up my neck and shoulders eased as Jamie's hand rubbed along my spine. My eyelids grew heavy as I gazed into those hooded royal blue eyes gazing back at me.

We hadn't had a moment like this since...

Green light flashed.

Of course, the moment was ruined before he could kiss me. Kiss me and *not* spook off. I just wanted one kiss. One. Before the onset of this war. Nausea rolled in my stomach in answer.

Reluctantly, I stepped out of the circle and warmth of Jamie's arms, and my friends had the good graces to not say anything as they busied themselves with the sky or their feet, Thea standing between Apalla and Ethan.

Electricity charged the air, and lightning struck the wooden planks of the observation deck. Amara's blood red eyes glowed against the inky blackness of the starless night sky.

"The witching hour is nigh," Amara said. "Are you ready to call upon Raziel?"

"Let's do this."

My circle took their places at each cardinal direction.

Like a million times before, Apalla began the circle casting by summoning the first element.

It was a simple prayer, but no less powerful. Short and simple since the final verses of the spell to call Raziel were complicated and cost a high energy toll to fuel the spell.

I call upon the element of air,
Wind of the east hear my prayer.

My first element whispered as it rushed to join our circle. My long black locks blew in the breeze, whipping behind me as a cyclone raged.

I call upon the element of fire,
Flames of honor answer my desire.

The element I shared with Jamie burned bright as white flames ignited around the circle, glowing but not burning the castle's wooden observation deck.

I call upon the element of water,
Liquid of splendor lead evil to slaughter.

Storm clouds gathered in the sky above Ethan, thunder rolling as the condensed water converged on us, and a gentle rain pattered against the wooden boards of the deck.

I call upon the element of earth,
Soil of nature, to our powers give birth.

Flower petals and leaves blew on the breeze as trees and plants shook fourteen stories below. Vines wound up the side of the castle, clinging to the stone walls.

I call upon the ultimate power of Spirit,
Answer our call, to glorify Heaven above all.

Lightning struck my chest, lighting up the sky with its brilliant glow. Electricity charged the air and sparks danced in my hair as it expanded from the polarity.

The white light of Spirit haloed around me.

"Now," I shouted. White light beamed from my hands, connecting to the other four witches forming my circle. Amara sat cross-legged on the stone wall surrounding the observation deck, outside of the circle of white light connecting the circle.

Together, we chanted, charging the spell with our combined powers.

Seek and ye shall find,
The magic of Heaven that binds.
Archangel Raziel, Keeper of Magic,
We seek your knowledge to avoid fate so tragic.
Tome of Secrets we explored,
To learn of Raziel, whom we implore.
Angel who holds wonder and mystery,
Only thee can inform us of truthful history.
Secrets of the Universe come from the Divine,
Pass your lips like flowing wine.
Knowledge and wisdom that we now lack,
Turn the tide against evil's diamondback.
Raziel, come to Earth to share your brilliance,
So, we may fight Darkness with holy resilience.
By the power of air, fire, water, and earth,
This circle calls on you to fill our dearth,
Four elements bound by Spirit's witchery,
To glorify Heaven through holy victory.

And with the final word, the white light connecting our circle expanded, filling the space between us before shooting into the sky above like a beam signaling space beyond.

Brilliant white light flashed in the circle, and my friends shielded their eyes to keep from being blinded by the light, but Amara and I did not flinch as Raziel emerged from the light, the ethereal glow of Heaven wrapping around him like a golden halo as the white light faded.

Standing seven feet tall with flawlessly white angel wings, Raziel filled the observation deck with his heavenly presence. Like Gabriel, Raziel stared at me with unsettling eyes—golden irises with a pupil of white that glowed in stark contrast to the darkness of his skin.

Tucked under his robe-clad arm was a scroll to match the peacock feather quill he held in his right hand.

A band of pink and white wrapped around Raziel's left ring finger, the colors stark against his cocoa skin. Hearts and angel wings and flower petals inked on his skin in an inch-thick soulmate glyph, the colorful ink edged by miniscule writings circling his finger.

Jophiel, Spirit whispered. Raziel was soulmates with Jophiel, the Archangel of Heavenly Beauty.

He wasn't as imposing as the Book of Raziel the Angel made him out to be. Was he an angel with awesome power and could destroy me?

Yes. But was he glaring menacingly at me like he would smite me? No. Raziel considered me with what may have been a look of blatant curiosity.

"Hayden Black," the angel boomed in a voice that shook mountain tops.

Literally. The mountains of the Crystal Mines quaked in the distance, earning a glare from Thea. A beam of green light shot from the emerald embedded in the top of her staff, blasting into the earth without destruction, and the quaking ceased at the command of the Heart of Earth.

With a voice of thunder that could be felt all the way to the center of the Earth, Raziel announced himself. "I am Raziel, the Angel of Secrets and Mysteries of the Universe and the Keeper of All Magic."

"Gallistur, Revealer of the Rock," I declared his name. "Yeah, I know who you are."

"You did not until the young Prophetess discovered The Book of Raziel the Angel: The Tome of Secrets." Raziel smirked.

"But I knew when I summoned you," I pointed out, waggling my eyebrows.

"Then you know my answering of your call—"

"Wasn't it a summoning?" Jamie asked.

"No. A summoning is irrefutable." Amara's red eyes pulsed with power. "Raziel is not bound to answer us. He did so of his own free will."

"You could have mentioned that sooner." I shot a daggered glare at her. "The Tome of Secrets made it sound like Raziel would kill us." Turning back to the Raziel, I said, "So, I need to know—"

Raising a flat palm, the angel interrupted me, "I will reveal the mysteries of the universe in answer to a single question."

"One question?" The book said nothing about limited questions.... "You mean one for each of us?" I asked desperately, but nausea rolled in my gut as Spirit answered me.

"One question from *you*, Salem Witch, as you are the one who called."

"But it wasn't just me." I gestured at the circle. "We all summoned you."

"But only you called me with *your* spirit," Raziel spoke, his voice reverberating through the air. "Therefore, only you may ask a question."

My accusing gaze shot to Amara. "Did you know about this?"

"I did not know."

"How didn't you know?" Jamie growled, red flames igniting in his hair. "You're a celestial. He's a celestial. You reside in the heavenly realms together."

Amara chuckled darkly. "You would think a Nephilim would understand the upper realms better—"

"You act like I've been there before," Jamie snapped.

"I'm more interested in why Amara insinuated that her and Raziel don't live in Heaven together?" Apalla probed. "So, you two don't know one another?"

"I live with the dead," Amara answered, ignoring Jamie's sass. "As the Angel of Secrets, Raziel resides in a different realm of Heaven."

"There's more than one realm?" I asked, my curiosity piqued. "I thought it was just the Garden?"

"Just the Garden for mortal souls to rest within, but there are many tiers of realms for different purposes."

"Like the underworld."

"Hell is a reflection of Heaven, but a perverted, incomplete, imperfect creation compared to the greater realms above." Raziel lifted a hand, gesturing to the sky. "Hell is comprised of torturous places to punish souls. But Heaven is tiered for different purposes to execute the plans of the Creator. For example, the armies of Heaven, led by my brother, Michael, train in a realm separate from the Garden. How could mortals find peace amid a warrior's environment?"

"As celestials, Raziel and I are permitted to travel between realms, but it is atypical as we each have a higher purpose, therefore we tend to reside in the realm aligned with our role," Amara explained.

"But you're the Keeper of the Veil," Jamie insisted. "You have to know when Raziel crosses from the upper realms to Earth."

"Meaning you know when he comes to Earth to answer questions," I accused.

"I may be the Keeper of the Veil for *mortal* souls, but that does not make me omniscient. Celestials have free rein to cross as they desire."

"Tell that to my father," Jamie grumbled.

"Yet you seem to know everything else." I scowled at Death. When I approached her with the Tome of Secrets, Amara had known of other mortals who successfully called Raziel, though she had never been present. "You knew how to summon Raziel, so how could you not know the rules binding him?"

Amara's red eyes narrowed on me with deadly focus. Her mouth opened, revealing a row of shark-like teeth, but before she could snap a retort, Raziel answered, settling the matter.

"Amara did not know."

"No!" we shouted together, throwing our hands up.

"That wasn't my question," I yelled frantically. "I-I—"

"Relax, child." Raziel raised a placating hand, his soulmate glyph shining with colorful light. "That is not a mystery of the Universe. I merely offered a confirmation as a courtesy to cease this needless argument."

Collectively, my circle breathed out a sigh of relief.

"Thank Goddess," Apalla muttered under her breath.

"Bloody angels," Jamie grumbled.

Running a hand through my long black locks, I inhaled deeply to calm my racing heart. "Bloody angels" was right. I could have sworn Heaven enjoyed nearly killing me from a heart attack.

But the angel in front of me was my only chance to win this war. I needed his help, which meant I had to be... well, not my angsty self.

"So much for incurring your wrath like the Tome of Secrets warned," I said sarcastically.

Oh, crap.

So much for not being myself. I really needed to think before I spoke. One of these days, my mouth would get me into trouble. Besides all the times it already had, namely in my interactions with the Supreme Council. Probably could have been more diplomatic, but it was too late now.

Raziel chuckled humorously, unfazed by my apparent rudeness. "I like to think I am one of the more tolerant angels, seeing as I enjoy interacting with mortal souls."

"Then why did the Tome of Secrets warn us against incurring your wrath when invoking you?"

"Ah, yes." Raziel smiled, his pearly whites flashing under the silver half-moon. "I intentionally wrote that into the book to sound ominous and intimidating. Mortals were too fond of summoning me after I helped Noah with the plans for the Ark. I ended up with a backlog of summons."

"But you can ignore summons."

"Yes, but the physical pull of a magical summoning is rather agitating." Raziel shrugged his shoulder, his bald head gleaming in the moonlight. "How would you like incessant phone calls? I needed a break. Honestly, I forgot about the book for a few centuries until the Creator told me you would call upon me, Salem Witch."

My circle and I stared at the angel, dumbfounded. Man, celestials were weird. It was a wonder they conceived mortal children.

Pfft, angels.

But our time with the angel was running short, and I needed answers, which the Angel of Secrets sensed.

"Choose your question wisely."

"How do I defeat Lilith?" I asked without hesitation. I didn't have to think about it. It was the most important question of my entire life. The *purpose* of my entire life.

A thousand other questions burned at me—how to free my mom and Kova, how to destroy the Voice of Command, who my sire was, if Jamie and I would end up together—but defeating Lilith... it was the task bestowed on my soul and nothing was greater than fulfilling the Creator's purpose for me.

"Ah. That is one secret I cannot disclose."

"What? Why not?"

"Lilith's demise is not clear to me."

"But you're the Angel of Mysteries," Apalla scolded. "You *have* to know."

"I am an angel, but angels are flawed, and while I know close to everything, I do not actually know everything."

"That's the most ridiculous thing I've ever heard." Jamie scoffed.

"Gabriel is rolling his eyes at you, son."

Jamie sneered. "Yeah, sure, of course you know that but can't answer our actual question."

But I remained quiet. Because I understood why.

"Celestials do not know everything, Jamie," Thea answered in a calming tone. "We are not complete and perfect. Powerful, yes, but we are not omnipotent, omnipresent, nor omniscient."

"Lucifer," I said quietly.

"What?" Jamie demanded of me.

"What do you mean 'Lucifer'?" Apalla asked with a quizzical look.

Glancing around my circle, then once at Raziel, I said, "Because Lucifer, the first to fall, was once an angel. And he convinced a *third* of angels to fall with him because he believed he was greater than the Creator." I threw my chin up in defiance. "But he's not. Even angels are less than the Creator, but power can make one arrogant. You don't know everything because those few shortcomings remind you of who is greater."

"Wise beyond your years, Hayden Davina Black." Raziel raised his hands and placed one of each of my cheeks. "Your father is proud of you. Proud of who you are and who you have become these past seventeen years."

Tears welled in my eyes. Raziel knew. He knew who my father was. The desire to ask burned inside my heart, an ache so deep, I didn't know if the gaping hole in my chest would heal unless I learned his identity.

"Because I could not answer your question, you may ask another."

A thousand questions raced through my mind, but ultimately, I had to ask the question that would win the Salem War. I gnawed on my bottom lip. But what was the right question? This is why I made a list... a list of countless questions, but I could only ask one.

I needed to save Kova. With her held captive, Lilith could channel the power of four elements. I wasn't sure how Kova kept the Mother of Demons from channeling Spirit—at least she didn't channel Spirit when she punched a hole in the wards—but it was a small mercy for which I was eternally grateful. Kova's powers could make a difference in this war, and taking it away from Lilith would even the playing field, but...

My demons.

Driving my fingers into my hair, I tugged on my black locks.

It was a massacre when Lilith used the Voice of Command against my demons. She couldn't command them to attack my witches because I prevented it years ago when they first arrived in Asylum—and continuously reissued the command as new recruits joined my army—but her command prevented them from fighting her demons, leaving them more than vulnerable.

They would be slaughtered.

Seventeen thousand demons would be reduced to ash if I didn't break Lilith's Voice of Command.

Kova, the Salem Witch, or a dark army of seventeen thousand demons?

Inhaling, I silently sent a prayer to the Creator that I was making the right decision.

"Tell me how to break Lilith's Voice of Command—both past and future commands."

I couldn't look at Jamie and Apalla as gasps left their mouths. Thea and Ethan remained silent, but their gazes burned into my back. Was I ashamed of my choice? Yes. Was it the wrong choice? I prayed not.

"You cannot sever the Mother of Demon's Voice of Command without losing your own powers, Princess of Hell. Do you still wish to know?"

Lose my Voice of Command? I never wanted it to begin with, but I had used it when necessary—to keep demons from hurting mortals and one another or in battle against Lilith's armies. I couldn't usurp Lilith's Voice by telling the demons to never listen to her... there were magical restrictions on the Voice. But I had countered her future mandates by commanding they not hurt witches unless in self-defense and to avoid fatal harm whenever possible if they must defend themselves.

Was it an enormous loss to lose my powers? Part of me said yes, because it was a power I wanted in the war to come. And after. If I defeated Lilith, hundreds of thousands, if not millions, of demons would remain loose in the world, and the Voice was invaluable to leash demons.

But the other part said I was being selfish. I didn't want to lose the Voice because I was afraid of forfeiting any power, even if it was a dark power.

Tossing my head back, I let my black locks ripple in the wind. "Tell me."

"Regalia is still refusing to send aide to Asylum."

"Shocker," I said with an eye roll before tipping my head back to blow out a breath. Not like we didn't already know this.

"If somebody hadn't insulted the *entire* Supreme Council, Regalia and Elizabeth might be willing to help us in our hour of need."

"How many times I can I say, 'I'm sorry'?" I snapped.

Truthfully, I wasn't that sorry. But I was sorry about the consequences—that Asylum would wage this war alone. Without reinforcements from the Supreme Council or any other witching community in the world since Regalia expressly forbid their aide, and she technically was the High Priestess, even if I refused to acknowledge her title.

"They weren't exactly fans of mine to begin with," I pointed out.

"We've known we would be on our own," Jamie added. "This isn't news. The Supreme Council has been silent since Hayden kicked them out of Asylum right before her Earth Trial, except to demand our troops transfer to Jerusalem."

Zola coughed. "Can Asylum survive this war with the Blairsville Knights?"

I shared a long, uncomfortable look with Jamie. We had discussed this at length. Even with all the engineering and modifications to the Spellery, and my brilliant ideas—seriously, I loved that water cannon, even if it was Harbor's idea—Asylum's military force, even with the civilian witches fighting and Blairsville's reinforcements, was pathetically small compared to the number of demons Jackal and I estimated in Lilith's army.

"We need every hand we can get," Jamie replied vaguely.

"The more witches we have, the fewer lives that will be lost." I grimaced at the casualness with which I talked about death. There was no intimacy in it. Just hard numbers.

"We aren't at a complete loss," I asserted, trying to lighten the somber mood that had fallen on the Council's chambers. The usual crowd was present—Isleen as High Priestess, Kane as General since my father officially passed, Professor Periwinkle, Dante, Naida, and Zola as the elemental Representatives—minus one key player, who had been missing for months now. My heart twanged with guilt. It should have been me who fought Lilith, not Kova.

"We have the Heart of Earth, a true Prophetess, and a witch who can mind control demons." All but Isleen stared at me in shock. Whoops. I guess Kelsey and I forgot to disclose the extent of her mind control powers to the Council. "And we have a Nephilim with the power of holy flames, and we have the Salem Witch. We have *me*."

"What about Death?"

The room shifted uncomfortably. Every witch who knew about Amara was still extremely unhappy that she was training me, which they reminded me of daily.

"Death is a neutral entity in the Universe. Amara can't choose sides. At least not through direct interference."

"But we have another advantage," Apalla added, her eyes flashing gold. Frowning, she glanced between me and Thea, but an almost imperceptible shake of my head made Apalla cover her tracks. Whatever she thought she knew, she kept it to herself. No need for us to ever discuss it. "Lilith will hunt Thea. She will drop everything to obtain the Maiden."

"And Lilith wants to kill me herself. Which is something we can use to our advantage. Wherever I am, she will follow."

But Naida couldn't give it a rest. It had been the same argument, week after week, for months on end.

"If you ask me," Naida sneered, "Hayden has an over glorified opinion of her significance to the Dark Mother." Naida shot me a tight smile as she flipped her shimmering blue hair over her shoulder with extra attitude. "It's difficult to believe she would attack Asylum instead of Jerusalem, where the Supreme Council resides."

The tension in the room tightened as everyone held their breath, waiting for my response.

But I didn't bite off Naida's head. My fiery temper didn't flare at her words because something she said tugged at my gut, and Spirit whispered through my mind.

My piercing blue eyes narrowed, my brain whirling as I thought through every word, every syllable.

Anyone can betray anyone, Spirit whispered. *Do not allow the pettiness of vanity to blind your mind to the truth.*

I cocked my head at her. "How did you refer to Lilith just now?"

The color drained from Naida's face as the vein in her forehead pulsed. Magic extended from me, my powerful tendrils sensing Naida's erratic heartbeat.

"I-I-I..." she stammered. "W-well, y-you s-s-see... the-the thing is..."

My hand slammed on the table in a fist. The elements exploded from where my hand hit the wood.

Air blasted into Naida, toppling her chair. She hit the ground with a thud, but I charged her as silver flames ignited in my hair. Water surged around the Water Representative, as I commanded the element to swallow Naida in a sphere. Forcing her head above water, I froze the sphere. Naida was a water elemental, but her magic was pathetic compared to my might.

"*You're* the spy. You are the one feeding Lilith information. You've probably been in league with her since the day I arrived in Asylum," I accused vehemently.

"Don't be ridiculous," Naida denied fervently, struggling futilely against the ice holding her captive. Her magic surged under the surface, but mine shredded hers to ribbons. "I-I would... I would *never.*"

"That's how Lilith discovered Thea is the Heart of Earth," Jamie growled, unsheathing his broadsword to press the tip threateningly into Naida's neck. "Even with mine and Harbor's Binding Spell."

I threw myself at Jamie, pressing against him before he could skewer her. I didn't need twin telepathy to know what he was about to say next.

He thrust an accusatory finger at the water witch. "You told Lilith before we cast the binding. YOU'RE THE REASON MY SISTER IS DEAD."

"If Lilith didn't know Thea was the Heart of Earth, she wouldn't have attempted to kidnap Thea, and Harbor wouldn't have used her Glory."

"That's how Elliot recognized you at the Grimoire Games. He couldn't see through my glamour talisman—he just knew what you looked like." Apalla added, nocking an arrow on her bow.

Not that she needed to, but we all felt better with a weapon in our hand while the serpent's spy slithered in our presence.

"You poisoned me," Thea accused with the most anger I had ever heard from her, but it was mild compared to the tempers raging in the room. "Before the Supreme Council's visit. You touched me during the 'etiquette lessons' you insisted on."

"Only Lilith's loyal demons call her the Dark Mother. Those who are loyal to me refer to her as the First Eve or the Mother of Demons," I accused. "Isn't that right, Jackal?" I asked my loyal demon as he scampered onto my shoulder, spreading between me and Jamie as I pressed into his chest to keep him from running Naida through with his flaming broadsword.

"Correct, Princess."

In a flash of black, Jackal morphed into a panther at my side, saliva dripping from his jaws as he growled menacingly. Prowling forward, he circled Naida where she stood paralyzed by fear.

"No," she gasped. "No, I'm not... I don't..."

Isleen was as unthawing as a winter blizzard. "The audacity of your feeble attempts to deny it."

Apalla snorted. "And the ignorance to assume we're stupid enough to believe her ridiculous assertions that Lilith will attack the Supreme Council. As if Hayden would allow Asylum to be vulnerable and unprepared."

"Not only are you an idiot, but you think we are, too." Kelsey popped out a hip as she slapped a hand on her waist.

"We trusted you," Isleen whispered with a deadly soft voice. "The Council trusted you for *years*."

Tears pooled in Naida's eyes as she shook her head, her blue hair rippling like waves in the ocean. "I didn't mean to," she half sobbed, half screamed in her nasally voice. "You have to believe me. I didn't want to. But the Dark Mother... she has such terrible power. She... she showed me things—no, she made me see things, horrible things that would happen if I didn't help her. She tricked me."

"You allowed her to manipulate you." Jamie stepped into me, but I pushed him back, dragging his broadsword away from Naida's neck. "You didn't have to give into her."

"Do you have any idea what power she possesses? She burned me with hellfire." Naida's voice quivered as she swallowed her sobs. She threatened to burn the entire town down if I didn't help her. What was I supposed to do?"

"Fight her," I growled. "Like Harbor did at the *cost of her life*."

"She's the oldest demon in history. The original demon, and you think I have the power to stand against her?"

"Yes. Because it isn't about power, Naida. It doesn't matter how much power you do or do not have. Standing up to Lilith is a *choice*. And you chose wrong." Waving my hand, I melted the ice holding her. "Thea," I called her name as I slid Jamie's broadsword into its sheath, extinguishing the holy flames as he shook with barely contained fury.

Metal shackles materialized around Naida's wrists and ankles as Thea waved her staff through the air, the emerald shimmering with magical light.

"As if you could have done any better in my shoes," Naida shot back.

Fire flooded my veins, and my blood boiled from the heat of my rage. Naida's pathetic excuses grated on my last nerve.

I had to attend to war preparations and train Spirit magic.

"I did," I answered coldly. "I've stood against Lilith since the day I arrived in Asylum, and I will continue to stand against her until my last."

Jamie's raging royal blue eyes didn't leave Naida as I dragged him away from her.

Meeting Isleen's eye, I told the Council, "Lock her up. Dungeons, prison, wherever you keep evildoers. We don't have time for a trial, but I can't have her running off to join Lilith. She knows too much about our plans—if it isn't too late already."

"Jackal, help Isleen, then find me."

"Yes, Princess." The black panther bowed ceremoniously.

I spun on my heel and stomped from the room, Apalla, Jamie, Ethan, and Thea flanking me in silence as we ignored the chatter of the Council behind us. We marched silently through the winding hallways of the Parthenon until we exited the building into the bright sunshine of the warm May day bathing Asylum. It was nearly June, which meant I had a little over a month until my birthday.

My last birthday if I didn't pass my Trial.

As sunlight soaked into my pale skin, I inhaled a deep breath and allowed myself to relax. Closing my eyes, I exhaled slowly. I repeated this again, and then again, and again, until my rage quelled to a low simmer.

"You know, I hate being suspicious, but dang, that gut feeling is never wrong."

Jamie's body quivered with fury. I didn't need to see him to sense the unbridled anger inside him. My eyes fluttered open as I turned and leaned into him—the others didn't flinch at our emotional intimacy.

"It was the right call," Apalla agreed as her eyes flashed gold. "Naida is the traitor."

"We knew there was a spy other than Elliot... for years, we were blind to not figure it out sooner."

"If we had known three years ago..." Jamie trailed off, and I knew where his thoughts were... Harbor. "I should have known... I-I should have seen it."

"You couldn't have known..." I began, but Jamie cut me off.

"Harbor and I knew... we always knew Lilith and Naida often sided with one another. Even before you came to Asylum, we knew those two were closer than any on the Council..."

"Jamie, *none* of us figured it out. Not me, not Isleen, not *Kova*," I emphasized her name. "Kova is an immortal Salem Witch. If she didn't know, then none of us could have figured it out."

Apalla shook her hair, her golden curls flying in a halo around her head. "The question is... why couldn't I see it?"

"Probably for the same reason you couldn't see Elliot. Lilith must have shielded them using dark magic."

"At least you caught Naida. There's no telling what kind of damage she could have inflicted by relaying our plans to Lilith."

"I wouldn't have if she hadn't called Lilith by her demonic title. Only by the grace of Heaven did I catch her traitorous words. I just hope it wasn't too late."

Jamie's heartbeat settled to its normal cadence under my hand, and I stepped away, breaking the contact between us.

"I can't believe I didn't see it before," Apalla complained as her eyes flashed gold three times in rapid succession as she used her Daughter of Apollo powers. "I'm not even talking about my True Sight. I should have figured it out. She just seemed so surface level mean, I never imagined she was evil to her core."

"We know now. All we can do is work with what we have," Ethan said reassuringly as he rifled through his potion kit for whatever potion he was going to brew up next.

"There's no point in worrying about Naida anymore," I agreed with Ethan, meeting Jamie's eye, trying to read his mind.

"You have your Trial to worry about." Apalla brushed past me. "Come on, let's train with Amara."

"You know, I wouldn't mind taking a day off from Death. Seriously, is that too much to ask?"

Jamie threw his head back and laughed. "If you take a day off, I'll surpass you in combat."

I snorted and shoved him playfully. "You wish."

CHAPTER FIVE

THE DESCENT INTO HELL IS SHORT AND STEEP

Blood red eyes flashed in the shadowy corner of my bedroom. My heart hammered out of my chest, and I lunged out of bed, the power of Spirit crackling around my hand as silver flames burst to life along my shoulders. Air tousled my hair as the element answered my call, and ice coated my fingertips in sharpened claws. Wicked vines extended from my potted plants on the windowsill, snapping defensively.

Death emerged from the dark corner, a shadow compared to the warm mango light of the dawn peeking through my windows. Her candy-apple red hair flashing in the light of the flickering silver flames burning in my bedroom hearth.

"Goodness, Amara." Clutching my heart, I released the power of the elements, ceasing the wind, snuffing the flames, melting the water, and receding the vines into their pots, but I let the black lightning zap my skin until it absorbed into my body. "That was insanely creepy."

She smiled that disturbing grin with teeth filed to points. I didn't care what my friends said—her adult form was far more sinister and ghoulish than her appearance as a little girl with jade green eyes.

"So," I started, leaning a hip against my dresser, "why is Death visiting me at the break of dawn?"

Amara swept across the room, her black dress flowing around her as she gracefully moved to sit on my bed.

"You are disappointed by Raziel's limited answers."

Shrugging, I schooled my expression into a mask of indifference. "It's okay, I—"

"Perhaps you can trick your friends, Hayden, but you cannot fool me. I know you are scared, and rightfully so. Lilith is not a foe to underestimate, and you are still so young to bear the weight of the world. A weight that is far heavier than the burdens suffered by any of your predecessors."

Hanging my head, I stared at my feet and massaged the back of my neck, releasing some of the tension from the stiff muscles. I had been training hard. Harder than ever, and you could see it, both in the hardness of my body and the hardness of my eyes.

"You wonder why you are the strongest Salem Witch in history." Amara rose off the bed to press a gentle hand under my chin to lift it so I would meet those uncanny red eyes. "It is because no other Salem Witch had to face a threat so great. The Creator has gifted you more power so you would persevere, because It is the one whose power flows through every Salem Witch to allow them to win their Salem War."

"Were any of them this scared?" I asked, my voice quivering from emotion.

"All of them," Amara said, releasing my chin. "All of them were probably more scared than you are."

"How do you know?"

Amara smiled. "Death sees everything, especially the Salem War, where so much death and destruction occurs."

"Is that why you're here?" I asked. "To tell me it's okay to be scared?"

"No," she said, patting me on the cheek, then swept toward the hearth. "I came here to teach you one final lesson."

My spine straightened as I perked up, pushing off the dresser to join her next to the fire, the warmth of the flames sinking pleasantly into my demon-blooded body. "But I still have so much to learn—I can't spook, and my birthday is seven days away..."

Amara raised a porcelain hand to silence me. "My final lesson will provide you with answers you do not know you are seeking."

I opened my mouth, then closed it, frowning at her. What did that mean?

"This is not a lesson in the elements, but rather a lesson in knowledge."

"I didn't know Death was so academic," I teased.

"All knowledge flows from Spirit, Hayden."

"Then why hasn't it given me the answers I need?"

"Spirit will always tell us what we need to know, but as flawed mortals, we rarely listen."

"I'm listening," I raged, throwing my arms wide. "I've been listening."

"Are you?" Amara said calmly, raising a single red eyebrow. "Humans and witches drown out the voice of Spirit, whether they know it or not. It is difficult to know when Spirit speaks to us, and even harder to hear everything it whispers. Sometimes, it is as clear as the words I speak to you, but other times, it can feel like we are stuck in a void, the silence stretching on endlessly."

"Yeah." I snorted, crossing my arms over my chest. "No kidding. So, what is this knowledge Spirit hasn't told me yet, but I need to know?"

"You need to know about Alice Parker's Trials."

"What?" I blinked at her in surprise. "You think that will help me defeat Lilith?"

"Whether you will find a solution to defeat Lilith, I do not know, but to defeat Lilith, you must understand your Trials, and Alice's journey might help."

"Why not tell me every Salem Witch's?"

"Because we do not have time for such a lengthy discussion, and the other stories of legend will have such a profound impact on you. Kova was your mentor, your mother figure, and one of your closest friends. She was a constant presence in your life in the absence of your parents. You have a profound bond with her, and therefore, her story will have far more meaning to you."

"Kova mastered the elements in seven years... faster than any other Salem Witch."

"Except for you."

"Except for me," I echoed hesitantly. I hadn't mastered my fifth and final Trial, and I wasn't sure I would with my looming deadline getting closer with each ticking second. "How did it begin?"

"Alice was not claimed as the Salem Witch until she was ten years old, later than most. Like you. It was not until she was twelve that she conquered her Air Trial and unlocked fire magic."

"What was her Trial?" I winced, recalling the brutal pain of dropping fourteen stories in my Air Trial.

"Alice killed a bobcat terrorizing the town."

I deadpanned. "She what?" I asked incredulously, my eyes flaring wider. "A bobcat? That's it?" I raged, tilting my head back to face the heavens as I shouted, "Are you serious? I fell off a *castle*!"

Amara chuckled darkly. "The bobcat was fearsome."

I spun back to face her, an "are you kidding me?" look on my face. "Dude, I could have killed a bobcat no problem when I was twelve, with only air magic and a dagger."

"Ah, but you forget, Hayden, Alice could not reveal her magic. She had to kill the beast without a sword, with only her air magic, in the center of the town square, where she was surrounded by humans who feared the existence of witches and magic. If anyone witnessed her using magic, she would have hung. And in 1692 Salem, magic was forbidden by the Athenian Council, who feared detection. Given the witch hunts in the Old World, they were right to exercise caution, because even without using magic, the Salem Witch Trials came to pass."

Releasing a haggard sigh, I begrudgingly agreed with her. "Okay, you might be right. I would have hated 1692 Salem. How did Kova learn magic if it was forbidden?"

"In secret. She and her soulmate, John—the first reincarnation of your father—"

"The first *what*?"

"John Parker, Alice's husband, was the first incarnation of your father's soul. He and Alice were married before her Water Trial—Alice changed her last name from Corey to Parker—and soon after, she conceived their daughter, Ariel."

Though I had come to terms with Dad being Kova's soulmate and knew he was stuck in a cycle of reincarnation, I didn't know his first life was during the 1692 witch trials... It was weird to think he was alive over three hundred years ago and had lived how many lives since? How did they have their soulmate sighting if he died before Kova turned seventeen?

"Alice and John frequently snuck to the Misery Islands off the coast of Salem. Humans had little reason to visit the islands and even less means, but for a witch with the power of air, it was of little challenge for Alice to disappear in the dark of night."

"So Kova and my dad... they grew up together?"

"As the best of friends," Amara said, a glimmer in her eye. "John supported her for years as she struggled through her Trials. He stood by her side when she faced an army of demons led by a Prince of Hell."

I gasped. Kova had faced a Prince of Hell and lived?

"She was not yet fifteen when she faced Asmodeus, the Sin of Lust, and repelled him. But she did not pass her Fire Trial until she stood before the witches of Salem and professed her identity. An identity she hid so fiercely from the public, but also denied to herself—she is the daughter of Archangel Uriel and the Salem Witch. In accepting all of who she is, she passed her second Trial."

Holy... Kova had faced Asmodeus. I was a Princess of Hell because I was the blood granddaughter of the Mother of Demons, but the Princes... the Princes weren't just demons... they were like Lucifer—powerful fallen angels who turned against the Creator and were repelled by the angels who did not betray the God and Goddess. And Princes were beyond powerful.... They were the embodiments, the immortal physical vessels for the Seven Deadly Sins—Wrath, Gluttony, Greed, Envy, Sloth, Pride, and Lust.

"Asmodeus was the ultimate enemy in Alice's Salem War," Amara said, pulling me from my thoughts. "But she did not face him in her Water Trial. Alice and John married, but as the husband, John provided for Alice and insisted on continuing his job as a mariner, despite Alice begging him to stay in Salem. John died at sea,"—pain stung my heart for the tragic love story—"but Alice passed her Water Trial by forgiving John and Uriel for abandoning her and leaving her alone in Salem to endure the bitter work of her Trials.

"But as the daughter of Uriel, Alice mastered earth magic faster than any Salem Witch. She showed tremendous strength as she suffered through childbirth during her Trial. After Ariel was born, Alice sent her daughter away to protect her from the growing Darkness and magical unease in Salem, but on the same night, Alice faced Asmodeus again and claimed victory." Amara's hand curled into a triumphant fist. "But it was not without its struggles, for Alice reached her lowest point after losing her husband and daughter, and she did not want to carry on. But in facing Asmodeus, she found her strength."

Earth is finding your strength when you have nothing left. It is hitting rock bottom and using it as the solid foundation on which you rise again. When all rock and stone have eroded away, the only thing left is you and your Maker.

The words Kova had spoken to me before my Earth Trial filled my mind. Kova was Alice Parker, the Nephilim daughter of Uriel... she understood the essence of earth better than any other witch. She told me the key to passing my Trial, for she had survived her own Trial three hundred years before I was born.

"Shortly after Ariel's birth, Tituba was arrested for witchcraft."

"The first woman to be accused in the Salem Witch Trials."

"Correct, but Tituba was not a witch, and while she was one of the few who escaped with her life, Alice was not.... Later that spring, Alice's adoptive parents were arrested, then so was she. Alice lived the summer in the rotten, deplorable conditions of the dungeons, but with the power of spooking, she spirited away in the middle of the night to fight the armies of demons looming around Salem and plotted against Asmodeus, who used the human vessel of Judge Hathorne to spread his evil."

"That's so totally unfair," I muttered. "I got jibbed on the magical abilities."

Amara chuckled with amusement, then sobered. "Convicted of being a witch, Alice was hung with seven others, including her adoptive mother, at Proctor's Ledge, mere days after her adoptive father was crushed to death. On her final day, her final Trial triggered, and she faced her death, accepting her immortal soul would live beyond the grave."

"But she didn't stay in the Garden." It wasn't a question.

"She wanted to." Amara smiled bittersweetly, her pointed teeth making her grin disconcerting to anyone other than me. "More than anything, she wanted to enter the Garden of Eden and live with her parents and soulmate. But Alice was selfless. As a Nephilim, she was granted the power of resurrection by the Creator. Knowing Asmodeus would spread his evil to the ends of earth, Alice made the sacrifice to return to the mortal world, knowing she could never die and enter the Garden.

"When she returned from the grave, she did not merely destroy Asmodeus's mortal host, but she summoned his immortal, fallen angel body and killed it, forcing the Sin of Lust from its host. But as a Resurrected Nephilim and a fully realized Salem Witch, she used the power of Spirit to chain Lust and banish it to Hell.

"If Lust desires a corporeal body, it must settle for a weak mortal instead of the immortal, angelic body of Asmodeus," Amara concluded smugly. "After she ended his reign of terror, Alice portaled to the Old World, where she ended the witch hunts terrorizing Europe, then returned to the New World to lead a pilgrimage from Salem, Massachusetts to the land now known as Salem, Wisconsin, and founded Asylum."

"She never told me..." I blew out an exasperated sigh and ran a hand through my wild black locks.

"She could not reveal the truth of her identity to you."

"Yeah, but she could have told me what Alice went through and acted like she knew because she's a Parker."

"I believe Kova did not tell you because she did not want you to be bogged down by more weight than what you already shoulder. Her Trials were dark, and so are yours. It would be discouraging to hear hers as you struggle with yours, and Alice could not bear to see you disheartened. She knew you needed to find your own path. And there are times she struggled to let you make your own choices and suffer the consequences of your mistakes, but she knew it was how you would gain the strength you need to survive the Salem Witch Trials, for it is no simple feat—a harsh truth, which she knew well."

"But her Trials... they were so different from mine."

Amara raised an eyebrow. "Were they?"

"Well, yeah." I shrugged. "Mine are more physical. Lots of magic and fighting. I fell off a building for my Air Trial, faced Lilith in her Lair, lost one of my best friends, and barely survived Lilith's Island. Kova's weren't any easier, but the way you tell it, they were more... subtle."

"In a sense, yes. Alice's Trials were designed for her to grow as the Salem Witch in the capacity for which she was needed. She would not bring the Salem Massachusetts trials to an end through a display of strength and power and magic, but through a subtle, unseen effort. True, yours are much more physical, but so is your war. Yet, the fundamentals of the Trials remain the same."

"Because we master one element, then progress to the next."

"While true, that is not what I was referring to." Amara cocked her head as she regarded me, folding her hands into the open-mouthed sleeves of her dress. "Take, for instance, your Water Trial. What did Heaven test you with?"

"I had to find my path to forgiveness," I said without hesitation, ignoring the pain twinging inside my chest.

"And by what means did Alice pass her Water Trial?"

"By forgiving her husband and mother for the actions that caused her so much pain. But it's different."

Amara cocked her head at me, those unsettling red eyes penetrating my soul. "How so?"

"I... well, I..." I faltered. "I guess it's not.... I was thinking Kova had to forgive others. I had to forgive myself for Harbor's sacrifice because it was my fault. Harbor's death... it seems like *more*, because it didn't hurt just me. It hurt Harbor and Jamie...."

"Forgiveness, like so much else in life, is a choice. While the consequences of your actions bear more weight, because your Salem War bears more weight, it does not mean finding forgiveness for yourself was any more difficult to choose than the type of forgiveness Alice chose."

"The Trials aren't about mastering magic," I whispered, the revelation dawning on me. I had understood the importance of free will for so long, but in my desperation to pass my Trials, save my friends, and not die, I missed the most important lesson of all. Air Trial—I was selfless but cunning, able to see the nonobvious solution. Fire—I accepted myself, both the good and the bad parts. Water Trial—I forgave myself for my mistakes. Earth—I found strength, even when I had nothing left. "It's about our choices."

"Many believe the Salem Witch is a symbol of power, and in a sense, she is. But she is so much more than that. The Salem Witch is not born with power but given it by Heaven. It is through her choices alone that she can master an element and assume complete control of its magic before gaining the powers of the next element. Power, like Light and Dark, is not born to a person, but is a choice presented to each of us. Just as a Nephilim may choose to walk with Evil or a demon may choose to step into the Light,"—she winked at me—"our bloodlines do not decide who we are. Our choices do.

"Your Trials have been covered in a layer of magic and battles that did not manifest during Alice's Trials, but imagine if you had made a different choice in any of your Trials. If you had chosen, like so many others, to remain in that celestial plane or pass on to the Garden. If you succumbed to your darkness, rather than accepted it. If you had not found your ability to forgive and heal. If you had not found your strength in the Creator. If you had made a different choice, what state would the world be in? It is for those reasons that our decisions outweigh our abilities."

"You know, for the first time in almost five years, I feel like I finally understand the purpose of my Trials." I looked Amara dead in the eye. "Part of it was to make me stronger, but mostly, it was to learn the power of choice, of free will, is greater than any other gift."

"Except for love," Amara said, her tone soft as emotion sparkled in her eyes in stark contrast to her normal stony mask. "But together, the two greatest gifts from our Creator—free will and love—are the strongest force in the Universe. Nothing can overcome it."

Spirit prodded me. Her words held weight beyond what I understood. Weight that my future self would soon understand.

"But one thing I don't get is how Kova is more powerful than when she was just Alice, before she resurrected?"

"After you passed your Earth Trial, you were wallowing in your room—"

"Hey now—" I balked at her words.

"It is true and you know it," Amara said without pause. "Your power erupted because your mortal body could not contain the sheer force of Spirit living within it. If you do not pour out, Spirit will do it for you."

"It's because she's immortal, isn't it?" I asked, then licked my lips. "You said an immortal body can hold more magic, so when Kova resurrected..."

"As an immortal, Alice channels the undiluted power of the Spirit within her. And Spirit is infinite."

"Are her powers infinite, too?"

"No, for no mortal or immortal can compare to the power of the Creator. Yet, Spirit speaks to us all. It lives inside each of us. But how we respond to it is what matters. Do we listen? Do we converse back? Do we act in accordance with what Spirit tells us? It depends on how we receive the power and what we pour into Spirit. But even an immortal cannot wield infinite power, for only the Creator is pure and wise enough."

"Is... is Kova happy?" I asked. Shrugging one shoulder, I added, "Not right now, obviously, since she's nailed to a cross, but in general.... She's been alive for *hundreds of years*. Is she happy here?"

"Immortality, like mortality, comes with its own unique set of challenges. As for whether she is happy or not... that is something you must ask her. But she never wanted to resurrect. She would have preferred to stay in the Garden with her soulmate and adoptive parents and Uriel."

"Then why did she?"

"Because the world depended on her. And because it was the path of the Creator. She sacrificed her desires to fulfill the purpose the Creator tasked her with."

"Do all Resurrected Nephilim get a power boost? Can they wield Spirit, too?"

"No, they cannot." Amara shook her head, her long red hair shaking behind her like the red stripes of the American flag. "While their power magnifies exponentially because their bodies are immortal, they do not possess the power of lightning but rather the powers of Spirit in their faith and connection to the Divine Mother and Father. The manifestation of lightning is bestowed only on the Salem Witch to fulfill her sacred duty."

"It doesn't seem like enough...." I stared out my window at the breaking dawn. "Not when immortality sounds like a punishment."

"It is a punishment for those of us who seek things above," Amara agreed. "But Lilith is immortal because she fell from Grace and aligned with Darkness to gain power. Alice resurrected, not for power, not for immortality, but because it was the path the Creator laid at her feet." Amara rested a hand over her heart. "While her immortality is a shackle—especially since her soulmate cannot join her in immortality—only an immortal living within the Grace of Heaven can wield the unparallel power as she does.

"Immortality is what makes angels' powers so devastating. The Princes are petrifying because they are fallen, but retained their immortal physical bodies. No mere mortal weak in faith can withstand their lure. Despite their immortal powers, there is a limit to how much power they can wield, but it is vastly beyond that of any mortal. Their powers are beyond that of a Salem Witch's, although, I do not think they could survive *you*," Amara said with a smirk, humor and mischief dancing in her red eyes.

"Apparently, Asmodeus didn't survive Kova, either." A wicked smirk tugged at my lips at the thought of my mentor absolutely wrecking a fallen angel.

"If Kova had not resurrected and mastered Spirit, she would not have succeeded in ridding the world of Asmodeus's powerful Sin."

"Then why does sin persist in the mortal world? Why do mortals fall victim to it?"

"The Sins are entities and do not need physical bodies to survive. They simply choose corporeal forms to strengthen their powers, especially when they can merge with a being as powerful as a fallen angel, but Alice destroyed the fallen angel and banished Lust to Hell. Princes cannot leave Hell easily. Asmodeus used Hathorne to try to claim enough power to manifest his immortal vessel on Earth.

"Lust cannot merge with another fallen angel—for they were bound to their own demonic duties upon their fall from Grace—but Lust must claim a vessel already on Earth, and it can only do so by slowly forcing its essence into the world, escaping Hell in fragmented doses. Lust spreads throughout the world, wreaking havoc on the masses, but its powers are significantly weaker without a vessel."

"Holy... If Kova hadn't succeeded in killing Asmodeus..." I shuddered and forced down the bile rising in my throat. "Even I find the thought terrifying.... But if Asmodeus is dead, the Deadly Sins are missing one from their ranks."

My thoughts spun in a vortex, scrambling to make sense of what Amara told me... something nagged at me, but I couldn't figure out what exactly.... Spirit nudged me, urging me to grab hold of the thread and trace it to the end.

The Sins were stronger with a physical vessel. They could inflict more damage on the world. Mortals wouldn't be as powerful as Asmodeus, but wouldn't Lust want to claim a new vessel?

"Can... can someone who falls from Grace devolve into an archdemon?" I asked, my stomach flipping with dread.

Amara gave me a pointed look, the glimmer in her red eyes telling me to reason it out for myself.

My mouth tasted of ashes as the truth slammed into me like an anvil dropping on a cartoon character.

"Elliot." I seethed. "He lusted for power, and last Samhain, then on Lilith's Island... he had more magic more than what naturally belongs to him. I knew he was channeling demons, but I never suspected..." I huffed out a sigh as I ran a hand through my wild black hair, my fingers tangling in the knots.

"He isn't channeling demons."

"Then how did he get so powerful?"

"To descend to the status of a Sin, of a Prince of Hell, Elliot must transform into a pure demon."

My mouth gaped open, aghast at the idea of Elliot as a full-blooded demon... the havoc he would wreak... I would have to kill him sooner than later, but how? I couldn't bring myself to kill Lilith, and she was *the Mother of Demons*.

Nausea twisted my stomach as intuition slammed into me. "Why do I get the feeling I won't like how he's becoming a Sin?"

"Elliot drank demon blood until he consumed enough that his heart pumps black blood instead of red. His transformation was slow at first, but now, he no longer needs demon blood to sustain him. He is one of the Seven Deadly Sins, representing Lust."

I retched, bracing my hands on the mantle as I fought the bile threatening to rise in my throat. "Oh goodie," I said sarcastically. "I needed more nightmare fuel." A shiver ran down my spine at the thought. "That's completely revolting."

"Unfortunately, Elliot is not your greatest threat."

"That is not at all reassuring. To anybody else in the world, Elliot transforming into the Archdemon of Lust would be the apocalypse. The fact that I have bigger concerns shows how insane my life is. New Prince of Hell in town? Eh, just another Thursday. What's new?" I let loose another sigh. "But you're right—Lilith is my greatest enemy. I have to stop her from claiming the power of the Maiden before my seventeenth birthday. Mastering my Spirit Trial, freeing Kova and my mother, and defeating Lilith are the most important things in the world." I flopped back on my bed, bouncing off the mattress. "If only I knew how to do any of the above." I scrubbed my face with my hands to clear the chaotic thoughts rampaging through my head.

"Quintessence isn't enough." I sat upright, my piercing blue gaze meeting Amara's deadly red one. "It's the most powerful spell I've ever cast, but Eve couldn't kill Lilith with it."

"True," she mused and smiled that creepy smile. "But Eve did not have the advantage of being part demon. Your very bloodline gives you leverage."

"That doesn't give me confidence," I said, throwing my hands in the air. "Especially since no other Salem Witch has wielded this power."

"I used this spell before. In my mortal life," Amara declared confidently. "Everything I taught you, all my earlier warnings, are based on personal experience. You have more knowledge than Eve did the first time she used Spirit."

"Personal experience from your mortal life?" I rocketed to my feet, my eyes narrowing at the personification of Death. "Quintessence belongs to the living. You said Death cannot wield the Spell of Salem because it contradicts the natural death of a mortal body and its natural return to the earth, so how do you..." My eyes glazed over as I trailed off, and my intuition flared like a punch to the gut. My sharp gaze snapped back to Amara's as understanding dawned on me. "No way... you... you're her... you're *Eve*."

"I am Eve," she confessed with a satisfied smirk. "Formed by the Creator from the dust of the earth and a rib from Adam's body. I was the not only the first witch, but I was the first Salem Witch, created by remnants of Goddess's magic lingering in my body, and the mother of both the human and witch races. And when my mortal life ended, I accepted the Creator's gracious offer to become Death incarnate, for my soulmate is Azriel, the Archangel of Death, and I could not bear to live in the Garden while he alone ferried souls across the veil."

Her words hung suspended in the air before understanding sank in.

"Holy crap," I shouted, flinging my arms in the air. "Why didn't you tell me before?"

Not only was she Eve, but she was the soulmate of the patriarch of the House of Black.

She smiled weakly, emotion flicking through those normally plain eyes. "For the same reasons Kova did not share her true identity with you. The Heavens did not want me to share the truth of my past life until you deduced it for yourself. It was best you did not know, for if you did, you would learn from me and attempt to fight Lilith in a similar fashion. So, heed this warning well—if you copy me, you will *fail*. But this way, you will battle her in your own unique way, free of the mistakes of the past."

I reflect on my training with Amara.

True, she taught me how to harness Spirit and control the black lightning. She taught me how to channel the element through my body, but she never taught me how to *use* it.

I formed my own style of fighting with lightning. She never gave suggestions except to describe how the magic should flow through my body. Everything I did with Spirit was developed through my own skills and intuition. She had been the perfect master to teach, but not influence.

What a sneak.

"But I know now," I argued. "I have a week before my Trial, so what's to stop me from grilling you for info?"

"Because it is time for us to part ways."

"What do you mean?"

Panic pumped in my heart because my only teacher was about to disappear a week before my seventeenth birthday, when I would either pass my Trial or die. No pressure.

Amara shook her head with resignation. "I cannot give you the answers you need to free your mother and defeat Lilith. Nor can I guide you to pass your final Trial, for your path vastly differs from any other Salem Witch, even mine. As it should be. I could not defeat Lilith on my own. But *you* can."

"How?" I cried, completely at a loss. "I still don't know how to kill her, even if I can bring myself to deal the final blow."

"There is one..." Amara stiffened as she said the next word. "Being... who may have the answers you seek."

A shiver crawled down my spine when she said the word "being".

"Again, why do I get the feeling I'm not going to like this 'being'?" I asked, torn between wanting to know what creature could help me and fear of what kind of creature it might be.

"The Devil." Amara stared me in the eyes unflinchingly.

Laughter bubbled out of me, and I flopped onto my bed, bouncing off the pillows and blankets as I clutched my stomach, my body shaking with laughter. One look at Amara's face, and I completely lost it, succumbing to another fit of laughter.

Finally getting a grip, I wiped my eyes and sat up.

"I-I'm s-sorry," I stuttered, still laughing. "But did you say I have to deal with the Devil to get the answers I need to defeat the very woman he enticed to fall from Grace? Talk about irony. He practically made her into the Mother of Demons. Why would he help me?"

"Think about it, Hayden," Amara crooned softly. "What does Lilith want? What is her goal?"

"Power," I answered without hesitation. "She wants enough power to rival the Goddess."

"Exactly. When Lucifer fell from Grace, even with all the powers of Hell, he could not defeat the Divine Masculine. Why would he want Lilith to succeed in conquering the Divine Feminine, the other half of the ultimate power of the Creator?"

"He wouldn't," I surmised. "Because she would be superior to him. But... Lucifer couldn't defeat God... so Lilith can't defeat Goddess. But, given enough power—the Power of Three—Lilith could obliterate the ties existing between Heaven and Earth. She would unleash Hell on Earth, rendering the Armies of Heaven unable to reach us, which Lucifer would love. But Lilith would become the Supreme ruler of Earth. Which doesn't fit into Lucifer's plans. Why would he want her to reign as queen over him?"

Amara nodded solemnly.

I sighed, rubbing my hands against my face. "Which is why he might be willing to strike a deal with me." Strengthening my resolve, I asked Death, "So how do I summon the Devil?"

"Summon him?" Amara looked at me in alarm, the red of her irises glaring against the white around them. "Are you insane? You cannot summon him here. That would unleash him with free rein on Earth."

"Uh, okay." I stared at her in confusion. What was I supposed to do? Send him a wand message?

"You must descend into Hell."

"Ugh," I groaned. "I was really hoping you weren't going to say that. I'll call the circle," I said, grabbing Nightmare and my amulet athame off the hook by my bed and strapping the sheaths to my thighs. "This is going to be so much fun." I added extra sarcasm to my voice.

"They cannot accompany you."

My head snapped up. "I'm going into Hell alone?" I asked incredulously.

Amara, the personification of Death, looked downright uncomfortable. "If anyone besides you descends into Hell, they will not survive the ordeal. Even if they did, they cannot leave."

"What do you mean?"

"If a mortal enters Hell of their own volition, there is no guarantee they can leave. Ever. The act of descending into Hell is symbolic of falling from Grace. It would forfeit their free will to Lucifer, who is eternally unwilling to relinquish fallen souls and return their free will."

"Fantastic." I worked my jaw back and forth. "So, what? I'm a demon, so I can't fall from Grace?"

"Yes. And no." She tilted her head. "Your choices have set you on the path illuminated by Heaven's Light, so should you choose, you can fall. However, you are not just any demon."

"I'm a greater demon."

"You're a *Princess* of Hell," Amara emphasized. "You are free to enter Hell whenever you wish, without the repercussions of falling, so long as you do not side with evil. By Lucifer's and Lilith's laws, no one can stop a Prince or Princess from moving freely within the underworld."

"Which means he can't stop me from leaving," I concluded.

"Magically, no, he cannot prevent you from leaving Hell." She bobbed her head in agreement, then waved a hand at my person. "But physically, the Devil will throw his power at you to chain you to the Pit. You must outmaneuver him."

"Terrific," I deadpanned. "How do I get in and out of Hell?"

"Getting there is the easy part."

"This just keeps getting better," I said sarcastically with an eye roll.

"I will channel your demon essence and combine it with my power to create a one-way portal to Hell."

"One way, huh?" I snorted. "And the getting back part?"

"That I cannot help you with, but Lucifer knows the way out. You must bargain with him for the answers you seek. Ensure safe passage home is part of the bargain."

"Is that all?" I asked, raising a single eyebrow at her.

"No. Beware of the Devil in all his forms," she warned darkly. "If the Enemy can talk angels out of Heaven, he can talk you into Hell. Permanently. Be mindful of the voices you listen to. Fear is a powerful ally. The Devil will try to use it against you. He will attempt to persuade you to abandon your soul to him for all eternity."

"Then I will use it against him," I replied fiercely. "What does the Devil fear most?"

Amara cocked her head as she pondered my question, her red eyes glazing over pensively. Then, she answered with wisdom. "Pride always comes before a fall. And none have fallen as far as the Morningstar. Therefore, he is filled with pride for the perversion he pervades through humanity. You want to know what the Devil fears? The entities he has not perverted. Chastity. Temperance. Charity. Diligence. Kindness. Patience. Humility."

"The Seven Holy Virtues."

"Yes, Hayden. And the Seven Holy Virtues are Heaven's warriors against the Seven Deadly Sins. But these seven are aspects of something far greater than the individual Virtues."

"And what is that?"

"Love, Hayden." Amara patted a bony hand over her heart. "The Devil fears love. And if you, who are so full of love, act in love, it will be the most powerful weapon you wield against him."

Coming from Death, it just sounded wrong. But...

Warmth settled in my chest at her words, Spirit filling me with a humming force as it responded to her declaration of love. My mind flickered to a blond-haired Nephilim. Then to my dad and Salem. To Kova and Mom.

As cliche as it sounded, Amara was right. Love gave me a purpose. It gave me a reason to fight. To fight for the ones I loved and to fight with the power so lovingly given to me by a loving Creator. And as Spirit buzzed pleasantly through my body, I knew it agreed.

"There is one more thing."

Rolling my eyes, I threw my arms up in exasperation. I was making myself dizzy with all the eye rolls in this conversation. "Just hit me with it."

"Time works differently in Hell."

"Time does what? How can it work differently?"

"Hell is the realm under the Earth. Like Heaven above, which is built on eternity, it does not feel the weight of time the way mortals experience it on Earth. Lucifer excels at taking pure and good things from the Creator and perverting them. Hell was fashioned after Heaven, but from a demented perspective, to counter the Creator's pure creation."

"Please tell me it's in a different time zone. I seriously don't want to deal with time travel." I pinched the bridge of my nose.

"An hour could pass in Hell, but a day might pass here. Or it could be the opposite. You could enter Hell and by the time you leave, mere minutes have passed. There is no logical correlation between time here and there. I suspect Lucifer has some limited control of the time scale, but it is sporadic, and with a week remaining before your seventeenth birthday, you cannot afford to lose any time. I do not know when you will return, but you must do it before the clock strikes midnight."

"Or you'll whisk my soul to the Garden?" I joked, earning a small smile from Amara. It kinda wasn't a joke.

"Whatever you do, get in and out as quickly as possible. Be wary of the Devil, for there is no greater manipulator. Also, try to not be yourself."

"Hey," I grumbled.

She shot me a stern look, so much like the other Salem Witch who was my mentor. "We both know you are not the best at self-control, and you are likely to insult him."

I opened my mouth to argue, then closed it. Shrugging, I conceded, "Fair enough."

"He's not known to be forgiving," Amara warned.

"Never thought he would be," I said, my expression darkening as I fell into a pensive state, absentmindedly massaging my jaw.

"Be warned. While Lucifer personally cannot physically harm children of the Creator as it is part of his punishment for falling, I do not know if this protection encompasses your physical body since you are part demon. I doubt Lucifer will face you in battle for many reasons, including your military prowess,"—she gestured at my sword and dagger—"but primarily because he has spent thousands of years using words and manipulation to deceive mortals and lead them astray from the path of Light. For him, words are more effective than the sharpest of forged weapons. Do not let him twist your mind. And one more thing. When you return—although, I do not know when that will be—I will no longer be here."

"I figured as much."

"I wish..." she swallowed roughly. "I wish I could be."

Gently, I reached out and placed my hand over hers where they were folded over her chest.

"I know, Amara. I know." I smiled at her, a bittersweet taste on my tongue. "You can't take sides, and I don't blame you for that. If anyone can understand maintaining the balance between Dark and Light, it's me. You do whatever it is you have to do. I won't love you any less." As I said the words aloud, I realized I did love Amara, for all this time, she had been teaching me out of love her beloved descendants. "Love is the most powerful force in the Universe, right? Even love can overcome death."

Tears welled in her terrifying red eyes, and rivers ran down her cheeks. Unexpectedly, she reached forward and pulled me into the tightest hug of my life, cutting off my air flow. When my vision tinged black around the edges and spots danced across my eyes, she released me, and I sucked in a blessed breath.

"On your last night, Death will be on your side," she whispered into my ear. Pulling back, she placed both hands on my shoulders. "How many mortals could find it within their hearts to love the personification of Death?"

Reaching up, I placed my hands on hers. "Oh, but Amara... Eve, you're so much more than Death. You ferry souls from this world to the Garden, but you also bring us back. You breathe life into us when we enter a new life here on Earth. If that isn't a miracle, then I don't know what is. You are an extension of the Creator, just like me, just like every being ever made."

"Thank you, Hayden. You remind me so much of myself," Death said with a smile.

"Well, I am descended from you one way or another.... You are the mother of humans and witches."

Amara tossed her head back and howled with laughter. "I suppose you are." Like a loving mother, she pressed a pale hand to my cheek. "I wish I had more time to teach you, but..."

"It's time to go," I finished for her with a sigh.

Throwing on my magically charmed leather jacket, I secured my silver wand in the hidden pocket in my sleeve, then checked my charm bracelet of weapons had everything I needed. I was headed toward the fight of my life. I would need everything in my arsenal. Weapons and words. Which would win me the battle to leave Hell?

My eyes flicked over my body reflected by the polished surface of my full-length mirror. Fully grown, my body had filled out in the last five years since my father gifted me this jacket. Muscle defined my body in places I never knew it could. Every inch of battle-ready muscle was toned to perfection.

I wasn't the same lost witch that came to Asylum.

I was a warrior witch.

Pulling on my beat-up, black leather combats, I grimaced. These boots had seen better days. But a small smile danced across my lips. These boots had seen me through it all, and I would gladly walk the last mile in them.

"I'm ready."

Shooting me a wicked smile, she pressed her right hand to my heart and her left to the crown of my forehead. Her magic sprang forth, swallowing me in a cloud of gray smoke. Charcoal smoke spilled from her palms, blanketing my vision as her power swirled inside me to find the part of my essence that was demon. Latching onto it, Amara pulled, channeling my essence and fusing it with her magic to fuel the connection to Hell.

Spirit magic mingled with mine, the powers of the first Salem Witch mixing with those of the Reigning Salem Witch's, drawing on my demon genes to open a portal to Hell.

Amara's dark gray magic cleared from my vision as she sucked her powers into a ball of swirling blacks and grays to hover between her hands.

The powdery magic flowed around us, twisting and curling into shapes like paint strokes on a canvas.

Closing her eyes, she turned from me, but kept her hand on my heart as she raised the other hand, her palm flat and facing the wall. Black and gray smoke poured from her open palm, swirling as it slowly floated away and hovered in the air, the smoke thickening as it undulated and expanded.

Power burst from the magic like a sonic wave pushing through us. My black hair whipped behind me in the rush of power, but I did not waiver. Flecks of light mixed with the gray and black as the smoke flowing from Amara's palm ceased, and her magic expanded into an ominous portal.

"Your powers... they're gray and black... like mine."

I stared at her with wonder.

"It is fitting that the alpha and omega, the first and the last, should have the same magic. Although, yours is greater than mine," Amara said with a wink. "And you will end what I began."

"Guess it's time then," I chewed my bottom lip as I eyed at the portal stretching and ten feet tall, mentally preparing myself for the challenge ahead.

Was I nervous about descending into Hell? Absolutely. But all I could think about was how much easier this would be if my friends were by my side. I knew without a doubt they'd be willing to follow me to Hell, but that was why I didn't ask Amara to share our plans with them. If they knew, they would try to follow me, and I couldn't let that happen. I couldn't let them fall.

Silently, I thanked the Heavens, for bringing such unbelievable family and friends into my life. After learning about Kova's Trials, gratitude for my friends swelled in my heart. Kova didn't have many people helping her through her Trials. As for me... my friends had been there for me through it all. But I had finally come to the part of my path that I would have to walk alone, and I was okay with that if it meant saving my people.

"Any last advice before I hit the road to Hellsville?" I asked Amara from over my shoulder as I walked to the portal.

The magic of the first Salem Witch prodded me in the back, pushing me toward the thing that both excited me and terrified me. Excited me because I might finally find answers to my questions—like who my father was and how to free Leyla and Kova. But terrified because I was descending into Hell to meet the Devil face to face. How many mortals had survived such an encounter?

None, Spirit seemed to whisper. *None without the power of the Creator living within them. Remember to whom you belong, and you will not fall.*

Inhaling a deep breath, I closed my eyes.

"Death is your gift," Amara whispered as I stepped into Hell.

The portal sucked me in.

Amara's portal was nothing like Silas's when we traveled to Lilith's Island. Maybe because Silas's earth magic opened a portal between two places on *Earth*. It was smooth and quick, even easier than spooking, which made me nauseous.

Amara's portal wasn't sending me somewhere on Earth. It spirited me across realms to the lowest, deadliest realm under the Earth. Hell—the Pit that devoured the souls that fell into it. And I willingly portaled there.

I must have been insane.

Because Amara's portal was like spooking while riding a bucking bronco and trying to hang on to the reins for dear life. It was worse than the time I clung to the roof of an airplane as I fought demons.

The turbulence jarred me back and forth, ramming my body into random objects. At least I think it was objects, but I was blinded by dark magic as my body rocketed through time and space until my side crashed into hard marble as the portal spit me out on the other side.

"Agh!" I shouted as I slid across the slick marble floors, my fingernails clawing at the smooth stone.

A strangled yelp left my mouth as my spine slammed into the wall, and the back of my head cracked against the cold marble.

Coughing as I rolled to my back, I summoned water magic to heal the gash on my head before any blood surfaced.

"She could have at least warned me it would feel like I was the personal punching bag for a herd of rhinos." I groaned.

"If you thought that was awful," drawled an unnervingly creepy and foreign female voice.

Leaping to my feet, I unsheathed Nightmare, the light of blue hellfire bouncing off the polished surface of the black blade. Drawing my amulet athame, I slipped into my stance, raising the dagger so the light glimmered off the unblemished blue crystal in the pommels of my bonded weapons.

"Then you should count yourself lucky you won't be leaving that way. Welcome to the Pit."

CHAPTER SIX

At the Devil's Door

"Who are you?" I demanded of the woman standing before me. Actually, she was more lounging than standing against the polished white marble wall of the corridor. The woman didn't bother to look at me, just kept examining her false nails. Thick black hair, not much different from mine, fell in large, loose ringlets and was dyed red at the ends. Her mocha skin emphasized her ruby red eyes with snake slit pupils.

The magic pouring off the female demon was unbelievably strong, and if I had been anybody else, I probably would have peed myself. In some ways, her nonchalant demeanor made her more intimidating than Lilith. Like nothing could harm her.

Without looking up, she responded in her uncaring drawl, "Oh, you don't know? I'm the Red Demon."

"Who?"

The strange woman snapped her gaze to meet mine. Her snake-slit eyes watched me with venomous intent, and I would be lying if I said it didn't make me uneasy. This was not an enemy to underestimate.

A forked tongue darted from between her lips as she hissed, agitated that I didn't know who she was. "I am Lucifiana Morningstar, daughter of Lucifer Morningstar and Lilith Nightfall."

"Ah, crap," I groaned.

She arched an eyebrow at me, a twinge of annoyance in her expression. "What kind of reaction is that?"

"You're kind of my aunt, right?" I shrugged. "I dunno. I wasn't expecting to meet another Lilith down here."

She surged at me, closing the distance between us in a blur to shove her nose in my face as she narrowed those blood red eyes. "I am nothing like my mother. I am the Red Demon, leader of my father's legions. I am—"

"Okay, okay." I threw my hands up in surrender, still holding tightly to both weapons. "Nothing like Lilith. Got it, got it. Didn't mean to offend you. Just surprised, that's all. Not every day you meet your long-lost aunt."

Lucifiana snorted and flipped her hair as she stepped away. "You're the long-lost relative, girl."

I opened my mouth to argue, then shrugged. "Fair enough."

"Well," Lucifiana drawled, gesturing down the hall, then let out an exasperated huff. "Do you want to see him or what?"

"Uh, the Devil?"

She rolled her eyes so hard she could probably see her brain. "Of course, the Devil," she sneered. "Who else do you descend into Hell to see?"

"Hold up." I gestured at her with my dagger. "You're going to bring me to him?"

She nodded, accompanied by another eye roll.

"Just like that?" I asked, raising a skeptical eyebrow. "Why make it so easy?"

Lucifiana looked at me like I was an idiot. "What?" She snorted as she gave me a once over. "You think you're a threat to him? In his domain? My soldiers told me you were intelligent, *mutt*. How disappointing they were wrong."

I grinned wildly. "Dear old granny didn't like it too much when I swooped into her lair and rescued my dad. Just saying."

Lucifiana grinned vindictively. "I would have loved to see the look on her face when you barred her lair from Asylum with a column of holy hellfire. Not much rattles my mother, but you have a delicious knack for driving her insane," she crooned.

It was my turn to snort. "The woman needs therapy, that's for sure."

She looked me up and down once, sizing me up, then pursed her lips. "Just enough wickedness to fit into our family. You're alright, kid. Follow me."

With a wave of her hand, she turned on her six-inch stiletto heels and sauntered down the hall, her hips swaying like a supermodel on the runway.

Keeping a tight grip on both my amulet athame and Nightmare, I followed her leisurely pace, my chest puffed out and chin raised high. If I had to walk through Hell, I would walk like I owned the place.

As I followed my demonic aunt, I got the sense that she had no interest in further small talk, which was fine because it gave me an opportunity to study the corridor and the demons that appeared at intersections of connecting halls. The demons reeled back in shock before fleeing, and as much as I would have liked to think it was in response to my presence, I doubted the demons noticed me. They fled from my auntie, who didn't pay them any mind.

The corridor was made of white marble, polished to gleam. Both the walls and the floors were made of the stone, giving the corridor an ironically cold feel. Torches of blazing royal blue hellfire hung from the ceiling and braziers mounted along the walls burned with smokeless fire, yet the smell of sulfur and brimstone stung my nostrils.

And it was freezing here. My charmed leather jacket repelled the frigid temperatures, but my legs started to numb under my jeans. A tendril of fire magic coursed through my body, fighting the unbearable cold.

"This isn't anything like I thought it would be..." I muttered to myself.

"You thought it would be warm." Lucifiana didn't phrase it as a question.

"Well, yeah. That's the reputation, isn't it?"

"To any being other than a demon or angel, yes, it would be unbearably hot, but your body was made to be comfortable in this environment."

"If my demon blood makes me able to withstand Hell, then why is it so cold?"

"Because he intends for it to be cold and uninviting to those like your father."

I froze in my tracks. "My father?" I asked, my voice an octave too high. Amara said he was waiting in the Garden, but what if she was wrong? Fear for my father's soul seized my heart.

"Keep moving," she snapped, not bothering to look back. Recovering from my shock, I ran to catch up with her, demanding answers.

"You know my father? Is he... he's not..."

"I wasn't referring to my sister's mortal brother." She rolled her eyes. "But no, he is not here, mutt."

Surprise slapped me across the face again, but my legs didn't stop moving, my mind set on getting answers from my demonic aunt. "You know who my biological father is?"

"Of course." She scoffed, flicking a red and black curl over her shoulder. "Not that I can tell you thanks to Leyla's spell."

"What did you mean be 'those like my father'?"

Shrugging like she didn't give a care in the world, she drawled, "Figure it out."

Nothing more was said as she led me down the main hallway until we came to a massive door, larger than the main doors of the Spellery, made of a black crystal with gold metal adornments around the edges. Ornate filigree was etched into the stone in thin silver lines, but the golden etchings in the black stone around the entrance captured my attention. Etchings of angels in full armor, their wings spread wide and swords in hand as they charged into battle against demons.

With a wave of her perfectly manicured hand, Lucifiana used magic to open the door, and it slowly swung open into the room behind it. Lucifiana sauntered into the room with me hot on her heels, my longsword and dagger still drawn.

My eyes darted around, on high alert for danger. Lucifiana's red stilettos clicked against the black marble floor that replaced the white marble from the outside corridor as she strutted across the chamber The black iridescent floor was polished to such perfection that it felt like I was walking on an oil spill as it reflected the red soles of Lucifiana's shoes.

Even the sconces of raging blue hellfire were made of polished black metal. The chamber was a massive underground cavern, like something you would find behind a waterfall in a fantasy book. The vaulted ceiling was swathed in shadows so dark that I couldn't be certain if there was a ceiling. Hell's walls were made of slate gray stone, as dull and depressing as anything I had ever seen. Then again, this was Hell, so that was probably the point.

"Just a pinch of depression and bloodthirsty demons. What's not to love?" I muttered under my breath, and sheathed Nightmare and my amulet athame as Spirit advised me to do. Even for a demon princess, this place was beyond bleak.

I followed my aunt across the black marble floor, but I stopped when we reached a set of stairs carved into the marble of the cavern floor. Lucifiana strutted up the steps, her hips swishing back and forth, but my gut rolled and intuition slammed into me, telling me not to follow her.

As she reached the top of the stairs, she twisted to the left and draped her sensual, curvy body over a throne carved from a single, massive slab of red ruby, her black heels with red soles dangling off the armrest. The ruby glittered in the light cast from the blue hellfire blazing in the braziers mounted around the cavernous throne room.

As seductive as she was, the Red Demon was not the one who captured my gaze.

Sitting on a sharp black throne, built from bones and skulls and glass, was the fallen angel himself. He wasn't the DFevil with red horns and a tail that I expected—he was so much worse. He was cunning and handsome, with golden blond hair and glowing bronzed skin. Wearing only black jeans, he positioned his eight-pack abs on full display, letting them contract with each breath. His pecs bulged and his arms were the kind that gym bros envied and gym girls drooled over. But it wasn't the muscles that captivated me. It was the face he wore—the face of a man I loved but aged a decade to thirty years old. His eyes flared open, and I was almost lost in his royal blue irises.

He looked like everything I had ever wanted.

And that made him dangerous.

"Hayden Black—the girl I've heard so much about," the Devil spoke, and I had to suppress my reaction to the shiver snaking down my back. No one should wield that kind of power with just their voice. A voice that made me feel inexplicably drawn to him. "Hello, darling. I do believe we are long overdue for a little chat."

And in that moment, I knew this battle would not be won with blades. This was a battle of the tongue. It was a dance of cunningness mixed with willpower, and something in my gut told me I wasn't going to win this fight, no matter how well I played my cards. But maybe he would let me win.

"Lucifer," I spoke with unwavering confidence, turning the name over in my mouth. "You know who I am?"

His smile was devilishly charming, and I understood why so many humans and witches succumbed to his compulsion. Unlike Lilith, whose black soul oozed repulsiveness, Lucifer was the opposite. His black soul was of the night sky, the darkest ebony with specks of light, and that's when I understood why he was called the Lightbringer. Despite his darkness, his light was glorious. Angelic, dare I say.

But he was *Lucifer*—evil and loving it.

"And pray tell, child, why wouldn't I know of you?"

Part of me didn't want to answer, didn't want to give anything to him freely, but the other half of me knew I couldn't afford to not answer.

Shrugging my shoulders, I rocked back on my heels and looped my thumbs through belt loops in my jeans, trying to exude a casual air despite my heart pounding in my chest and the blood pumping in my ears. "Guess I didn't expect you to know me."

His cunning grin reminded me of the Cheshire Cat, similar to my own wicked smirks. But it looked wrong on that face. "Oh, I know you well, Hayden Black. I know more about you than you know about yourself, darling." The words rolled off his tongue like a reverent prayer, so soft and sensual, I almost missed the message.

The words sank in, and I was no longer relaxed, but staring at him with wide eyes and my lips slightly parted. We had never met. Dad whisked me away to the human world the same day of my birth and we definitely hadn't met since I moved to Asylum. And I would remember encountering the Devil, no matter how young I was.

And yet, he claimed to know me.

Every fiber of my being screamed at me to demand what he knew about me that I didn't know. But he wasn't an angel. He was the Devil, and the look on his face told me he knew the storm raging within me.

"Lilith's immortal life and mine have been intertwined since the day she fell. The Eveningstar to my Morningstar, if you will. So, given your most unique... ah, parentage, I have sustained an unusual interest in your mortal life since discovering you growing within your mother's womb."

I didn't miss his sly smile when he mentioned my parentage. There was something there, something I was missing. Narrowing my eyes at him, I studied his face closely, but the more I tried to read him, the more I grasped at straws.

After a long pause, I finally spoke. "You know my parents." I already knew this. Lucifiana had told me as much on our walk here.

"Tsk, tsk," he clucked his tongue at me, and let me tell you, it was strange for the Devil to mimic a mother hen. "Now darling, surely you know, I don't give out answers for free. Payment is required."

"It wasn't a question." His response, demanding payment for answers, confirmed what I suspected—he knew who my biological father was. Which begged the question—how did my father know Lucifer?

Lucifer grinned wickedly at me, pleased with my retort. "Then, my darling Hayden, why would a lady such as yourself bother to travel all the way to my domain to bother with the likes of me if not to bargain with me?"

"Maybe I wanted to meet you in the flesh."

"And?" He grinned knowingly. I couldn't get the answers I sought without striking a bargain. It would be foolish to think I could manipulate the Devil, the master manipulator, and live to see the light of earth.

"You have the answers I seek," I answered honestly.

"But to risk making a deal with the Devil, you must know I am the only one with your coveted answers."

"Probably not the only one, but I wouldn't have come if I didn't think you'd give me the info I need."

"And what makes you so sure I'm willing to give you answers?"

"Because," I started slowly, knowing I had to be careful with how I proceeded. "You are the Devil, and the Devil is known for his love of bargains. Didn't you just ask me for payment? So, I'll offer you a deal."

Lucifer looked amused, and my heart hammered faster in my chest. Swallowing through the thickness in my throat, I forced my beating heart to calm itself. It was the last thing I wanted to do, but what other choice did I have?

You always have a choice, Spirit seemed to whisper.

Lucifiana snorted from where she lay draped on her red throne. "As if you could offer any payment of value, mutt." She spit the last word out, but it lacked malice, especially since she winked at me.

Intuition slammed into me like a punch to the gut. She was trying to communicate a specific message. Calling me "mutt" was more than a lame insult. It should mean something to me, but the only reason I could think of was because Leyla's father—my grandfather, Edward—was a witch. But Lucifer also mentioned my parentage. That couldn't be a coincidence.

Lucifer's eyes sparkled as he glanced mischievously at his daughter. "What is it you want to know, Little Warrior?" he asked, his voice far too nonchalant, like he was controlling the game.

Because he did. He always had. I had to outsmart the Devil, who had been manipulating mortals for countless millennia, longer than Lilith had been alive. No pressure.

"Oh, no." I wagged a finger at him. "I'm not sharing my questions. We make the deal first."

He sat straighter on his black throne, his interest piqued. "Oh." He raised an eyebrow at me. "And what exactly are we exchanging in this deal?"

"You will give me answers to all my questions. Truthful answers with a complete and thorough explanation."

"That seems reasonable." He smirked, and I couldn't help but feel like this was going exactly as he wanted it.

"And," I continued, wiping the smug smirk off his face. "You will guarantee my safe passage back to Earth."

"Hmm," he mused, leaning forward on his black throne. "Now that depends entirely on what you bring to the table for this little deal of ours."

"What do you want?" I asked flatly, no inflection or fear in my voice.

"Isn't it obvious?" He traced his fingers around his lips. "I want you soul."

"Not gonna happen, Luci," I snapped. "Try again."

"I could take it, you know," he drawled, leaning casually back in his throne. "There is nothing to stop me from doing so. As of now, we do not have a deal, so I am not obligated to ensure your safe return to Earth."

"Try it, and I'll burn the Pit to ash and dust with my holy flames," I growled and white holy flames erupted along my skin and danced in my black hair like an angelic tiara.

"Hmm," he hummed, unfazed by my threat, but as Lucifiana sized me up, she shifted on her throne, as if she was shying away from the flames even as she turned her nose up in dismissal.

She was afraid of the flames I could conjure at will. Rising from her throne, she leaned in to whisper something to her father. I strained to hear, but despite the dead quiet room, no sound reached my ears. Air magic whistled around me, yet nothing. The demonic duo must have had a spell to prevent me from eavesdropping.

Lucifer's lips twisted into another disconcerting smirk as he listened to his daughter. As she stepped away from him, he nodded to her. "Very well."

He turned back to me, still relaxed on his throne as the Red Demon draped herself over her own, though she was visibly less comfortable than before. Something about me worried her. Smart demon.

"Little Warrior, I know what I desire that you can give me. Something only you can give me."

"And what is that?"

"Lilith." He said it so simply, like I could serve her to him on a silver platter.

"Dude, you do realize I'm literally here because I—you know what? Yeah, alright, I can give you that. Killing two birds with one stone works for me. I can drag her crazy butt down here, and you two have at it. Distract her for a few more eons, if you would. Thanks for taking this one for the team."

"You misunderstand, child," Lucifer's voice boomed in a cold command. "I want you to defeat her, then give her to me."

"I'm failing to see the conniving, underhanded betrayal in this." I crossed my arms over my chest as I narrowed my eyes.

What game were you playing, Devil?

"Because there isn't one," Lucifiana snapped. "Lilith has always been wild, unpredictable. But this, what she is trying to achieve—it crosses a line that cannot be undone once crossed. She thinks overthrowing the Goddess will make her the supreme power of the mortal realm, the Dark Mother, as she calls herself. But instead, she will throw not just the world, but the entire cosmos out of balance, and Chaos will reign, not Lilith."

"And don't you want that?" I challenged. "You are the Devil and his daughter."

"Mortals have always possessed narrow minds, assuming I aim for the mass destruction of Earth as they know it, that I strive to usher in a new age of darkness where Hell reigns on Earth. But I don't want that at all."

"You don't?" I raised a skeptical eyebrow, not buying his good-guy act.

"Darling," he drawled, then licked his lips slowly and sensually. Ugh. "Why would I want to destroy my playground? It's the game itself that I relish, not the win. Earth spiraling into Chaos—now what fun would that be for me? I win and the game is finished. No more fun to be had. But this way... this way, I can continue playing with humans' frail little minds as I please, corrupting them, breaking them, bending them to my will—"

"Got it." I held up a flat palm. "I don't need to know anymore."

He pouted, and holy, the look almost brought me to my knees. I wasn't sure how I didn't melt at his feet right then and there.

"But I have so much more vile darkness to share with you," his voice silky smooth like melted chocolate.

And the feeling was gone.

"Maybe another time. Do we have a deal or not?"

He wiped the pout off his lips, returning to his cool, relaxed exterior. The ease with which his entire demeanor changed... it was beyond unsettling... it was intoxicating and terrifying at the same time. The Devil wasn't wicked like me. No, he was evil because he was so sickeningly good at making himself irresistible.

"I will trade you answers for Lilith, nothing more."

I scowled at him. "Complete and truthful answers. And immediately. No stalling."

"Yes, yes." But he frowned, annoyance laced in his expression. "I will not stall to provide complete and truthful answers, and you will supply me with Lilith. Pleased?"

"And my safe passage to Earth."

"Ah," he sighed. "No."

"Excuse me?"

"Safe passage from my domain is not part of this Devil's Bargain. Only answers."

"Fine," I growled. "What do you want in exchange?"

"Nothing," he replied. "I will not make a deal regarding your exit from Hell."

"Fine," I snarled, my hands curling into tight fists at my side. "But if any creature here tries to stop or harm me, I will incinerate everything in my path."

Lucifiana cackled madly, her curls swaying. "If I wasn't already convinced you were Leyla's daughter, your deranged desire to burn everything in your path validates you as part of this unhinged family."

"Uh, thanks?" My face contorted as I pondered if that was a compliment or an insult, but I didn't have time to dwell on it as Lucifer rose from his throne, his eight-pack rippling.

Methodically, he made his way down the throne stairs. His descent was maddeningly slow as he drew out every movement, taking his sweet time as though he knew the wait was excruciating for me.

I needed my answers, then I needed to get out of Hell. After what seemed like eons, his feet touched the smooth, polished floor beneath our feet—his bare and mine clad in dirty old combats that clung to life at the seams. Tired of waiting for him, I strode forward, closing the space between us.

"How does this bargain thing work?"

"It is an unbreakable bond," Lucifiana declared.

"Duh." I snorted. It was a deal with the Devil. I wasn't stupid enough to think I could strike a deal and double cross him without consequence. If I had learned one thing from the Trials, it was that every decision—every action or inaction—had a consequence. "But what happens if I break it? Or if he breaks it?"

"I cannot break the Bargain. The powers of the Universe bind me irrevocably. But if you break the Bargain, I claim your soul," Lucifer said, his voice seductive as he leaned in to brush his nose along my collarbone.

Wrapping a hand around his throat, I forced his face away from my jugular. Only a fool exposed her neck to a predator.

"Just initiate the Bargain." I shoved him away.

"I consent to the terms we laid out. Do you consent?"

"Yes."

"Say it."

"I consent," I growled the words, weary of Lucifer's games.

A dagger appeared in Lucifer's hand, and he grabbed my hand and slid the sharp silver blade across the fatty flesh of my palm.

A hiss whistled through my teeth as I bit back my reaction to the stinging pain. I had endured worse and, undoubtedly, worse horrors awaited me. I was just peeved he touched me without permission.

But I *had* given him permission, I realized. By saying I consented, I allowed him to inflict harm, and I questioned if the consent stopped there. Or could he physically harm me in any way now since I agreed to his Bargain?

"Dude," I snapped at him. "Next time, ask a woman before you touch her."

Amusement flashed through the Devil's eyes as he glanced at me, as though my anger was no more threatening than a Golden Retriever stealing its owner's underwear, but he said nothing as he sliced his palm open to match my wound.

Cupping my hand, I willed my water magic to grab hold of the blood so it didn't drop to the floor. I refused to give any more of my blood to this place than I had to, and a roll of nausea in my gut told me that once this forsaken Pit tasted my blood, it would crave more. No. I would give only what was required and not a drop more.

Lucifer let his hand fall to his side, his black blood dripping onto the floor and soaking into the stone. I repressed a shudder as the ground greedily swallowed the black liquid. As though the cavern literally consumed the blood.

The dagger disappeared as Lucifer raised his hands. I wasn't fond of his little conjuration and banishment powers. Maybe jealous that he could make things appear and disappear at will. But this was the Devil, and I'd be a fool if it didn't make me a little uneasy. He made to touch me—the left hand poised over my heart and the right one raised to the same height as my forehead—pausing at the last second to ask, "May I?"

Perhaps he couldn't touch me without permission. Or it was a ruse. Either way, I did not trust the Devil, and it was safer to assume he could harm me and chose not to than to assume I was safe.

Meeting his blue eyes—cold blue eyes meant to look like the ones I loved so much but could never replicate his warmth and love—I nodded stiffly, my head barely bobbing.

At my nod, he placed his hands on my heart and my head.

Before he sliced open my flesh, he made me say the words aloud. No, I was not safe from physical harm. The Devil was trying to coax me into false security, but I would not be fooled by the Great Deceiver.

The placement of his hands was opposite of Gabriel's whenever my Trials started or ended, and I remembered what Raziel said about the Devil perverting the Divine's creation.

I mirrored his pose, pressing my blood-soaked hand to his bare chest, the red liquid staining his skin over his heart. If he had a heart.

His black blood oozed onto my leather jacket—which yuck—but my red blood was in full contact with his skin.

I gasped in disgust. "Is my blood soaking into your skin?"

The Devil chuckled at my discomfort, his eyes flashing with amusement. "Relax, Little Warrior. It is the nature of the Pit and its inhabitants to claim anything it can for Its own. Though you are a mutt, you are a demon. It is in your nature, too."

My gaze shot to where Lucifer's hand pressed against my heart, and I released a relieved sigh at the sight of his black blood dribbling down the front of my leather jacket and onto the dark crystal below.

"Apparently not in my nature," I muttered with a smug smirk. "Now what?"

"You each state what you bring into the Devil's Bargain. If both of you are satisfied, you state, 'I agree'," Lucifiana explained, watching intently from her throne, her spine rigid and eyes sharp.

"That's all? You first, Luci." I waggled my eyebrows at him.

His lightless blue eyes narrowed, but he let the nickname slide for the second time. I probably shouldn't push my luck considering I hadn't secured safe passage out of Hell yet, but eh, what was the fun in facing the Devil if you didn't rile him up a bit?

"I, Lucifer Morningstar, will provide complete and truthful answers to Hayden Black's questions in a timely fashion."

"And in return I, Hayden Black, will provide Lilith to Lucifer Morninstar after I have defeated her." Looking him dead in the eye, I added, "Assuming I defeat her." When Lucifer's eyes sliced into me, I shrugged. "I could die first. Never know with the Trials."

"I agree," he said with a lazy, almost sensual smirk, then in his deep, sultry voice, whispered almost mockingly, "Last chance to back out, Little Warrior," like he knew I couldn't afford to abandon the Devil's Bargain, no matter how fatal it could be.

No more fatal than the Salem Witch Trials... except that he would claim my *eternal soul*.

"I agree," I snapped.

As the words left my lips, dark, dirty magic swept over me, nuzzling against my skin, whispering dark thoughts. I shivered at the touch of the unholy magic. Unsettled in my own skin, I wrenched myself away from Lucifer and summoned holy flames to devour the dark magic desperately trying to cling to my soul's essence. When I felt the last of the vile magic release its feeble hold on my physical body, I released my flames.

Lucifer raised two fingers to his chest and ran them through my red blood yet to be absorbed. I nearly vomited as he brought both fingers to his lips and tasted the blood.

"There's hardly any mortality in your blood," he commented casually, unperturbed by his disgusting act.

"I'm only a quarter demon," I disagreed with a frown. My eyes narrowed at him. What was his point? The Devil didn't say the comment off-handedly, as much as he tried to exude a casual façade. Nothing the Devil did was without reason.

"Ah, yes, Little Warrior, you are a quarter demon, but that does not necessitate your other half is mortal."

My heart stopped in my chest. Thoughts whirled through my head as I tried to fit the pieces together.

Lucifer and Lucifiana knew the identity of my father and intentionally dropped strategic hints about him. First, Lucifiana mentioned something about his kind, as though my father was neither witch nor demon. She had called me a mutt—part demon, part witch... and what else? Then Lucifer basically said my father isn't mortal. Neither would tell me outright but purposefully dangled the information in front of me. But Lucifer made a deal to answer my questions, so he was willing to hand me the information... but Leyla's spell... he couldn't tell me outright.

I surveyed Lucifer, examining his full six-foot height. Easily a foot shorter than Gabriel, he stood barely taller than me. I hadn't met any other angels except Gabriel and Raziel, but I was willing to bet the other archangels stood exactly seven feet tall.

"Were you always this short?" I blurted out.

Lucifer's eyebrows twitched in surprise as his lips pursed in disdain.

But Lucifiana threw her head back and cackled. "Holy hell, girl, evolution deprived you of survival instinct."

"Sorry, I didn't mean it as an insult," I muttered. "I was just wondering if you used to be seven feet like the other archangels?"

"That is your first question?" he growled as a shadow darkened his face, his expression menacing. I didn't flinch. What was the Devil to a demon princess?

When I nodded, Lucifer threw his head back and howled with laughter. "You are a curious creature, Little Warrior. My daughter is right." He considered me from head to toe, sizing me up. "You do not fear me nor worship me as others. You are an interesting soul to corrupt, for neither fear nor desire drive you. Only your own darkness threatens you." Amusement flicked through his blue eyes. "Yes, I stood at seven feet like my brethren, before the Earth came into being and I chose to fall."

Spirit magic zapped through me, and I stepped back in shock, my jaw dropping open as I realized a blatantly obvious law of creation magic that had previously escaped me. My father had mentioned it to me last year... Hell came before Earth.... Heaven and Hell were created before Earth.... Angelic magic, even that of a fallen angel, was older than the Earth itself....

"It was you," I whispered, staring at Lucifer with wide blue eyes. "You helped my mother cast the Binding Spell to shield my father's identity."

"Did I?" He smirked villainously.

I scoffed. "Unless Leyla had easy access to another celestial." Leaning back on my heels, I looped my thumbs through my belt loops and smugly puffed out my chest.

"And what makes you so sure she needed a celestial to cast the spell?" He smirked, mirroring my pose and positioning his arms to make the muscles bulge. But a glance at those blue eyes that did not replicate the emotion of the ones he sought to mimic, and I felt no attraction for the Ultimate Seducer. He was toying with me, and I knew it, but it didn't matter as long as I got my answers, and he got his fun.

"Because she needed magic older than the Earth itself to perform the spell to muzzle anyone who knows my sire's identity. You two"—I gestured at Lucifiana lounging on her red throne—"clearly know the rules better than anyone considering how carefully you've dropped hints. If you could say all those things, then they don't fall under the spell's restrictions. And Leyla needed a nearly endless power source to charge the spell. As a demon princess, her power isn't infinite." I cocked my head at the Devil, then smirked wickedly enough to rival his devilish grin. "Oops, I forgot. Your power isn't infinite either. Sorry," I mocked. "But it's close enough."

"Careful, Little Warrior," he growled, venom in his voice.

My heart thumped rapidly in my chest, threatening to burst out of my body. Not out of fear, but in anticipation of the answer I was closing in on. Would I finally know the identity of my sire? "The thing I don't understand is why? Why protect another man's child?"

He raised an eyebrow. "Would you believe me if I said I did it out of the bottom of my heart?"

He was deflecting. Stalling. He made the Bargain to provide complete and truthful answers, but I suspected if I asked another question before he gave me all the info, it nullified the magic that forced him to tell me everything.... Trickery of the Devil trying to sidetrack me with useless information. I would have to play this carefully.

"Ha," I barked out a humorless laugh. "Not in the slightest. I doubt you even have a heart." Shrugging my shoulders, I added, "No offense."

"We can simultaneously be human and monster," Lucifer said, not an ounce of regret for the monstrous evil within him. No offense taken then. "The capacity to commit great evil exists within us all—mortals, demons, and angels." He paused, considering me with morbid curiosity. "But so does the potential to conceive the highest good. Angels aren't perfect creatures. After all, I was the first angel to fall, but I did not fall alone."

"So, what?" I challenged, not falling for his façade of the wounded animal who regretted his fall from Grace. "You protected me because there is a miniscule sliver of good shining within you?"

"Because," he growled, infuriated at my overstepping accusations. "I may have fallen of my own volition, but I still care deeply for my family."

"Doubtful." I scoffed. "Evil is not Good, but disguises as what is good. It lies, steals and destroys. You could return to Heaven, but in countless millennia, you've *chosen* not to. So, how much do you care if you've chosen eternity without them?"

"My brothers and sisters in the stars think they are virtuous by aligning with the Creator." He pressed a veiny hand to his tanned chest. "I merely wish for them to understand what I came to understand long ago. The reason I fell. They are naïve, they do not see the truth—"

"The truth is that you helped my mother for your own selfish reasons. I want to know why. Now," I barked. "No more stalling per the terms of our Bargain."

The Devil regarded me coolly, his nostrils flaring with anger as he stewed. Lucifiana swung her legs off the arm of her ruby throne, sitting straighter as her eyes bounced between me and her sire. He gritted his teeth as the magic forced him to answer.

"I did it because it is in my best interest for you to defeat Lilith, Little Warrior." Then he muttered under his breath, "You are as infuriating as your father."

"Why? Aren't you and Lilith on the same side?" I knew he didn't want her plan to succeed, but did he really want me to beat her for eternity?

"We parted ways long ago due to creative differences."

"Creative differences?" I scoffed.

He shrugged his sinewy shoulders, and the movement almost distracted me. Almost. "Lilith and I have different ideas of how Darkness shall reign, and I am sick of her wasting demonic power on her selfish plans. Plans that only elevate her power. Elevate her *above* me. Why would I want her to reign when it was I who showed her the beauty of the Darkness in the first place? If it were not for me, she would never have come so far."

"You mean *fallen* so far," I corrected. "Though you fell further, Luci."

His threatening smile was a feral flash of teeth. "Epodic, isn't it?" the Devil mused, ignoring my jabbing nickname. "That you were created to fight the Dark Mother when your father has been such a warrior against evil." There it was again—the wink paired with his devilishly cunning smile. "You shall be her demise, Hayden Black. You are doom to the Mother of Demons. I knew it from the moment you were born, and the choirs of Heaven sang triumphantly, and that is why I assisted Leyla in hiding the identity of your sire."

Spirit zinged through my body, leaving a pleasant tingling sensation on my skin. He was telling the truth. But there was more. More hints about my father....

My father—a warrior against evil.

I was dangerously close to the truth. A truth the Devil wanted me to know. Was that because the Devil would tell nine truths to get me to believe one lie? Or because the truth would help me defeat Lilith?

And I believed his reasons for wanting me to beat her. Evil was loyal to none, not even to other Evil, and so the two darkest beings in existence battled amongst themselves.

But before I could defeat Lilith, I had to sever her hold on Leyla's freedom, thus separating the power of the Mother from the power of the Crone.

"How do I liberate my mother from her imprisonment to Lilith? And not just her physical body. How do I return her free will?"

"Only a Master of Spirit can return one's freedom."

My heart fluttered in my chest as hope brimmed within me. "Perfect. Once I free Kova—"

"Ah." The Devil clucked his tongue condescendingly. "Now the complication with Leyla's unfortunate situation—"

"Unfortunate situation? That's an understatement. She's *nailed to a cross.*"

He continued like I hadn't said anything, "—is that you are the only person who can save her."

"Last I checked, I'm not a Master of Spirit, and given the countdown to my birthday is deadly close to zero, I probably won't master Spirit this week."

"If you want to save your mother, you'll have to," Lucifiana said from her ruby throne, her eyes flicking between me and her father.

"Why can't a fully realized Salem Witch do it?"

"If it were any demon other than my *mother*," she spit out the word, "then the half-breed could restore Leyla's freedom. But since the Mother of Demons—"

"Let me guess," I raised a hand, stopping her. "Only a blood relative of Lilith can use Spirit to free my mom?"

The Devil and his daughter nodded.

"Technically, I could free my sister—"

"Then why don't you?" I roared at my demonic aunt, throwing my arms in the air.

"By killing her," she drawled with a pointed look.

"Oh." All the hot air left me.

"I am sorry," she said with a twinge of regret. "Lilitu demons are not Masters of Spirit but Masters of Death. To free Leyla, I must suck her soul from her body and place her in Hell. She would be immortal here, but..."

"She could never leave," Lucifer finished for her, no trace of emotion in his tone as he watched me carefully.

My gaze snapped to the Red Demon. "Lilitu demon sounds a lot like Lilith..."

"She was the first lilitu demon, if that is your question," Lucifiana confirmed. "Lilitus are a class of demons known for their abilities to suck the life from a mortal vessel. You are probably familiar with succubi, but I am a soul eater, which is a far rarer lilitu, as we are spawned by a union between my demonic parents." She gestured a perfectly manicured hand at her father.

Lucifer glowered at his daughter. "Which is why you are the youngest of your siblings, Lucifiana, as I have no desire to procreate with Lilith again. Yet I wonder why I endure your existence, Daughter."

Lucifiana's smirk was absolutely feral. "Perhaps you should have spawned more useful children if you wanted to be rid of me, Father, for I am the most competent."

Gotta say the family banter was weird. They were joking, but kinda not joking, in a totally twisted way.

"Lilith, however," Lucifer drawled, compelled to answer my question by the Bargain binding him. "Is the first lilitu, and therefore, her power is unrivaled. She is the only lilitu that can steal the power of free will from both mortals and demons.... A power even I do not possess."

"In a dark, kinda twisted way, it's rather poetic. She fell from Grace of her own free will and obtains the power to steal free will from others? The Universe has a sick sense of humor sometimes."

Lucifer smiled mischievously as he waggled his eyebrows. "Oh, you have no idea, Little Warrior."

"Nope, I'm not even gonna ask because I straight up don't wanna know." He opened his mouth, but I raised a flat palm. "Seriously, dude, if it's not relevant to beating Lilith, I don't wanna know what kinda twistedness you've indulged in for the last thousand eons."

Did I just call the Devil "dude"? He didn't seem to appreciate it. Oh well. We had a deal. "How I do become a Master of Spirit? Ya know, other than by passing my last Trial?"

"Isn't it obvious?" He drawled, an amused smile dancing on his lips. The expression of delight on his face made my stomach flip. "You have to die."

CHAPTER SEVEN

When Extremes Meet

"Sorry," I said, shaking my head in disbelief. "For a second there, it sounded like you said I have to *die*."

"That is exactly what I said, Little Warrior. Only by dying and resurrecting can you conquer death." One corner of his lips curved up in a sadistic smile. "Death shall lose its grip on you, and the grave shall have no claim to an immortal body once you have broken the chains of mortality. It is an enticing offer, do you not think?"

Bringing my hands up, I smacked them together in a slow clap. "Wow, I gotta hand it to you. You are an excellent manipulator, trying to convince me to die and resurrect."

"That is a truthful answer, Little Warrior."

"Oh, I have no doubt. I'm sure it worked for Alice Parker in 1692, but here's a little secret. Kova is *Nephilim*," I mock whispered with an eye roll.

"Resurrection is the only way other than passing your Spirit Trial by which to become a Master of Spirit." The Devil shrugged like he didn't care one way or another. "At least, to my knowledge."

"I'm starting to think your knowledge isn't all that great, Luci, considering you're living in this"—I gestured to the cavern as I glanced around, wrinkling my nose in disdain—"*Pit*."

"Careful, *girl*," Lucifer growled from where he stood, his hands clenched at his side, with blue hellfire burning around the curled fists. "Best remember, you are in *my* domain."

"Best remember, I am not one of the sorry souls you corrupted, Luci," I snarled, taking a menacing step forward. "I am the *Salem Witch*, a Daughter of Heaven, and I will not cower before you."

"We are done here."

"Not even close, Angel Face." I sobered instantly, pointing a finger forcefully at Lucifer. "Assuming I master Spirit and free my mother, how do I defeat Lilith? I wasn't able to kill her—"

"Because you can't," the Red Demon barked savagely. "I beheaded her once. Her head just re-grew," she finished with an eye roll.

My mouth gaped open. "You..."

I kicked Lilith into a volcano in self-defense, but to actually behead your own mother, even if she was immortal... it was so beyond twisted.

The Red Demon shrugged like it wasn't the most deranged mother-daughter relationship in the history of creation. "She stole my boyfriend. Not like it was the first time I fatally maimed her. Not likely to be the last. One time, I drove a wooden stake through her heart just to see—"

"Lucifiana," Lucifer barked at his daughter. "Focus. I am growing bored of this tedious conversation with Heaven's chosen champion."

"Oh, right," she drawled with an exaggerated eye roll. "Her body is literally indestructible. I blew her up, and her particles snapped back together." She snapped her fingers, the crisp sound echoing through the chamber.

"It's good to know I'm not the craziest one in this family," I muttered.

Lucifiana beamed at me. "Thank you," she said, batting her eyes like it was a compliment.

"But I meant *morally* I wasn't able to kill dear old granny."

Lucifiana pouted, pursing her red painted lips. "Mortals are no fun. At least try a couple of torture techniques. You usually accidentally kill your victim." She shrugged, then continued filing her nails. "Never know what will end her."

When did she get the nail file? Was I seriously the only one who couldn't spook? Ugh.

Rolling my eyes, I ignored the Red Demon. "If I can't kill her, how do I put her down for eternity?" I directed my question at Lucifer since I didn't have a blood-binding agreement with my demonic aunt.

"I do not know," he stated simply, running a hand down his torso to hook the thumb in the waistband of his black jeans.

My eyes bulged in their sockets as I stared at him, mouth hanging open. "I think I misheard you. Because for a second there, it sounded like you said you don't know."

"You did not mishear me, Little Warrior. I do not know how to defeat Lilith. If I did, I would have leashed her long ago."

"But... I mean..." I stuttered as my brain struggled to comprehend. Then I exploded with fury like fire. "But you were supposed to have the answer. How could you not know? You're the Devil, for crying out loud." I jabbed a forceful finger in his direction, pointing accusingly at him. "You're the one who seduced her into falling from Grace. You're the Enemy. You've spent eons with her. You know her better than any other being except the Creator, and you don't know how to beat her?"

"Yes," he snapped at me, those royal blue eyes darkening as a shadow of rage claimed his face, and he surged at me, pushing his seductively flawless face dangerously close to mine. "I am the Devil, not the Creator. Even I admit—I am not omniscient. My power, though near limitless, is limited." He added with a grumbled, "Thank you for the reminder."

"You must be kidding me," I raged with complete disregard for the Devil's murderous expression. "I came all this way, braved Hell and the Devil, because I was told you have the answer to stopping Lilith, and you're telling me you don't have the faintest clue?" I thrust an accusing finger at him. "This is great." I threw my hands in the air, my voice rising three octaves to hysterical. "Just great. I'm in Hell with a Devil, who, throughout eternity, hasn't figured out how to beat her because he's, what, too lazy? Too stupid?"

"Careful, Little Warrior," he growled maliciously as his dark power coiled around me, prodding and poking in search of weakness in my defenses so his evil might infiltrate my mind, a stark reminder to keep on my best behavior given my vulnerability. I still had to make it out of here alive. "Just because I am helping you does not mean I care. Your death would be nothing more than a minor inconvenience as it would incur the wrath of your father, whom I do not particularly care to deal with." Lucifer flicked his fingers over his shoulder like he was bored and had nothing better to do than brush the nonexistent lint off his broad, bare shoulders. "That is all."

I paused. My father? Who was my father that Lucifer didn't want to enrage him? My father, who was a warrior against evil. My sire had to be alive. And powerful, if he was a threat to the Devil.

Lucifer and Lucifiana mentioned him too much for it to be a mere coincidence. His identity was significant. And not just to me, but in how I would wage and win the battle against the Mother of Demons. I just didn't understand why.

Fear is a powerful ally. The Devil will try to use it against you. Amara's warning drifted through my mind.

Then I will use it against him. What does the Devil fear most?

Pride always comes before a fall. And none have fallen as far as the Morningstar. Therefore, he is filled with pride for the perversion he pervades through humanity. You want to know what the Devil fears? The entities he has not perverted. Chastity. Temperance. Charity. Diligence. Kindness. Patience. Humility.

The Seven Holy Virtues.

Yes, Hayden. And the Seven Holy Virtues are Heaven's warriors against the Seven Deadly Sins. But these seven are just parts of something much greater than the individual Virtues.

And what is that?

Love, Hayden. The Devil fears love. And if you, who are so full of love, act in love, it will be the most powerful weapon you wield against him.

If the Devil was full of pride—and he was certainly brimming with arrogance—then humility, its opposite, was the best weapon to fight him with. Even if I did it begrudgingly.

Spirit whispered through my mind, guiding my next words.

"I am sorry for my words. I should not have offended you."

Lucifiana scoffed, not bothering to look at me as she inspected her nails. "Maybe you take more after your father than I thought. What Princess of Hell willingly apologizes?"

I shot her a curious glance, unsure what to make of her offhanded comment. She made it sound like my father would be the kind of man who could swallow his pride to apologize, even to the Devil.

The saying "kill them with kindness"... whoever said that must have been referring to old Luci, because my apology grated him. The dark presence, the power searching mine for a weakness, faltered at my words. As though speaking the apology aloud weakened the Devil's magic.

This whole Bargain... I had been playing the game wrong. I was determined to meet the Devil blow for blow, showing my unwavering resolve to fight evil with my aggressive nature. But Lucifer, the King of Hell, didn't fear the darkness of a Princess of Hell. Not the way witches on Earth feared me. In the depths of Hell, I needed to act like a Daughter of Heaven whose Spirit irritated the Devil's demons.

"Maybe you don't know how to defeat Lilith, but there has to be something you've learned in the last six millennia. Something from her fall from Grace?"

"Lilith's soul has long been lost."

"Gee." I snorted. "Ya think?"

Lucifer glowered at my sarcasm. Like I cared.

"As I was saying," he shot a hardened look at me, "Lilith's soul is lost. When she first fled the Garden because Adam attempted to assert dominance, three angels hunted her. The Creator sent my brothers, Senoi, Sansenoi, and Sammangelof to return her to the Garden."

"Right, but they never did. When they found Lilith, she was spawning demons and refused to return with them. For her disobedience, the angels swore to kill one hundred of her children every day. What's your point?"

"Do you really think my mother would allow the angels to kill her demons without seeking revenge?" Lucifiana drawled, propping her chin on her hand.

She was right. "Lilith would never endure such a slight without inflicting pain and suffering in return."

"Precisely." Lucifiana nodded, then scraped her file against her red nails, sharpening them in to claws.

My piercing blue gaze stabbed into the Devil. "Tell me the story. The whole story." Of course, I knew the legends, but the Devil was the only other being who lived through the events of Lilith's fall. Creator only knew what information the legends missed.

"Lilith returned to the Garden, but of her own volition, without the angels. Sneaking in, she discovered Adam already had another mate."

"Eve."

Lucifer nodded. "For her vengeance, she stole Adam's seed, which she planted on Earth to bear lilium—earthbound demons—to replace the children the angels slaughtered."

"What does any of this have to do with Lilith's lost soul?"

"Because, until that pivotal moment, she was still human—a being with a soul. But when Adam discovered what Lilith had done, he called out to the Creator, for Lilith committed many atrocities. First, she fed Adam the fruit of the first tree—the Tree of Knowledge. For her crimes, the Creator cast them both out of Eden but allowed the humans to live in Jerusalem, the Promised Land, where the powers of Heaven are absent and replaced by the power of Mother Earth, who sustains this world and its inhabitants."

"So, basically, Adam and Lilith fell, but the Creator provided everything for them to live comfortably on Earth?"

"Essentially, yes."

"I guess the Creator does love us despite our sins," I muttered, not loud enough for them to hear, but judging by Lucifer's scowl, his angelic body had superior hearing. "Keep going. I want the complete and truthful answer to my question about her soul."

"When Lilith ran from the Garden, the Creator did not intend to punish her until she refused to return against Its wishes and instead chose to spawn demonic children. Even so, God and Goddess allowed her free rein between the Garden and the rest of Earth. But when she returned to the Garden and left with Adam's stolen seed to spread darkness, the Creator sent my brother, the Warrior Archangel, to confront Lilith. He went forth, casting her out of the Garden and forbidding her return until she sought absolution from her sins."

I snorted, crossing my arms over my chest. "Doubt it was high on her priority list."

Lucifiana barked out a laugh at my jest, but Luci didn't seem to find it humorous.

"When Michael confronted her about her dark path, she realized she could separate her Light from her Darkness. In front of the Warrior Archangel, she ripped her soul from her mortal body, inviting Darkness to take its place and casting out her Light forever, never to return. I assume her soul was destroyed when she discarded it."

"Holy," I breathed the word as Spirit traced my skin. The thought of separating my consciousness from my soul gave me the wiggins. What possessed someone to do that?

Lucifer shrugged. "Michael cast her out of Earth, sending her to the Hell planes for a year and a day, in the hopes her misery might motivate her to seek her soul and pursue forgiveness from the Creator."

"But it backfired?" I guessed. "Hell wasn't torture for a soulless being. Lilith had no desire to atone for her mistakes, but with the forces of Darkness within her, Lilith became the Mother of Demons."

"And yet, the tides are shifting," Lucifiana said, flicking her black and red hair over her shoulder. "It seems many demons, despite my mother's muzzle on their free will, fight for a new power. Part demon, part witch, they call her their Savior. Interesting development, wouldn't you say?" She quirked an eyebrow.

"Quite the contrary, Daughter," Lucifer argued. "It was my understanding that the demons call her the Demonic Angel."

"Not sure what you're talking about," I denied, earning a wicked smile from my aunt.

"Curious. I heard she is quite the duality." The Devil circled me, his fingers dancing over my neck and collarbone as his body pressed against mine in an attempt to seduce me. But his cold skin lacked the warmth I was used to, and his hollow eyes held no temptation for me. "Part Hell, part Heaven, she wears her Darkness and Light equally. Warrior by birth, Savior by choice."

Heat crawled up my neck as my pale skin flushed bright red, and I averted my gaze, bashful of the praise. Well, as much praise as one can receive from the Devil. Wait, was the Devil praising me for trying to save a bunch of demons by bringing them to walk the path of Light? No. The Devil had a reason.... To lead me to the identity of my sire. So, what did my dual nature have to do with my father?

I was the Salem Witch and a demon. It would have been easy for me to give into my darkness, but I chose to follow my calling. Not because I was an angel. Not because it was my birthright—

Spirit zapped through my soul, the truth whispering through my mind like a hauntingly beautiful melody. And the answer slammed into me like a ton of bricks as the puzzle pieces slipped into place—the subtle clues from Lucifiana and Lucifer, my natural ability to fight before I tapped into my magic, my silver flames birthed by merging hellfire and holy flames. Power rippled through me like a wave crashing on the shore, Spirit humming as I let the knowledge settle in my gut where my intuition whispered the truth I had always known deep in my soul.

The Devil chuckled deep, dark laughter that reminded me of silky dark chocolate. The thrall of his power alone shook me from my stupor.

"Judging by your face, Little Warrior, you have unmasked the identity of your sire."

Lucifiana snorted. "Took the mutt long enough."

I nodded numbly, my eyes glazed over as I stared at him standing shirtless with muscles rippling across his torso as he lazily ran a hand through his golden-bronze locks, the veins in his forearms bulging at the movement.

He was beguiling and seductive in an ominous and foreboding way. The Devil was a terribly attractive sight to behold, but it was just a mirage. The Enemy had the face of an angel, but the fallen angel was a gruesome creature. And it was this angel that struck fear into the hearts of men older and wiser than me.

But I wasn't afraid of him. Cautious, but not afraid. Because he has no power over me, and somewhere, deep in my soul, the core of my being knew it before I did. And it had nothing to do with my demon blood.

And it was the ace in my hand in this war.... The pivotal secret, hidden so fiercely thanks to my mother's love for me.

"Hey." My vision snapped into focus, staring at those hollow blue eyes that held none of the warmth of the ones awaiting me in Asylum. "One last question.... Why?"

"Why did I fall?" He knew what I was referring to but asked anyway. "No one expected an angel to set the world on fire." Lucifer smirked at me. "But with this smile, I can get away with everything when it comes to mortals."

"A man with charm is a dangerous thing," I remarked drily. "But that doesn't answer my question. You didn't fall just because it was unexpected. You fell for a reason."

His lips tugged into a vicious frown, displeasure written on his face. "I, like Lilith, fell for power." Lucifer held up a tan hand, letting his dark blue magic dance at his fingers. "The Creator was unwilling to share, so I aligned with Evil, who gave me exactly what I desired," he raved like a lunatic. "I am the Morningstar, who brought light to the darkest depths of the Pit." He gestured around the throne room—one small portion of the vast realm that was the underworld. "Hell is my domain, and I am beholden to none of the Divine."

Fearlessly, I met his eyes. "I think we both know that's not entirely true."

"Foolish of you to presume as much, Little Warrior," the Devil cooed in his low, silky voice. "If the Creator controlled me, then why has It allowed Darkness to spread amongst mortals so thoroughly?" He whispered it like a prayer, his voice reverent as he tried to enthrall me. And part of me wanted to give in, to let him, to fall for his temptation. The dark, flawed part of me. And I let him get alarmingly close to whisper in my ear, "Why does It allow such unsavory actions in the world? Such heinous crimes? Why not remove your demon blood, as your mother asked?"

"All the forces of Darkness cannot overcome the Light." I shoved away from the Devil and fled several steps to put some distance between me and the beguiling charm of the Enemy. "Mortals were granted freedom of choice because we were made in the image of the Creator. But the gift of free will creates the opportunity for evil to creep in." I recalled Amara's lesson as understanding filled my spirit. "The Creator doesn't force us to be good. It wants us to willingly choose love instead of evil," I stated defiantly. "It's not about defeating the Darkness. The Creator could have vanquished you long ago. It's about mortals choosing love instead of hate because we want to. And I walk in the Light. You have no power over me. The Creator is within me. You will not deceive me." My voice echoed around the cavern, the fierce confidence and rebellion clinging to the echo.

"Are you sure about that, darling?" the words rolled off his tongue like honey and the level of power in his voice alone was overwhelming as he prowled toward me. The depths of his power were almost endless. "It would be so, so easy to seduce you, especially in this form."

He brushed his nose over the skin of my neck, nuzzling against me as his dark, revolting power caressed mine, calling to me with its twisted temptation. "You are not like the others. The frail little humans who so easily fall to the Darkness. They cannot withstand the might of the power we wield. But you, Little Warrior, you are not like other mortals, other witches. Your soul... it has darkness in it. And is smells delicious... surely you can taste the sweet nectar the Darkness offers. The power it offers. It can give you everything you want. It can help you beat Lilith. It can help you survive the Trials and your seventeenth birthday. You just have to give in. Give into the darkness inherent to your soul. You know you want to, Little Warrior. I can sense your desire. You are tempted so."

The lure of the Devil called to me, his sensual compulsion tempting beyond all reason, beyond all faith, beyond all emotion.... Royal blue eyes flashed through my mind. The Devil's compulsion was nearly inescapable as he donned a mirage of the person I loved most.

But that's all it was—a mirage.

The Enemy sought to mimic good, to pretend to be something virtuous and beloved with the intention to deceive and manipulate to his own ends. But the thing about the Devil was... he could never get it exactly right, and as I looked into those royal blue irises that lacked the warmth of the eyes I stared into every day, the mirage shattered, crumbling to dust because it was broken and bent from the beginning.

Swaying forward to lean into the Devil, I spoke softly, "You're right... I am tempted..." I trailed off, letting my sensual words linger in the air. "I want to..." I licked my lips, flicking my eyes to look into those cold blue eyes. "I'm tempted..."

The Devil leaned into me, inhaling my scent as he took a deep breath in through his nose.

My hand shot out, quicker than lightning, and clamped around his neck, my fingers digging brutally into his throat, crushing his windpipe. Holding the Devil at arm's length, I grinned my signature smirk. "I am not tempted by you, Devil. You forget, I have been a demon my whole life. I know the wickedness of your ways, and I will not fall victim to your deception." Glancing him over once, amusement claimed my lips. I snarled, "You cannot compare to the real thing." Shoving him away, I sent him stumbling backward. "No matter how hard you try, you will always fall short of the purity of what is good."

"What is good." Lucifer scoffed, rubbing his throat. "What would a demon princess know of what is good? You believe you are virtuous, Little Warrior, but your soul is as dark as mine."

"No," I said with fierce conviction, "it's not. My soul has its darkness, but it also has so much light." I pressed a hand to my heart, finding the sliver of silver light within me, just as Death taught me. "You... you have no soul. We are not the same. Which is why I am not bound to this Pit like you and will take my leave now."

"Ah," the Devil drew out the word, then clucked his tongue. "And how do you plan to leave, Little Warrior?"

Freezing, I schooled my expression into an emotionless mask. He knew I didn't have a way back to Earth. Amara said her portal was a one-way ticket, but she had seemed confident I could find my way back.... Right?

"It seems I am correct," Lucifer drawled, his tone amused. "Lucifiana, remind me, daughter, did the portal close behind the Salem Witch? Or was she foolish enough to leave it open in the depths of Hell?"

Lucifiana grinned a shark-like grin. "Her portal slammed closed as soon as her feet landed in this realm. There is no return for her."

"Then it seems, Little Warrior, there is no escape for you."

"Escape for me?" I scoffed, stalling. "Demons belong in Hell, but I'm not a soulless demon. I'm a Daughter of Heaven, and I will return to the Light." I prayed Lucifer didn't see through my thinly veiled attempt to distract him from the fact that I didn't have an escape route.

"Hmm... is portaling one of your powers, Salem Witch?"

Falling silent, I didn't break eye contact with the Devil as I gripped the hilt of Nightmare. My magic sang with life in my veins, my magical radar keeping tabs on Lucifiana, who still lounged lazily on her throne atop the dais.

"Like I thought—powerless."

Without flinching, without expression, I took a careful step backward. "Our definitions of power are very different, Luci. You think I am powerless, but I know while I have the Creator, all power is in Its name. A name no soulless demon can utter." Taking more steps backward, I steered toward the massive doors Lucifiana and I had entered through. I didn't know how I was getting home, but I needed to get away from the Devil and my aunt.

Dark magic blasted out of the Devil like a sonic wave. The power of Spirit moved faster than lightning, protecting me from the lethal magic, forcing it to skirt around me and slam into the walls of the cavern. I didn't dare turn my back on the Devil as I summoned a personal cyclone to lift me in the air and fly me to the door. Dropping to the ground, I willed the cyclone to smash into the doors to fling them open.

But nothing happened. Summoning winds stronger than a tornado, I shot them into the door again. Then again and again. To no avail. Holy flames burned into the doors in a fiery torrent, but the marble didn't budge. With the force of a waterfall, my third element crashed into the doors, splashing off the unmovable surface. Rumbling the earth, I shook the crystal of the doors, but for all the magic of the elements, the doors endured the abuse.

"It is no use, Little Warrior," he called, leaning casually on his heels. "I sealed those doors. There is no escape."

"So, what?" I demanded, stalking toward the Devil with dangerous intent. "You're going to trap me here forever? To what end? What use am I to you?"

"I want to know what you're made of, Little Warrior," the Devil crooned. "I want to know how much like your father you truly are."

My piercing blue eyes—the eyes I inherited from my sire—narrowed in suspicion. My black hair rose in the air as static electricity crackled between the strands, and a crown of silver flames sparked to life atop my head. The five elements surged around me, more intense and threatening than before. "You want a fight, Luci?" I raged, my eyes flashing silver. "I'll give you a fight."

"Oh, no, no, no." He clucked his tongue as he shook a patronizing finger at me. "I don't want a fight... at least not with you." He shared a vicious look with his daughter.

"Try to stop me, and I will kill every last demon standing between me and my freedom, *Luci*. Or I will persuade them to my side. They seem to like the idea of free will."

"We shall see about that, Little Warrior. The funny thing about demons is they are like obedient dogs. They come when I call." The Devil's magnetic blue eyes glowed blood red.

A summoning....

"You should have known better, *Niece*, not to play with the Devil. I always cheat." Lucifer spun on his heel and sauntered up the gleaming crystal stairs to drape himself over his dark throne. Snapping his fingers, he commanded the demons.

My eyes widened in understanding. The Devil wasn't man enough to face me himself. He was calling his demons to attack me. Countless demons against one Princess of Hell.

Hidden stone doors burst open from the smooth, black crystal walls, and demons poured into the cavern in droves. Brimstones, hellhounds, agony, inferni, spiders, killer bees, agony, abyss... every type of demon in existence filtered into Lucifer's hellish throne room. More demons than I could count until they blurred beyond the doors.

Thousands of demons surrounded me, with more to replace the ones that would undoubtedly fall to my sword and sorcery.

Lucifer's eyes flashed deadly red as he commanded, "Attack the Salem Witch."

Air raged around me in a cyclone, silver holy hellfire burned in my hair like a tiara for the Daughter of Heaven fighting in the midst of Hell, water swirled around me, and earth rumbled under my feet as the elements hailed to my beckoning call. And Spirit, the ultimate power of the Universe, filled me with endless power.

Black flashed as I unsheathed Nightmare, brandishing the blade as I slipped into my stance.

Lucifer hissed, his spine straightening as he rocketed upright, every muscle taut and stiff at the sight of my longsword. Lurching to his feet, he stepped toward me.

"That sword," Lucifer boomed from the top step of his throne. "Where did you retrieve that sword from?"

Lucifiana's sharp red gaze snapped to her father, then back to me, the confusion written across her flawless features. Intrigued, she straightened, lowering her red stilettos to the floor, but didn't rise.

Spirit lightning crackled, striking demon after demon in a brilliant display of a heavenly thunderstorm. Magic poured from every orifice of my skin. Air blew, fire burned, water flowed, and the crystal stone floor rumbled in answer to my magic. But Spirit. Spirit regenerated my magic as quickly as I expelled it. As long as I had Spirit, I would never tire in warfare against the evils of this world. Or rather, the underworld.

"What does it matter to you?" I snapped, thrusting the black blade through the black heart of a pit demon.

White fire soared in an arc as I spun, slicing Nightmare through the torsos of five charging brimstones. Holy flames slammed into the front line of demons, sizzling on impact until the demons were reduced to dust. But for every demon that fell to my blade or to my magic, another took its place.

"Because it is mine," Lucifer growled with all the contempt of Hell.

I nearly faltered as an agony demon's grotesque hand curled around my forearm. It yanked on my arm, almost shattering the bone with its vise-like grip as it shook me like a dog does a toy. Wind swirled around me, and I twisted midair until I was horizontal, and I jabbed Nightmare through the agony demon's black heart. Black dust exploded around me as I fell to the ground, my legs twisting under me, so my combats landed lightly on the black stone floor without a sound.

White flames burned in a circle, driving back the demons. A radius of fifty feet black dust surrounded me. Demons on the edge of the circle blinked at me, hesitating to charge after the deadly display of heavenly magic. My head snapped up to look the Devil in the icy blue eye.

"What?" I demanded, my voice reverberating with the power of the Salem Witch as spiritual power flowed through me. Rising to my full height, I maintained eye contact with the Enemy. "What do you mean Nightmare is yours?"

Joints cracking sounded through the air as the Devil squeezed his clamped fists tighter, popping the knuckles. "Nightmare is my longsword, given to me by my eldest brother, Michael, when I was created. It was my bonded sword in Heaven."

Lucifiana's red-painted lips parted as her jaw dropped and her eyes widened at her father.

"It's not your sword anymore," I said, twisting the pommel in my hand. "Nightmare bonded to me the moment my mother handed it to me."

Lucifer's eyes flashed as he bristled. "Leyla had Nightmare?"

Cocking my head, I considered him. How did he not know Leyla had Nightmare for decades before it bonded to me? Did she know it belonged to him before the Fall?

"Ha," I laughed. "The better question is if Lilith knew Leyla had the sword. Man, you two must really be estranged if she didn't bother to return Nightmare to you."

"Lilith did not know about Nightmare."

"Shocker," I said flatly. If Lucifiana didn't know the details of her sire's angelic past, it was unlikely Lucifer shared openly with Lilith. What a cut-throat family I was born into. Extended family? Not sure how that worked. "Then I doubt my mom knew."

Grumbling something under his breath, Lucifer shook his head.

"Funny," I said, lifting my sword to inspect the Enochian script etched into the black blade. "Nightmare was in my mother's possession for decades. But neither Leyla nor Lilith knew Nightmare's name. Tell me, Devil, can you read Enochian?"

The Devil bristled, glowering at my taunting. A fallen angel couldn't read an angelic language. Even mortals struggled to comprehend the language.

"I lost the tongue when I fell."

"Which is why Nightmare bonded to *me*, a witch who inherently understands the language. It is no longer your sword, for it belongs to me and I belong to it."

"Nightmare will submit to its rightful owner. Perhaps it passed hands through the eons because of thievery, but it rightfully belongs to me."

"Your logic is a bit flawed there, Luci. I didn't steal Nightmare. So, how did you lose it?"

"Nightmare did not fall with me, but Michael stole it as he pushed me from the heights of the celestial realms. And I want it back. Now." He held his open palm out expectantly, as though I would willingly relinquish my cherished weapon.

The blade hummed in my hand, speaking to me with its energy. It was thrilled to be bonded with me, and it would not willingly submit to its previous owner. Not without a fight.

A wicked smirk claimed my lips. "Be careful what you wish for, Luci. This sword is mine. I will return Nightmare to you. And me driving it through your soulless body will be the last thing you see."

"Ha," he barked out a humorless laugh. "I am immortal, child. What could you possibly do to me?"

"Invincible and immortal are two different things." To prove my point, I waved my hand through the air, shooting arrows of white fire into the hearts of the demons around the circumference of my dust-filled ring. "Demons are immortal. Not invincible."

"I am not a demon."

Brandishing Nightmare in front of me, I said, "No, you're a fallen angel. And angels can die. You would know, seeing how many died by your hand when you and the Sins fell from Grace." I swiped a hand gently along the polished black surface of my loyal longsword. "Nightmare belongs to me, now and forever. My mother gave me this sword, and I will not relinquish it because you feel entitled."

"It is mine," the Devil roared with a fury that shook the walls of Hell.

"It *was* yours," I roared back, my voice backed by my tremendous power. "Nightmare chose *me*. Heaven chose *me* to wield a celestial's blade. Perhaps God and Goddess think I will redeem Nightmare after the failures of its previous owner."

Black and blue power blasted from the Devil like beams of light shining from his palms. Black lightning surged forward as silver light surrounded me like a halo. Lucifer's unholy powers slammed into me, bouncing off the shield of lightning and light surrounding me.

Flinging my arms wide, I unleashed a blast of pure, unfiltered magic. The power of Spirit. White light and black lightning threw Lucifer backward, and he crashed into his throne, crushing it to rubble beneath his body.

Half a dozen brimstone demons charged me, their three-inch slate horns angled to stab into me. Holy flames burst out of my palm as I swiped it through the air in an arc.

Killer bee demons buzzed angrily overhead, but a twist of my wrist smashed them against the stalactites protruded from the ceiling. Black blood splattered down on me as the sharp stones wounded but didn't kill the bees.

Spider demons crawled over the cavern walls, their pinchers pinching and legs scuttling. Red hourglasses gleamed in stark contrast to their dark bodies. Sticky webbing shot from spinnerets on their rears. Raising walls of earth, I separated myself from the charging demons and let the gooey black webs stick to my walls. Earth magic sang to me, and I thrust my arms wide, throwing the walls of rock across the cavern to squash the spider demons like bugs.

For every demon I killed, another flooded through the open doors and into the chamber.

I was in Hell.... Lucifer had an unending supply of demons. I would have to decimate them all if I wanted to survive this. An impossible task for anyone without the power of Spirit.

White light beamed as lightning zapped through the air, the electricity expanding like veins. Rays of light shot from me, bouncing from demon to demon, crisscrossing and intersecting as the power of Spirit magnified, building on itself until it wove into a blinding net of raw power. With a push of my magic, Spirit obliterated the demons filling the cavern. But there were more. But as long as I had breath in my body, I would fight, I would glorify my Creator using the powers gifted to me until I breathed my last.

Wraiths zoom into the cavern with blinding speed that no mere mortal eye could track. But the power of Spirit slowed their attack in my mind's eye, and I could see with unbelievable detail every twitch of their muscles. I could see the puss oozing from their decaying skin and the rot eating away at their green, putrid flesh.

With deathly calm, I slid out of the way, sidestepping the wraiths. As they crashed together in a tangle of gangly limbs, I spun, slicing Nightmare through their necks on the back slice. Four more wraiths attacked with unparalleled strength and speed, but I disposed of the threat with unwavering confidence, even as the cavern filled with a fresh wave of demons.

Recovering, the Devil cursed as he rose to his feet, blue hellfire smoking in his golden hair as he summoned dark powers to rebuild his throne, his cold, dark eyes never leaving me as I obliterated his army with the strength of my magic and the skill of my sword. I was a witch and a warrior, and I would not fall to demons.

As tirelessly as Darkness fought, it could not overcome the power of Spirit within me, the power of Light that repelled the vileness of the soulless demons, who did not join me out of the desire to obtain free will.

Smoking husks of demons piled around me as they slowly disintegrated, stacking as a barrier to the attacking demons endlessly flooding into the room. I was a fearsome force, a whirlwind of elemental magic as I struck down every demon.

Maybe it was the elements or my magic, or the power of Spirit, but it was like I could sense what the demons were about to do before they did it, even if I couldn't see them. Surrounded by demons, I was at a severe disadvantage.... Impossible odds for anyone... except for me.

I sliced through dark and demented flesh like it was butter, and magic plowed through the rest.

A massive pit demon smashed at me with his club, a growl rolling off his troll-like lips. Ducking, I rolled between his legs, then stabbed Nightmare into his backside. Dust rained on me.

Dozens of inferni demons charged me. Inferni were basically balls of blazing fire with limbs like burnt and charred firewood logs. Most witches hated inferni because they were mostly incorporeal, and their hellfire was searing hot.

But I wasn't most witches. How foolish of them to believe hellfire posed a threat to me. Inhaling a breath, I called upon my magic of air and water, mixing the two elements to breathe out frost. My frigid breath misted over them, freezing them in place. But regular water couldn't extinguish hellfire. Only holy water.

So, their fiery little bodies began to melt the ice entrapping them. I called upon my inherent fire powers and pulled the hellfire off their bodies, snuffing their life force. Channeling the hellfire, I mixed it with my holy flames, turning the neon blue into a flickering silver. Flames slammed into the looming pit demons.

A massive hellhound teleported into the chamber directly above me. Leaping out of the way as it came crashing down, I used the power of air to throw myself clear of where it crunched into the floor with a vicious growl. My side hit the ground and my leather jacket squeaked as I slid, shooting flames out of my hands to kill the demons in my path. Skidding to a stop, I clamored to my feet, the elements swirling around me in a ball, protecting me from the surrounding demons.

But the hellhound... it must have been the size of a house...

"Forfeit, Little Warrior. You know how this will end," Lucifer taunted from his throne. "Either you will die here in Hell, or you will die at Lilith's hand. There is no other option. And I will reclaim my sword. Nightmare shall live with its rightful owner."

"Not a chance, Luci." I jumped and spun, cutting Nightmare through the neck of a pit demon as black lightning crackled, incinerating demons in droves as I moved toward the humongous hellhound.

Spinning, I swept Nightmare in an arc, severing three more heads before I pointed the lethal tip at the Devil. "Nightmare's rightful owner is me. You may have wielded it first, but Goddess granted it to me. Fitting, too, for a Princess of Hell and Daughter of Heaven to bond with a sword from the Heavens that was once owned by the Morningstar, who fell so far."

The Devil bristled at my boldness.

"You cannot protect everyone in the mortal world, Hayden." The Devil purred as I slashed Nightmare through the neck of a spider demon, severing its head from its grotesque body. "Especially if you cannot save yourself."

"That's the thing Luci," I grunted as I stabbed an agony demon through the eye. Silver flames exploded out of me in a ring, incinerating every demon in the room, but more kept filtering in. I spun to face the Devil. "You think I won't win. You think I can't fight forever against your demons. But you and I both know that with Spirit within me, I won't tire until I've killed every demon in Hell. You think I can't save everyone, but that doesn't mean I won't try."

With a wink, I spun and slashed my blade through another demon, then another, then another, not even working up a sweat. The demons degraded into shriveled husks of skin and bone, smoking until they disintegrated into dust.

As I killed demon after demon, faster than they could disintegrate, their bodies stacked up around me, again forming a barrier between me and the living demons.

Magic shot from my palms. First air, then fire, then water, then earth, then lightning, blasting through demons, leaving nothing but dust in the wake of my fearsome power.

But the hellhound blundered toward me, tossing demons to the side as it plowed through the crowd of its comrades. This beast was nothing like my pet hellhound, Buddy.

"What was the point of striking a Bargain with me if you were just going to kill me?" I faced the Devil after swiping Nightmare through the necks of three brimstone demons. I jabbed a finger in his direction. "Isn't it in your best interest if I beat Lilith?"

Nightmare sank into a pit demon's black heart as he raised his club, attempting to strike me from behind.

"Like I said," drawled the Devil, completely unfazed by the carnage in his throne room. "Your death is a minor inconvenience. But since you transferred your blessing to the Heart of Earth, making yourself vulnerable to Lilith, you are a liability. If you cannot survive this, then you cannot survive her, and she will claim the power of the Maiden."

My eyes widened in shock. How did he know? Thea was the only other being who knew.

Razor-sharp claws flashed in my peripheral. Spinning, I ducked under an agony demon's clawed hand as it swiped to take off my head. Jabbing up, I stabbed through its spine into the back of its neck, killing it in an explosion of dust.

Raising Nightmare to point the lethal tip at the Devil, I spoke with the ferocity of a Princess of Hell and the confidence of a Salem Witch, "I will burn this Pit to the ground and leave nothing but ash in my wake."

The hellhound's clawed paw stomped on me from overhead. Stabbing up, I ripped Nightmare through its paw pad as I threw myself clear to stand under its belly. The hellhound howled in pain as black blood spurted from the bottom of its paw. Sprinting for the side of the hellhound, I threw the elements in front of me, clearing a path through the demons. As I got out from under the beast, I summoned a whirlwind to toss me in the air.

With the graceful reflexes of a feline, I landed on the hellhound's back, the blue hellfire burning along its hackles a welcomed warmth compared to the cold of Hell. Rising to my full height, I smirked, then ran up the giant hellhound's spine like a gazelle, hacking apart the wyvern demons diving at me from overhead.

As I reached the head of the hellhound, I took one, two, three steps, then leaped into the air, twisting like a gymnast in a full layout. The hellhound's jaws gaped open as he snapped at me with lethally sharp canines. I threw Nightmare, directing the sword with earth magic as I summoned a gust of wind to blow me free of the canine's fangs.

Nightmare pierced the soft, fleshy uvula and sliced clean through and down the hellhound's throat. A strangled grunt sounded from the hellhound, followed by what may have been a bellowing burp, and it exploded into a mushroom cloud of dust.

I didn't miss a beat as my feet touched the ground, my amulet athame sinking into the eye of an agony demon and dusting it. Holding out my right hand, I summoned Nightmare, letting the black blade cut through the demons standing between me and it. With both blades in hand and the unlimited power of Spirit energizing my elemental magic, I became a one-witch army.

As I decimated his army before his eyes, Lucifer snapped his fingers at his daughter. "Lucifiana, stop her."

With an eye roll, the Red Demon swung her legs off the armrest of her throne and rose on her fragile stiletto heels. Sauntering down the throne stairs, she tossed away her nail file to brandish her red claws. Poisonous red magic swirled around her hands, the powdery magic dancing at her fingertips as she stalked toward me as predatorily as a panther.

Without missing a beat, I gripped both my longsword and amulet athame in one hand while simultaneously shoving Nightmare through another demon's heart and clamping my free hand around a charm on my bracelet. Black magic blasted from my hand, enlarging the weapons to full size and attaching the sheath to my thigh. Ripping a throwing knife from the leather strap around my thigh, I spun and released the blade, letting it soar across the room in a blur. The black metal sank into Lucifiana's heart.

Smiling, she gripped the hilt of the knife and pulled it from her chest, the blade coated with dust. "What that supposed to hurt?"

I smiled back as the magic of the elements blasted the demons clawing at me. "No. but the potion on the blade will render you immobile in three... two... one.... And there it is. Feel anything?"

Lucifiana stood paralyzed with a creepy smile on her face as another surge of demons attacked me.

Thank goodness for Apalla's Prophetess gifts. She wasn't sure why at the time, but she had a vision and insisted I dip my throwing knives in a special Paralysis Potion. Bet she already knew I was in Hell, whatever the time was at home.

Black lightning crackled as I spun away from the frozen Red Demon to stab Nightmare through the eye of an eight-foot-tall agony demon. It roared in agony, its voice fading as it disintegrated.

While flames flew off my body, the arrows of fire finding their mark between the gaping jaws of hellhounds.

Wading into the legions of awaiting demons, I fought like an avenging angel—taking out dozens of brimstones with every strike, destroying beast demons like pit and agony demons, and using the elements to obliterate the wyverns, pelicans, pterodactyls, and other winged demons flapping overhead.

"I'll have to deal with you myself," Lucifer growled, rising from his dark throne.

As Lucifer descended the dark steps, his demons did not stop their onslaught, and I fought with a bitter rage, each strike of my blade fierce and deadly.

Swiping a hand through the air, he called upon his dark powers, the dark blue and black swirling around his hand as incorporeal darkness solidified into a tangible, serrated blade.

I met his first strike with Nightmare, the impact shaking the cavern as power blasted from where our two blades met. But the magic was not on the fallen celestial's side, crashing into the sea of demons and reducing them to smoking piles of ash in an instant. Lucifer's smug grin disappeared.

My eyes snapped up from where they were locked on the interception of our blades, and I smirked. "It seems Nightmare remembers you, and it will not allow you to claim it ever again."

Thrusting away, I spun Nightmare through the air. Lucifer's eyes tracked the movement, distracted by the impressive move, but I had already released the hilt as I gripped the metal with earth magic. Dropping to the ground, I spun in a circle, kicking Lucifer's legs out from under him.

He hit the ground with a crunch but maintained his grip on his dark blade. Kicking to my feet, I directed my magic to stab Nightmare downward, but Lucifer rolled, dodging the lethal tip so it clanged against the polished marble floor, trailing sparks.

As I grabbed Nightmare from the air, Lucifer regained his footing, his eyes flashing as he growled, a deep, guttural sound that shook the stalactites overhead.

Stabbing down, Lucifer embedded his serrated blade into the marble floor, the Pit splitting willingly for the Devil. As his blade struck, a wave of pure force blasted me backward through the air, over the heads of the demons filling the chamber.

Righting myself with air magic, I hovered overhead. The elements raged around me, my magic begging to unleash their power. Inhaling deeply, I concentrated on the ebb and flow of the elements, of the power coursing unrestrained through my veins. Even in Hell, the power imbued in me by the Creator held strong, unyielding, fearless, and unfathomable.

The elements engulfed me in their flood until I was fully immersed by the power of not just four, but all five elements, for the element of Spirit was alive and working all around me.

Lucifer ignited in a column of blue hellfire in response. "Salem brat," he said in with a resounding metallic voice. He spat on the ground as he ripped his sword from the marble floor. The façade he had so carefully crafted crumbled as his rage heightened, and the true nature of the Devil began to show.

"Oh no, hellfire." I mock fainted. "I'm so scared of an element I can control."

"You've never felt fire so cold."

I grinned wickedly. "Oh, you want cold? I'll give you cold."

Commanding the water circling around me, I froze it into javelins of ice. All at once, I launched the javelins at Lucifer. The ice rocketed toward him, the points frozen into savage knives. But the Devil was crafty, twisting and turning to dodge, and using his dark magic where he could not avoid.

But when it came to the battlefield, I was just as cunning. Without waiting to see if my javelins struck true, I charged.

Ice froze on the floor, and I hit my knees, sliding over the frozen surface. As I rocketed past Lucifer, I raised Nightmare to block his strike, but my amulet athame found purchase, tearing into the tender flesh behind his knees.

Lucifer yelped in pain, leaping away from me as black blood splashed to the ground. That should have brought him to his knees.

I was on my feet in an instant.

The Devil attacked with blinding speed, and like with the wraiths earlier, Spirit seemed to slow his attack in my mind's eye. He was powerful and fast—faster than Lilith. Before the Fall, he was an angel. Lilith was merely human.

But Lucifer couldn't land a blow as Nightmare and my amulet athame caught his strikes. Blue hellfire ignited at his feet as his rage heightened, anger flashing in his eyes every time I countered his attack. I slashed and stabbed, letting my reflexes take over as I battled sword to sword with the Devil himself.

Nightmare crashed against his dark blade, the grating noise of clanging metal resounding through the air from the force—a clash of Heaven's chosen champion and the Devil.

"Touch me, and you'll burn, Luci," I purred, summoning white fire to enshroud my black Nightmare. "After all, I am my father's daughter."

Thrusting against his sword, I pushed him away with the power of the elements. His bare feet slid over the sleek marble floor before he ground to a halt. With a sadistic smirk, he prowled forward with the grace of a deadly feline.

But I was no lesser than him. He had countless eons to hone his craft, but I was just as fierce and just as powerful with the elements.

But it was not just my magic that set me apart, but the skill I had honed throughout the years, the innate abilities I possessed as a warrior witch.

Every stroke of my sword, every step of my feet, every movement of my body was part of my nature—automatic, instinctive, and fatally confident.

I kept moving, my feet strong and steady, every step smooth and confident in this dance with the Devil as I matched my tempo to the speed of Lucifer's blade, easily catching the serrated edge on every strike.

He was fast. But I was faster.

Not that he needed to know that.

Feigning stumbling, I stepped backward thrice, drawing a smirk to the Devil's face. Dodging a swipe of his blade, I twisted my torso in a half circle to deliver a sharp, forceful cut to his abdomen. I struck decisively, and a fan of red droplets sprayed the wake of my black Nightmare.

Releasing a guttural roar that shook the cavern, Lucifer's eyes flashed with dark rage as he magnified the force and speed of his attacks. But I was better.

Dodging a sloppy, enraged attack, I pivoted in a half circle as I sheathed my dagger to deliver a two-handed blow with Nightmare to gouge out a chunk of flesh from Lucifer's bare shoulder. Spinning away, I unsheathed my amulet, the blade hissing against its scabbard.

Not letting Lucifer recover from his gushing wound, I leaped into the air and spun, my tornado roundhouse kick mixed with a blast of air striking him in the chest to send him sliding back.

Growling venomously, he pushed off the ground, charging at me like a raging bull at a matador's red flag. Heels digging into the ground, I mirrored his movements, running full speed at him until we clashed in a storm of swords and magic.

My hand moved fast as lightning. The air hissed as Nightmare traced a short, luminous arc through the air, missing the Devil's neck by a hair's breadth as he threw himself backward.

We collided again, Luci spitting fire as I summoned rain in a clash of the elements. Regular water wouldn't extinguish the flames, but the flames vaporized the raindrops, releasing tendrils of steam. And steam was water and air....

With a smirk, I formed a wall of water between me and Lucifer, like a shield. When he struck, the water froze, blocking his attack, then melted instantly as I deployed an attack of my own.

Pushing the wall of water into his flames, the water evaporated in a torrent of fresh steam. My magic grabbed hold of the steam, unfurling in Luci's face.

He released an agonized scream.

Fire did not hurt him, but steam wasn't his element.

The elements provided the opportunity I needed. And I saw my opening. So simple, so easy.

Silver flashed as my amulet athame gouged into the Devil's wrist. And black flashed in the other direction, clawing a nasty cut across Lucifer's ribs, the sinewy muscle splitting to the bone.

Tossing back his head, the Devil howled in pain.

Thrusting my dagger forward, I cut through flesh and bone until his severed hand bounced against the floor.

What? It would regrow.

His sword of shadows tumbled from his severed hand and a bolt of my lightning incinerated the dark blade. Black blood dripped to the floor from the severed stump.

As the Devil's head snapped forward, his eyes glinting with undiluted rage, I stepped into him, my blade flashing in the light of the blue hellfire torches, and the Devil froze.

Nightmare's tip pressed into his throat as the Devil stood weaponless before me, his hands raised in surrender. Well, one hand. Black blood dripped to the floor from the severed stump.

"It seems we are at an impasse," he drawled in his seductive voice.

"An impasse?" I laughed humorlessly, summoning a cage of black lightning to crackle around the Devil. "My blade is at your throat. My power cages you. You are at *my* mercy, Luci."

"Am I?" He quirked an eyebrow. "Because you need a way out of Hell, Little Warrior. And seeing as you cannot open a portal, you need me. But I will not do it for free."

I pressed Nightmare further into his neck. "Free?" I scoffed. "Your payment is that I don't skewer you here and now."

"Hmm," the Devil hummed. "I think not. Because if you kill me, you remain stuck here, and time is ticking, Little Warrior. You would not want to miss your Trial. I am only consenting to opening a portal—for payment—because it is clear you will not stop slaughtering my demons until I do."

I scoffed. "As if you care about the lives of demons."

The Devil slapped his hand to his chest, feigning pain. "I'm wounded. Of course, I care about the lives of demons."

"Only because they serve as your pawns in the war against Good. Now... back to what you are going to do in exchange for me not running you through with a blade that was once yours." I smirked wickedly, a mocking tone lacing my words.

Spirit zapped through me, alerting me to the threat bearing down on me. Spinning, I caught Lucifiana by the throat as she lunged, vampire fangs and razor red nails ready to shred me to ribbons. Black lightning shot from my hand, electrocuting her body like a hundred tasers on the highest setting. Lucifiana's muscles went limp from the searing shock of my power.

Releasing her throat, I let her red leather-clad body drop to the marble floor with a thunderous crash. Summoning a squall, I pushed the wind into her limp body, sliding her over the floor with such force that her spine slammed into the bottom step of the stairs leading to their thrones.

My black lightning surged around Lucifer, the bolts multiplying as I channeled my power. His scowl deepened as I strengthened his cage. Without sparing him a glance, I squared off against the Red Demon.

Groaning, Lucifiana rolled to her back, her muscles twitching from the shock-induced spasms.

Not waiting for her to clamor to her feet, I unleashed the power of the elements. Air, then fire, then water, then earth. A gust of wind carried my burning flames across the cavern to plow into the Red Demon, blasting her body off the ground. She flew up six stairs, slammed against the corner of a stair, then pounded down the stairs until she crumpled in a heap at the bottom. Water blasted into her like a hose from a firetruck. A block of marble rose from the floor, shooting Lucifiana's body ten feet into the air. A bolt of black lightning the size of my waist shot from my chest, blasting into Lucifiana. She crashed into her red throne, spasming with uncontrollable contractions.

"A piece of advice, Auntie... know yourself and know your opponent, and you will never fail." Popping out a hip, I smirked at her, then snorted. "Too bad you never experienced the true power of Spirit." I glanced around, gesturing to the Hell around us. "Living down here, a soul eater wouldn't know the Grace of Heaven."

Scowling, she managed to look up at me, her red and black locks curtaining her face, swaying as she twitched violently.

"Second piece of advice... don't get up or I'll put you down harder this time. Remember, Hell feels cold to me, so I didn't even break a sweat." Spinning on the heel of my combat boot, I faced Lucifer, diminishing some of the power crackling around him. "Now, Luci, I want a portal out of Hell that leads to Asylum at the time it currently is in my timeline. No time trickery involved. Just a simple return to the correct time and place, according to me."

"Ah," the Devil drew out the word in a mocking tone as he glanced between me and his daughter, who slowly regained control of her convulsing body as she struggled to sit upright. The Devil smiled his disarming smile. Disarming to someone who wasn't me. "I would love to do exactly that, Little Warrior. But I cannot. You see, my banishment to the Pit prevents me from creating a portal directly to the mortal realm."

"Then how do demons escape? Lilith's been moving her armies to Earth for millennia. Or is she more powerful than you?"

The Devil's lips curled into a snarl as a low, threatening growl reverberated in his chest like the monster he was. "It is not a lack of power, but a law of the Creator. Lilith, while immortal, is a fallen *human*, thus my mother and father allow her to maintain her ties to the mortal realm. I was never mortal, therefore I am bound to live in a celestial realm, whether it be above or below the Earth, but not Earth itself."

My eyes cut to the Red Demon, and Spirit whispered to me. She had been on Earth. The energy of the mortal realm clung to her too intimately. She had walked the mortal realms recently.

"Then how is it Lucifiana comes and goes as she pleases?"

"And how would you know of my comings and goings, mutt?" my aunt asked monotonously from her scarlet throne.

I smiled a humorless smile. One that conveyed the threat I posed from being attuned to the whisperings of Spirit.

"The Creator sees all," I merely said.

"I cannot create portals, mutt. It is not the power of a soul eater."

Her words rang true with Spirit.... Or maybe it was because I was a demon princess and inherently understood the nature of demons.

"But it is within the powers of a celestial... or a fallen celestial." I gestured to Lucifer, dragging the tip of Nightmare gently along the skin of his neck, drawing a faint line of black blood. "So, how do you do it?"

"And why would I share the mysteries of my powers with you, Salem Witch?"

Nightmare twisted deeper into his jugular. "Because my sword is at your throat." Silver power glowed in my blue eyes at my command.

"Impudent of you to assume a mere sword can kill the Devil. Generations of mortals and angels have sought to kill me, yet all have failed."

"Impudent of you to assume I am like the rest," I said, pressing Nightmare farther into his flesh. "I am no mere mortal. I am the Salem Witch who wields a sword from Heaven and the ultimate power—Spirit." Black lightning sparked to life around me as white flames engulfed my longsword.

Lucifer jerked backward, pulling away from the searing flames, but a wall of hard air slammed into him from behind. Air magic cornered him, blocking him from escaping the flames of Heaven. Hissing, he cringed away from the sword, but he could not escape the bolts of black lightning surrounding him like a cage.

"So, kill me then, Little Warrior." The Devil hissed like the serpent he was. "Your power surpasses any other, so eliminate the greatest threat to mortals."

All decisions, whether it be action or inaction, have a consequence, Spirit whispered lovingly from realms far away from this Pit. Even in Hell, Spirit never abandoned me. The Creator never abandoned me. *He is not yours to slay. Not today. Your mission is to drive out Lilith's darkness with your light.*

As the words of wisdom drifted through my mind, I lowered Nightmare, but kept the black lightning shocking around Lucifer.

"Because I know who I am. And killing the Devil won't end Evil. Fire against fire, even holy flames against hellfire, and the world chokes on the smoke. Killing you isn't the answer."

"Weak," the Devil hissed the last syllable with a vindictive smile. "You could not kill Lilith, and you are too weak to kill the source of Evil. Physically, you could, but your weakness—"

Black lightning shot into him, silencing his words before he could utter the impending insult. "Careful, Luci. I said killing you isn't the answer, not that I won't do it," I warned darkly. "I refuse to kill Lilith because she was human. Somewhere, that humanity still exists. There is redemption for people like us, no matter the mistakes we've made—Lilith included. You are not mortal, therefore you have no humanity, for there is no good inside you, so it will not stop me from ending you. You may have been the first to fall, but you are not the source of all Evil. Despite what you may think, Evil existed before you."

The words rang true in my soul as I said them, as I spoke from a power greater than myself. "Destruction is not the way of the Creator, so it is not my way. I kill you, and eventually another being will take your place—probably one of the Seven Deadly Sins or another angel who fell with you. Killing what is evil is not enough. The only way to defeat it is with love."

The Devil scoffed at my declaration, the deadly flash of his eyes a clear indication of what he thought about love. "Love," he sneered. "Mortals always think love is the answer. But love is so fickle. Do you have any idea of the dark thoughts that cross the minds of mortals? The cheaters and liars and thieves. If love is so powerful, then why is it broken so easily?"

He spat on the floor, blemishing the pristine black marble. Until the Pit drank in his spit.

I had to fight the urge to gag. Disgusting.

"And that is why we are up there," I pointed a finger upward, "and why you are trapped down here." I gestured around us. "We are nothing without love."

"So cliché." Lucifiana yawned as she shifted on her throne, as though the conversation bored her. Man, life must get boring for an immortal. No wonder the Devil aspired to such deceit and trickery. What else did he have to fill the time?

"It's not cliché," I countered even headedly. Temperance was a Virtue. Not one that I was usually good at, but it weakened the Devil and his sins, making it one of my strongest weapons. "It's a lesson mortals know but have failed to truly embrace since the dawn of humanity. Lilith fell, cursing every other mortal with her sin. But love saves us from being doomed to Hell." I emphasized the word with a burst of earth magic that shook the ground.

"And you think a demon princess is saved?" Lucifiana eyed me with intrigue, a different look than her previous disinterest.

"I am," I said with conviction. "I found love when I had nothing left. No mother, no father, no family. But the Creator loved me and set me on Its righteous path. I've known love beyond what you can imagine. It is why I have survived the Trials. Humility. Chastity. Diligence. Kindness. Charity. Temperance. Patience. The Seven Holy Virtues are products of love. And they will be the end of Evil. Not me driving a sword through your heartless chest."

Lucifer rolled his eyes, but Lucifiana regarded me with a different look. Longing, perhaps? It was hard to tell with those red eyes, so similar yet so opposite of Amara's. Both were unsettling, but while Amara's were otherworldly, Lucifiana's were dark and brooding and stained with the evils of a fallen world. Eyes were windows to the soul, and Lucifiana's revealed the brokenness and twistedness of hers.

What I didn't say was I needed a way back to Earth. Amara wouldn't have sent me here on a one-way ticket if I couldn't book travel back. So, it was possible. Lucifer just didn't want to send me back that way because I could destroy the entrance between Hell and Earth. But it was one of many.

Like the Satanic Temple in Salem, Massachusetts. Did Kova block off that entrance? Years ago, I blocked the entrance to Lilith's Lair with a pillar of holy hellfire. But back then, I had only unlocked air and fire magic. Now, I had Spirit magic, making my power infinitely greater. And the Devil knew I could destroy whatever portal he sent me through.

Instead, I added, "My father isn't the type of man to kill you, and I don't think he wants me to bear the burden, either."

"You assume he was in a position to kill me."

"I am certain of it," I said, my voice unwavering in my conviction of the truth. "Now, let's try again. How do you send demons to Earth? How does Lucifiana travel between the realms?"

"You certainly are as daring as any other Princess of Hell." Lucifer's eyes shot to his daughter, who bristled at the comparison. "But you lack a certain demented quality of the others," he cooed, soothing his daughter's wounded ego.

Eyeing me and the danger of the elements swirling around me, he said, "Because you embrace your darkness, I will tell you how my demons travel between the realms. I do not aid Lilith, nor does she assist me. Our armies move separately."

"That's not an answer," I snapped.

"Aways in such a hurry, mortals," he drawled. "Immortals are never so rushed."

"Immortals have the luxury of time. I do not. Perhaps if Lilith had hurried her plans, she would have succeeded before I was born."

"She has contingencies, but none are worthwhile pursuits. Not compared to obtaining the power of the Maiden through you or Thea." The Devil shrugged, like it wasn't likely. "As for how I move the armies, I open a portal to another realm. One containing another portal connected to Earth." He shrugged. "More or less."

"Open it," I demanded.

"No," the Devil said simply, his expression unchanging.

"Do you forget who holds the power here?" I snapped, letting the lightning glow brighter.

"What are you going to do?" he questioned mockingly. "Kill me? You already admitted you do not aspire to be the witch who ends Satan."

My heart stopped beating in my chest. I was a fool. I revealed my hand too soon. If I had kept my mouth shut, I could have tricked him into opening the portal under threat of death.

Deceit and manipulation and threats are not the means to win this battle, Hayden. Those are his weapons, not yours.

"But I am willing to work with you."

"Work with me?" I deadpanned, my skepticism written clearly on my face.

"Well, of course, Little Warrior," he cooed. "Negotiations always accompany my business dealings."

"What are you proposing?" I eyed him skeptically, cautious of the game the Devil was playing. Whatever he had to offer couldn't be virtuous.

"A Devil's Bargain."

"Why? What else could you possibly want from me?"

"Your soul, Little Warrior," Lucifer drawled, his eyes flashing with seductive sensuality, "would make a stunning trophy in my collection. The ultimate jewel in my crown."

"Never gonna happen. I will die before I offer my soul to you."

Lucifer chuckled darkly. "I assumed as much. Be careful of the words you speak, Little Warrior. They may come to pass sooner than you think."

A scowl tore across my mouth at his words. I was wary of his games, and the longer he talked, the more opportunity he had to manipulate me.

Black lightning zapped into him, sizzling as it burned into the flesh of his torso.

Steam unfurled from Lucifer's nostrils as he glowered at me, taking a menacing step forward.

The power of Spirit surged to meet him, blocking his approach.

"Enough," I barked the command. "Name the terms, Devil."

"I will give you safe passage to an interim realm where you can obtain a second portal directly to Earth at the time and place of your choosing. In exchange, you will promise not to harm Elliot Fox."

"What?"

"When you return to Earth to face Lilith, Elliot will be with her. You have the power to kill him. I want you to spare him."

My piercing blue eyes narrowed to slits. "Why such an interest in Elliot?"

"That information is irrelevant to the Bargain. All that concerns you is that harm shall not come to him by your hand. Ever."

"Ever?" I scoffed. "You want me to promise that? I despise Elliot. If he threatens to harm my people—"

"Then you may defend. But nothing fatal. And nothing to diminish his powers."

I narrowed my eyes at the Devil. Why? Why did he want to preserve Elliot and his unnatural powers?

It struck me like lightning.

Elliot's stronger powers... drinking demon blood... devolving into the Sin of Lust... Lucifer was behind it, not Lilith. What did the Devil have to gain from strengthening the magic of a witch who walked with evil?

The whispers of Spirit drifted through my mind. Kova—Alice Parker—had destroyed the immortal vessel of Asmodeus, a Prince of Hell, during her Salem War. That was over three hundred years ago, in 1692. The Seven Deadly Sins waged war against the Seven Heavenly Virtues every seven hundred years. A War sanctioned by the Devil, not the Mother of Demons. Because Lucifer and Lilith had "different ideas of how Darkness will reign," as Lilith had said months ago when she nearly killed me on her island.

"Elliot is the new earthly vessel for the Sin of Lust."

It wasn't a question. Amara had confirmed Elliot was drinking demon blood to obtain his new powers, but the Devil's interest in Elliot revealed that he bolstered Elliot's powers, not Lilith. Smart of the conniving fox to align with both Luci and Lilith. While Lilith refused to supply him with more power, Lucifer did. "But why Elliot?"

"Because he aligned with Darkness. He chose us. Only one who willingly falls can obtain the power of a Sin."

"True, but you don't give a crap about Elliot. He's a mortal vessel. Replaceable. So, why do you care so much about making a deal with me?"

"Because, Little Warrior, striking another Devil's Bargain is exactly what you do not want to do. I sense your desires, Little Warrior, and you absolutely loathed striking the first deal with me. You felt like you betrayed the Creator. And that feeling... that feeling of guilt and shame is the next best thing to claiming your soul. The Salem Witch, Champion of Heaven, dealing with the Devil... tsk, tsk, tsk." He clucked his tongue. "How disappointed the Creator will be with Its beloved daughter for betraying It a second time."

You will need every lesson you've learned, especially those from the Trials, to survive an encounter with the Devil. Amara's words echoed through my mind.

He was goading me. Trying to get a rise from me. I wouldn't kill him, and he knew it. But he knew I had a temper... a temper that tended to get the better of me more often than I cared to admit. The Devil knew my deepest desires... and the darkness in my heart. I didn't doubt his abilities. But I knew he would use my fears against me. Not in a physical way, but, mentally, he sought to undermine me and reduce my faith in myself and my Creator.

"This is going to come back to bite me, isn't it?"

Nightmare slid into its sheath as I dropped the cage of Spirit, and I replaced it with my amulet athame, its dual tone blade flashing in the light of the blue hellfire torches. Pressing the tip to my left palm, I dragged the dagger across the soft, vulnerable flesh. Red blood pooled in my hand as I sheathed my dagger, ignoring the hand Lucifer held out expectantly.

Raising an eyebrow, he asked, "Are you not going to seize the opportunity to inflict pain on my person, Little Warrior?"

"I will not stain my amulet athame with your black blood for this regrettable purpose. Summon your own dagger."

The same silver blade from earlier appeared in his empty hand, amusement dancing in the Devil's cold blue eyes. Always playing the game. Even the warrior witch, who could end his immortal existence, did not inflict enough fear into the Devil's heartless chest to change his ways. He would play the game until the end of days.

Black blood flooded his massive palm as he sliced open his flesh. Pressing his bloody left hand to my heart, his right hand pressed against my forehead. I mirrored the pose, allowing my red blood to seep into his smooth chest for his skin to greedily consume my blood.

"I, Lucifer Morningstar, will provide you with safe passage to an interim realm where you can obtain a second portal directly to Earth at the time and place of your choosing."

"In exchange, I, Hayden Black, will not harm Elliot except in self-defense of myself or another. I will not kill him if I can incapacitate him with nonlethal means."

"I agree."

"I agree," I echoed.

Dark magic curled around me, aggressively scratching the surface of my skin, searching for a weakness to take advantage of so it could burrow into the depths of my heart, mind, and soul. The unholy magic caressed my skin with a sickening touch, but this time, I didn't pull away before summoning white holy flames to engulf my body in a fiery baptism.

Yelping, the Devil leaped away from me, scrambling to avoid the searing flames that would mercilessly burn a soulless being like him.

"You could have pulled away first," he growled, running a hand over the spot on his chest tinged red in the shape of my hand.

Waggling my eyebrows, I said, "As if you would have."

"Ah, admitting you are like the Devil," he said smugly.

"Not at all," I disagreed. "I simply know my darkness and acknowledge it. I said I wouldn't kill you. Doesn't mean I won't protect myself from your darkness."

"Mm-hmm. You are not as in control of your darkness as you think. Remember, Little Warrior, if you kill Elliot, your soul is *mine*. Wouldn't want your darkness to get the better of you when dealing with a new Prince of Hell." A sadistic grin twisted his lips, yet it did nothing to lessen his seductive aesthetic.

With killer calmness, I said, "Killing Elliot would serve you, not me. The Sin of Lust will persist past the expiration of Elliot's mortal body and will claim another vessel. Like I said, it's Chastity's destiny to end him. Not mine."

The Devil's eyes narrowed to slits. "You know about the Apokalypsis War." It wasn't a question.

"Open the portal, Devil," I said with a knowing smile.

A portal burst to life mere feet from us at the snap of his fingers. The portal swirled with blue magic, but it wasn't ocean blue like Harbor's magic. It lacked the purity of her power. Darkness tainted this portal, like I could see the evil infused in the magic. I would have to deal with the Devil one day, but other than my bargain to leave Hell, today was not that day.

Shoving away from Lucifer, I kept Nightmare raised as I cast a wary glance at Lucifiana to make sure she stayed put like a dog on a leash. Slowly, I backed toward the portal.

"Oh, and Hayden?" Lucifer slipped his hands into his pants pockets as he surveyed the black dust coating his floor, piled up to his ankles. His cold blue eyes snapped to mine, the blue darkening into black orbs that swallowed the whites of his eyes. "Please, for the love of the Creator, never return to Hell."

A wicked grin seized my lips. "No promises."

CHAPTER EIGHT

CRAWLING FROM THE DEPTHS

"You must be kidding me."

In a flash of light, the Devil's portal slammed shut behind me, leaving me stranded in the middle of a dirt path lined with dark green hedges towering overhead as the plants disappeared into the shadows above.

Spinning around, I stared down the hedge-lined corridor that stretched into an endless expanse of shadows. Magic flew out of me, sweeping over the plants caging me in. But these weren't normal plants, and this wasn't an endless hallway.

It was a labyrinth.

The hedges stirred, their leaves quivering as the branches shook.

My magic sensed it before my physical senses saw the movement. Sharp-tipped branches pierced toward me.

Throwing myself out of the way, I summoned a gust to carry me clear of where the hedge's branches speared into each other as the hedge on either side of the aisle tried to skewer me. These weren't plants of the earth. They were *demons*.

A demonic plant. Seriously? Was that Lucifer or Lilith? Either way, not a fan.

As the branches stabbed into each other, they intermingled, twisting and twining around one another until a hedge replaced the empty air I had previously occupied.

Well, crap.

I stood from my crouch, Nightmare in hand as I stared down the foreboding corridor of evil plants.

If these plants were demons, then...

White holy flames ignited in my hands as I summoned a raging inferno to blast the hedges on either side of me.

The leaves of the hedges reacted so fast, my eyes couldn't track the movement as they piled together to form a shield. A magic-resistant shield.

Holy flames spit at me as they bounced off the wall of leaves. As I ceased the flow of ineffectual heavenly fire, the hedges shuddered, the wind whistling through their leaves and branches like a venomous hiss.

Well, crap. Again.

With both blades in hand, hanging at my sides, I stared down the hallway to where the hedges disappeared into the darkness. Darkness that I did not trust.

Lifting my blades, I cautiously stepped forward, eyeing the hedges on either side in case they decided to attack me. They didn't, but something told me if it weren't for my demon blood, the hedges would seek to end me. Even if Lucifer would have let my friends return to earth, the journey was perilous to a mortal, and I was thankful for Amara's foresight.

Swiftly, I stalked along the hallway, my guard up, even knowing the hedges would not attack unless I attacked first. But that did not mean Lucifer didn't lay other traps for me.

Nausea rolled in my stomach. I was headed the wrong way. No, not exactly, but this corridor carried me past the place where I needed to turn, yet there hadn't been an outlet. How much longer would I have to walk before I could turn again?

Because the tug in my gut told me to turn to the left. To the center of the labyrinth, where something powerful awaited the next demon to stumble across it.

As I slid my foot forward, my ankle caught on an invisible wire hidden by magic. Tripping the trap wire, I fell toward the ground. The marble flooring slid aside, revealing a row of spikes sharpened to deadly points and tipped with poison.

Air magic ripped out of me, forming a hard wall between me and the spikes. Earth rumbled, forcing the block of crystal to slide back in place to cover the spikes as air magic placed me on my feet.

Frowning at the floor, I thanked the Creator for the power of the elements and strode off the slab of stone covering the deadly bed of spears.

I had been right—traps riddled this labyrinth to prevent souls like me from escaping against Lucifer's desire. But I refused to give him even a sliver of my soul.

Staring at the hedges, I let thoughts whirl through my mind. Perhaps I could use the Voice of Command, but something told me it wouldn't work. Lucifer likely already commanded the demonic plants. My elemental powers hadn't worked on the magic-resistant creatures... but that didn't mean I couldn't use my powers to fight them. They were demons. And I had never lost a fight to a demon. Not even Cain. I would overcome these feeble demons, too.

Magic stretched out of me, gently prodding at the hedges, seeking a weakness without alerting the demonic plants to my intentions.

Water pumped through the green leaves, and their roots embedded in the marble stone underfoot. Water and stone. Maybe I couldn't harm the hedges, but I could control the elements *around* them. Just like Professor Periwinkle taught me in my first air magic lesson—command the air around the pebble to lift it, don't lift the pebble itself.

My hand curled into a fist as determination spread through my body like fire flooding my veins.

Water responded to my call. The leaves of the venomous hedges twisted and crunched as I commanded the water inside the plants. The leaves turned brown as they crumbled and writhed as if in pain from the extraction of the life-giving element.

As the water drained, I called earth magic to shake the stone. Power rumbled under my feet as I cracked the stone with a thunderous clap, crunching and breaking it to uproot the hedges embedded in the crystal floor. Brown, wrinkled roots spit out of the ground, slicing open against the shards of razor-sharp crystal poking up from the floor.

Fire ignited in the roots, using the fallen brown leaves as kindling to catch fire to the waterless branches. Sparking from power and nature, my flames soared into the sky like a bonfire started by a pyromaniac.

Me. I was the pyromaniac.

A low squeal ripped through the air, as the hedges cried out in pain as I destroyed the barrier separating me from the next leg of the labyrinth. But I wasn't done.

Air whipped from me like a spinning cyclone, blasting the hedges aside to clear a path. My hair blew on my summoned wind, but I remained unaffected as I crossed the threshold of black ashes that remained in place of the hedge barrier that once kept me from my destination.

Another wall of demonic plants separated me from the center of the labyrinth. I cracked my neck. With the power of Spirit filling me ceaselessly, I could do this all day. Power ignited at my fingertips, dancing joyously over my skin as though the prospect of destroying evil beings delighted it.

But my work here wasn't to destroy hedge demons—that wouldn't stop Lucifer's demons from using this intermediary realm to sneak into Earth. I would have to destroy the entire labyrinth and the strange magic I sensed.

I felt the call in my soul as surely as Spirit whispered the truth. I needed to get to the center of the maze. That was how I escaped this hellish realm. And that was how I would destroy it. Or at least destroy Lucifer's escape route. But this wasn't his only backdoor to send demons to Earth. Spirit knew he had others. Like the Satanic Temple in Salem. And if I survived this war, I would find and destroy every last one of them. Maybe Kova couldn't, but I was a demon, and demons had free rein to pass between Earth and the underworld.

The elements ripped out of me, punching a hole through the next hedge, and I stepped through, letting the elements work ahead of me as I followed the strange tug in my gut as intuition guided my steps.

Hedge after demonic hedge fell to my magic, but then I sensed something else. A demonic presence. Lucifer unleashed his dogs in the labyrinth.

A menacing growl echoed down the hedge-lined corridors.

Hellhounds, pits, inferni, brimstones, and agony demons.

Nothing I couldn't handle. But if they caught me, I would have to fight, and Lucifer was likely to send more to keep me busy. And if I was busy fighting, I wasn't burning through hedges. I couldn't afford to waste any more time in this labyrinth. I had to get to the center so I could return to Asylum. Who knew how much time had passed on Earth?

Spirit flooded my veins, buzzing like a live wire as it magnified the other four elements. Thrusting my hands forward, I channeled energy through my body, powering the elements with unprecedented force. Three hedges fell to a single blast of magic, and I ran through, following the internal compass that guided me.

Another three fell, then another and another.

But the demons were gaining on me.

A current of magic tapped me on my right shoulder, and I turned, sprinting down a length of passageway, away from the path of devastation I had left in my wake. Faster than an Olympic athlete, my powerful legs carried me away from the demons chasing after me, and I silently thanked Kova for her adamancy that I do cardio every day.

But I still *hated* running.

Another current of magic tapped me on the left shoulder, and I slid to a stop as I shot a concentrated dose of the elements through the hedge.

Spirit sang. I wasn't far from the center of the labyrinth now. But the demons weren't far from me either.

Sparing a glance down the hallway to my left, I saw a flash of glowing red eyes. A twirl of my hand sent a horizontal cyclone spinning down the hallway, throwing the demons back. The first row of demons flew into the air and tumbled overhead to crash into the demons in the rear. But air was intangible, and it only did so much against the battalion of demons pursuing me.

Magic tore out of me, and I dug my heels into the ground, pushing off as I sprinted through the hole in the hedge. My powers barely blasted another hole in the demonic plants before I threw myself through it.

Another hedge obliterated under attack, revealing a space no larger than ten feet by ten feet with a cast iron cauldron sitting in the center.

My combats skidded over the crystal floor as I slid to a halt in front of the cauldron filled with a thick, bubbling purple and gray and blue liquid, burning over blue hellfire. The brim of the cauldron rose to my waist, and the round container was about the size of a jacuzzi.

Man, what I would give for a hot tub right now. Hell was cold, which made no sense since, as a demon princess, I loved the heat.

What was I supposed to do with a cauldron filled with potion? I didn't dare touch it. Who knew what poison Lucifer filled it with?

Perhaps Spirit whispered the answer to me, or maybe it was knowledge inherent to my demonic blood, but I knew what the demented cauldron wanted to taste. The payment it required for its services.

Like the Pit.

A guttural roar sounded behind me, and I whipped my head back to stare through the burned hedges to find a small battalion of demons gnashing their fangs and clacking their claws against the marble as they prepared to charge down the straight and narrow path directly to me and the cauldron.

With a unanimous roar, they charged.

Holy flames burst from my hand, forming a wall to shield my back. But it would only hold the demons for so long.

The first demon crashed into the wall, sacrificing its soulless body to consume some of the holy flames. Then another, and another.

I drew my amulet athame.

A thunderous boom resounded through the labyrinth, the sound bouncing off the hedges and echoing around me as a black crocodile demon with beady red eyes and blue hellfire burning around its ridges emerged from the shadows. Another resounding boom filled the air as it stepped forward, its heavy leg crashing into the stone and leaving a paw print carved into the crystal.

The crocodile demon must have been the size of a truck.

Holy crap. Crocodiles were ridiculously fast runners.

A second wall of flames burst from my hand, and I spun to face the cauldron. Touching the tip of my athame to the fleshy part of my palm, I dragged the blade across my skin, splitting my palm open for the third time.

Red blood pooled in my hand, and I scowled as I flipped it over the cauldron, letting my lifeblood drip into the mix of purple and grey and blue. My mortal blood touched the gooey substance in the cauldron, and a ripple of power surged over the surface, changing the color to pure black as the surface stilled.

I felt the first wall of flames disappear as a final demon sacrificed itself to my fire. But I couldn't turn around to summon another wall. It was as if my body was locked in place. Frozen as the blood dripped from my palm. Even my magic didn't want to move through my body.

Terror clamped around my throat, and I forced myself to swallow as another drop of blood hit the smooth surface of the cauldron.

Closing my eyes, I willed my beating heart to slow itself. Fear wouldn't get me anywhere. Not in a place like this.

But my second wall of flames was diminishing, and the demonic crocodile would snatch me in its jaws any second now.

Another drop of blood. How much more could it need?

With my eyes still closed, I pictured Asylum. I pictured my home in the simple cabin built in the Wicked Woods behind the Spellery student apartments. A home built by my mother's and father's hands. A home where Kova, my mentor, had raised me and trained me to become everything I was today.

A fourth drop of blood.

I pictured the Spellery castle, where I honed my magic through the years. Where I won my first fight against Tuck and Leo. Where I found my first friends, who turned into not just my circle, but my family when I had none. My mind flickered to the top of the observation deck of the Divination Tower. So many dark memories formed there... but so many powerful ones, too.

The lagoon, the twins' secret getaway that they entrusted to me, flooded my mind. Kova must have made it for herself as a special escape when she was still Alice Parker. A place to go when the weight of the world was too heavy for one person to bear alone.

A fifth drop of blood.

Asylum was her home. She made it when her last home was destroyed. And now it was my home, too. Did she know then that the next Salem Witch would come to care for it so much?

My second wall of flames extinguished.

A final drop of blood hit the surface of the cauldron, and power burst from it.

A demented roar sounded behind me, and the hot breath of the crocodile demon steamed around me.

My eyes flared open as black magic exploded from the top of the cauldron, ripping through the air to slam into the hedge on my right. The black magic would be ominous if it wasn't *my* signature color.

I lurched forward as the power holding my body in place released me. My hands caught on the edges of the cauldron before I slammed into it, and air brushed over my back, alerting me to the threat behind me.

Throwing myself to the side, I narrowly dodged the snap of the crocodile demon's jaws. My side slammed into the crystal floor, my shoulder dislocating from the impact as the breath rushed from my lungs.

Air forced itself down my throat as my magic acted of its own accord to keep me alive. Clenching my teeth to bite down a scream as my dislocated shoulder jostled from rolling over the unyielding stone, I rolled to my feet and drew Nightmare from its sheath.

Ah, crap.

The oversized crocodile stood between me and the swirling black portal. What I would give to spook. Seriously, the angels couldn't have given me that one?

I rolled my eyes, hoping Gabriel could hear my thoughts.

Lightning crackled over my skin and white light glowed around my shoulder as Spirit and healing water magic mingled to shove my shoulder back in place.

A grunt passed my lips from the expected pain, but I didn't miss a beat as the crocodile demon lunged. Nightmare slashed against its hard scales, leaving a trail of sparks in its wake. My deadly blade did nothing against the demon's protective scales, and the crocodile's teeth gnashed dangerously close to my side as I barely skirted around it.

Slamming my fist into its nose, I used a blast of air to throw the crocodile away from me, but in the confined space of the hedges walling in the cauldron, the crocodile was mere feet from me.

But in a way, I had the advantage.

As the size of a truck. The crocodile could barely fit the front half of its body into the cranny protecting the cauldron and my black portal. It could barely turn its head to attack me, and its bottom jaw hovered in the air around waist height.

And I saw my opening. All I needed was for it to attack.

Thankfully, the crocodile obliged with a ferocious roar.

Brutally sharp, triangle-shaped teeth snapped at me with unprecedented speed. But I was faster.

Ducking under the crocodile as it lunged at my torso, I curled into a ball and pushed with all the strength of my legs. Momentum carried me over the slick surface of the stone floor as I slid under the crocodile's chin. A tongue of holy flames lashed out of my hand and slammed into the crocodile's jaw, pushing it closed with the force of my elemental attack.

I was halfway to the portal.

Leaping to my feet, I shoved Nightmare into its sheath, then ducked, pressing my stomach flat to the ground as the crocodile swiped its snout at me. Its nose slammed into the hedge wall.

Lifting its head, the crocodile jumped into the air. It was going to slam its massive head down on me.

Scrambling, I shoved my legs under me in a crouch, and using the strength coiled in my legs, I threw myself through the black portal, black lightning crackling at my fingertips.

The crocodile's chin bounced off the crystal floor, and it lurched at me, opening its maw to swallow me whole.

As I passed through, magic washed over me, and my powers thrummed through my body as they recognized the magic of home.

Vicious jaws of the crocodile demon stretched wide, aiming to clamp around my lower body.

Twin bolts of lightning shot from my open palms, blasting into the cauldron and shattering it to pieces.

As the demon's jaw snapped closed, the portal slammed closed on the crocodile's neck, severing its head from its torso. The severed head dropped to the ground, disintegrating.

I slammed into the ground, my leather jacket protecting my skin as I skidded over jagged rocks and debris. Coughing on the dust cloud swarming me, I pushed to my feet, scanning the hill I stood atop.

The hill above the Crystal Caverns—where I received my amulet athame nearly five years ago. Figures that Lucifer's evil cauldron would send me to the spot farthest away from the action just to spite me.

Because as I stared at the town, one thing was explicitly clear...

All of Asylum was under siege.

CHAPTER NINE

OPERATION: BLACK

Tree trunks burned like torches, heat scorching the air as smoke stung my nose. I choked on the stench of sulfur and blood tainting Asylum.

Darkness had descended on the town, the smoke from hellfire burning Asylum clogging the air.

Hell was empty, and all the demons were in Asylum.

Wielding Kova's magic, Lilith had penetrated the wards.... My heart stopped as I realized the treacherous consequences of my descent into Hell.

My Salem Witch magic resealed the wards when Lilith attacked after my Earth Trial, but when I left the mortal plane, my magic disappeared with me, breaking the power of the circle we channeled into the wards. Without my powers fueling the wards instead of the Resigned Salem Witch, who was currently channeled by Lilith, Asylum was vulnerable.

And Lilith knew it. Not because of Naida, but because of the magic she wielded from crucifying both my mother and Kova.

Curling my hands into fists, I cracked my knuckles.

Trees and buildings were ablaze with hellfire. Bursts of fire flashed around the town below, followed by splashes of water as witches attempted to quench the inferno, to no avail. They needed holy water to snuff the perpetual flames.

Hellfire burned bright.

Earth rumbled as witches fought for their lives, the tremors reaching my feet at the top of the mountain, far from the thick of battle. Wind screamed in my ears, and I sensed the magic as air witches blasted winged demons from the sky.

Storms brewed overhead, the clouds and smoke blotting out the light of the full moon from hanging in the sky above.

The full moon... it was the eve of my birthday....

I had been in Hell for *seven days*....

Seven days... how long had Asylum been under attack?

Asylum needed me. Everywhere. But I couldn't be in two places at once. But from up here, I could see most of the battle waging endlessly on. Magic burst from me in like a shockwave, sweeping through Asylum and carrying information back to me.

A ring of hellfire trapped fifty witches as they futilely fought thrice the number of demons. Demons could pass, but witches could not. Water witches channeled hoses of water from Lake Luna, but it did nothing to quench the dirty flames. A witch in the center of the ring worked her mind control, holding dozens of demons at once so her comrades could fell the beasts. But her control was slipping as her magic depleted.

My eyes flared open, and magic gathered in my palms. Colorful hellfire rose off the ground, gathering in a ball to fly through the sky and sink into my open palms as I consumed the power of the evil flames.

A strange silence hushed the town as witches and demons stared at the sky in bewilderment. A resounding crash erupted as battle broke out again.

The earth surged underneath me, launching me into the air. Air magic swirled around me, directing my trajectory. Splaying my palms as I tore through the sky at a breakneck speed, my fire magic leaped into action. When my magic touched the evil fire, the flames turned black and rose into the sky, rushing to its new master as my superior magic ripped the power away from lesser demons.

Silence descended on the town as the battles ceased. Every eye—both witch and demon—tracked my path overhead.

A war cheer ripped from the lungs of the witches fighting for Asylum. Battle crashed into motion, the sounds flying to my ears as my people fought with renewed vigor.

Slamming into the ground, the impact softened by the magnitude of my power, I unleashed the power of the elements. Air, fire, water, earth, and Spirit blasted out of me like an atomic bomb, my impeccable control directing the elements to tear into the demons and leave the witches untouched.

Nightmare and my amulet athame were in my hands before the elements finished their brutal attack that shredded three hundred demons to ashes.

The witches around me released a guttural cheer. "The Salem Witch is back! Hayden Black has returned! We are saved!"

Raising Nightmare into the air for all to see, I summoned white holy flames to coat the blade as a message to all—a message of hope for witches and a message of doom to demons.

Seven hundred demons prowled toward us, emerging from the shadows of the buildings on the west side of the town, cornering me and the witches between them and Lake Luna.

With a wicked smirk, I growled, "Come and get it, beasties."

Witches brandished their swords and summoned their magic, but I raised a hand, signaling them to stand down. Kneeling on one leg, Kelsey threw her arms up, shaking with effort as she struggled to hold the line of demons.

"Conserve your strength," I commanded Kelsey and the others. "These are *mine*."

I charged, moving faster than the demonic eye could track. Twisting and twirling, slicing and stabbing, I ripped through the demons, hellfire burning, lightning crackling, air blowing, water whipping, and earth quaking as the elements fought, my magic waging the war without explicit commands.

Nightmare sliced through the neck of the last demon. The demon's corpse exploded into dust before its goat-horned head bounced to the ground.

My magic range, which extended to most of the town, didn't detect any demons in the immediate vicinity. Spinning, I faced the haggard witches covered in red and black blood and demon dust. Burns and scrapes and dirt and claw wounds littered their bodies.

"Any casualties?" I called.

Heads shook in response, weary expressions staring back at me as the witches muttered to one another, checking each other for injuries.

"Any lethal wounds?"

A pause, then, "Here!" someone shouted from near the lake. A couple more shouts sounded out.

"Kelsey—"

"On it," she said, pushing her neon magic through the crowd, clearing the uninjured—more or less—away from the injured.

"Any healers?" I asked as I ran to the first girl who shouted for help for her friend.

"Most of them are out of magic," Kelsey said. "And those who aren't are at the Spellery. We can't spare a field medic."

The blood drained from my face at her words as I skidded to a stop on my knees beside a twenty-year-old man, bleeding from a gaping wound in his abdomen.

Water rose from the lake, glowing silver as my magic purified it before it coated my hands. I was a terrible healer, but I could heal him so he didn't bleed out.

"Hayden, over here," Kelsey called from twenty yards away.

Rising, I sprinted to the next witch, healing her in a flash of silver light and water. Then the next and the next until half a dozen witches were healed... or healed enough. A superior doctor like Ethan would have to dress the wound beyond my rough field healing.

"We have to get the wounded to the infirmary. The Spellery is our base of operations, like you planned." A pained expression painted Kelsey's face as she stared at the castle looming in the sky above.

"Then let's move."

"It's not that simple, Hayden."

"I'll take care of the demons, you—"

"We've been fighting for *three days*," Kelsey emphasized, cutting me off. "You weren't here, Hayden. When Lilith pierced the wards, we were driven back to the Spellery within the first twelve hours. It's the only reason any of us are still alive. Excursions of Knights—like this one—deployed to try to close the wards, but without you, everything has gone wrong. Nobody can get near Lilith, and the demons have isolated the battalions to pick us off one at a time."

Guilt panged through me. The Devil knew. He knew the time difference between Hell and Earth. He knew my friends were fighting for their lives. That's why he stalled me with his army of demons. It wasn't about testing my abilities, but about distracting me for longer, so more of my people would fall in the battle against Lilith.

Kelsey gave me a once over, truly taking me in for the first time. "You look like hell," she remarked. Leave it to Kelsey to pad nothing.

"Thanks," I snorted. Magic whispered softly to me, warning me of the threat charging at me. "I just got back."

Spinning in a circle, I sliced my sword through the abdomens of four demons, the holy flames coating my sword jumping to their bodies and incinerating them.

"We need to spook these witches to the Spellery. Where's Jamie?"

Kelsey shook her head, running a grimy hand through her disheveled platinum locks. "He's been fighting nonstop, Hayden. Seriously, I don't think he has slept. He's out of magic. No way can he spook."

Guilt tore through me again. Jamie had stepped up to lead my war. It was my responsibility, and instead, he tirelessly fought in my stead. I had to make this right. I had to save Asylum.

What I would give to spook right now.

"Then how do we get everyone back?"

Kelsey opened her mouth, then closed it and shook her head in defeat. "I don't know," she admitted, tears welling in her eyes. She was hanging on by a thread. They all were. "My powers are exhausted. I can't even send a telepathic message. We've been communicating with wand messages, but my wand was destroyed. Lots of us have lost our wands to hellfire. And there must be thousands of demons between us and the Spellery. We will never make it back alive."

"I have an idea." Sheathing Nightmare and my dagger, I splayed my palms, standing in a T position.

The power of Spirit zapped through me. As I expelled magic, Spirit renewed my powers, refilling my reserves as quickly as I depleted them. If I didn't use my magic, it bottled up like a mentos in a soda bottle with the lid screwed on. Such was the vast infinity of Spirit. If it could renew me, then it could give life to others.

Black lightning crackled in my palms, mixing with divine silver light before shooting into the chests of the witches around me. It was like the time I transferred my energy to the witches from Lilith's Island. Then, I had depleted my magic... but seven months later, my bond with Spirit was strong and unyielding, and I did not drain as Spirit poured power into me.

Color returned to Kelsey's face and light danced in the eyes of the witches as Spirit filled them with life and power. Gasps rang out as my energy transferred to them, followed by murmurs about their renewed strength.

"Listen up," I yelled, silencing the mutters. "We need to return to the Spellery, the injured included. No witch left behind."

"But I can keep fighting," someone called out. "My magic is back."

"Yes, but we need to join the Knights and other witches. If we fight in broken groups, the demons will pick us off. So, we're returning to the Spellery to regroup. I need volunteers to carry the injured." Hands shot into the air. Nodding, I beckoned them forward. "The rest of you will defend. Encircle the injured and those carrying them. I will be at the front to protect everyone. Kelsey will bring up the rear. We're going to move and move fast. Do not stop. If something happens and you fall behind, Kelsey will send me a telepathic message, and I will come to you. Understood?"

Agreements rang out from the witches as they fell into formation.

"Keep an eye out for demons attacking the rear," I said to Kelsey, leaning in. "If you're attacked, use your mind control, but send me a message. Got it?"

She nodded, summoning neon yellow magic to dance at her fingertips. "Let's do this."

Power blossomed in my chest as the elements heralded my call. A call unlike any other witch's power. An undeniable magic granted to me by the grace of the Creator.

And with a roar like a lion, I released my power like a bomb.

Air, fire, water, earth, and Spirit tore through the air, blasting through the winged demons in the sky above and the terrestrial beasts roaming the town square.

Witches rushed forward with a shout of victory, waving their swords in the air and firing magic haphazardly at the enemy as others carried the injured in cradles or on their backs.

A wave of holy flames surged from my hands, rolling up State Street to incinerate the demons crawling toward us.

I smirked. Dusted.

"Go, go, go!" I shouted, ushering the back of the escape caravan forward.

"Hayden, get to the front," Kelsey shouted. "I've got this."

Nodding, I burst into a sprint, my feet barely touching the ground as my legs, honed from the years of ceaseless training with Kova, carried me past the others.

As I leaped past the witches at the front of the caravan, Nightmare slashed through the air to slice through the neck of an agony demon. I lunged from demon to demon, cutting them down as effortlessly as a child sliced butter with a knife.

Lightning zapped out of me. Thick, black electricity crackled through the air, blasting into demons and frying them to crisps before they could cross a claw with a witch's sword.

But then we hit the cobblestone street of University Avenue. I had always loved the old European architecture Alice Parker had instilled in Asylum, but as the witches struggled over the uneven surface, I cursed her.

Slamming a flat palm against the ground, I willed my earth magic to sweep the avenue. Cobblestones quaked and shook as my magic spread, shaping and pushing and pulling them into place until the stones smoothed into an even surface.

"Why didn't one of us think of that?" shouted a familiar voice. Terren Reed—the former Earth Major. "Faster people, faster," he shouted, urging the others on.

I flew into the air to meet a pterodactyl demon head-on before it swooped. As its dust rained into my hair, I landed in a crouch on the roof of the town's weapons store—Kova's favorite store, where I bought my first Yule present for her, a jewel encrusted dagger.

My heart panged, but I ignored it as I leaped from the rooftop to stab Nightmare into a spider demon crawling on the walls of the store on the opposite side of the street. And then I leaped to the next rooftop and the next wall, and I did it again and again, all the while shooting magic out of my body.

The going was slow compared to my normal speed, but I reminded myself that most witches weren't me and forced myself to stay with the main body of witches.

As fast as a demon appeared, my lethal black blade cut mercilessly into it, and a blend of the five elements tunneled around the witches in a swirling mix, protecting them from attack as I slayed our enemies in droves.

Kelsey relayed telepathic messages as she brought up the caboose. *We're passing the Black Cauldron. Clear the lawn to the Spellery.*

On it, I thought back. I wasn't sure if she could hear my thoughts. We probably should have tested that.

I shot like a bullet through the sky, landing in a feline-like crouch on the path to the school before I leaped forward, sprinting past the witches again, allowing my powers to protect them as I dove headfirst into the throng of demons.

With stony determination and unperturbed calmness, I sank my athame into the skull of a brimstone, then shot a tongue of holy flames down a hellhound's throat.

I was a one-woman army, and I finally realized what it must have felt like to be Kova for the last three hundred years. To have this kind of power, to protect my people. And like when I faced Lilith, when I was alone and powerless, I didn't need my magic to win, but I *did* have it, and I would use every last drop of it to fight like I had everything to lose.

And that thought, the desire to not lose another life to this Salem War, made me fight with more ferocity than ever before as I cut through soft flesh, spraying black blood on my clothes and on the demons converging on me.

I was the warrior witch.

Slashing and slaying and cutting and stabbing every demon clouding my vision.

And then there it was.... Its stone walls mere feet from me, if not for the layer of black demons clinging to it like ivy.

White holy flames soared through the air, the fire flickering in my eyes as I channeled my rage into the element that burned away the taint clinging to the castle walls.

The Spellery.

Spinning on my heel, I stared at the train of witches following me, my eyes tracking each witch as they blundered up the hill to the Spellery, followed by a relentless pursuit of demons.

Air, fire, water, earth, and Spirit.

The elements answered my call to shelter the witches as they struggled toward me, and the battle turned into a blur. Magic raged around the castle as I tracked each witch's escape route until the final witch passed through the massive doors of the Spellery, so only Kelsey trailed behind the others.

Two tongues of holy flames ripped from my palms and sailed over her shoulders to slam into the wyvern demon just before its claws tore into her back.

Gasping in a breath, Kelsey hit the ground, shielding her head as dust rained on her. Her head snapped around to look at me as I blasted another wyvern from the sky.

Lurching to her feet, Kelsey sprinted the last fifty feet to where I stood outside the castle doors, protecting the Spellery and the witches seeking shelter inside. Searing hot holy flames arced out of me, incinerating every demon within a hundred-yard radius.

Tense silence fell over the Spellery lawn as the immediate demon threat decayed to dust.

Kelsey stormed toward me, raising a hand.

A stinging slap cracked across my cheek, and I was impressed by the force of Kelsey's slap, even if she howled in pain compared to the light tingling of my skin.

Waving her hand to dull the pain, Kelsey asked, "Where have you been? You've been gone for an entire *week* and left us here to fend for ourselves."

"I was serious about the being in Hell thing," I grunted as I drove my sword through a pit demon that appeared from around the corner of the castle, followed by more of its brethren. "Apparently, time works differently down there."

A bolt of lightning zapped through a row of pit demons.

"Then do you know—"

"It's the eve of my birthday?" Fiery ropes of holy flames extended from my palms, and I whipped them like a conductor, slashing at the demons charging the castle. "Yeah, I know. What time is it? It's impossible to tell with the unending darkness and all."

With a wave of her wand, Kelsey read the time. "Noon. You have exactly twelve hours until midnight, and then you—"

"We'll burn that bridge when we cross it."

"That's not the saying."

"It is now. Lilith—she's using the elements against us, right? That's how she breeched the wards again."

"When you went to... Hell"—her face twisted in confusion as her brow scrunched—"it must have stretched your magical ties too thin to maintain the magic of the wards across realms. But it's worse than that. She's been using our own magic against us. Though, she's not very good at wielding the elements of the Salem Witch. Even Jamie can't get close to her."

"All of them?" I asked in alarm. "Even Spirit?"

"No, not Spirit. But the other four, yes."

"Because she can't. I wasn't sure if that had been a fluke or not after my Earth Trial—if she couldn't access Spirit or didn't know how."

"Your circle thinks Kova is using the power of Spirit to kill herself repeatedly."

Black lightning veered off to the side, blasting into the night sky as I jerked at Kelsey's declaration.

Kova was killing herself? Why?

"So, Lilith can't channel Kova's full powers to wield holy flames and Spirit," Kels answered before I could voice my question aloud.

"Can a soulless demon wield the powers of Heaven?" I asked. But something in my gut tugged at me. Even if Lilith couldn't command Spirit, if Kova was fully alive, her powers would magnify Lilith's. By Kova keeping her soul on the other side of the veil, Lilith couldn't steal her free will like she did to Leyla. Like Amara had taught me, *neshama*—soul—was the creation that gave mortals free will. If Lilith claimed a soul, she owned its free will.

Black lightning blasted from my palms, incinerating another group of demons. Thinking of demons—where were mine?

"Jackal and the others are hiding. They're helping as much as they can, but Lilith..."

"The Voice of Command."

"The Voice of Command," Kelsey echoed in agreement.

"One thing at a time. We need to free Kova and seal the wards. It will cut off Lilith's army and reclaim magic for our side while reducing her powers. Then we worry about breaking the Voice of Command."

"Raziel told you how to?"

A dark shadow fell over my face. "Yes."

"Then why didn't you do it *before* you left for Hell?" Kelsey threw her hands into the air with an eye roll, then muttered, "I swear, I'm the only logical one around here."

"Because I have to forfeit my Voice of Command, too."

Kelsey blinked at me. "Oh."

I shrugged as I speared an ice dagger into the eye of an agony demon. "I don't mind losing the power, but I didn't want to relinquish it and let demons ensue chaos on the town, especially when I was gone. It's gotta be a last-minute thing."

"Well, it's last minute, so let's do it now."

"I can't," I grunted. "I need my circle, and we need to be in close proximity to Lilith."

Kelsey rolled her eyes. "Of course you do. What's the point of being a Princess of Hell if you have to operate within the confines of magic? Isn't the whole point of being you that you get to break the rules?"

"Sometimes." I shrugged. "I don't get to pick which ones I break. The Universe decides for me." The power of the elements shot into the sky, piercing the soft flesh of the winged demons flying overhead and slicing off the stingers of killer bee demons.

"Step one, free Kova. Step two, free demons."

"And step three?"

"I haven't gotten there yet," I yelled as I directed the elements to decimate another dozen of charging brimstone demons.

"Even if we free Kova, it won't stop Lilith from channeling her if she's used a channel charm."

"Has Apalla found a counter-channel charm?"

"No. She's been fighting as nonstop with the rest of us. We need every hand to fight."

"Change of plans. Track down my circle. Find Isleen. Get them back to St. Salem's. Have Isleen and Apalla hit the library to find the spell. It's top priority. They do their intelligence thing, and I'll do my fighting thing. You and the rest of the circle prepare for what's to come. While you do that, I'll clear out the vermin around the Spellery." I winked at her and spun on my heel, summoning the elements to my palms.

The ground shook as a massive boar with gleaming ivory tusks emerged from the Wicked Woods, stomping on trees as it stampeded toward us and leaving depressions in the mud from the weight of its steps.

"Seriously, Lilith?" I shouted. "Pig demons? You must be kidding me."

The boar released a guttural roar, its beady black eyes glaring at me.

"Uh, you sure you got this one, Hays?"

I grinned wildly at Kelsey. "Oh yeah, this is nothing compared to the Devil. It will probably be fun."

Kelsey groaned. "There is something seriously unhinged about you."

Staring at the overgrown pig, Kelsey missed the demon descending on her from behind.

A bolt of lightning tased the demon.

Kelsey blinked, stunned by the lightning bolt flying past her face. Shaking her head, she cleared the shock from her nerves. Thrusting her arms out, she sent her will into the minds of witches nearby to relay my message to find my circle.

With a single nod, she turned on her heel and sprinted through the double doors of the Spellery in search of my circle.

Twisting my wrist, I closed the twenty-foot-tall double doors to the entrance hall and sheathed my longsword and amulet athame. Closing my eyes, I pressed my palms together. Magic gathered between my palms. Power coursed through my body, and black lightning crackled through my long hair as it floated softly on the breeze.

My eyes flew opened, and I thrust my arms outward, black lightning shooting out from my palms in every direction to zap from one demon to the next, leaving piles of ash in its wake.

Power rippled through my body as I increased the voltage, ripping through demons until every demon in a fifty-foot radius was dust blowing in the wind.

But the pig demon was still stomping toward me.

How was I going to kill this thing? It was massive. Like as big as a house. But I didn't know its weak spots.

When in doubt, aim for the joints. They were almost always soft and fleshy. And the spine. If the back wasn't covered in armor-like flesh, I could pierce between the vertebrae.

If I could cut through all the fat on porky.

A block of earth rose under my feet, launching me four stories into the air, so I sailed above the pig demon. Holy flames streamed from my hands.

Porky released a wild scream, steam unfurling from its nostrils as the white fire seared the armored skin on its back. Dense smoke rose from the smoldering flesh, the pungent stench filling the air. But my flames didn't kill the demon. Not even close. It would take a devastating wildfire to kill the pig demon, something I couldn't risk with all the witches fleeing to the Spellery. Which meant I had to carve it like a Christmas ham.

Air magic threw me at the pig demon like a missile. Porky snapped at me, its pointed fangs closing around air as I anticipated its attack and dodged.

Landing on its snout, I stabbed Nightmare into its beady, black eye, eliciting another roar from the overweight beast.

Not waiting for it to recover, I cartwheeled over its head like an acrobat and drove Nightmare into its ear—you never knew what might kill a demon. But that wasn't it.

As I landed on its back, I wrinkled my nose in disgust. The melted flesh stuck to the bottoms of my combats, and the acrid smell of burnt demon flesh nearly made me faint. Using the magic of air, I diverted the stench away from my nostrils, so I didn't breathe it in.

Lifting Nightmare, I summoned air, then I thrust down, driving Nightmare between Porky's vertebrae with the assistance of gravity and air magic.

The pork stick shook in pain and rage, its body quivering like a seismic wave. Nightmare's hilt slipped from my grasp as I flew backward. My back hit the pig demon's unburnt flesh, and I bounced off, falling off its back and tumbling through the air.

Magic swirled around me, righting me before I crashed into the earth, and lowering me until my feet lightly touched down.

Crap.

Nightmare was still lodged in its back.

Porky bucked and kicked, screaming in pain as it tried to twist so its teeth could pull Nightmare free. A twinge of regret panged through me at the sight of an animal in pain, but this wasn't an animal. It was a demon in the form of an animal, a manipulation so cleverly crafted by Lilith.

An idea sparked in my mind.

With a grin, I straightened from my crouch and thrust my hands forward, unleashing a menacing stream of flames to sizzle into the side of the pig. Sprinting toward its rear, I held the stream of fire, dragging it with me to burn its side. The smell of rotten bacon filled the air, and I gagged, but my feet kept moving.

The tail. I had to get to the tail.

As I reached Porky's hind leg, I jumped, summoning a gale to lift me. Rising in the air, I stuck out my free hand and summoned Nightmare with earth magic. Its leather hilt slammed into my right hand as I twisted in a layout.

White flames coated Nightmare's black blade, and air pushed on the longsword, accelerating its speed. Nightmare flashed through the air, its lethally sharp blade slicing through the soft flesh of Porky's curly tail.

Black blood spurted from the stub of the lost appendage. A roar that shook the earth escaped the disgusting demon as its knees crashed to the ground and it collapsed into a smoking heap of decaying flesh.

Landing in a crouch, I watched as the massive demon slowly decayed into a shriveled husk. I hated when demons didn't dust right away. How rude of them not to clean up after themselves.

Silence permeated the air as the pig demon disintegrated with excruciating slowness.

"Hayden," a familiar voice shouted my name.

As I spun toward his voice, a hard body slammed into me. Warm arms embraced me as Jamie's natural smoky scent drifted to my nose, and he pulled me tightly to his chest.

"Jamie," I sighed his name, sinking into the feeling of his arms.

And then his hard chest was gone. He had pulled away to hold me at arm's length, scanning for injuries. When he decided I was unharmed, his royal blue eyes shot to mine, brewing with anger.

"Where have you been?" he demanded.

"The underworld."

He deadpanned. "WHAT?"

"Don't worry. Hell was boring. I thought the Devil would at least be a challenge, but I was disappointed."

"The Devil—what—Haywire!"

I held my hand up, cupping my palm around his cheek. "I promise I'll answer all of your questions later, but for now, we need to level the playing field."

"Where have you been?" screeched the unwelcome voice of my least favorite water elemental.

Well, second least favorite. I still didn't like Katrina.

Mareena stormed up to me, covered in red and black blood and drenched with water, her blonde hair dripping water on the floor. "I brought reinforcements for *your* war." She pressed the tip of her sword to my heart, digging the blade into my leather jacket. "And you haven't been here!"

Rolling my eyes, I pushed her blade away from my chest. "Sorry that my dance with the Devil took so long. I would have been here sooner if I didn't have to kill all the demons in Hell."

"All the... what?" Mareena paled at the realization that my words were literal.

"What?" Jamie snapped, his hands grabbing me by the cheeks as he pulled me toward him so he could re-check me for injuries.

"Jamie, focus. I'm fine," I said, peeling his hands off my face. "Mareena, how are your soldiers?"

"Dying," she growled with contempt, and a sharp pain of guilt stabbed me in the gut. "Because of you."

"This is probably a stupid question, but the Supreme Council didn't happen to change their minds and send reinforcements, did they?"

"No, and they're not going to. We're on our own." Kelsey snorted. "Not that I'm surprised, knowing my grandmother. You provoked Regalia. She doesn't forget a slight. No one can hold a grudge like a Kensington."

Tipping my head back, I breathe out a sigh. Kova had said my behavior with the Supreme Council would come back to bite me. But it wasn't hurting just me. Asylum was paying the price.

"We don't have enough warriors," Mareena snapped in her high-pitched, nasally tone.

"It's not just the Knights and your demons, either." Thea grimaced as she said, "All of Asylum. Witches of all ages are fighting. And we're barely surviving."

The blood drained from my face, and I visibly paled.

"Lilith's army is infinite. For each demon I kill, two more take its place." Jamie shook his head. "And with the wards open, they keep coming. There's nothing to stop her army from marching in. And we're getting slaughtered out there. I'm the only witch who can summon holy flames, and nobody can control hellfire except you."

"Then we're going to stop her army from marching in. We did it once, we can do it again." Hardening my face from an expression of regret into a mask of death, I extended my arms to my sides. "Get ready for a recharge."

Without asking permission, I shot a concentrated dose of Spirit into the other witches. Power flooded into them in a flash of silver light, and I sensed their magical signatures intensify beyond their normal power levels. Gasps sounded as they stumbled under the intensity of the magic renewing within their bodies.

"Better?"

Jamie stared at me with wonder as red flames sparked in his grim-covered blond locks. "Is that how you feel all the time? Like Spirit is constantly re-energizing every cell in your body?"

"Like that and more," I said with a knowing smile. "Circle, listen up." I barked out commands, "Thea, spook Kelsey to Luna Pier, then head to the northern tip of the lake. Kels—you're filling in for Palla."

She nodded with a look of unwavering focus.

"Jamie, take Ethan to the west side of the lake, then come back for me. I'll connect my magic to each of yours when I'm ready to summon the element. When we're done casting the circle, move. Meet at the cathedral. From there, we begin stage two of Operation: Black."

"What's stage two?"

"Rescuing Kova and closing the wards." I met Jamie's eyes with hardened determination.

"What should I do?" Mareena asked.

My eyes flicked to her. "Do you have healing abilities?"

"No."

I considered her for a moment, then said, "Gather all the healers, so I can pour Spirit into them and restore their magic."

"What is the circle casting for?" Mareena demanded, not budging from where she rooted her feet, glaring at me with her hands on her hips.

"Leveling the playing field. Lilith wants to set the town on fire, and we need firefighters," Kelsey explained. "A regular witch can extinguish hellfire by dousing it with holy water."

"Harbor could bless holy water by herself, and we had reserves stocked for emergencies but ran out on the first day."

"And we need it, desperately," Ethan added. "For fighting and healing burns."

"I can't make holy water by myself, but with a circle this powerful, we can bless the entire lake."

Mareena's eyes bugged out of her skull. "That's why you want the healers."

She scrambled to do as I commanded, screeching at the healers in her high-pitched nasally voice. As the healers rushed to me, I zapped them with the power of Spirit, rejuvenating their powers as I conversed with my circle, drafting the spell to bless the lake.

When the final healer was refreshed on magic, Mareena rushed back to me.

"Move out," I instructed my circle, then instructed Mareena. "Help Silas manage the healers and let me know when they need another dose of Spirit."

Red and green light flashed as Thea and Jamie spooked with the others.

I couldn't be everywhere at once, especially if I was going to rescue Kova and take on Lilith. With the lake blessed, water elementals could kill demons in seconds instead of relying on weapons. It could turn the tide in this war, give my warriors at edge, and reduce casualties. I flinched at the thought of all the fallen witches.

Red light flashed, and smoke stung my nostrils. Without looking, I took Jamie by the hand. A tugging sensation pulled at my stomach, making it roll with uncomfortable nausea, but I ignored it as we appeared above the center of the lake, suspended in the air before gravity grabbed hold of us.

Releasing my hand, Jamie spooked to his position on the south side of the circle.

Curling my hand into a fist, I froze the water into a patch of ice. Landing in a feline crouch, I willed the ice to wrap around my ankles, balancing me on my island of frozen water.

Swiveling to face east, I sent a tendril of my magic to connect with Kelsey's and called upon my first element.

I summon the power of air,
Whose life-giving essence,
The Creator breathed into Adam and Eve.

I turned to the south. My magic surged toward Jamie's, happily mingling with his. Not releasing my connection to Kelsey, I continued to cast the circle.

I summon the power of fire,
Whose holy flames burn evil from my veins,
Leaving light in its place.

Turning to the west, I connected with Ethan, not hesitating to call upon the third element.

I summon the power of water,
Whose depths cleanse away pain and sorrow,
Providing healing and love from Heaven above.

Lastly, I turned toward Thea and connected with her emerald green essence.

I summon the power of earth,
The dust of which was used for form Eve's body,
And to which we all shall return.

The last element, Spirit, was mine, and mine alone to summon.

East, South, West and North,
I call you forth.
Mind, heart, blood, and body,
I call you to this sacred space for witches to embody.

Air to travel as wind will blow,
And heat of fire for it to glow,
Deeper than the ocean's flow,
Earth to make this spell grow.
And the fifth is soul to make the spell hold.

I summon the power of Spirit,
The fifth element who belongs solely to Heaven.
When all others are gone,
We find within Spirit eternal life.

Great Spirit, Divine Above, Creator of All,
Answer this holy, reverent call.
This circle is cast,
Heaven's light unbroken.
So mote it be,
This magic has spoken.

My eyes fluttered closed as I gave myself to the power of the elements. Five elements surged from me, rushing through the water beneath my feet. Simultaneously, each individual element originated from its pillar of the circle to join my magic and the power of its elemental brethren.

The ice melted under my feet, and I splashed into the lake, sinking down, down, down, until I stood on the sandy bottom.

Water swirled around me, faster and faster and faster. My eyes flared open, glowing with the silver light of the Salem Witch. I shot up, breaking through the surface with the force of a hurricane. Water rose under me, swelling into a tidal wave. My feet landed atop the crest of the wave, and I rode it like a pro-surfer riding pipe, pulling the holy water behind me until the tidal wave crashed into the earth.

Surfing past Kelsey, leaving her unharmed by the crushing wave, I threw my arms forward, channeling the magic of the circle to crash into the demons throughout the town, burning their essence, but leaving my people untouched by the powerful, destructive wave.

Surfing up University Avenue, I willed the water to wash through the streets, over the buildings, and into the demons attacking the Knights and witches throughout Asylum.

Riding the tidal wave to the base of the hill the Spellery sat atop of, I willed every drop of holy lake water to spread through Asylum, as far and wide as the waves would flow. As my wave dissipated, water witches leaped into action, using their magic to control the holy water saturating the streets to fight the swarms of demons in the sky overhead.

Unsheathing my blade, I took off running down University, sprinting for the cathedral. I spun and ducked and stabbed and jabbed at the flying demons that my wave of holy water hadn't doused as they landed on patches of dry earth where the holy water had evaporated.

Lilith's army fell at my hand, their dust blowing on the wind raging at my back, pushing me faster through town.

It felt like flying as the elements hurried my pursuit, their power lifting me so my feet barely touched the ground.

Even without my feet on the ground, I felt the earth tremble so forcefully that I skidded to a stop. Witches fell to the ground, unable to maintain their balance as the earth rose and fell beneath them.

Bending over, I slammed my hand into the earth, counterattacking the earthquake with the sheer force of my will. Thea's magic mixed with mine under the ground, and the shaking subsided.

"Everyone alright?" I called to the witches on the street.

Heads nodded and strained groans responded, but nobody was seriously injured.

Grabbing a random nearby witch by the wrist, I hauled him to his feet. "What was that?" I demanded.

"That would be *Lilith*." He hissed her name like it was a curse on his lips. The witch couldn't have been any older than sixteen, and I recognized him from the Spellery, so I was impressed he said her name aloud. "She's channeling Kova's power of the four elements, but she hasn't used holy flames and Spirit."

Like Kelsey had said.

"Has she made an appearance anywhere?" I asked, helping another witch to their feet.

"So far, she has stayed out of the battle, electing to use the powers of the Salem Witch and the Mother from afar. Nobody has got close to her. Not even Jamie or Thea."

"I've heard. Where is her base of operations?"

His expression darkened. "The cemetery."

A wicked grin crept onto my face.

Thanking the witch, I burst into a sprint down the avenue, eager to meet my friends at the cathedral. As I rounded the corner and skidded into the town square, I plowed into a group of witches fighting off a wyvern demon.

Shooting holy flames out of my hands, I engulfed the wyvern in a furnace of heavenly power. Winged demons landed in the square, but the water witches splashed them with holy water, scalding their feathers and hides.

Other than the winged beasts, few demons remained in the area. For now. The wards were still open. As much as I wanted to stop and help, I had to get to my friends so we could save Kova.

Reluctantly, I spun on my heel and ramped into a sprint. Shooting across the lawn outside the cathedral, I once again thanked Kova for forcing me to do cardio. I wasn't even out of breath.

Bursting through the double doors of the Cathedral, I barely skidded to a halt before I crashed into my friends.

"What's the plan?" Jamie didn't waste any time.

"Kelsey, where is Apalla at with finding the counter channel spell?"

"She's nearly there." She cocked her head as she communicated telepathically with the Prophetess. "Actually, she thinks she has a spell that will work. She's gathering the ingredients."

"Tell her to focus solely on that." I met each of their eyes. "Nothing else is as important."

"You felt it, too," Thea whispered.

It wasn't a question. She was more than a little disturbed that Lilith could control Thea's earth.

"We all did." Isleen's voice was ice as she spooked into the Cathedral. "Our top priority is rescuing Kova. It won't just steal power from Lilith. The power of two Salem Witches will tip the scales in our favor. What do you need me to do?"

CHAPTER TEN

REBEL SPIRIT

"Move out," I commanded like a war chief.

Thea and Ethan disappeared in a flash of green, while Isleen spooked with Kelsey.

Jamie reached for my hand, intertwining his fingers with mine, but he didn't spook.

"I need you to promise me something," he said, his royal blue eyes staring into my piercing blue ones. "I need you to promise me that you won't die."

Doubt filled my gut, and intuition told me not to make that promise. Maintaining eye contact, I fought the urge to look away.

"Jamie... James." I rested a hand gently against his cheek. "I'm the Salem Witch. I will do whatever it takes to keep my people safe. If I die in the process... I don't relish the idea. I'm certainly not ready, but if it happens while protecting my home, then at least I'll go knowing I did everything I possibly could to fulfill the Creator's plan."

Jamie's head dropped. When he spoke, emotion clogged his voice. "I had a feeling you would say that." Lowering his forehead to mine, his hands gripped either side of my face and he massaged circles into my jaw. "But I'm going to do everything I can to keep that from happening."

My lips twitched into a soft, half smile. It was all I could manage while standing there, staring into Jamie's sorrow-filled, ocean blue eyes. He had lost his sister... and I didn't think he could withstand the pain of losing me. But I couldn't withstand the pain of failing the world. Reclaiming his hand, I pulled it to my lips and pressed a gentle kiss to his palm.

"Let us go to war with smiles on our faces because we are friends of Death herself. Lilith cannot win, for Amara is helping us."

His lips twitched into a grim smile. "I guess even Death has a heart."

I snorted. "Let's go save the Salem Witch."

Squeezing my hand, Jamie spooked. An instant later, we appeared in the Wicked Woods around the cemetery.

Isleen had spooked Apalla into the trees under the guise of a powerful Cloaking Spell to hide from Lilith and her demons. I felt my bestie's familiar magic wash over us, encompassing us in her spell. I had absolute faith in my best friend and knew Lilith would sense us before she ever saw us.

The power of Spirit muted our magical energy signatures, preventing the demons from sensing us, but I had never extended Spirit to dim the magical potency of other witches before. I prayed my magic worked as well as I thought it did.

Standing hand-in-hand with Jamie, a mere five feet from the edge of the forest where the trees ended to reveal a massive clearing, my eyes scanned the demon-filled cemetery. Dark mounds protruded from the ground so thickly that I couldn't distinguish headstones from demons, even as mausoleums towered over them.

There.

In the center of the clearing, surrounded by demons, loomed a dark figure surrounded by an aura of evil and magic. Lilith laid casually on her back, lounging on top of a white marble mausoleum with a single leg dangling over the edge.

Purple velvet, so dark it was almost black under the swirling gray maelstrom in the sky above, hugged her curves like a second skin. The strapless cocktail dress ended mid-thigh, so an inch of skin showed between the edge of her dress and the tops of her thigh-high purple pumps.

How the heck did she fight in that outfit?

With her head titled back to stare at the sky, she held a single hand in front of her face, lazily twirling her wrist as she summoned the elements to her palm one at a time.

Air in the form of a mini cyclone. Purple hellfire. Water as a hurricane. Earth in the form of venomous purple flowers.

But not Spirit. Never Spirit. For the soulless could not wield such considerable power.

On the front steps of the mausoleum, under Lilith's dangling foot, towered a massive X-shaped cross. Two shackles hung from the top of the X, taut from suspending Kova's weight by her wrists. Magical cuffs encircled her ankles... not that it was necessary. The Salem Witch was knocked out cold, her body swaying in the breeze.

Rage flooded my veins at the sight of my mentor crucified, compounded by the sight of my mother hanging from a cross next to

Kova. Grinding my teeth, I swallowed my scream of rage and the desire to throw all of my magic at Lilith in one shot.

Clamping down on my magic, I willed it to a low simmer instead of a fiery inferno. Despite our proximity to Lilith, I wasn't concerned about her detecting our presence, but I needed to control my temper, or my energy signature would alert her. For all I knew, Lilith was aware of my return, but if she wasn't... then my reappearance was an edge we didn't want to reveal.

Without taking my eyes off my enemy, I asked Apalla, "Do you have the counter channel charm ready?"

"Yes," she said, using air magic to muffle our words as she held up two bottles filled with a potion. "If you can get me close, I can douse them both. Once the liquid touches both of them, the charm will take effect."

"No." I snatched a potion vial from her hand, looking at my friend with aghast horror. "No way am I letting you or anyone else get anywhere close to Lilith." At the hurt in her eyes, I softened my tone. "Palla, it's not that I think you can't handle it. But this is my responsibility. Kova is my mentor and my father's soulmate. Lilith is my grandmother and the enemy in *my* Salem War. *I* have the power of the five elements. Lilith has control of four. It has to be me. You get that right?"

"Doesn't mean we have to like it," Jamie grumbled.

I wasn't sure if he intended for me to hear or not, but I ignored it. This was my war, and I had been absent for long enough. "Palla, use your vial to apply the potion to Kova. I'll take care of Lilith."

"She's erected a Reverse Barrier Spell around the cemetery." Isleen worried her lip. "We can spook in, but not out. Quite genius to trap you and anyone who tries to rescue you."

"How do you know that?"

Isleen smiled wanly. "Leyla used to cast a Barrier Spell to prevent her mother from bothering her at... inopportune moments. I can sense the magic of the spell, and it's the exact opposite of Leyla's spell."

"This doesn't change the plan," I said, my eyes cutting back to Lilith lounging on the top of the cemetery. "You all know your missions. Here goes nothing. Commencing phase two of Operation: Black."

Thea disappeared in a flash of green, the light of her magic mixing with the red flash of light as Jamie spooked, their energetic signatures cloaked by Apalla's light magic.

Kelsey, Isleen, Apalla, Ethan, and I remained crouched in the forest, invisible to the army of demons lurking mere feet from us.

A roar tore through the gloomy night as the earth rumbled fiercely under my feet. Thea's emerald green magic swirled in the air above her.

Demon after demon fell to the Heart of Earth, succumbing to the rampaging power of the Earth.

Lilith bolted upright, rising in a flash as she glared at the child goddess. With a vicious snarl, the Mother of Demons leaped from her perch and landed in a crouch, her heels sinking into the soil. Demons fled from the Dark Mother, frantic to flee her line of sight and clear a path for their dark mistress.

"Now," I told Isleen.

The High Priestess gripped Apalla and Ethan each by an elbow and spooked, taking Apalla's Cloaking Spell with her.

Lilith froze mid-step, her spine ramrod straight. Whirling around, her eyes scanned the tree line where I hid in the shadows.

But Lilith and the rest of the world falsely believed I possessed the blessing of free will, gifted to me from the Goddess. I wasn't Lilith's target. Thea was. Because Thea was her means to obtain the power of the Maiden and ascend to the Power of Three. But Lilith was Darkness incarnate. Why settle for Thea's power when she could force me to forfeit mine under the threat of torture and death to my friends?

A scowl tore across her mouth, but she turned around, setting her eyes on Thea, as I expected.

"Kels, time to go."

She rose to standing, one hip popped out with the attitude of the witch of terror. "What if Elliot shows his ugly mug?"

"He won't," I said confidently.

Her eyes landed on me, skepticism apparent on her face.

"Elliot isn't as aligned with Lilith as you'd think. Lucifer is amplifying his powers. And Elliot's goals are self-serving. If Lilith wins, good for him, but he lusts for dominance over the witches of Asylum. His priority isn't to protect Lilith when he could be proving how much better he is than us."

With pursed lips, she mumbled, "As messed up as he is, his psychological complex gives us an advantage."

"Couldn't agree more. But if he does show, you can take him." I winked at her, a feral smirk on my lips. "Now, move."

Bursting into action, I launched myself into the cemetery with a spurt of air magic.

On queue—because I could always count on my Angel Boy—brilliant red and white flames sparked to life from the southeast, far from either Thea or me.

Lilith froze in her prowl from the mausoleum to Thea, spinning to watch the holy flames burn her armies to crisps.

Thea disappeared in a flash of green light. Lilith's head swiveled, ignoring Jamie's slaughter charge as her eyes narrowed at the spot where Thea disappeared.

With Lilith distracted, I unleashed my silver holy hellfire, incinerating every demon in a twenty-yard radius.

With fury in her aura, Lilith spun toward me, her lips curling into an evil grin as she forgot Thea.

Drawing Nightmare with my right hand, I beckoned her toward me with my left.

Grinning maniacally, Lilith changed directions, her focus on her new prey—me.

Demons threw themselves from her path, but they were equally afraid of me, not daring to attack for fear of my flames... and fear of what their mother would do if they got in the way of the battle that belonged to her. The crowd of demons pushed and pulled, swaying as the demons fled from the Dark Mother.

A brimstone demon was thrown back from the undulating crowd and landed in front of Lilith. Dark purple magic blasted into the demon, incinerating him on the spot. Lilith didn't so much as glance at the patch of smoking black grass as she stepped over the charr.

"Ah, the Salem Witch," she purred. "Hello, Hayden. Nice of you to finally join your own war. I was convinced you finally realized what I have known since the day Gabriel claimed you."

Silently, I raised an eyebrow at her, my mouth shut.

"You are a *failure*. You will never beat me."

"Is that so?" I asked nonchalantly, lifting Nightmare to study the name etched into the blade from Heaven. The blade that had once belonged to Lucifer.

"Absolutely," she drawled. "I have been alive since the beginning of mortals, and no woman, no witch, no *goddess*," she spat the last part, "has bested me."

"I did." I prowled forward. "Or did you forget? I did not need magic to overpower you. I did not need my blades to best you. It is time someone put you down for the rest of eternity."

"And who is going to do that? You?" Lilith threw her head back and laughed maniacally. "I channel both your mother and a fully realized Salem Witch. You're nothing more than a half-baked wannabe playing pretend. Even with the power of the elements, you cannot defeat me."

"Funny. You have been alive longer than any other human, known the Goddess for eons, yet you still do not understand the vast power or the ways of the Creator." Brandishing my black Nightmare, I said, "Did you know this blade is a sword from Heaven, once belonging to the Morningstar?"

Shock slapped Lilith across the face.

"It seems the Creator designed Nightmare to bond to me to redeem it from the past of sin Lucifer stained on it. And what better way than to use it to defeat the first mortal to fall to his beguiling trickery?"

Fuming, Lilith took a menacing step forward and conjured her sickled sword. With distance still between us, I slipped into my stance, summoning the elements to swirl around me. Lilith channeled the elements from Kova and had a power boost from obtaining the magic of the Mother, but I was the Salem Witch. The most powerful Salem Witch in history.

And I was other things too.

I was the first warrior in history to best Lilith. I did it without magic. And I would do it again.

"On the contrary, Granddaughter, that blade seems cursed. Its owner shall always fall from Grace. And you will be the same. How poetic that you shall fall to me when I fell because of Lucifer."

"Perhaps." I cracked my knuckles. "Whether I do or do not, one thing remains absolutely certain."

"Oh?" She smirked smugly at me, her serpentine fangs poking into her lower lip. "And what is that?"

"I will fight until my last breath."

"That can be arranged," she snarled, lunging forward, her blade flashing off the light of the flickering purple hellfire burning in the braziers mounted to the mausoleum walls.

Lilith's sickle crashed into mine. She was stronger... ridiculously stronger than the last time we crossed blades.

But so was I. It wouldn't be easy for her to best me, either. My strength had grown exponentially since I passed my Earth Trial and wielding Spirit strengthened my soul.

Sparks spit at me, metal grinding against metal as she slid her blade down the length of mine. Without a thought, my fire magic extinguished the sparks, and I swiped at Lilith with my dagger as I deflected her next attack with Nightmare.

Nightmare's pommel slammed into her sternum, a whirlwind of air crashing into her with the sword and throwing her backward twenty yards.

A grunt escaped her lips as Lilith's back slammed into the ground. Staggering to her feet, Lilith's eyes grew wild as it dawned on her that I wouldn't be so easy to beat, even with her channeling the Mother and a Salem Witch.

She didn't know how to properly wield the elements. Not like I did.

Charging her, I sliced upward, forcing her to dance to the left to escape the slice of my blade, but I was already twirling in perfect time to strike a hard elbow to her gut, knocking the air from her lungs. Dancing out of the way of her blade, I caught another blow with my athame and deflected a wimpy breeze of air she cast at me.

"What the—"

I threw myself backward, narrowly dodging the deadly slice of Lilith's second sword. She had summoned a pair of katanas to replace her sickle. I didn't even see her swap the blades.

Gripping a blade in each hand, she cut at me, coordinating her attacks to force me to dodge and parry twice the number of blows and limit my opportunities to strike, all while throwing measly elemental attacks at me, which I easily deflected with my superior magical skill.

But I was a warrior, and even at my young age, I was more of a warrior than the fallen human who fought me so vehemently. I would not be bested in swordsmanship by her.

Despite her twin blades, Nightmare and my amulet athame were a lethal team, capable of playing offense as easily as defense against the katanas. But if I needed one hand free to douse her with the Anti-channeling Potion. Reluctantly, I sheathed my dagger, knowing it put me at a disadvantage.

Lilith snorted as I slid my amulet athame into its sheath on my right hip. "Are you so arrogant that you believe you can best me with a single blade? I have the Mother and the Crone *and* Alice Parker. Your magic is outmatched, and even if you can beat me in combat, you will not do so with a single blade."

Striking out with Nightmare, I didn't respond as I attacked in a flurry of jabs in rapid fire. Catching her blade, I dodged a strike from her other katana, then circled her blade with mine until I rapped the flat of my blade against her wrist, sending one of her katanas flying into the skull of one of the demons watching us with rapt attention.

Pushing off her, I ducked under a swipe of her other katana and sank a dagger of ice into her gut.

A blast of purple hellfire slammed into me, throwing me to the ground. Using my momentum, I rolled to my feet and blocked her weak blast of water magic.

With a roar of rage, Lilith threw handfuls of purple hellfire at me repeatedly. The flames couldn't harm me, but her flames filled the sky, hindering my vision.

White holy flames flew from my body to meet the hellfire, obliterating Lilith's dark purple flames.

As flames of Heaven and Hell dueled, I charged forward and threw a tongue of white flames at Lilith. My heavenly flames licked Lilith's hand as I closed the distance between us. Lilith stumbled backward, shaking her burnt hand as she hissed.

Leaping in the air, I aimed a kick at her head, but Lilith tricked me. While I thought she was distracted by her burnt hand, she was feigning. Her hand snaked out and wrapped around my ankle. My spine slammed into the earth with help from Lilith's air magic, forcing the air from my lungs. But I had suffered whiplash enough during my years of training. Air magic returned the element to my lungs.

Lilith hovered above me, twirling the hilt of her blade as a scowl tore across her beautiful face.

"You are nothing more than a pathetic little girl with delusions of her grandeur. You have never amounted to anything, and you never will." She paused, cocking her head. "The only significance you possess is the potential to serve as a magical battery for me to obtain the Power of Three. But you are useless with your blessing from my *mother*, unless you willingly yield to me."

Raising the katana overhead, she aimed to stab the long blade through my gut and pin me to the earth.

Kicking up, I drove the steel heel of my combat boot into her wrist. A shriek pierced the air as bone shattered. Metal clanged against stone as her remaining katana clattered against a headstone. I landed on the balls of my feet in a graceful crouch.

In a furious rage, Lilith threw herself at me. The force of a full-grown man slammed into me as Lilith used her enhanced physical strength against me. Scrambling, we fought for control, each struggling to grip the other by the wrist or throat.

But for all my strength, for all my training, Lilith was made from the clay of Eden and possessed physical strength equal to Adam, and I was just a seventeen-year-old girl.

Lilith's hand seized my right wrist, but I clung to my longsword as her other hand tightened around my throat. Lifting me by the neck, Lilith smiled a victorious, serpentine smile, those purple snake eyes flashing with triumph.

My feet hovered half a foot above the ground as I kicked futilely, my feet scrambling for purchase.

"Any last words, Granddaughter?" she snarled, her nasty breath infiltrating my nostrils like an unwelcomed parasite.

Gripping the vial of Anti-channel Potion in my left hand, I swung my arm in a perfect left hook and smashed the glass bottle against Lilith's bloodless, porcelain cheek. The glass shattered, biting into my hand and slicing gashes into her face.

Grim satisfaction drove away the sting of pain and a shot of healing water magic tore the glass shards from my hand and stitched the fragile flesh together.

Lilith's slitted purple eyes widened in utter shock as the strength fled her body. Her grip loosened around my throat, and I yanked my wrist from her grasp.

"You lose," I growled as I raised my arms up and slammed them down on her elbows, forcing her to release my neck.

One foot touched the ground, earth magic twisting around it to stabilize my base leg as I pulled my other knee up and drove the bottom of my foot into her stomach. With a burst of wind, I sent her flying backward with a single kick until her spine slammed into the corner of another mausoleum and she crashed to the ground in a heap.

"Go. Go. Go," I shouted at my circle as I sprinted through the army of demons, decimating them with magic and blade.

Red flames flashed ahead of me, signaling my friends' position. Pivoting directions, I tore through the crowd of demons, keeping my eyes on my friends, who barely fended off the army of darkness converging on them.

Kova hung between Isleen and Ethan as they dragged her through the cemetery, one of her arms draped around each of their shoulders.

Swallowing the vomit rising in my throat at the sight of my mentor's mutilated face, I ripped through Lilith's demons with the might of five elements, destroying them by the dozens.

Thea, Jamie, and Apalla surrounded the trio with Apalla protecting her mother's side with beams of sunlight shining from her palms, Jamie and his white holy flames protecting Ethan's side—closest to me and Lilith—and Thea leading the charge from the middle, cutting a path through the black sea of evil with her purifying emerald magic.

Furiously, I twirled my longsword, slicing through demons as all five elements surrounded me, annihilating any demon that got too close. I was a deadly storm wading through a sea of black like a hurricane tearing through the ocean.

As fast as I moved, there was a lot of ground between me and my friends, and panic rose in my chest at the sound of a demoness's shriek.

"I do not remember giving you permission to leave," Lilith screeched at the top of her lungs.

Demons skidded to a startling halt as they frantically turned to bow to her, mistaking her rage as aimed at them.

Spinning, I locked eyes on Lilith standing on a white marble headstone, towering over us and the demons despite her short stature.

Lilith's purple snake eyes sliced into me as she pulled her arm up and back before thrusting it forward. A black dagger flew hilt over tip through the air.

Ice flooded my veins as I recognized the frozen hellfire blade. Time seemed to slow... or maybe I did as I lifted Nightmare to deflect the hellfire dagger that had ripped into my skin once before.

But the evil blade sailed past my head, clearing my scalp by an inch.

It wasn't intended for me.

A chill slithered along my spine—like someone had walked over my grave, and I just *knew*.

As though I was moving in slow motion, I turned to trace the trajectory of the blade. Horror pierced my heart as I tracked the blade spinning toward Jamie's chest.

"No!" I screeched, summoning air magic to stop the blade before it could pierce his vulnerable flesh.

Before my magic could act, before *I* could act, a flash of blue cut in front of Jamie, catching the blade before it buried itself in Jamie's chest.

Ethan faced Jamie, his arms spread to either side as he sheltered Jamie's body with his own. The obsidian blade's leather hilt protruded from the center of Ethan's back, surrounded by a dark circle of blood staining his denim jacket.

Red blood splattered Jamie's face as Ethan coughed.

Horror filled those royal blue eyes as Jamie caught Ethan under his arms before he collapsed.

Time crashed back into motion.

"Ethan," I bellowed my friend's name with the ferocity of Heaven and Hell, striking fear into the heartless chests of the surrounding demons.

The sight of Ethan collapsed in Jamie's arms, surrounded by an unending mass of demons, spurred me into action.

Spinning, I summoned an unbelievable ball of crackling black lightning to my hand. Thrusting it forward, I willed the power of Spirit to rip through the air.

Lilith's smug grin disappeared as my power slammed into her, throwing her backwards through the hole gaping in the wards. Crashing to the ground, Lilith plowed through a dozen agony demons as they marched through the wards.

The wards... they should have sealed after we severed the channel between Lilith and Kova.... Why were they still open?

Blinking, I struggled to comprehend the magic... the black tinge around the edges of the hole...

That demon!

Lilith knew I would come for Kova—she'd be a fool to think I wouldn't. She had a backup plan for if she lost the powers of the Salem Witch. She had needed Kova's powers to open the wards, but Lilith's dark magic held them open, the wards weak from Lilith tearing through them with the powers of the Salem Witch who constructed the wards in the first place.... Goddess, the magical logic made my head hurt.

I needed a circle, but Ethan...

Air whipped around me, a tempest brewing in the sky. Fire burned, leaping at demons, eager to burn them. Hail rained from the sky, hammering demons in the heads, but my friends remained untouched.

The ground rumbled as vines and roots ripped from the earth, tangling around demons and squeezing until they ruptured.

Lunging forward, I buried Nightmare's blade into the nearest demon, then the next and the next as I charged forward, black lightning rippling over my skin and shooting in every direction to electrocute demons. The rage-fueled magic of the elements, of Spirit, did not cease as I rejoined my friends.

Tumbling to my knees, I clasped Ethan's hand in mine, keeping the other clamped tightly around Nightmare. Magic swirled, protecting us while I grieved my fallen friend.

"He-he saved me...." Jamie's shell-shocked blue eyes met mine as he cradled Ethan in his lap, tears streaming down his cheeks. "What were you thinking, you idiot?"

Ethan coughed, blood splattering against his shirt. "The least... I could do... was save... her... brother," he wheezed, every word labored.

"Harbor? Why?" Jamie choked on the congestion clogging his throat. "Why for her?"

"Because he loves her." I gasped, tears streaming down my cheeks.

"And because..." He coughed up more blood, drenching the front of his shirt as his chocolate brown eyes met mine. "Because I already lost my love... I didn't want anyone else to suffer the same fate."

"I'm sorry," I sobbed. "I thought Lilith was aiming for me... if I had been smarter, faster, I could have—"

Ethan shushed me. "There's nothing... you could... have done."

"Thank you," I whispered through the thick emotion clogging my throat. "For saving him."

"It was my honor... and the greatest sacrifice I could ever make," Ethan said with a faint smile. "But I should already be dead from this wound." His smile fell into a frown. "Yet my soul is clinging to the mortal realm."

"Tonight, Death is on your side," I muttered to myself. *Death is your gift*. Amara wasn't claiming Ethan's soul yet, letting him linger painfully in his mortal body. Why?

The gravestone next to my head exploded into rubble as purple hellfire slammed into it. The debris flew past me, leaving us unharmed as my magic pushed it aside.

Lilith's hellfire punched through my weakening elemental barrier. Weakening because I wasn't paying attention and losing myself to my emotions.

The wards...

CHAPTER ELEVEN

THE SPELL OF SALEM

Lurching to my feet, I fueled my powers into the tempest of the elements swirling in a protective bubble.

"Isleen," I barked her name. "I need a water elemental."

Isleen's pale blue eyes snapped to Ethan, then back to me.

With a subtle shake of my head, I said, "I'm going to clear a path for you through the demons. Sprint until you clear the Reverse Barrier Spell, then you and Kelsey use telepathy to find Dani Sanchez."

"Come on out, Hayden," Lilith called as another ball of purple hellfire blasted against my elemental dome. "Come out and face me. Unless the Salem Witch is too much of a coward to face the wrath of the Mother of Demons."

Closing her eyes, Isleen inhaled a slow breath, and my magic sensed her erratic heartbeat evening as she calmed herself. Flicking her eyes open, she met my gaze and nodded.

At my command, the five elements swirled in a ball in the cup of my hand. Funneling magic into the elements, they expanded larger and larger, the magic growing denser as the elements condensed into a concentrated shot.

Throwing my arm forward like a baseball pitcher, I hurtled the elements down the gravel path leading from the cemetery to the heart of town. Magic blundered through the demons clogging the lane, shredding their dark flesh to pieces. Dust swirled like leaves on the wind, the path clear of demons.

"Go, go, go!"

Isleen sprinted down the aisle toward Kelsey, who held a circle of demons around her at bay without breaking a sweat.

Throwing my arms wide, I ignited a row of holy flames on either side of the gravel to prevent the demons from snatching Isleen as she raced out of the cemetery and crossed the threshold of Lilith's Anti-Spooking Spell.

We were down another witch.

Knowing my air elementals would find me a water witch, I turned my back on the holy flames. We had to fix the wards, but first... I wanted my demons.

And Raziel had told me exactly how to free them.

Sheathing my longsword and amulet athame, I used earth magic to unsheathe the throwing knives from their leather pouch. All except the one I threw at Lucifiana in Hell because the blade was still down there.

Thanks to Apalla's vision, I had dipped each blade in a Paralysis Potion, and now Lilith would taste my venom. The blades hovered in the air, waiting to be thrown.

Lilith sneered. "What an intimidating sight. Hayden surrounded by knives." She rolled her slitted purple eyes. "I am *immortal* and *invincible*, girl. Your knives will not harm me."

I threw the first knife with lethal precision.

Lilith dodged the blade, but the tip nicked her cheek, drawing a faint line of black blood.

Not enough.

Apalla shot golden sunlight into Lilith's eyes. With an enraged roar, Lilith threw her arms up to block the penetrating light, but it was too late. My second knife sank into her gut, and black blood gushed forth.

Green vines wiggled from the soil at Thea's command, each one thicker than my leg, and snapped around Lilith's wrists and ankles.

My third knife was already spinning handle over tip through the air. Sinking into her fleshy thigh, my blade pierced her femoral artery, drawing enough blood for the spell.

"What is this?" Lilith roared, her words slurring.

Apalla's Paralysis Potion—brewed by our potions expert, Ethan—coursed through Lilith's veins, and her movements slowed as she struggled against Thea's vines. The potion would give us just enough time to finish the spell.

I hoped.

"Stop them," Lilith commanded, her voice magnified by the Voice of Command.

But not for much longer.

Jamie, Apalla, and Thea jumped into action, their weapons rising to meet the charging demons as my friends protected me from the dark army. I couldn't fight and perform the spell—Raziel had made that extremely clear.

Water magic pulled Lilith's black blood off her body to swirl in a ball in my hand.

Sitting cross-legged on the damp, trampled cemetery grass, I returned my throwing knives to their pouch and withdrew my amulet athame.

Blood I take and blood I give,
Black blood taken, but ancient demon lives,
By this athame, pure blood drawn,
Bind this spell, no longer her reign to live on.

The blue crystal in the pommel of my dagger sparkled as I charged the amulet athame with the spell. Dragging the tip across the flesh in my palm, I released a hiss of pain. Too many nerve endings in the hand. Of course, breaking Lilith's spell would require pain. I had lost track of how many times Lucifer and Lilith caused me to slice open my palm.

The sounds of battle raged around me. Fire blasted, sunlight shined, and earth trembled, but the raging fight did not disrupt my focus—nothing could. Not even Lilith, as the Paralysis Potion wore off faster than it had with Lucifiana.

By immortal blood, she did conceive,
Unbreakable spell of command.
Her ancient spell will now sieve,
Broken by Light, hear my demand.

Lilith's torso writhed as she struggled to move her legs, to no avail. The potion was wearing off quicker than we anticipated.

Purple hellfire blasted from her palms, but Jamie met it with his white holy flames. Once I started the spell, I couldn't stop. Jamie had to protect the others from her hellfire.

With blood of old and blood of new,
I call about this concocted brew.

Water magic pulled my red blood off my palm and merged it with the black blood of my ancestor. The bloods mixed, and I gagged at the revolting sight.

Power from Heaven from above,
I call upon the power of the Dove.
Holy breath to speak this spell,
Holy flames to power it well.
Holy water to cleanse it pure,
Holy ground to make it mature.

The elements wrapped around me as I called upon each one with a line in the spell, forming my own personal circle like on Samhain. But this time, there was something more.... Spirit infused the elements, blessing each as holy, like Heaven itself wanted my demons free of their shackles.

Lilith's leg twitched, and overcoming the power of the potion, she stepped forward, dragging her other paralyzed leg behind her.

"Hayden," Jamie cried my name, but I couldn't lose focus. Not now, not when I was so close.

Authorities of Heaven and forces of Hell,
I ask you to hear this spell and listen well.
Ancient one claimed realms for her own,
And enslaved creation with her tone.

Lilith's other leg broke free as the Paralysis Potion completely wore off. But the spell... if I could just finish the spell.

But I have come to topple her throne,
For pain she caused, I will atone.
Nevermore shall subjects bow,
Without free will or choice allowed.

The mixture of our bloods expanded, stretching farther and wider than the amount of blood I collected possibly could have without the assistance of magic.

Hellfire rained on me. Jamie sheltered the girls with his body, calling holy flames to coat him like a cloak, but I remained unharmed by the evil fire.

With her black blood and my red veins,
I break her unholy chains.
Lilith's Voice of Command is nullified,
And in sacrifice, my Voice has died,
To void her powers, I pay the cost,
Millenia lost, but her spell is uncrossed.

Blood mixed with the holy manifestations of the elements, the power bottling and intensifying as I held it between my hands. It was like a bomb, ready to explode.

Roars sounded from demons, closer than before, as my friends sheltered themselves from Lilith's hellfire rain. But as my spell cast, the hellfire sank into my body, my fire magic protecting me like it was second nature.

Lilith stormed toward us, and Jamie rose to meet her, his broadsword flashing as Apalla fought demons with sunlight. But my spell...

By the power of Spirit within me and all things,
I power this spell with blood and power,
For this shall be its last ungodly hour.

As the last word passed my lips, black lightning flashed, and a great clap of thunder split the sky in two as I sealed the fate of demons everywhere on earth and below the earth.

The Voice of Command would be no more.

Not for me. Not for Leyla. Not for Lucifiana. Not for Lucifer. Not for Lilith.

It was gone, severed forever by the seal of our shared blood.

Then something happened inside me. Something I never felt before. It was like a pair of giant incorporeal scissors reached into my core—the center of my power—and snipped a string like the Fates cutting the cord of a mortal's lifeline. A string connecting me to the power of the Voice of Command. As it drifted away, the power diminished... the glow dimming as it sank out of reach, then faded altogether.

"NO." Lilith screamed an infernal scream unlike I had heard before. Gasping, she clawed at her chest where that severed cord had once stretched taut.

In a rage, Lilith ripped her hands away from her chest and summoned her magic. A ball of purple hellfire the size of a basketball hurtled at Jamie.

Leaping to my feet, I threw my body in front of him.

The hellfire absorbed into me, but the blow was jarring as I crashed into Jamie, and we smashed into the ground in a tangle of limbs.

"*You,*" she accused as I extracted myself from Jamie. Glaring daggers as she stalked toward me, Lilith curled her hands into fists at her sides, her chest heaving as she seethed with rage. "What did you do?"

Magic lifted me to my feet without me asking, and I stood tall with the power of the Salem Witch at my beck and call.

"You don't own them anymore, Lilith," I yelled, the power of the Salem Witch lacing my voice and magnifying it tenfold. "Demons—you have your freedom. Join me if you wish, otherwise... prepare to die."

"You can't save everyone, Hayden," Lilith said, repeating the words Lucifer had said to me mere hours ago. An evil glint in her purple snake eyes made my skin crawl, and nausea slammed into my gut so strongly, I nearly doubled over.

My heart dropped out of my body as I followed Lilith's line of sight to my friends behind me. She would kill each of them before she killed me. Go for the pain, not the kill. Wasn't that the way of demons?

Never again.

Lilith would not claim the life of any more of my friends.

"Thea," I shouted. "Gorgonize her!"

A beam of green light shot out of Thea's staff and slammed Lilith in the chest. The power of earth ripped through the Mother of Demons, rippling over her skin. As Thea's emerald magic surrounded Lilith, covering every inch of her skin, it left behind a scaly gray tinge as it transformed the Mother of Demons to stone.

"Way to put the hurt in the dirt, Thea."

Jamie groaned as Apalla rolled her eyes.

Pffft. Fire and air elementals just didn't understand earth.

Lilith's stony tomb wouldn't hold for long, but we needed it to last until I could remove the taint of dark magic and patch the hole in the wards.

"Sage, I need sage." I looked at Apalla frantically. She was the spell master. If anyone would have it, it was her.

"My emergency..." A nasty cough wracked Ethan's chest. "Kit." He patted the breast of his jacket, his hand shaking as he pulled out a travel-sized kit of potion ingredients.

Thank the Creator for healers.

As he passed me the potion kit, he sighed deeply, and his body went limp in Jamie's arms.

Pressing my lips together, I fought the tears that pricked the back of my eyes and released his hand, lowering it to the ground. Standing, I reclaimed my sword and turned to Thea, who maintained a magical green bubble of protection around us. Her powers would repel the demons until Lilith broke through her stony sarcophagus.

Yellow light flashed as a pale-faced Isleen spooked with a blood-covered Dani Sanchez. Without asking, I shot Spirit into her chest, the power sinking into her. She gasped, her spine arcing as Spirit regenerated her depleted magic reserves.

"Whoa," she exclaimed, her eyes wild with exhilaration. "That's what I call magic."

A slight smile flitted across my lips. "Form the circle."

Pulling the sage smudge stick out of Ethan's kit, I strode toward the opening in the wards and sent up a silent prayer to the Goddess that this would work. The sage stick was ridiculously small. Only two inches.

Red flames sparked at the end as Jamie used his fire magic to light the bundle. A light breeze blew on the sage, snuffing the flames so the smudge stick smoldered, releasing sweet smoke into the air. My magic wrapped around the smoke, air and fire mingling to spread the sage smoke and direct it to the dark magic holding the wards open with its claws.

The sweet smoke pressed against the darkness, the purifying properties of sage cleansing Lilith's dark magic little by little.

"Palla, now," I commanded, and she began the chant.

I call upon the element of air,
Here and now, I cast this spell,
Bind the wards and seal them well,
With breeze from Heaven to blow away Hell.

Air whipped into a cyclone blowing outside our circle and beyond Thea's green bubble to blow demons away. The magic of the first element seeped into the wards, and the air shimmered with sunlight as a patch formed over the gaping hole. The edges of the wards moved as the hole shrank, our sage and magic devouring Lilith's dark magic.

I call upon the element of fire,
Here and now, I cast this spell,
Bind the wards and seal them well,
With flames from Heaven to burn away Hell.

Fire ignited, warming the air to what must have been uncomfortable for any normal witch. But I relished the heat seeping into my bones. Sparks flew as Jamie's red flames spread through the circle and mingled with the air to repair the wards.

I call upon the element of water,
Here and now, I cast this spell,
Bind the wards and seal them well,
With rains from Heaven to wash away Hell.

A monsoon raged inside our circle, the power of water absorbing into the wards as the element added to the inherent magic that naturally made the wards self-repairing. Dani's powers, although weaker than the rest of my circle, fed off the powers of the rest—for a circle was always greater than the sum of its parts—and the water mixed with the elements, healing the wards with its natural affinity.

I call upon the element of earth,
Here and now, I cast this spell,
Bind the wards and seal them well,
With vines from Heaven to prune away Hell.

Emerald green magic billowed out of Thea. Vines slithered over my feet to extend past her bubble and wrap around demons and beat them to death against the earth.

Man, the Earth could be vengeful.

Colorful flowers bloomed to life, decorating the cemetery as her powers merged with the other elements. With the Heart of Earth's powers, the hole in the wards was nearly shut. All it needed was a little push.

I call upon the element of Spirit,
Here and now, I cast this spell,
Bind the wards and seal them well,
With Soul from Heaven to overpower Hell.

Unrelenting Spirit crackled as a black lightning bolt burst from my chest and joined the silver beams of light pouring from my palms. Together, the purity of Spirit's powers slammed into the wards, pouring their energy as the hole shrank and shrank and—

The wards snapped shut with a resounding, "BOOM!"

A blast of magic surged past us like a raging wind from a rocket taking off, but we stood unaffected. Demons were blown off their feet, clearing half the cemetery.

Except one.

The Mother of Demons clawed her torso free of its stone sarcophagus, purple hellfire burning in her black locks and in her immortal eyes.

Raising her hands into the air, she summoned a blob of dark purple magic that undulated and convulsed like a thick, inky substance as it expanded into the clouds above.

"Oh, crap," I cursed, sensing her magic.

A spark ignited her brutally dark magic.

Hellfire rained down on us.

Throwing up my hands, I drew the hellfire to my open palms, absorbing her devastating flames before they could sear my friends. Sucking the power into my body, I converted it into raw energy. Throwing my arms wide, I unleashed the energy with the roar of a lion.

A sonic wave of power arced out of me in a half circle, blasting into the demons not swept away from the blast of the wards.

Lilith threw her arms up, crossing them over her face as she slid backward, her stilettos pounding into the soft ground, rooting her in place.

The last of her stone prison chipped away with the power of the wards sealing, freeing her lower half from Thea's gorgonization.

A beam of dark purple light shot from Lilith's palms and slammed into Thea's magical bubble of protection, popping it like a balloon, so the green magic rained around us.

"Oops." Lilith fake gasped.

But it didn't matter. The bubble only would get in my way.

"Thea, break the earth," I shouted with a wink. "To the depths."

The child goddess stomped her foot against the ground like a line dancer winning a competition. The earth trembled, fractures splitting the surface. Cracks dove into the depths of the earth, the ground rumbling as the earth split into a gouge running the length of the cemetery. Demons fell into the void as the earth separated under their feet. Coffins protruded from the sides of the ravine, some shaking loose into the hole from the earthquake.

A wave of cool air enveloped us as the smell of stone and mildew and candle wax wafted from the gaping abyss.

Planting my feet, the heels of my beat-up combats digging into the dirt, I faced the mausoleum with my arms spread wide to the sides, fingers extended as my palms pointed at the fissures in the earth.

Closing my eyes, I tunneled inward toward the bright white light glowing in my gut and reached for the power of Spirit living deeper than the rest of my magic. The power of a soul that infused every fiber of my being—both my physical body and my ethereal soul of light.

Power from something greater than me filled my body to the brim until it was ready to burst from the overflowing light.

Unleashing my magic, I uttered the spell so unique, so powerful, it had only been used once before in all of history. Against the very enemy I faced now.

"QUINTESSENCE."

The word ripped from my throat, a powerful command that ricocheted through the air, the earth, the trees, and every living being around me. Black lightning shot into the gorge at my feet and into the sky above, illuminating the night and surrounding us in Spirit.

Magic rumbled below my feet, the power of the Spell of Salem infusing life into the dead.

A skeletal hand shot up from the ground.

Wiggling its fingers, an arm of bone emerged from the soil by the mausoleum. Connected to the arm was a skeleton that crawled from the chasm depths. Another arm protruded from the ground, writhing as the skeleton clawed itself from the earth. Then another. And another.

The stench of rot and mildew and incense filled the air like the musty air of a tomb.

Shock slapped the smug snarl from Lilith's face, replacing it with profound fear. Her face paled as her eyes darted around the cemetery, frantically searching for Death.

"Don't bother," I shouted. "Amara has no need to fight you."

Lilith's eyes widened at my casual use of Death's name.

"This is my fight," I shouted triumphantly, lifting my hands to shoulder height as black lightning crackled through my fingers. "Prepare to confront a Master of Death."

An army of skeletons rose to standing all at once.

Black lightning crackled through the air, charging every molecule with electricity and infusing every dead warrior as they brandished their weapons. Empty pits stared at me. The skeleton's jaws clacked open and shut, and bones cracked and popped as they awaited instruction.

"Warriors, attack!" I shouted, commanding my army of the dead.

As one, they charged against the enemy.

Black ash plumed in the air like a mushroom as my skeletal army hunted the demons fleeing from the petrifying sight of an undying army.

My shrewd gaze cut through the cemetery, scrutinizing the battlefield. The wards were at our backs. We could go outside, spook, and re-enter Asylum somewhere else, but Lilith's endless army would overwhelm us before we could get off a shot of magic. And we couldn't spook out of the cemetery thanks to Lilith's spell. Which meant we had to follow through with plan A—going *through* the cemetery to meet Kelsey outside the radius of Lilith's spell.

Five elements blasted a beam of energy through the army of demons. Black dust hovered in the air until a swipe of my hand blew it away on a wicked breeze. My skeletal army used the opportunity to push back the demons, fighting on either side of the path to clear it for our escape.

Grabbing Thea by the scruff of her dress, I threw her like a pitcher throws a softball. Green magic swirled around her as magic directed her trajectory. Apalla flew after her in a mini tornado of gold and pink magic.

When Apalla was at the opposite end of the cleared path, I wrapped a cyclone around the other four witches. Twisting my arm, I whipped them across the path toward Apalla and Thea, then sprinted after them, pumping my arms with my weapons in hand.

Gold and pink magic wrapped around the witches and lowered them to the ground as Thea blasted demons with beams of green magic from the emerald in her staff.

Elemental magic blasted out of me on its own, like Spirit was directing the elements to fight on my behalf as I raced toward my friends.

Flying past them, I clashed against the demons. Black lightning crackled with devastating ferocity, frying the demons that approached. But for each demon I blasted, another took its place, even with the closed wards ceasing the influx of demons. *That* was the sheer number of demons that had entered Asylum during my excursion to Hell.

And my witches had endured against this overwhelming dark army.

If Lucifer hadn't distracted me, if he hadn't attacked me with his demons and detoured me through the labyrinth, I would have been here sooner. I would have saved Kova and closed the wards sooner, and there would be fewer demons inside Asylum. Fewer deaths inside Asylum.

Stabbing Nightmare through the jugular of an agony demon, I spun to check on my circle slowly following me through the crowd of demons as we fought for our lives. But after I cleared the initial path, we barely moved.

I needed more witches, more warriors.

Dani and Isleen suspended Kova's limp body between them while Jamie hiked Ethan onto his back, holding him in place with one hand while his other wielded his broadsword. Apalla and Thea were free to use their magic unshackled, and Kelsey awaited us beyond the cemetery.

A trickle of magic leaked from me, connecting with Kova's essence to heal her while I directed the rest of my energy on fighting the demons bearing down on my circle.

Even with Dani's help, with two witches down, we were falling apart under the sheer number of demons. I couldn't spare the minutes it would take to use my water magic to fully heal Kova—if I even could. I wasn't exactly a skilled healer.

But Spirit was, and since I unlocked its full power, it inherently knew how to heal without my concentrated will directing it.

Steadily, I pumped the power of Spirit and a splash of water magic into Kova's body, letting Spirit guide the healing touch to mend Kova's wounds. I didn't hit her with a jolt of lightning for fear of how it would react to her being on the brink of death.

Kova was using the power of Spirit to kill herself continuously, so Lilith couldn't steal her free will. As a Nephilim, she would resurrect, but I wasn't sure how my Spirit magic would react with her temporarily dead immortal body.

Even with my healing magic steadily pumping into her, Kova remained unconscious. If she woke up, she wouldn't be in any condition to fight.

But I wasn't out of tricks yet.

"Thea, can you control the Terracotta Army?"

Her brow furrowed as she shot a beam of emerald light into a group of brimstone demons, incinerating them in a blink of an eye. "I awakened the clay warriors yesterday when the Spellery almost fell to Lilith's demonic army. Most were destroyed in battle. The remainder are guarding the Spellery."

Not good.... We were down another chess piece.... An entire army unusable. Or most of an army. But I was glad Thea protected the Asylumnites.

My secret advantages were running out, but at least the wards were sealed, and we had Kova back... sorta. I had to get her to the Spellery to heal her.

Fight back with your Spirit, Hayden, the loving voice of the Goddess whispered to me. Calm composure washed over me and renewed my faith in myself.

Summoning my power into another concentration shot, I jump in front of Thea and thrust my arms wide, releasing the five elements in a coordinated attack. Wind blasted the demons backward, white fire licked at their skin, water flooded the ground, black vines writhed in the soil to coil around demons, and black lightning bounced from one demon to the next. Elemental magic barreled through the demons, but it wasn't enough against the unending hoard of evil raging against us.

"Where is Death when you need her?" Apalla shouted as her bow twanged, shooting off a spelled arrow.

Emerald green foliage grew out of the earth at an alarming rate, twisting and squeezing around each demon it touched until the life drained from the evil beings. Golden sunlight filtered from Apalla's palms, blinding the demons charging toward us. Brilliant red flames burst to life as Jamie burned our enemies to crisps.

"Switzerland," I yelled back. "You know she can't take sides. Death comes for us all. But she's helping us as much as she can."

My eyes fell on Ethan's lifeless body draped over Jamie's shoulder. Helping by letting him cling to life long enough to give me the sage to cleanse the wards.

A light gasp sounded behind me, followed by a pain-filled moan.

Kova groaned as she struggled to lift her head. "Not all." She laughed, followed by a chest-wracking cough.

"What?"

"Death doesn't come for us all," she repeated with a weak grin. Blood dribbled down her chin as she coughed, and I directed the flow of water magic to heal her insides.

I snorted. "Glad to see torture hasn't dulled your sense of humor."

"Never." She scoffed, then hacked louder than a car horn, spitting more blood down her front for it to soak into blood-drenched rags that were once clothes.

Spinning, I slashed with Nightmare and released a burst of holy flames as we fought our way along the path.

"Hayden," Kova said my name again, her voice thick and raspy. I couldn't spare a glance back as I encountered five troll-like pit demons. "Hit the demons with Quintessence. But instead of pouring out Spirit, pull their life force into you."

"You're telling me to suck the literal life out of these demons? And that will work?"

"I have no idea," she admitted with a rattling cough. "But it's worth a shot, right?"

"Jamie, Thea, cover me."

Red and green magic extended toward me as I released my hold on the elements to summon Spirit to my hands, the black electricity crackling over my skin as the power built inside me.

My nerves sang, on fire like a sparking wire.

Ready to burst, I unleashed a thick bolt of black lightning from my chest. It rocketed forward, slamming into one demon, then the next, and the next, until my power touched every demon.

"Quintessence!" I screamed, pulling the magic toward me. Black lightning surged toward me, striking my chest harmlessly. As the lightning fed into me, orbs of energy absorbed into my skin, and I watched in awe as demon after demon fell with each orb that sank into my body.

Demons crumbled to dust, revealing an open lane for us to flee down with a stunned Kelsey standing beyond the perimeter of Lilith's spell on the cemetery. A circle of demons surrounded her, frozen in place.

On either side of the path, demons swarmed, repelled by my skeleton army. I threw black lightning outward, sending the energy I had gathered into the skeleton army.

Kelsey thrust her arms out, and her magic rippled across the clearing, slamming into the demons and forcing them to freeze. Her arms trembled from the exertion of mind controlling so many at once.

"Go," I shouted, pushing Thea forward. Jamie hurried after her, carrying Ethan on his back.

Isleen and Dani stumbled behind them, weighed down as they dragged a barely conscious Kova. Despite being awake, Kova's feet barely found purchase on the ground as she tried to help the witches carry her weight.

Ushering them to move, I guarded their backs and cut down frozen demons as they slowly regained control. Kelsey kneeled on a single leg, her entire body shaking with effort as she grappled to maintain control.

Pushing my friends harder, I shouted at them—as if it would make them run faster—as I cut down paralyzed demons.

A demon with full control rocketed toward us, leaping over its brethren in a frantic attempt to stop us. Leaping into the air, I twisted, spinning my longsword in an arc to slice the demon cleanly in half, turning it to ash.

Another charged toward me as I landed in a crouch. A tongue of holy flames incinerated the beast.

Demons quivered, their fingers and fangs twitching as they fought for freedom from Kelsey's mind control.

A battle cry roared out from the air witch as she struggled to contain the demons. Sweat streamed down her tomato-red face, and she had a single, quivering arm raised, but she held off most of the demons.

Some escaped her grasp and stormed toward us. My skeletal army engaged the enemy, preventing them from touching my circle as they sprinted down the gravel path.

Stumbling outside the perimeter of the Anti-Spooking Spell, Jamie spun in place to face me, waiting for me to get to the other side. Sheathing his sword, he summoned white flames to his hands, then launched them at the frozen demons.

Kelsey dropped like a sack of potatoes, her magic faltering.

Demons surged toward us like a tidal wave.

Summoning a gust of wind, I rammed it into Isleen and Dani's backs, lifting them off the ground and tossing them through the air.

"Apalla, go!" I shouted.

Dropping her hands and ceasing the beams of sunlight, she sprinted. Wind raged around her, and I added my magic to hers to launch her after Isleen, Dani, and Kova. Apalla reached for the women, her fingers splayed as she stretched toward Kova's ankle.

Her hand wrapped around Kova, and they disappeared in a flash of pale yellow light.

Sprinting after them, I grabbed Thea by the scruff of her shirt and hauled her alongside me, her feet barely scraping the ground as she shot off green magic.

"When we cross the wards, grab Kelsey and spook," I told her. "Spook as many of the skeleton warriors as you can. The Spellery. Go!"

Spinning in a circle, I released Thea's shirt, throwing her with my bare hands the way a shot-put thrower throws that heavy metal ball.

Sailing through the air, Thea surrounded herself with green magic and dropped next to Kelsey.

Emerald green light flashed like a light show as Thea disappeared with Kelsey and my entire army of the dead.

Demons flew at me, unrestrained by magic or undead warriors. Claws clawed, fangs gnashed, and fire burned as Lilith's demonic army stampeded toward me.

"Hayden!" Jamie screamed my name, terror rattling his voice as demons attacked.

But the power of the elements protected their master, and Nightmare seemed to fight with its own mind as I sprinted for the edge of the cemetery. Not much farther.

"Jamie!"

I lunged for him, the power of the elements propelling me across the Anti-Spooking Spell boundary. Frantically, I threw myself at Jamie and Ethan, nearly toppling the three of us from the force of my momentum.

"No!" a screech rang out from the center of the cemetery, Lilith's shriek high and desperate.

Red light enveloped me, and nausea tugged at my gut as my body was sucked into a tube, and I was thrown through time and space. My blood-stained combats slammed into the mud-covered floor of the Spellery's entrance hall.

The Spellery was in chaos.

Kelsey collapsed, her hand slipping from Thea's to catch her face before it smashed into the ground.

Jamie sank to his knees, tears spilling down his cheeks as Ethan slipped off his back and hit the floor with a thump.

Sheathing Nightmare, I whirled in a circle in search of every face that went into the cemetery with me. I breathed a sigh of relief when I ensured everyone was...

Vomit surged up my throat at the sight of Ethan's prone body, but I forced myself to swallow the bile.

"Healer! Healer! We need a medic over here!" Apalla screamed, running toward a ward of healers.

Witches rushed past her, but a couple acknowledged her and ran off in various directions. Despite the exhaustion in her hazel eyes, Apalla sprinted into the room, followed by a team of healers with a stretcher.

A haggard-looking Isleen and Dani carefully transferred Kova to the stretcher, groans sounding from all three women.

Spirit shot from my hands, my black lightning infusing power and life force into the healers, who desperately needed the power I had to give.

"We need holy water!"

A teen witch—the one who provided me with Lilith's location—hurried forward with a waterskin. Snatching the skin from him, I pulled the holy water out using my magic and dispensed some to the healers.

Willing the water to coat my hands like gloves, I placed both palms on Kova's chest and released the power in my gut. Silver light illuminated the water as it slowly roamed Kova's body, healing cuts and scratches.

With a sigh, Kova sank into the stretcher and passed out. I held the healing magic until the last drop of holy water sank into her skin. Nodding, I motioned for the healer to work his magic, and his assistants rushed Kova's stretcher from the room.

Apalla sank to her knees, sighing in relief. Except for minor injuries, my Prophetess and her mother were unharmed. But I shot another bolt of life-giving Spirit into them, rejuvenating their depleted magic. Again.

And I would do it more before this war was over.

Thea swayed on her feet, her eyes dimmer than before. I shot a bolt into her, the power of Spirit mixing with the Heart of Earth in an explosion of green and black that swirled around her. Thea's spine straightened, and she gasped in a breath as the sparkle returned to her eyes.

Witches rushed every which way, all of them splattered or coated in blood. Most carried Knights or injured witches, hauling the wounded soldiers toward the healers. But it was becoming more and more difficult to cross the massive hall as a layer of blood and grime covered the floor.

With a flick of my wrist, I evaporated the blood and cleared the floor, causing every eye to turn toward me as a momentary silence blanketed the hall.

Raising an eyebrow, I asked, "Does someone want to tell me what's going on?"

"What's going on?" A young male witch scoffed at me. "What do you think is going on? We're under siege by demons."

One of my favorite people cuffed the young man on the head. "She knows that. She's the Salem Witch." Dramatically rolling his eyes, Damien turned toward me with an exhausted smile.

Spotting his sister, he rushed at her, and Dani threw herself into his arms. Holding each other, the siblings silently wept, thankful the other had survived this long.

Pulling apart, Dani stood silently at Damien's side and wiped her eyes as she glanced at Ethan.

"To answer your question, she suddenly doubled her forces. She must have ripped the wards open in other places when she found out you were back."

"No wonder she seemed weaker than I expected," I muttered.

Her elemental powers weren't as strong as Kova's, which made sense now that I knew she opened other holes. But those must have closed when we cleansed and sealed the main hole.

"Demons are attacking from all directions. Some of us were able to retreat..."

"What is it?" When he didn't answer, I grabbed him by his shoulders and shook him. "What is it, Damien?"

"Half of Asylum is still out there, most of them surrounded by demons and unable to get back to the Spellery. They're fighting to stay alive."

My face blanched as the blood drained from it.

"It gets worse," he warned. "Elliot's leading the charge, and he's... he's different." Damien shuddered in horror. "More powerful."

My expression darkened. "I know. That's because he's no longer a witch, but has descended to one of the Seven Deadly Sins, a Prince of Hell."

CHAPTER TWELVE

THE SIEGE

A mix of shocked and appalled expressions stared back at me.

"How?" Isleen demanded.

Shaking my head, my black hair flying, I said, "Believe me, you don't want to know." I inclined my head at the room, silently conveying it was not something for civilians to hear, least of all teenagers—my classmates. I didn't want to mention Elliot's new status as a Prince of Hell. News like that... it could make them lose hope, and hopelessness decided the victor of the war.

"Jamie." His head snapped up, his eyes finding mine. "Jamie," I spoke softly this time. "Please, I need you."

With a sniffle, he wiped his eyes before carefully transferring Ethan from his lap to the ground. Silas and a healer rushed forward to tend to the body.

"I'm with you." He nodded at me. "What do you need?"

"Kelsey, status?"

Bleary-eyed and green-faced, Kelsey struggled to lift her head from where she laid spread-eagle on the ground.

A zap of lightning jolted into her, resupplying her with the magic lost in mind controlling an *entire army of demons*. A year ago, she couldn't control one, let alone an entire army. Our training sessions had paid off.

"Jamie, take Kelsey and Apalla to the top of the Divination Tower. Kelsey, you're my guide from the eagle's nest. Jamie and I are going out to fight with our feet on the ground, but I need someone to direct us where to go. When we're done torching demons in an area, send us to the next place. We'll take care of the rest. Apalla—cover Kelsey. Don't let any demons get to her, especially the aerial beasts. Take out as many as you can from the sky with your light and arrows. Jamie—give her a brazier of holy flames.

"Thea, Isleen—take the front of the Spellery. As Jamie and I take out demons, we'll send witches back to you. Don't leave the immediate vicinity of the school. We can't lose the Spellery, so I need the two of you to manage our defenses. There's a lot of open ground between the castle and everything surrounding us, so only deploy soldiers if it will save those fleeing toward the Spellery. Move out," I commanded like a war general, because I was.... I was the Commander-in-Chief of this war. *My* war. And I had to save my people.

Jamie took Apalla and Kelsey each by the hand and disappeared in a flash of red. Thea exited the front doors while Isleen waved down some Knights, corralling them to defend the front of the school.

"Hayden, what about the rest of us?" Damien asked.

I smirked wickedly. "Oh, Damien, I'm so glad you asked."

"Uh oh, I know that look. I do not like that—"

Black lightning and white light expanded from my hands. Spirit exploded in a display of light—white, silver, and black magic dancing around the room to pour into the mortals in the room, rejuvenating and filling their souls with energy as Spirit replenished their magic stores. Spirit was the ultimate healer and the source of life. With a flash of light, Spirit receded into my hands and left the witches looking refreshed and alive.

The room burst to life, drawing excited gasps as I refilled the energy missing from my mortal warriors and witches.

"Keep doing what you've been doing," I said, my silver wand pressed to my throat to amplify my voice. "Defend the Spellery, but don't leave the castle. I'm bringing everyone home," I said with a vicious ferocity.

A war cry rang throughout the room, echoing off the walls as Knights thrust their weapons in the air and chanted my name.

"Damien." Isleen rushed to us after having sent Knights outside to help Thea. "Where is the rest of the Council?"

Looking at my friend, I caught his strained expression as his chest visibly sank and his shoulder hunched as the joy deflated from his body.

"Oh no."

"Naida is still protecting Zola."

"You must be joking? After she betrayed us—"

"That was my call," Isleen cut in, waving me off. At the furious look on my face, she explained, "You weren't here, and I didn't have enough hands. She wanted to help, so I made her take a blood oath. If she betrays us, she dies."

I sighed and rolled my eyes. "I don't love it, but we don't have time to argue. What about the others?"

"Kane is dead, and Dante has been unconscious in the infirmary for at least half a day."

My heart plummeted into my stomach.

Not Kane... Not the mountain of a man with the greatsword longer than I was tall. Kane had always seemed larger than life, infallible. A savage fighter, he should have been the last to fall. He had taught... he had taught me so much.

"Kane is dead?" Jamie suddenly asked from beside me, his voice cracking. "You can't mean... no."

Jamie's knees buckled underneath him, and I caught him. His arms wrapped around my waist in response, but he couldn't hide the tremble of his body.

"I'm sorry," I whispered to him.

He buried his face in the crevice of my shoulder, and I drove a hand into his golden hair, holding him close to my heart. Kane mentored Jamie as much as he trained me. Probably more since Jamie had lived in Asylum his entire life. First my dad, then Kane.... How many more generals could we lose?

"With Kane gone, who is in charge of the Knights?"

"That would be me," I answered loudly, but nobody looked surprised by my declaration. Holding Jamie's head to my heart, I pressed the tip of my silver wand to my throat to magnify my voice. "Listen up, everyone. Damien is in charge of the Spellery while Isleen and I are out on mission."

Adult witches glanced at him uncertainly and others looked alarmed that I placed someone so young in charge, but I trusted Damien. I didn't know the other witches, and without the Council, there weren't any adults capable of running Asylum.

"Me? But Hayden—"

"I need someone who can stay calm in the face of chaos."

Damien smiled deviously as he pushed his glasses up his nose. "Girl, have you met me? I am chaos."

"Exactly." I grinned conspiratorially. "And that's how I know you'll keep this under control while I get our people back."

Collecting himself, Jamie righted himself and stepped away from me. We shared a look, communicating without words.

"Guard the Spellery. Stick to the perimeter. No witch goes out alone, and no group goes out too far. No unnecessary risks. I want every witch to return in one piece. Our mission is to recover our people, not lose more."

Witches scattered like I dropped a bomb, hurrying off to perform their duties or to rush into battle.

Damien pulled me into a quick hug, urging me to be safe. Dani threw herself at me, only releasing me after I squeezed her back. Together, the siblings rushed off to manage the Spellery.

"You don't have to do this alone," Jamie whispered in my ear, his warm chest pressing into my back as his hands gripped my biceps. "You're taking on too much. You can't be everywhere at once."

Twisting in his arms, I gazed into the royal blue eyes I loved so much, their warmth a stark contrast to the mirage Lucifer had donned.

"It's not too much. I haven't been fighting for three days straight. And even if I had been, I wouldn't lack for power. Spirit regenerates itself. It is life giving as much as it can steal life."

"It's not your power that I'm worried about. I'm worried about you worrying about everyone else when you should be worrying about your Trial."

"I'm not worried about my Trial. I'm worried about keeping my people alive through this war."

"And what about your life? What about fighting Lilith?"

My flat palms landed on his chest, and I leaned into him, brushing my lips over his. As I pulled away, Jamie's arms wrapped around my waist, and I sensed he wanted to pull me back in.

But I whispered, "Then we fight. Together." Snapping my piercing blue eyes to look into his, I added ferociously, "Let's go kick some demon butt."

Red light flashed, and we materialized atop the Divination Tower, next to Kelsey and Apalla, who had her bow in hand, shooting arrows in rapid fire.

Kelsey's pale face betrayed how bad things were. That, and the hellfire burning untamed through the town.

Stepping to the edge of the observation deck, I held my hands wide. I inhaled deeply, letting my magical range expand as my breath stretched my lungs, then I grabbed hold of the devastating hellfire and sucked it toward me. Hellfire of every color—different colors for the different types of demons that summoned it—soared into the air, pulling away from whatever surface it raged over to heed my call and absorb into my open palms. Smoke clogged the air above the town, but at least it wasn't burning. Yet. Demons would set more fires.

"Where's the damage?"

"Everywhere," Kelsey grunted as I felt her mind control magic stretch over the town. Apalla nodded her agreement. "Hit the cathedral first. Demons swarming twenty witches. They're surrounded and about to succumb."

Jamie took my hand, and the observation deck disappeared. My black combat boots slammed into the ground behind a swarm of demons surrounding the cathedral. Sounds of battle floated to me from beyond the demons as witches fought vehemently for their lives.

Jamie and I unsheathed our swords, letting the metal grate to alert the demons to our presence. The last row of demons turned on us. And we plunged into the chaos. Black blood drenched my clothing as more and more grime coated my body with every kill.

There must have been two hundred demons against twenty witches. Twenty witches with barely any magic left from the look of their weak elemental attacks.

"Jamie, get inside and spook them out. As many as you can. Then come back for more."

"What about—"

"Go!" I would be fine. I was the warrior witch, and once the witches were clear, I could unleash the full power of Spirit and obliterate these demons.

A black streak soared past me, ripping into the assembled demons. Black blood splattered as a prowling black panther appeared before me, casually licking the blood off his paw.

"Need a hand?" Jackal drawled as Buddy teleported to his side.

"I was wondering when you two would show up." I smirked before cutting into the demons with my loyal demons by my side.

Red flames burst out of Jamie from inside the circle of demons as he fended them off, then spooked again in a flash of red, disappearing with a group of witches.

"Buddy, Jackal, teleport me inside the circle."

Buddy bounded over, then pushed his face under my arm. Faster than spooking, we appeared inside the circle of demons.

White flames shot out of me in an arc, accompanied by black lightning. Air whistled and earth trembled. Rain poured in torrents at my command until the entire demon army was hacked into piles of dust, leaving a group of ragged, tired Knights behind my protective wall of elements.

Jamie spooked back, nodded to me, then spooked another group to the Spellery. As he disappeared, I called upon Spirit and shot it into the Knights still with me, refreshing their powers.

A group of witches are cornered on the north side of the river. Demons set fire to the bridge, so the witches can't cross and they're overwhelmed.

Jamie's hand wrapped around mine without me asking. Red light filled my vision, and my combats slammed into the cobblestone street on the south side of the river. The bridge connecting north and south was alight with blue hellfire.

My eyes flashed with power as I pulled the hellfire toward me. But instead of absorbing the fire and converting the raw energy into holy flames, I did it midair.

Blue flames flickered into white, and a squall of air caught the heavenly fire, spraying it outward in an arc over the heads of the witches caught between the river and a sea of demons.

Jackal and Buddy teleported next to me, a low growl reverberating off their lips.

Jamie sprinted across the bridge, diving headfirst into the throng of witches to fight while our troops retreated.

Witches clung to the cliff edge above the raging river below, their fingertips barely clinging to the cliff edge as feet stepped on their hands in a frantic attempt to not fall under the pressure of the attacking demons.

Earth magic shot from my fingers into the dirt at my feet. Blocks of stone ten feet wide shot across the river, forming a bridge of earth. Air swirled around the witches dangling over the river, and I lifted them to ground level.

"Jackal, Buddy." I pointed a finger at the Spellery. "Get my other demons and clear a path for the witches. Find me when they're safe at the Spellery."

With a graceful bow, the hellhound and panther shot up the hill in a blur of black, blending with the dark surroundings, and I prowled into the rising wave of demons.

Air blasted in front of me, followed by tongues of holy flames. Javelins of ice speared out of the river below, and I summoned a wave of water from the river. Earth rumbled as vines tore through the soil to pierce the soft underbellies of demons.

With a wild grin and exhilaration in my penetrating blue eyes, I charged as a lone warrior against impossible odds, dusting demons in droves until their forces dwindled to a pathetically small bunch that I pulverized with a blast of silver holy hellfire.

My eyes tracked the fleeing witches, searching for the blond-haired fire elemental escorting them to the Spellery. On the hill with Jackal, Jamie battled half a dozen demons single-handedly.

Tightening my grip on Nightmare, I made to join him in defending the witches until we could head to the next destination.

But before I could take a step, a guttural roar tore through the air, and Spirit prickled the hair on the back of my neck until I turned to face my newest opponent.

A taurean demon—basically a demonic bull with brutal horns, but this wasn't a rodeo and there weren't any cowboys to rope and ride this bull that rivaled the size of a pickup truck.

"Come and get it, Beef Boy," I snarled under my breath as I slipped into my stance, the motion as natural as breathing.

With a wild snort and a shake of its head, the taurean scraped its hoof against the cobblestone street, then repeated the motion as it lowered its gleaming black horns.

Its nostrils quivered as it snorted out a breath of hellfire and charged. The taurean beast was magnificent in a "I'm-going-to-gut-you-kind-of-way" as the green hellfire reflected off its polished horns. Dude had no idea who he was charging at.

Side-stepping in a single fluid motion, I sliced Nightmare through the air, the movement of the black blade imperceptible against the darkness.

"Moo?" the taurean grunted as it stormed past me and skidded to a halt in a cloud of dust. Its right horn clattered to the ground, severed from the bull's head. "MOOOO," he roared, swaying from his unbalanced horns as he turned in a wobbly circle to charge me.

He never got the chance.

My fist collided with his snout in a left hook. The force of my hit coupled with the unevenly distributed weight of his head sent the bull crashing to the ground, and before the cloud of dust could kick up around the taurean demon's body, I stabbed Nightmare into its black heart.

Taurean dust coated the cobblestone street.

Maybe I should get a cowgirl hat?

An image of Jamie wearing a white velvet cowboy hat popped into my mind, and I drooled a little. I definitely knew what I was getting him for his belated eighteenth birthday present.

Ugh. Focus, Hayden. War time was not boy time.

Black Cauldron, now, Kelsey shouted in our heads.

Jamie appeared next to me, and I lunged for his hand. I had barely made skin contact when he spooked.

Witches took shelter inside, and now they're trapped.

By demons and hellfire.

Jackal, Buddy, and Hyde—another one of my morphers in the form of a hawk—appeared next to me and surveyed the scene in a heartbeat. My loyal demons led their brethren in a charge against their own kind, tearing into the dark demons without mercy.

Like with the bridge, I summoned the hellfire and converted it into white flames to blast against enemy demons.

But holy...

The Black Cauldron's exterior was burnt to a crisp, and a swarm of demons crowded around it with barely enough room to breathe. Countless demons.... The witches would never escape on their own.

A twist of my wrist sent a squall of air blowing over the heads of the demons and into the gaping holes of the burnt wreckage, filtering clean air to the suffocating witches.

Maintaining a constant current of smoke-free air, I gestured to Jamie. "Spook them out. I'll handle the rest."

Red light flashed and smoke stung my nostrils as he disappeared into the wreckage.

Nightmare swished through the air as I spun it in a circle as a warning. Shouting commands to my other loyal demons, I flew against the enemy—an unbreakable force of magic and mayhem.

A whirlwind of elements and blades, I ripped through hundreds of demons with frightening speed—as fast as the lightning I wielded. Dust coated my hair as I passed through a cloud of ash so I could cut down the next demon. And the next and the next and the next.

Jamie appeared next to me in a flash of light, not missing a beat as he kicked the brimstone demon swiping its impish little claws at my thigh.

With a feminine squeal, it tumbled heels over head through the air until it impaled on an agony demon's spikes.

"Dude, wicked."

Jamie smirked. "That's not even what I was going for."

"Either way—he's dusted, Angel Boy."

In perfect synchronicity, Angel Boy and I danced into the crowd of demons, sashaying and slaying in harmony with fluid strokes of the sword as we fought like master swordsmen. And I imagined the fear we must have struck into the hearts of our enemies.

But their fear wouldn't last long as we obliterated the mass of demons, unhindered as Spirit renewed my powers endlessly, and I shared the benefits with Angel Boy.

Get to Capitol Hill, Kelsey's voice floated through my mind. *Massive demon blockage slowing the retreat.*

As I killed the last demon at the Black Cauldron, Jamie took my hand, spiriting us to the Parthenon. We jumped into battle, cutting and slicing, twisting and spinning, dodging and lunging until every demon was dead and every witch had fled to the safety of the Spellery's castle walls.

Kelsey told us the next location, then the next. And the next. We must have hit twenty more spots before Kelsey finally called for us to return.

That should be the last of it. Isleen has eyes on the last group heading back to—What? Thea, no!

Alarm rang through my body as my frantic eyes met Jamie's. Spirit whispered the answer before Kelsey screamed a single word in my mind.

ELLIOT.

Jamie lunged for my hand and spooked us to the front of the Spellery doors. Weaponless and wandless, Isleen sheltered Thea's body with hers as a curved blade swung at her.

I lunged forward, swinging my sword at Elliot's arm. The blade cut clean through his elbow, spurting black blood as he bellowed in pain. I couldn't kill Elliot because of my Bargain with the Devil, but I was allowed to wound him within reason. And chopping off the arm he used to stab Isleen with seemed reasonable to me.

I thrust Nightmare into his abdomen, letting the black blade sink up to the hilt. Blood flew from his mouth, splattering my face, but I didn't care.

"Too late," he cackled, black blood staining his teeth.

"Hayden, kill him," Jamie shouted at me.

But I couldn't. I hadn't told Jamie about my adventures in Hell yet, and I wasn't about to tell Elliot about the Devil's Bargain.

The Devil made me promise not to kill him, but Elliot was a Prince of Hell now... a full-blooded demon and one of the Sins. He couldn't die by ordinary means, which meant...

"I have a better idea," I growled, then grinned viciously at Elliot, baring my teeth.

Yanking the sword from his gut, I let him fall to his knees. Sheathing the blade, I wrapped a hand around his throat and lifted him off the ground until his legs dangled beneath him. Silently, I extended my free hand to Jamie.

Wordlessly, he took it and enveloped us in red light, so we appeared outside the perimeter of the cemetery. Spinning in a circle, I whipped Elliot through the air like a discus thrower, launching him with magical precision, so he flew through the air until his back slammed into the top of the mausoleum, mere inches from Lilith's head.

Lilith sat up in alarm.

"Just returning your pet." I glowered at her.

Jamie seized my hand, and we disappeared, returning to the Spellery.

Thea cradled Isleen's head in her lap, tears dripping soundlessly off the child goddess's cheeks, her ebony skin a stark contrast to Isleen's ashen face.

My throat went dry, and I had to croak out my next words, "Jamie, get Apalla."

He disappeared and returned with my best friend. Apalla's hazel eyes landed on me first, filled with worry. I opened my mouth to speak, but my voice failed. All I could do was shake my head and point at her mother's lifeless body.

"Mom?" Apalla whispered, her hazel eyes widening in disbelief. She took a wobbly step forward. "Mom?" She called again, her voice cracking as tears filled her eyes. "Mommy?" She whimpered. "No. Mom!"

She rushed forward, falling to her knees beside Isleen's body. Wrapping her arms around her mom, Apalla pulled her body to her chest. "Mom, please wake up. Mom. Mommy, please." She sobbed. "Please, open your eyes. I never ask you for anything but this one thing. Mom, I need you to wake up."

Apalla shook Isleen, screaming in her mom's face as tears streamed down her cheeks in uncontrollable rivers.

"Mom!" she screamed, and my heart shattered as hot tears poured from my eyes.

Numbly, I sank to my knees beside my best friend and wrapped my arm around her shoulders. In the background, Damien shouted at people, ordering them into the castle to give us privacy.

I didn't know how much time passed, but the cold seeping into my bones suggested it had been a while, but that may have been from despair.

"Hayden," Jamie touched me lightly on the shoulder. "We should bring her in."

"Okay," Apalla said weakly. "Let's... let's bring her inside. She'll be warmer in the castle."

"Apalla," I spoke her name gently.

"I know she's dead, Hayden." She turned to me with puffy red eyes filled with unimaginable grief, tears flowing in rivers. "But let me do what... what I need to do to get through this."

With a nod, I wiped the tears from my face and willed my water magic to stop my water works. I needed to be alert to lead Asylum in a war that had suffered too many casualties already. Taking Jamie's hand, I clamored to my feet, and we made to pick up Isleen's body, but Apalla waved us off.

"I want to... need to do this by myself."

Nodding, I accepted Jamie's hand and stepped away. Thea pressed into my side and wrapped her tiny arms around my stomach. Burying her head in my leather jacket, she sobbed. Jamie wrapped an arm around my shoulders, his mere touch bringing warmth to my cold and numb body. His natural smoky scent stung my nostrils in a familiar, comforting way as we watched Apalla lift her mother's fallen body and carry her inside the castle we had grown up in.

"We should go inside, too." Jamie tugged on my hand, guiding me and Thea toward the doors.

As I took the first numb step, a cruel laugh pierced the air, rooting me in place. She wasn't nearby, otherwise Spirit would sense her. But her voice echoed around us, as though it came from the sky.

"Hayden Black," she snarled my name with contempt. "You cower and hide amongst your tiny witches and those traitorous demons, too afraid to face me yourself. You, the Salem Witch—the most powerful mortal in the world—only dare face the Dark Demons when you are surrounded by pathetic weaklings that you use as human shields. You claim the Creator is omnipotent and Its power flows through you, but all I see is treachery and cowardice.

"Enough. Enough of your fleeing and hiding. It is time you face me alone. Just you and me. The battle that was always meant to be. I will wait for you outside the cathedral. You have until midnight, or I will unleash the full wrath of Hell on Asylum, and every man, woman, and child will die at my hand... because of you. The choice is yours, Granddaughter."

CHAPTER THIRTEEN

THE LAST STAND

"Hayden, you can't possibly plan on fighting her," Jamie growled, his hands balled into fists as he shook with barely contained emotion.

Glowering darkly at him, I didn't move from where I leaned against the wall of the student lounge in the Spellery. Most of the witches were either in the infirmary, training hall, or collapsed on a cot in a random room.

My demons, freed at last from Lilith's Voice of Command, patrolled the Spellery's perimeter, but based on their reports, it didn't seem they were necessary. Lilith's demons had pulled back. Not a single dark entity had been spotted within sight of the Spellery. Unless you stood on top of the Divination Tower and looked to the southwest—then you'd see the cathedral overrun with demons.

It was unholy in the greatest sense of the word. Lilith knew it would infuriate me and offended the Creator, which is why she chose the cathedral as our final battleground. But it was the cathedral of the Creator, whose Spirit resided in me. Not her.

"Jamie." I sighed, pinching the bridge of my nose. "We've been through this. I have to face Lilith—"

"Not on your own," he exploded, throwing his hands in the air as red fire ignited in his grime-coasted golden locks. His royal blue eyes simmered with rage.

"Anyone wanna help me out here?" I pleaded with the rest of the room, but my circle avoided my gaze. Rolling my eyes, I huffed out a "fine."

"Look," Kelsey finally chimed in. "I'm not saying Hayden's idea is good. Because realistically, it sucks. Like really bad. Entirely blows."

"Thanks for the vote of confidence, Kelsey," I grumbled, rolling my eyes as I crossed my arms over my chest.

"I'm not finished." Kelsey said calmly. It never failed to amaze me when she was the voice of reason. "But it is the only plan we have with an hour until midnight. We don't have much choice but to let Hayden fight her."

"You want Hayden to fight Lilith when she isn't a master of Spirit?" Jamie rounded on her.

"I'm the last person to agree with Kelsey on anything, but what difference will an hour make?" Apalla asked quietly, her face strained as she glanced apologetically at me. "No offense, but if you haven't mastered Spirit yet, then what could you possibly do in the next hour that will change that?"

"Seriously, Apalla?" Jamie accused.

"Back off, Angel Boy, she's right," I snapped, then sighed and scrubbed my face with my hands, which probably rubbed more black blood and dust on my face. "None of my Trials were brought on intentionally. Each one started in the middle of a major throw down."

"You think your Trial will start while you're fighting Lilith," Thea said calmly. It wasn't a question.

"I have no idea, but it's my best shot, because either way..."

"Because either way, you die," a familiar voice finished for me.

My neck cracked as I whipped my head up. The room turned to stare at the woman standing in the entrance to the lounge.

Leaning against the wooden door frame was the familiar fiery red hair and hunter green eyes belonging to my mentor. Even bandaged, Kova had a sharp and strong appearance, like she was bigger than life. And in some ways, she was.

"Kova," I breathed her name and rushed her. Grabbing her roughly by the shoulder, I pulled her into a bear hug.

"Oof," she grunted from the force of my hug, but returned my embrace with equal fervor. "Hey, now," she exclaimed, pulling back from me. "When did you get so tall?"

I snorted. "I'm still two inches shorter than you, Kova."

"Considering I'm the Nephilim and your mother is short, I'm a little upset you've caught up to me."

Maybe it was because she stood barefooted on the wooden floor, and my combats gave me extra height, or because she hunched slightly from her injuries. Or maybe it was the power of Spirit alive within me, but I seemed as tall as Kova.

I grinned maniacally and lightly punched her on the shoulder. "Maybe you shouldn't have gotten yourself captured, then I wouldn't have caught up."

She grinned back, her parched lips bleeding. Only two Salem Witches could joke about such morbid things.

"Now," she said, her tone growing serious as she sobered to the reality of our situation. "What is your plan to face Lilith?"

"That's it."

She blinked at me. "What?"

Jamie threw his hands in the air in exasperation. "Finally, someone who is on my team. Thank you, Kova."

"Oh no, Jamie. I'm sorry, but I agree with Hayden. She has to fight Lilith, but she needs a better plan than simply to *fight Lilith*."

"What?" I scoffed. "Like you have a better plan?"

She opened her mouth to respond, then snapped it shut and grumbled, "Fair enough, kid."

I sighed. "Guys, I appreciate your concern. I really do."

"But?" Kova raised an eyebrow at me.

"But I can beat Lilith," I insisted. "I've done it before with less magic than I have now. I can beat her again," I said with unwavering conviction.

"You what?" Kova's mouth hung open, her hunter green eyes wide. "You beat her?"

"You were already taken," I explained, my voice gentle. "On Lilith's Island, after she beat you, I faced her."

"But how?" Kova asked. "You were out of magic. Hunter... he... he..."

"He died," I whispered, and a strangled gasp left Kova.

Pressing a hand to her mouth, she lowered her head to stare at the floor, drops of water plopping onto the floor below.

"I... I felt his soul leave this plane... when I was captured, I spent time on the other side of the veil, and he was in the Garden... but I had hoped... I had hoped I had imagined it."

In every lifetime, he passed away, but it never got easier for Kova. If anything, it seemed to be more anguish each time.

"I killed Cain."

Her head snapped up, her mouth ajar.

"And then I faced Lilith. Without Nightmare, without magic, without anyone, and *I won,* Kova. I won." My piercing blue eyes bored into hers.

"Then why is she..."

"Why is she still alive?" I snorted, then laughed humorlessly. "Because I couldn't bring myself to kill her."

It was absurd. I couldn't kill the demoness who had taken the lives of so many of my friends and comrades. I should hate her. I should want to end her.

But I couldn't do it.

Kova stared at me, the expression on her face saying, "are you kidding me? You can't kill the Mother of Demons? What is wrong with you?"

Before she could speak, Apalla asked, "You can beat Lilith even though she's supercharged by channeling the power of the Mother through Leyla?"

"Yes," I said unflinchingly.

"I'd feel a lot better if Lilith didn't have the power of the Mother," Jamie grumbled, crossing his arms over his chest.

"If we can free Leyla, it would give Hayden the upper hand."

"So, let's free her." Kova made it sound so simple.

"Only a master of Spirit can free her."

Kova pointed to herself, but I was already shaking my head.

"A master related to her by blood."

"Well, crap." Kova sounded like me.

The room fell into solemn silence.

"So, you see the ultimatum here. I can't beat Lilith until I free Mom, but I can't free Leyla until I become a master of Spirit, which I can't do until my Trial starts."

"But Hayden, if you fight her but refuse to kill her, she will eventually win and while you have the blessing of free will from the Goddess, Thea does not," Apalla said, always the voice of reason. "Lilith will imprison her, like she did to Leyla."

"And she will finally obtain the Power of Three and transcend into an unbelievable power," Jamie shouted, flapping his arms wildly in the air.

"And if I don't, I die, and Thea definitely becomes the Maiden." I didn't dare look at Thea as I said the last part, maintaining the ruse that I had the free will blessing. No one knew I had transferred it to Thea last year... and it was my final ace. The only card that would stop Lilith if I couldn't bring myself to kill her.

"I don't have to win right away," I argued. "If I'm right, my Trial will start while I fight. Then I can pass it and free Mom."

Kova didn't hide her doubtful expression. "And if your Trial doesn't start before midnight?"

"Then it's no different than if I don't face Lilith, but I have to try."

"And if you can't kill Lilith?" Apalla squeaked.

"I'll burn that bridge when I cross it," I said, eliciting groans from the room.

"That's not even the saying," someone muttered under their breath.

"I like my version better." I shrugged.

Kova sighed, letting her head fall. Shaking her head, her hunter green gaze snapped to mine. "Okay."

"Okay?" Jamie echoed in disbelief as he uncrossed his arms. "Okay? You're going to let her go through with this?"

"She's the Salem Witch. If it's her wish, then by law, we are not to stop her, but more so, it is her duty to protect this world. Who are we to get in the way of that?"

Jamie whirled on me, desperation in his eyes as he pleaded with me. Taking both my hands in his, he begged, "Hayden, please, please don't do this."

Swallowing roughly, I said the words I knew could make him understand. "Jamie, your sister gave her life to save us—to save my life so I could one day fulfill my duty as the Salem Witch. Harbor was sixteen when she sacrificed herself. So who am I to be so selfish and cowardly that I don't fight Lilith? If not for you, if not for Asylum and every other witch in the world, then I'm doing this to honor her."

Blinking rapidly, he fought the water threatening to spill over his eyes. Then, ignoring the audience in the room, he pulled my face toward his to press our foreheads together and breathed in deeply, like he was trying to memorize my scent.

Sighing, I breathed in his natural smoky smell, and memorized the feel of his thumbs tracing circles on my cheeks and his forehead pressed to mine. I wanted to freeze this moment forever and just be with him.

"I can't convince you, can I?"

I shook my head, my mouth set in a grim line. I'm not sure if he saw, but he knew my answer all the same.

Stepping closer, he pulled me into his body and wrapped both arms around me. Whispering in my ear so only I heard, he said, "Whatever happens, promise you'll come back to me."

All I could do to respond was squeeze him tighter.

Taking a shaky deep breath, he stepped away from me, his royal blue eyes swimming with unshed tears. Closing his eyes, he looked away from me.

Apalla replaced Jamie, her eyes red and puffy from mourning her mother's death. I stepped into her embrace, hugging my bestie tightly. No words were needed, especially when she was already consumed by grief. Grief that I could not soothe.

Next was Kelsey. We had grown close these last couple of years, and Kelsey had grown as a person. No longer was she the mean, vindictive bully I had met on my first day in Asylum, but a person I genuinely considered a friend.

Thea's little arms wrapped around my midsection, and I had to bend to hug her. Hoisting her up, I pulled the little girl into my chest and spun her in a circle.

The Sanchez siblings rushed me together, tears streaming from their eyes. I met their solid embraces, half my body tugged by each sibling. It was awkward and uncomfortable, but I loved every moment of it.

Releasing the siblings, my piercing blue eyes—the ones I had inherited from my mysterious sire—met Kova's hunter green eyes—the ones she had inherited from her mother—that matched my dad's so perfectly, and I wondered how I never realized she was in love with him.

"All these years," I said, eliciting a confused look from Kova. "All these years, you knew Hunter was in the human world, raising me. Didn't you?"

Kova's face split into a mischievous smile. "Of course I did."

"I'm sorry." My bottom lip trembled.

Kova stepped forward, cupping my cheeks with her hands. "Whatever for, kid?"

"You were separated from him for twelve years because of me. And when I was finally here, he was gone. You never really got the chance to be with your soulmate, and now you have to wait another seventeen years."

"Eighteen," she corrected.

"What?" I sniffled.

"Eighteen years. Your father hasn't reincarnated yet. I get the feeling he's waiting for something."

"Oh," I sniffled again, and Kova used her thumbs to wipe away my tears. "That's even worse."

"It's not your fault, Hayden. And if I could, I would do it all again. I may not have gotten as much time with Hunter in this lifetime as I would have liked, but I got to spend four wonderful years raising his daughter as my own. Something I haven't experienced in over three centuries. You are both my daughter and my best friend, Hayden Black. And I love you to Eden and back."

My lower lip trembled as emotion filled my voice. "I love you too, Kova. To Eden and back."

Pulling me into her tight embrace, Kova held me with a sympathy that could only come from a fellow Salem Witch who understood the weight of the world resting on my shoulders. A weight I refused to drop.

But time was running short. I pulled away from Kova, wiping my tear-filled eyes and drying the stains on her shirt.

"I love you guys. All of you." I met each emotion-filled pair of eyes in the room. "You're the best friends a girl could ask for, but you're so much more than that. You're my family and I couldn't have asked for a better one."

These past five years, I had lost so much, but I had built a family when I had none. Silently, I sent a prayer of thanksgiving to the Goddess and God for bringing me to Asylum. For Its greater plan that I didn't understand. Because I didn't want any of my friends to bear this responsibility. And because I was so lucky to have people who were willing to die for me as much as I was willing to die for them.

Teary eyes and sad smiles stared back at me, and I basked in the warm love of my family one last time before I faced the Mother of Demons.

A blob of black flashed, and Jackal appeared on my shoulder, his black cat tail wrapping protectively around my neck. "Princess, it is almost time."

Running a finger over his tiny cat head, I said, "I know."

"Princess?" I looked at Jackal over my shoulder. He smiled a shark-like grin at me. "I love you, too."

"Thank you, Jackal." Emotion clogged my throat. My demons had always revered and respected me, but never had they told me they loved me. Were they capable of love? Maybe they had lived in Hell for so long that they didn't know love until I loved them first. "I'm fighting for you, too. You and all my demons because I love you."

Jackal nuzzled my hand, then jumped over to Jamie to perch on his shoulder, and I gestured for my friends to exit the room.

"I need a minute alone with Kova," I said to the room.

Kelsey was the first to turn on her heel and march out of the lounge, followed by the Sanchez siblings, then Thea and Apalla. Angel Boy slowly and begrudgingly followed, pausing in the door frame to shoot one last longing glance over his shoulder.

But I avoided his gaze. If I looked into his eyes again, I would falter.

"What's up, kid?"

I blew out a heavy breath, my shoulders sagging. Then I said two words I had never said in my entire life—during the entire Trials. "I'm scared, Kova."

It felt so good to say it, to admit it aloud. I couldn't falter in front of my circle or the rest of Asylum. I was the Salem Witch. If I doubted, then what reason did they have to believe in me?

"I'd be concerned if you weren't." She wrapped a motherly arm around my shoulders. "Everyone is scared, Hayden. Every Salem Witch who came before you was absolutely petrified going into their final Trial. The worst enemy we shall meet is nothing less than our own fear, and fear is a crippling foe than any Darkness a Salem Witch has faced, even deadlier than Lilith. If you let fear in the door, then she will surely kill you. So, when fear knocks, let faith answer."

"I'm not afraid of dying," I said truthfully. "I'm afraid of dying without taking her with me. I can't kill her," I said hollowly, feeling defeated already. "Even if I knew how to, I can't bring myself to do it. She was human once. I can't take a human life. Not again. Not after Cain."

"But Hayden, she's not human. She doesn't have a soul," Kova insisted.

"Yes, I know that, Kova," I snapped. Slowly, I exhaled a heavy breath, staring at my feet. When I lifted my head to meet her hunter green eyes, I didn't flinch as I admitted with a slight quiver to my voice, "I know. But when I look at her, I see myself. I see everything I could have been, and if I had become that, I would want someone to redeem me."

"Then what are you going to do when you fight her?"

"I have absolutely no idea," I admitted. "I'm going to do what I do best and fight. The rest... well, hopefully Gabriel gets his angel butt down here." I straightened, pulling away from Kova's arms to face her, woman to woman. "When I fight her, I need you to hold Jamie back. You and I know how this ends, because you know who my father is, don't you?"

A spark of green fire flared to life in her hunter green eyes. "You figured it out?"

"With a little help from the Devil," I said with a smirk. I stared at my hands, at the magic burning under the surface. The magic that would save me was the same magic that would doom me. Would it be enough for me to put an end to Lilith's reign of darkness? "All this power, all this magic, yet it's the same magic that ties me to the Trials."

"Magic is an honor," Kova agreed. "Until it is a shackle."

My blue eyes met her hunter green ones filled with ancient knowledge and power. How did I never piece it together that she was immortal? Immortality that chained her to a life without her true love.

"Your immortality... how do you go on knowing you'll live forever?"

"I lost everything in the Trials," Kova said, then blew out a haggard breath and ran a hand through her spiky red hair. "I suppose losing everything made it that much easier to build a new everything." She gestured to the castle around her. "As much suffering as I endured, I don't regret any of it, because without the Trials, I would never have been able to create all of this. And this has given me so much to live for.

"They say don't look back, but for women like us, it's important to remind ourselves how far we have come. Of the things we've lost, the things we've sacrificed, and the things we've built for ourselves. The Trials are to teach us lessons to prepare us for war. So, how can you not look back when you are about to enter your final Trial?" She pressed a hand to her heart, a single teardrop shining in the corner of her eye. "Those memories and the memories I make in this lifetime remind me why I live this immortal life. The purpose for which I was created and the purpose which I still fulfill with my immortality make it bearable, even when I am separated from my soulmate."

I nodded, understanding deep in my soul what she meant. Fulfilling our soul's purpose was our highest calling in this mortal world, and as much suffering as Kova endured, she found solace in what she suffered for. Just like the Trials.

"How did you handle the unknown when you entered your Spirit Trial? When you were about to be hung at Proctor's Ledge and didn't know if you would save the world?"

Kova chewed on her bottom lip, looking up at the ceiling as she recalled the most terrifying event of her life. "The fear was overwhelming, but that was what Asmodeus wanted, so I refused to give it to him. Dying was easy. Coming back is when things got complicated. I certainly wondered if I made the right choices when I was being carted to my death, but then I remembered, I passed my Trials. I had the approval of the Goddess herself. What more could there be?"

"But what if I fail the Creator?" I asked quietly.

"You won't, Hayden. The Creator is greater than our worldly fears, and It has chosen you." She pointed at me with unwavering confidence. "The Creator will not let you fail. You have unparalleled intuition in any given situation, whether it be magic or combat. I've never seen anything like it." Kova pressed her hands to both my cheeks. "You are more powerful than I could ever be. You were born powerful. You were born with the powers of Heaven and Hell for a reason. But that is not what makes you special, Hayden.

"You're just an ordinary witch." She brushed back a lock of my hair. "What makes you special is that you chose to be different. You didn't ask for this responsibility, but when the Creator called you higher, your soul answered the call. It is your choices—who you choose to be—that make you truly special. I do not think it will be your powers that win this war. It will be your *choices*. And so far, your choices in these Trials have not been wrong. More or less," she added with a cheeky smile, then sobered again. "Listen to your intuition. It is your soul speaking, it will not lead you astray. The Creator will tell you what to do. And the Creator is never wrong."

"I've made my decision, Kova."

She nodded curtly and released her hold on my face, her hunter green eyes swimming with emotion.

With a deep breath, I squared my shoulders. Wordlessly, I marched out of the lounge to where my friends waited in the hall. With them by my side, I strode through the Spellery, savoring each step as we passed hundreds of witches and demons. When they spotted me, everyone stopped what they were doing to join me in my march to face Lilith.

As I exited the heavy, twenty-foot entrance doors of the Spellery, countless witches and demons swarmed around me. All of them were exhausted, on the brink of collapsing, but they persevered, standing in united solidarity with me against the Darkness threatening to devour our world.

The power of Spirit was alive within me, stronger than any force in the Universe. Unlimited and infinite. Calling upon its power, I unleashed the magic. Power infused the air and electricity crackled, charging the life forces of the mortals around me. I didn't dare touch the demons with my Spirit for fear of what it would do to their soulless bodies, but I could replenish the magic of the mortals until they stood straight and tall with the power of Spirit residing within them.

Accompanying me to my last stand against Lilith, the procession strode through my beloved town with a solemn silence. As I walked down University Avenue, the Spellery at my back, I savored the sights and smells. Despite the carnage and blood and destruction hewing Asylum, I marveled at the wonder of the town Kova had built and cultivated for three hundred years.

As I walked along the lake, the cobblestone road turned to grass beneath my feet, opening to the field containing the amphitheater, and just beyond it, the cathedral.

Lilith's demons swarmed the field, a dark, undulating mass of evil staining the holiest of places. But not a single ordinary demon stepped foot on the lawn of the cathedral. Holy ground. Kova had blessed the area around the cathedral.

Wow. We were dumb. Why did nobody think to bless the ground in Asylum so the demons couldn't step foot inside the wards?

Then again, my demons weren't permitted to walk on holy ground either... and not like I knew how to bless holy ground.

Lilith's slitted purple snake eyes landed on me, and her dogmatic demons followed her gaze.

As I walked, all the demons stopped.

They parted like the Red Sea, allowing my witches and demons to pass unharmed. No doubt Lilith was eager for what she mistakenly thought would be the fight in which she finally conquered me. Of course she wanted an audience. She wanted to kill me in front of my own people... and with me, kill their hope.

Jamie and Kova each took one of my hands, giving them a squeeze. Demons retreated from my approaching form until the only demons standing before me were Lilith and my mother, hanging from her cross not ten feet away.

When Kova and Jamie released me, they hung back as I alone strode to the center of the clearing around Lilith and stood directly across from her, mere feet separating me from the darkest force in the world.

She was unhinged. Evil to her core. Soulless.

Demons encircled us, a swarming crowd pressing in on us, but my witches and demons would not be boxed out. White holy flames burst from Kova's hands, and she used the fire like whips to corral the enemy demons. Witches and my loyal demons rushed forward, claiming spots at the front of the crowd to watch the action.

Elliot, the snake that he was, lingered on the edge of the circle, eyeing me warily after I sank my blade into his gut. Although he had reattached his severed arm with the help of demonic magic.

I might be bound by the power of a Devil's Bargain to not kill him, but he didn't know that. Still, he wasn't my concern right now.

I only had eyes for the viper in the skanky purple dress cut low to show off the serpent tattooed on her chest, its mouth open and fangs bared to bite into the golden apple inked on her skin. The apple she ate when she chose to fall. And the serpent I had met in the pits of Hell.

"Hello, Granddaughter," she sneered. "I must say I am surprised. I doubted if you would show. In fact," she shouted louder so our audience could hear, "You ran and left your people to die. You should never have returned."

Wordlessly, I unsheathed Nightmare and my amulet athame. It was fitting that the battle between Heaven and Hell would be fought with a sword from Heaven and a dagger that matched my dual nature—Princess of Hell and Daughter of Heaven.

Lilith scowled at me. "Tsk, tsk, you are in such a hurry when you know you cannot withstand the power of the Mother and the Crone combined forever. Eventually, you will falter, and I will seize what is rightfully mine."

"You underestimate my power, Grandmother. Last time we crossed blades, it was me who held the sword to your throat."

"Ha," she scoffed, then smiled coyly. "And look how that turned out. I have your mother. I have her power and two-thirds of the Power of Three. And you have... *nothing*. You are *alone*."

"You're wrong. I am never alone. I have everything I need right here." I tapped my heart with the tip of my athame.

"Aw, how sickeningly sentimental." She smirked before growling at me. "Even if you manage to hold a sword to my throat, I will outlast you. You know I will have yours and Thea's powers in the end."

"And you know I'll sacrifice everything to prevent you from obtaining the Power of Three."

"Oh, yes, you will." She grinned a viper's scowl, her eyes burning like the pits of Hell. "Your struggle will make it that much sweeter when you finally yield your power to me. First, I will incapacitate you and steal Thea's power, and then, one by one, I will torture and kill your loved ones in front of you until you give me the power that is rightfully mine."

Lilith didn't know I transferred the Goddess's blessing of free will to Thea. She thought I must be coerced into yielding.

"It is not yours to own," I said defiantly, my chin raised high. "I will never yield to you, Lilith, for my Creator is greater than all the forces of Darkness. My freedom is mine alone."

Lilith tossed her head and laughed a maniacal, insane laugh. "You think you are free, Hayden? You are not free. Freedom is an illusion, a trick of the Creator. Are you not a slave to the Trials?"

"I'm as free as a bald eagle in a national park," I said, eliciting groans from Jamie and my circle.

Lilith's feral smile slipped from her lips as she rolled her eyes.

"She did not just say that during a battle to the death." Jamie scrubbed his face with his hands.

Kova snorted from beside him. "Have you met Hayden? *Of course*, she said that during a battle to the death."

I waggled my eyebrows at them as I caught Lilith's sickle with Nightmare, not looking at my opponent as I jumped in the air and slammed my foot into her face in a tornado roundhouse kick, sending her stumbling across the field.

I struck with the speed of a viper. My longsword hurtled through the air, the tip aimed at Lilith's throat, but she deftly dodged the attack, then countered using a second sword conjured from thin air. I charged, swiftly executing attack after attack. My blade sang every time it struck hers, whether I was attacking or defending. My athame didn't stop, either.

All those years of practicing with both hands made me lethally ambidextrous. It didn't matter if my sword or my dagger was in my right hand, I could wield them equally well with either hand. And I did just that, never ceasing my onslaught of attacks. Yet Lilith blocked them all, matching me blow for blow. She never suffered a hit, but neither did I. With her channeling my mother, we were equally matched.

Or at least that's what she thought.

But I had conquered the Devil himself.

I was the warrior witch, and I would not be defeated even by a demoness like Lilith, no matter how ancient.

Swinging Nightmare, I allowed the black blade to scrape the length of Lilith's, grinding to a halt as I pushed against her. She matched my force with her own, pressing on my blade. With a sneer, Lilith shoved against me, throwing our bodies away from each other. I stumbled back, but so did she.

Magic surged within me, and the elements heralded my call. Rain came, wind blew, earth quaked, and fire burned. Sparks jumped between my fingers like electricity zapping between wires.

Lightning cracked through the air as a massive bolt slammed into Lilith, throwing her backward. Her swords thudded against the ground and her head snapped back as Lilith plowed into her demons.

Snarling, she lurched to her feet as the demons helped her up. Shrugging off their claws, she seethed at me and summoned her sickled sword to her hand.

Rolling my shoulders, I cracked my neck.

"I see you learned a thing or two from *Eve*," she hissed the name of her first nemesis.

A wicked smirk stretched my lips.

Nightmare parried the blow of her silver sickle sword with an ear-shattering clash of metal. Sparks flew as our blades ground apart. Moving with unparalleled speed, Lilith and I fought in a blur of feints and slashes as we moved across the open field with nimble litheness.

Darkness and Light exploded back and forth, plunging us into a strange battle of flickering color with the magic of the elements cutting through the ominous night.

In the flashing darkness, I wielded Nightmare, its black blade undetectable against the black sky as Lilith's silver sickle flashed in the light of the silver fire burning in a diadem atop my midnight black locks.

Metal clanged as Nightmare caught blow after blow from Lilith's sickle. I didn't need the light to see—it was like I sensed her every move before she made it. As though Spirit knew everything before it happened, and I intuitively plugged into the magic stream of the Universe.

As fast as Nightmare moved through the air, catching and parrying strikes, I jabbed and sliced and cut and stabbed with my amulet athame, seeking vulnerable flesh.

Ducking under an arced attack from her sickle, I lashed out with my amulet athame and sliced a thin line through her purple dress, directly over her ribs.

A line of black blood bubbled to the surface, and her forked tongue slid out between her teeth as she hissed.

Lilith backhanded me, the rings on her knuckles stinging against my skin as the force of her blow sent me stumbling back.

Water magic mixed with Spirit to heal the gashes torn across my cheeks before blood beaded over the wound.

One blow would not decide this battle.

The greater warrior would claim victory.

Slipping into my stance, the stance I had learned my first week at the Spellery, the stance I had intuitively known when I faced Tuck and Leo in my first tussle at St. Salem's, I faced Lilith with a calm determination, my brain calculating how to close the gap between us.

Twirling her blade over her hand, Lilith sneered as light flashed through the darkened night sky. "You should have run instead of facing me, Granddaughter." She waved a hand, gesturing to the witches and demons surrounding us. "Your foolish need to protect them will be your undoing."

"No," I growled, brandishing Nightmare menacingly. "It is my strength." I struck, my blow glancing off her blade. "Love is my reason to fight. Have you considered what is yours?"

Lilith's dark purple eyes flashed with rage, and she sliced at me with her sickled blade.

"I'll tell you what your reason is," I growled, catching her blade with ease as my eyes simmered with power and emotion. "You crave revenge. You want to watch the world burn because you feel slighted. But guess what, Lilith. *Life isn't fair*. That doesn't mean you slither into bed with Darkness."

"We are all bad in someone's story," Lilith stated flippantly in response. "What you consider evil was *freedom* for me. What you consider good was the tight shackles of slavery for me. Do you still not understand? It is all *lies*, granddaughter. The angels want you to think I am a monster. I did not start out evil. But if you are treated like a monster long enough, you become one."

"That's a lie," I snarled back at her. "No one made you fall from Grace. You chose to."

"Chose to?" she scoffed. "Of course, I chose to. As if I were going to spend the rest of my days living as an inferior to that ridiculous excuse for a man."

"So, you sided with Darkness and became evil." I rolled my eyes. "What a great idea. My marriage isn't going great, so I'll climb into bed with the Devil."

Purple hellfire lashed through the air as Lilith fired at me in a rage. White flames soared up to meet them, consuming them like a dragon eating fire.

Moving faster than the lighting I conducted, I closed the space between us and rammed Nightmare against her sickle while simultaneously slicing my amulet athame into the space between her ribs. Black blood gushed over my fingers, and my water magic grabbed hold of her blood. It wasn't blood magic—I didn't steal her free will—I simply willed her blood to flow out of the wound with the pressure of a waterfall, and Spirit spoke to me as her life force weakened within her body.

Lilith swiped at me with razor-like talons, her fingernails grazing my leather jacket-protected arm.

The blue crystal in the pommel of my amulet athame cracked across her cheek, staining her porcelain skin with a black and purple bruise.

Shoving away, Lilith stumbled backward, pressing a hand to her gushing wound.

It was time to end the Salem War.

Sparks came to life, dancing between my fingers as energy surged in my veins. Lightning streaked through the air, shattering Lilith's purple hellfire as quickly as she summoned it. Again and again and again.

As fast as she was, I was faster, and my black sparks electrocuted her hands.

Wind howled, earth trembled, water flowed, fire burned, but the elements left my people and demons unharmed. Only Lilith and her demons felt the sting of my magic.

I wielded my magic against her.

Magic flashed in my eyes as I flew forward on a squall of air. White flames arced out of me as I crashed into Lilith, and her nasty purple hellfire sparked to meet mine, protecting the demoness from my purifying power.

Telepathically, I commanded the elements with terrifying power. A dagger of ice sliced into Lilith's gut, earning a grunt of pain. Lilith lunged as I leaped away from her. A block of rock rocketed up from the ground, and the Mother of Demons slammed into it face-first with a sickening crunch.

Faster than it appeared, the rock wall disappeared, and there I was, slamming my fist into Lilith's nose. A fist that was hardened to metal by earth magic.

Bone shattered under my hand as a feral scream escaped Lilith's lips. Raising my foot, I kicked forward and slammed my heel into her knee, obliterating her joint. The Dark Mother dropped to the ground with a scream of rage and pain.

Wind whistled as it slammed into her, forcing her to her back. A ring of white holy flames ignited around us as her demons jerked forward to save her.

Javelins of ice formed in the air, then dropped, slicing into her clothes in strategic places to pin her to the ground. Vines snapped out of the soil, twisting and curling around her body to immobilize her.

Even as Lilith struggled, my vines tightened, fighting with the infused power of Spirit to counter her inhuman strength.

Lightning crackled around her like a cage, and silver light haloed around my body as I stood over Lilith. Nightmare pointed down, its tip hovering over her chest where her heart should be as my silver light reflected off the polished surface.

My witches and demons roared with victory, drowning out the infernal screams of Lilith's dark army.

"Kill her, Hayden!"

"End her!"

"Finish this war! Claim our victory!"

And I almost did... I almost shoved Heaven's blade into the black heart of the Mother of Demons.

Lightning streaked across the sky so brightly that I should have been blinded, but lightning would never betray its master. Lilith blinked as the flash of light seared across her vision.

Silver light beamed down from the full moon overhead, its light returning to Asylum as Spirit banished the darkness that blanketed the town. And as the light shined on me and Lilith, I stared into her soulless purple eyes. Purple eyes framed by a face identical to my own and hair as black as mine.

It was my face—sixteen years from now, at the age of thirty-three.

I looked at her face and saw everything I could have fallen to. Everything I could have been but didn't become by the grace of the Goddess and God.

Nightmare quivered in my hands from the force of Spirit coursing through me. And from the emotion filling every fiber of my being.

I couldn't do it.

I couldn't kill her.

Stumbling back, I lowered Nightmare to my side, my chest heaving from emotion and grief and turmoil shredding me apart inside.

I could end it. I could end this war by ending *her*.

Asylum shouted as much, their echoing words ringing in my ears as I backed away from the Mother of Demons, who struggled against my vines holding her prone to the cold earth.

I couldn't kill her on her island after she imprisoned Kova and killed my Knights, my dad, and my familiar. So, why did I think I could kill her now? Was this not the exact fear I had voiced to Kova?

Summoning her sickle sword, Lilith sliced through the vines holding her captive, then rose to her feet, her hair wild and dangerous around her face.

I stood there uselessly, my blades hanging at my sides as I warily watched the Mother of Demons.

If I couldn't kill her, how was I supposed to defeat her? How did I end this war and cease the slaughter of my people and stop her demons from overrunning the mortal world with their tainted darkness?

All this power. All this magic. All this natural talent. And I was as useful as an ashtray on a motorcycle.

And we both knew it.

Raising her sword, Lilith pointed the tip at me, then threw back her head and laughed like a maniac, the sound sharp and cruel. "Perhaps you are the greater warrior. You did best me in combat yet again, but you cannot beat me, Hayden. No matter how good you are, no matter how many elements you wield, you cannot defeat me. You are too *weak* to deal the final blow.

"I am ETERNAL. I am the Dark Mother, who channels the powers of the Mother and the Crone and soon, I will channel the power of the Maiden from dear, sweet little Thea. I will claim the power that is rightfully mine, and then I will take your power, too. I will force you to yield. Forfeit, Granddaughter, because you will *lose*."

Laughter and sick satisfaction glimmered in her dark purple eyes as she gazed triumphantly at me, like she had already won.

And she was right.

I could beat her. I *did* beat her. I had her at the mercy of my blade. With the everlasting power of Spirit, I never tired and my magic was stronger than ever.

But Spirit whispered to me lovingly, speaking secrets into my mind like a current of magic ebbing and flowing through the Universe. And I just *knew*.

Smirking wickedly, I played my last hand. The final blow against Lilith before midnight.

"I gave Thea my blessing."

Gasps rang from the crowd, including my friends. They had kept their secrets for years. But I had kept secrets of my own.

The sanctimonious smirk slipped off Lilith's face as the air of haughty arrogance transformed to rage. Lilith's nostrils flared as she seethed, realization hitting her that Thea was useless to her, but me...

I was her only means of obtaining the power of the Maiden. But Lilith couldn't beat me in a physical fight. She knew it. I knew it. Everyone who stood witness today knew it.

The clock chimed in the distance, the first stroke of midnight as the Spellery bells tolled. My seventeenth birthday.

But I couldn't kill Lilith. And I couldn't free my mother until I mastered Spirit, but my Trial... Gabriel hadn't triggered my Trial. I was about to turn seventeen without mastering the fifth element.

Midnight was here—the ultimate deadline.

I was out of time.

Two chimes.

Gazing past Lilith, my eyes found Kova's, and with just a look, she spoke volumes. She never spoke, never made a sound, just pressed her lips into a thin line, like she was holding back tears, but the look in her hunter green eyes told me she knew exactly what was about to happen. Because it had happened to her.

Her eyes were sad, but her face beamed with pride as she started toward Jamie, who was oblivious to Kova as he stared down the battle. She would hold him back, so he couldn't stop me.

Three chimes.

"Any last words while you still have your freedom? Because it is about to become *mine*, and when it does, you will not speak another word ever again." Lilith cackled madly, oblivious to the fact that I wasn't going to let her channel me. Ever.

She couldn't beat me, but I couldn't kill her. And if I couldn't kill her, then the least I could do was ensure she couldn't channel the power of the Maiden.

Six chimes.

My mother hung from her cross, struggling to lift her head to watch the duel between her mother and her daughter. Sorrow-filled lavender eyes found mine. Sorrow not for herself, but for me. She knew I was out of time.

Nine chimes.

Ignoring Lilith, I stared into Leyla's eyes, trying to convey all the love I felt, to tell her how sorry I was for not knowing my mother. Only my blood could save her, but in this instant, I was powerless.

Ten chimes.

"I'm sorry I couldn't save you." My words were soft.

One final breath to take, and it would be finished.

"I know who my father is."

And with those words, Leyla's lavender eyes shone with the light of the Heavens.

Eleven chimes.

I stared Lilith in the eye as I wordlessly brought my amulet athame to my throat, watching as Lilith's purple snake eyes grew as wide as saucers. The Dark Mother rocketed toward me on a wave of purple magic. "No!"

But it was too late—I had already dragged the blade across my throat.

Scarlet blood flowed from my neck. My amulet athame slipped from my grip, clattering to the ground. My lungs burned for oxygen as my white shirt turned crimson. The edges of my vision blurred as the blackness swallowed my mortal life, and my knees slammed into the earth. Collapsing forward, my vision went completely black.

And then I died.

CHAPTER FOURTEEN

THE TRIAL OF SPIRIT

The deepest peace I had ever known washed over me.

Bright white light flooded my vision, but I wasn't blinded by the ethereal white light, not like how it would blind my mortal eyes. Everything was completely white. I was surrounded by emptiness. No, not emptiness, but *light*. Everything was made of light—made of energy—the opposite of the materialistic form of everything on Earth. Even me—my soul—was a being of light.

Looking down at myself, I found my clothes to be a pristine white. I had worn all white once before, and I could definitely say it was not my color. I wore the same simple cotton shirt and pants from the celestial plane of my coma when I passed my first Trial. My feet were bare, but it didn't matter, seeing as I wasn't on the earthly plane anymore.

Catching a glimpse of my hair, I gasped. Reaching up, I pulled a lock over my shoulder and stared at the shimmering silver, then pressed a hand to my cheek below my eye. No doubt my eyes were silver, but I didn't understand. Gabriel hadn't appeared before I died. He didn't start my Trial.

"Woof!" a cheery puppy bark sounded from nowhere.

My head snapped up. Tears welled in my eyes as a smile split my face, my jaw popping from stretching so wide.

"Salem," I shouted, dropping my knees and flinging my arms wide for the fluffy yellow lab to bound into my arms. I buried my face in her rough fur, savoring the feeling I had missed for months. "I missed you, girl," I murmured into her fur, my tears soaking into her coat.

She ran her rough, wet tongue over my cheek as if to say she missed me, too.

"Loyal familiar you have there," came a familiar voice, echoing some of the first words Kova said to me. "Even Death could not keep her from rushing here to meet you."

With a smile, I released Salem and rose to my feet. "Well, Death is an old friend of mine, so something tells me she made an exception."

"I think she just might have." Amara winked as we stepped into each other's embrace.

We clung tightly to one another, like old friends in desperate need of the other's love. When we pulled back, Amara's hands gripped my elbows.

Death didn't look as scary on this side of the veil with her candy-apple red hair and motherly green eyes. The mother of the human and witch races.

"I was worried you would not figure it out in time," she admitted.

I couldn't help but laugh, the joyous sound echoing through the Heavens. "Oh, I figured it out. 'Death is your gift,' is a bit cryptic, don't you think? It was a dead giveaway." I winked a silver eye at her.

Amara tossed her head back and laughed, her candy-apple red hair rippling on an unseen air current. "Are you telling me you knew this whole time?"

Casually, I shrugged. "I knew what you were getting at, but I couldn't figure out *why*. It took that little visit to Hell for me to put final the pieces together."

"Then you know..." she trailed off, prompting me to answer the unexpected question.

"Yes." I nodded. "I know, and I am ready."

"Then let us walk." Amara offered her elbow, and I gratefully accepted, entwining my arm with hers. "It is time I led you to the Gates."

Salem bounded along with the energy of a young pup, rushing ahead, then turning around to race back toward us. But on this plane, she looked younger than I remembered.

"Amara, why does Salem look like she's only three years old? She was twelve when she died."

"Ah, astute observation from a keen mind." Amara winked a jade green eye at me—her original eye color from when she was Eve. "Everything in Heaven is thirty-three years old."

"What?" Startled, I stumbled to a stop, tugging on Amara's arm as I raised a hand to my cheek. "Do I—I don't..."

Amara nodded. "Even you."

It was a strange feeling, knowing I looked thirty-three even though I was barely seventeen. And dead. What did thirty-three-year-old me look like?

"That's why Kova doesn't age, isn't it? Because it's the age our souls appear when we are in Heaven."

"Yes. This is true for all immortals, except Lilith. Her immortality is born of sin and dishonor, not of selflessness and holiness, so she forever remains the same as the day she fell."

"But then why is my hair silver? I don't remember Gabriel starting my Trial."

"Because he didn't. Your hair is silver because you brought on the beginning of your Trial by yourself."

I stopped walking. "You can't mean... I didn't–I mean I didn't know..."

"It's okay, Hayden. Of course, you didn't know. That was intentional. Had you known, the power of your sacrifice wouldn't have meant as much. It was the selflessness of your actions that marked the beginning of your fifth Trial."

"Kova's Trial didn't start before she was hanged, did it? Her death triggered her Trial."

"Every Salem Witch faces the same start of their Spirit Trial. Each dies in sacrificing their life to save the world."

I swallowed. "So, my eyes are silver?"

"No," she said, surprising me. "Your eyes are not silver, nor will they ever be in this realm."

"But why?" I asked quizzically, surprised my heavenly Trial—the Trial of Spirit—did not change my eyes to swirling pools of molten silver.

Amara smiled, tugging on my arm to urge me to walk with her again. "You will understand in a moment."

We walked in comfortable silence, except for the occasional bark from Salem as she sprinted into the beyond, then ran back, panting at the joyful rush of her playtime. Joy manifested into a smile on my face as I watched my puppy. I had missed her, missed my home.

"Ah, and here we are," Amara said as a glowing ball of silver and gold light swallowed us whole.

Unlike before, the heavenly light blinded my vision.

Blinking as the light faded to reveal two elegant gates of simple design, I stared in awe at one wrought in silver and the other in gold to form a luminescent, pearly color that glistened in the light... not sunlight, for there was no sun, but everything was made of light. Even the Pearly Gates were made of light but appeared as simple round metal bars. In the center of each gate was a flat, circular disk. A shining silver moon adorned the golden gate, and the silver gate had a gleaming golden sun. The sight was so simple, yet awe filled me as I stood before the Gates to the Garden of Eden.

"Home." I sighed as a weight lifted off my chest. A burden I didn't know was weighing heavy on my soul for all my life.

"Home," Amara echoed.

"Can I go in?" I asked, taking a hesitant step forward.

"Not yet, Hayden," a deep timbre thundered through the air. The Messenger Archangel appeared dressed all in white as his pristine white angel wings swayed behind him. With a megawatt smile, Gabriel opened his arms wide. "Hayden Black, you brave and wonderful Daughter of Heaven."

With a broad smile, I leaped into the angel's waiting arms, wrapping mine around the giant angel. Lifting me off my feet, he squeezed tightly, like a father holding his child, before setting me down.

Gabriel stepped back, revealing a seven-foot-tall man, his broader shoulders more imposing and intimidating than any other angel could hope to achieve.

An enormous longsword was strapped to his left hip, a smaller dagger on his right. White heavenly fire burned along the top edges of his massive white wings. Golden blond hair with streaks of platinum gleamed like it was made of light. His deeply tanned skin was a sharp contrast to the pallor of my own. Despite the fierceness of his intimidating nature, a look of uncertainty painted his features.

But his eyes, those fierce blue, piercing eyes, were as familiar to me as my own. Finally, I stood face-to-face with the man from whom I inherited my eyes. My biological father...

Tears welled in my eyes and rolled down my cheeks, my lip quivering with emotion.

"Michael," I said his name with all the confidence in the world. "Hello, *Father*."

Joyful tears filled his crystal blue eyes as he stepped forward, spreading his massive, fatherly arms wide for me to leap into.

Throwing myself at him, I sank into his embrace. After seventeen years, I finally met my father. A father I had searched for for years.

And in his arms, an overwhelming feeling of protection and love wrapped around me.

The deep timber of the Warrior Archangel's voice rumbled in my ear. "You have no idea how long I have waited to meet you, my Little Warrior."

"And I, you," I choked out the words between sobs. "I'm sorry for doubting you. I'm sorry for being so angry with you."

"Ssh, ssh," he hushed my sobs, rubbing a hand up and down my back. "You have nothing to apologize for, Davina." My true name. He said my true name. "A daughter has the right to know who her father is. I am sorry you could not know sooner."

"I understand why Mom did it," I murmured into his shoulder, the words muffled. "She did it to protect me, and it worked. It was the last weapon I had against Lilith. It kept the world safe."

We finally let go of one another, stepping back to drink each other in.

"I heard you." I didn't intend for my voice to come out as a whisper. "I didn't know it was you, but I heard you."

Michael's giant thumbs brushed the tears from my cheeks. "I have always watched over you, my dearest Davina. Even if you did not know it, I was always by your side."

"We may not be allowed to raise our children, nor are we afforded the luxury of seeing them often, but we are always watching over our sons and daughters," Gabriel said, his words echoing Michael's sentiment, emotion clogging both their throats.

"All those times you called me 'Daughter of Heaven,' were you trying to tell me..." I trailed off and gestured to Michael.

Gabriel gave me a knowing smile. "Yes, I was alluding, not in so many words, to the truth of your parentage. However, I would have called you a Daughter of Heaven if your father was a mortal, for you are a child of the Creator, whether you are a child of a celestial or not."

"Not to mention, Dad likes to be melodramatic—comes with the gig as the Messenger of the God and Goddess." Harbor's familiar voice was like music to my ears.

"Harbor, you're here," I shouted as I threw myself at my chosen sister, her familiar black locks tangling in my silver ones. Her hard body crashed into mine, and I hugged my friend for the first time since my Water Trial... since her death.

Pulling away, she grinned at me. "They let me out of prison every now and again."

"Prison?" Gabriel scoffed. "Eden is not—"

"Relax, Dad, I'm joking," Harbor soothed her father, then turned away from him to roll her ocean blue eyes. She whispered to me, "Yeesh. As the Archangel of Water, you'd think he'd have more of a sense of humor."

"What do you mean, I do not have a sense of humor?" Gabriel asked, affronted at the suggestion. "I have had a sense of humor since long before you were conceived."

Harbor shot me a wink.

"I think Gabriel is funny."

"Thank you, Ethan." Gabriel crossed his arms over his chest. "At least my daughter's soulmate understands me."

My neck cracked as it whipped around to stare at Harbor and Ethan. I gestured at the two of them and raised a questioning eyebrow. "So, it's finally common knowledge?"

Harbor grinned wickedly. "So, you figured it out, huh?"

I scoffed. "Of course, I figured it out. It was kinda obvious."

"Not to James." Harbor grinned wildly at me. "I may have forgotten to mention it to him."

My jaw dropped open. "You hid your soulmate from Jamie?" I asked incredulously. "You two have twin telepathy—how didn't he sense your emotions?"

"My twin has never scored high on emotional intelligence." Harbor rolled her eyes. "Look at how he handled your first kiss."

Red stained my face as embarrassment flooded my body. At least, I thought I was blushing... I wasn't sure how that worked with a soul.

"He has the empathy of a rock," Harbor continued with a shrug. "It was easy to hide the depths of my true feelings for Ethan, especially when I knew I would be using my Glory and passing to the Garden."

"That's why you stayed in Eden, isn't it?" I gestured to Ethan. "You knew he is your soulmate, and he is mortal."

Harbor smiled a bittersweet smile, filled with love and understanding. A glint in her eye told me she sensed the feelings running through my heart. "I didn't know explicitly, per se. It's impossible to confirm until the Creator marks us, but I had my suspicions."

"Had your suspicions?" I asked with extra sass. "Girl, *I* had suspicions. How did you not know?"

"Okay, okay." Harbor held her hands up in surrender. "I had a pretty good idea that Ethan is my soulmate. Apalla confirmed it when she told me she had a vision of me dying and waiting for Ethan."

"She what?" Ethan asked, surprise evident on his face.

"But the true confirmation came when this"—she raised her left hand to reveal the band of blue and silver ink wrapping around her ring finger in the shape of ocean waves with a pair of angel wings in the center—"confirmed it when my soul crossed to this side of the veil."

"Apalla knew WHAT?" I shouted, the soulmate glyph completely forgotten.

Harbor scrunched her nose. "Oh, did I forget to mention that? Apalla knew I was going to sacrifice myself, because I made up my mind after Dad delivered the message on my thirteenth birthday. Of course, he conveniently left out the part about Hayden being twelve and not a new born baby." Harbor rolled her eyes, making sure Gabriel saw it, which he answered with an eye roll of his own.

Michael caught my eye, both of us grinning as we suppressed our laughter. It was funny how much Harbor and I were like our fathers.

"You told me about the message," I told Harbor. "But you and Apalla conveniently forgot to mention that she knew Ethan is your soulmate." I threw my hands in the air. "I had to figure it out on my own."

I would have words with Palla. How much did she know that I didn't know she knew?

"Dad didn't bother to tell me about my soulmate then, either." She slapped her hands on her hips, jokingly glaring at Gabriel. "Anyhoo, remember the vision Apalla had at Candlemas?"

"Yeah, I know the one." I thought back to my second year in Asylum, the bloody tears Apalla cried during a terrible vision of Harbor's fate, which Apalla didn't disclose to me until after Harbor used her Glory.

"In her vision, she saw my death and that I stayed in Eden because Ethan wouldn't be long behind. So, when she confronted me, I already knew about my fate, but," she faced Ethan, gripping both of his hands in hers as she drew them to her chest to rest above her heart, "knowing you would join me soon, it made my choice easier."

"All this time, you knew," Ethan stared at her with wonder and awe, his chocolate brown eyes glimmering with unshed tears of joy and love. "You knew we were soulmates, and that's why you decided against immortality? Against returning to your family?"

Harbor's ocean eyes filled with tears, the water making the blue sparkle under the lights of Heaven. "I didn't want to resign us to the same fate as Kova and Hunter." She hiccupped. "I want us to be together, in the Garden of Eden, and one day, when we choose to, we can reincarnate together. But being separated from you... I was selfish because I couldn't bring myself to do it."

"And I love you all the more for it."

Ethan kissed her, a chaste kiss, but with love conveyed through every touch, and my heart panged for the boy I wanted to kiss with all my heart and soul.

My thoughts flicked to Kova and Dad, who were separated after each mortal life my father lived and then for seventeen years until he was an adult witch and the soulmate glyph could reappear.

As though I had summoned him with my thoughts, the voice I knew like my own, said, "Well done, Hayden." Whirling, I found my dad standing in his ethereal form, his hunter green eyes shining with pride. "Welcome home."

"Dad," I screamed, launching myself into the embrace of the man who raised me.

"There's my girl." He grinned as he caught me in his arms, holding me the way only a father could. He whispered into my ear, "I am so, so proud of you, Hayden."

"I missed you so much, Dad."

I sobbed into his shoulder as he held me close.... I was taller than him now, but it didn't matter. Nothing could beat this feeling... the feeling of being reunited with my father after years apart and a fleeting year together. It wasn't the same as I felt in Michael's embrace, but I felt loved all the same.

When he released me, I asked, "Why didn't you choose to reincarnate? Kova is waiting for you."

"Yes, she is waiting for me." He smiled knowingly, a certain fondness in his expression as he mention of his soulmate. "But if she can wait seventeen years each time I die, she can wait eighteen years for me to meet my daughter when she sacrifices her life. Plus, Alice would probably kill me herself if I didn't wait for you."

I grinned at him. "I love you, Dad."

"I love you too, Hays. But you cannot stay here much longer."

"What do you mean?"

"You have a choice to make, Little Warrior," Michael said, using my nickname that, knowing my sire's identity, I loved so much. As the words rolled off his tongue, they held none of the cold animosity of the Devil, but the love and warmth of a father speaking to his daughter. "You, like Harbor and Kova, are Nephilim. You can either enter the Garden of Eden now, never to return to the Earth as Hayden Black, but one day, you can reincarnate if you so choose. Or you can return to Earth, without entering the Garden, to resume your life as you left it. But you will be immortal. And immortals do not die. Whenever you suffer a mortal death, you will appear here, on this side of the veil, before Death ushers your soul back to Earth." Michael gestured to Amara, who leaned against the broad chest of a massive angel with black wings—Azriel, her soulmate.

"Dad, what will you do if I enter Eden?" I asked my dad, Hunter.

"I will stay with you, but not for long."

"It's extremely painful for soulmates to reside in separate realms, but it is the price we pay to have such profound love," Harbor spoke reverently as she gazed lovingly into Ethan's eyes.

"And if I return?"

"Then I will watch from above as you defeat Lilith and finish this war. But then, I will return to Earth to a newly reincarnated life."

I shook my head, my long silver hair flying around me. "But I don't know how to defeat Lilith. If I did, I wouldn't have died."

Amara, who had been so silent that I forgot she was there, said, "You cannot defeat Lilith without first freeing your mother. And you cannot free your mother without mastering Spirit. And you cannot master Spirit without dying. Often, the most powerful magic comes in the form we least expect, but sacrifice to save the people you love...

there is no greater gift than to lay one's life down for her friends. It is such a pure and selfless act that it is the least expected."

"But I haven't mastered Spirit," I whined in frustration, shaking my head. Taking a deep breath, I faced my father, Michael, "If I enter the Garden, and one day I want to be reincarnated, I won't be Nephilim, will I?"

Michael smiled, his blue eyes sparkling. It was strange, yet oddly satisfying, to see my own eyes staring back at me after all this time. "Yes, and no. The mortal body you left was conceived from the physical union of me and Leyla, so if you reincarnate, your body will be that of the parents who conceive you. But your soul was fearfully and wonderfully made by the Creator and infused with the essence of Leyla's soul and the essence of my angelic being. You are not a body. You are a *soul*. And you are, and forever will be, my daughter, even in your next life. Eyes are windows to the soul, which is why, the true color of your eyes remains a captivating blue. It is the divinity of your soul shining through."

"I am a soul..." I said the words slowly, as though speaking them aloud was casting a spell of its own, manifesting the truth into reality. A reality I could see by looking down at my spectral body of light. "I don't think my soul can be described with the word 'divinity'."

"Why do you think you, a demon, do not flinch at the name of the Lord and Lady, *Yhwh*? Why can you summon holy flames?" my angelic sire asked.

"Because I'm Nephilim?"

He shook his head. "It is more important who one chooses to be than what they are born as."

It struck me then, because I chose to walk the path the God and Goddess set before me... Like I learned in my Fire Trial. "I reflect the Light of the Creator."

Michael nodded.

"Just as our brothers and sisters, led by Lucifer, fell from Grace willingly—"

"And we gladly repelled them from Heaven," Michael added with a growl.

Gabriel continued, ignoring him. "Lilith turned her back on our Creator."

"When Lilith fell, I was tasked with the duty of tracking her after our brothers failed to return her to the Garden," Michael said to my surprise. Legend and lore didn't disclose that my father—wow, that was still weird despite how right it felt—confronted Lilith during her fall from Grace. "She aligned with Darkness to rip her soul from her physical body in front of me and cast it away. Willingly parting ways with her mortal soul, she welcomed Darkness into her physical body and merged with Evil to become the Mother of Demons."

"Lilith had a mortal soul..."

I was a little mind blown by Michael's description. The Creator chose Michael, who confronted Lilith during her Fall, to mate with Leyla, the daughter of Lilith, to create... *me*. Me, who was chosen as the Salem Witch.

Spirit whispered to me, its tender, loving touch sweeping through my ethereal form more intimately than I had felt as a mortal. *My plans are greater than anyone can imagine. You were not an accident, but My beloved creation.*

"Lilith was human—mortal—before her fall.... If she could sever her soul and her connection to the Creator... then..." I trailed off, my eyes glazing over as I stared at the gated entrance to Eden. How could Lilith abandon something so beautiful and pure and holy? Something that called to my soul with an undeniable love?

Before I faced Lilith in my final battle, I had told Kova that if I had fallen like Lilith had, I would want someone to redeem me. Not kill me. Because of *this*. Because of the love awaiting me on the other side of those gates. Because I wanted my soul to live forever in the Garden of Eden.

It struck like lightning.

"I know how to beat her," I shouted in victory, thrusting a fist into the air. "I know how to beat Lilith!"

My excitement deflated as quickly as it had sparked.

"But I'm still torn. I want to go back. If I don't... what will happen?" I directed the question at Gabriel because he was the Messenger.

"I cannot tell you, Hayden. I am sorry."

"Well, that's helpful," I quipped sarcastically.

My soul was torn.... Every part of me screamed to enter the Garden. To walk through those pearly silver and gold gates to the eternal life of love and peace awaiting me. But a sliver of my soul... a small, almost imperceptible part of me remembered Earth and all the souls alive down there. The souls fighting to defeat Lilith and stop Darkness from overcoming the world.

Despite the heaping responsibilities, the insufferable burden of being the Salem Witch, that small sliver of my soul screamed at me to return to save everyone. To sacrifice my peace and happiness for the path of the Creator and the love waiting below.

Sensing the turmoil of my emotions, Harbor whispered, "Jamie is immortal."

I whipped my head up to stare at her. "What?" I asked dumbly.

"When James was a baby, Lilith knew what he was and killed him in his sleep. He crossed to this side and stood before us, outside these

Gates, as you do now." Michael gestured around. "He chose to return to Earth, and for the selflessness of his choice, I gave him my blessing, endowing him with the power of fire to summon holy flames and gracing him with his superior skills as a warrior."

I let out the breath I didn't know I was holding. "Holy... I did not see that one coming."

My biological father and Gabriel laughed merrily and shared a look. The look of two men who had spent an eternity together.

"Something finally catches you by surprise." Harbor nudged an elbow into my side. "With the power of Spirit, your gift of knowing has been a little too spot on."

I snorted. "My entire life these past five years has been a series of surprises, Harbor. It's only fair I get to be in the know at some point."

"True, though there are more to come, should you return," the Messenger Archangel warned.

"Oh, joy." My tone was sarcastic, but Michael and I shared a smile, and I wondered from whom I inherited which of my personality traits. Searching for my sire's identity for years, I rarely thought about who he was as a person, but about his name.

But now that I knew, I wanted to know everything about him and Leyla.... Were they soulmates? Did they love each other when they conceived me? If Mom wasn't imprisoned, would they be together? Did angels love mortals? Didn't Amara tell me no power was greater than love? Then love... love was more than enough. Did I...?

"Don't you miss him, Harbor?" I asked quietly as emotion clogged my throat. But I knew Harbor heard, and she understood. "You're here and Jamie is on Earth. Forever."

"I miss my brother like the Sea would miss salt if it were taken away from Her. But I find solace in knowing the Creator has a plan greater than what I can comprehend." Pressing a hand to her heart, she said, "Deep in my soul, I know I will see him again." She smiled with tears in her eyes. "Have you made your decision?"

I bit my lip, shaking my head. "I..." I sighed.

Never in my life had I been so torn. I was stubborn, decisive, and confident. But this choice... one that impacted not only my eternal soul but the lives and souls of billions of others... that was what the Trials were for. Each was a monumental decision with unforeseeable consequences. And the Trials led to this ultimate choice.

The Trial of Spirit.

"Yes, but I want to make this decision for the right reasons, not out of selfishness."

"Perhaps I can be of assistance, then," said a familiar voice, one I had not yet heard on this side of the veil.

Isleen appeared from thin air, along with countless other souls who had passed in the war against Lilith. Souls that had died long before I was born as they came face to face with the Mother of Demons or died on account of her actions. There must have been millions gathered outside the gates.

A man with hazel eyes and feathers braided into his dark hair stood hand-in-hand with Isleen, smiling like the sun. Apalla's father... he and Isleen were reunited at last.

"As your godmother, it is my Heavenly duty to guide you, not as the Salem Witch, but as a soul and my daughter's best friend."

I choked on my spit, my eyes bugging out of my head. "Y-you mean..."

Isleen's once cold eyes glinted with laughter. "And who do you think helped your mother give birth to you that fateful night? Who else would Leyla trust other than her best friend?" She gestured to herself with a graceful hand.

"But then..." The pieces fell into place inside my head. "You knew who I was all along?" I accused with laughter in my voice.

"From the moment the Knights brought you into Asylum. Only one witch would be living outside the wards, and I knew Hunter had disappeared." She touched both hands to my cheeks. "But when I saw you... your face is identical to Leyla's. You looked just like her when we were your age."

"The picture..." I trailed off, thinking back to the year of fire.

"What picture?"

"Apalla and I found an old picture of you and Leyla from when you were thirteen. It was a near replica of Hayden and Apalla," Harbor answered.

Isleen snorted. "I should have known after Apollo declared Apalla a Prophetess that she had the foresight to find those."

Harbor shrugged. "We didn't even use her powers. She found them in a box in the basement."

Isleen sighed in defeat.

"Wait a minute... if you were there the night I was born, then did you know...?"

"As Leyla's best friend, I knew the truth of her demonic heritage and was sworn to secrecy. Unlike the rest of Asylum, I knew Lili's true identity was Lilith."

Gesturing to Michael, I asked, "Then did you know..."

Isleen nodded, her hands slipping into the folds of her white cotton pants that matched the ones I wore. "I knew Michael was your father. And I am sorry I could not tell you, for I saw the anguish you endured."

"But if you knew all of this... if you knew Lili is Lilith and that I am the Salem Witch, why didn't you tell me?"

"Because it was not my path," Isleen stated simply. "Goddess appeared to me and made it clear I was not to go about my life any differently and was to keep Lili's hidden identity a secret until you discovered the truth yourself. If I had openly proclaimed against her, she would have killed me." Isleen glanced at her husband. "And if I told you, you wouldn't have undergone the experience you needed to grow as the Salem Witch."

"While I am seriously sick of the secrets"—I cast a narrow eyed glare at Michael, Gabriel, and my dad—"and am angry with all of you."

"Uh oh," Dad groaned. "She can hold a grudge forever."

I shot him a threatening look, then winked. "I understand why you let me figure things out for myself, Isleen."

"Oh, sure, she understands why Isleen kept secrets."

Rolling my eyes, I corrected Hunter. "I understand why everyone kept secrets from me." Pointing to Harbor, I clarified, "But I still have beef with you."

She waggled her eyebrows as she leaned into Ethan, her back pressing against his chest.

"But I get it, Isleen... why Goddess commanded you not to tell me. Otherwise, I might not have been able to accept my darkness and merge my holy flames and hellfire."

Isleen nodded. "It was my job then, as it is now, to guide you, yet let you choose your own path, even if you did not always know it."

"You and Kova," I grumbled.

Isleen placed a hand on each of my shoulders. "You've always had a rebellious streak, a hot temper and inner fire that could not be quenched. You get it from your mother, no doubt."

Michael scoffed. "Well, it certainly doesn't come from me."

"Your mother had an uncanny talent for getting herself into trouble—often dragging me into it. A talent, it seems, you inherited, especially given you drag my daughter into your trouble as well." Isleen winked a pale blue eye at me. "I suppose some friendships are fated. But when it comes to doing the right thing, you have never faltered, Hayden. When the Creator made you seventeen years ago, It presented you with the choice to become the Salem Witch. When confronted with this tremendous task, you accepted and were born into a mortal body. Twelve years later, you arrived in Asylum with nothing.

"You struggled to access your magic, unable to create a wisp of air, but eventually, you prevailed. During your Air Trial, not even thirteen years old, you sacrificed yourself for your friends. A year later, you descended into the Serpent's den to save your father. At fifteen, you stood between Lilith and Thea, shielding the Heart of Earth with your body. And not seven months ago, you risked your life and your Trial to free mortals from their enslavement to Lilith.

"And today you paid the ultimate sacrifice to protect your people. You were not chosen because of your angelic blood. You, a *demon*, were chosen because the Creator uses the most unexpected people to enact the will of God and Goddess and bring about the Kingdom of Light. Your decisions, even when wrong, were driven by the right reasons. Should you return, we will be with you," Isleen said, an air of finality in her voice.

I didn't need her to explain. I already knew.

Looking to Harbor, I asked, "Will you be with me?"

With a smile, she said, "Always."

Nodding stiffly, I swallowed the lump in my throat and blinked back the hot tears threatening to spill over.

"Dad, I..."

"I understand, kiddo." Hunter swept me into another tight embrace, a feeling of finality and acceptance. He knew what my decision would be. Whether it was what he wanted or not, he accepted me anyway.

"Michael," I called to my sire as I stepped out of my dad's embrace. "I..." I faltered, not knowing what to say to him. There weren't words to explain how I felt about him. How honored I was to be his daughter and at peace finally knowing his identity.

"It is okay, Davina." He placed a massive hand on my shoulder, giving it a fatherly squeeze. "I understand. And whatever decision you make, I am proud to call you my daughter."

The waterworks began, the tears spilling down my cheeks as I pressed my lips into a tight line, trying to stop the quivering of my soul-body. Gasping in a breath, I inhaled deeply, using the air to calm my aching soul.

"I've made my decision." I looked at Gabriel expectantly, knowing he saw my heart and soul and knew my choice.

"It is not me who will bless you this time."

I gave him a quizzical look. "Then who?"

"That privilege belongs to me," said a woman's voice, more ethereal and magnificent than any voice I had heard before. It was a voice I knew well.

An impossibly beautiful woman with black skin that glittered like stars twinkling in the night sky appeared before me. Her face was young—thirty-three like everything on this side of the veil—but radiated endless power and love. Straight silver hair fell past her shoulders, stopping at her waist, shining with the shimmering glow of a full moon. But it was her eyes that struck me, and as I peered into the shining silver orbs that lacked a pupil but held the wisdom of countless lifetimes, I understood why my hair and eyes turned silver during a Trial.

It was truly the mark of the Goddess.

"Goddess," I breathed the name.

She smiled, her teeth like beautiful white pearls against her night sky skin. "Hello Hayden, I have missed you so."

Joyful tears filled my eyes. "Goddess, I remember you from when I was made. You were the first thing I opened my eyes to. You and God, together."

"And I have always, and will always, be with you, even when you do not sense my presence. You are never alone."

"I know that now." I swallowed, fighting the tears. "I guess Amara was right... Death really was my gift."

"Death is *one* of your gifts. The real gift is your soul, taken from the essence of both your mother and father, both Heaven and Hell. She pressed a dark hand to my cheek. Despite your flaws, despite your darkness, you are fearfully and wonderfully made. And of all the souls I have made, I chose *you* to be my Salem Witch to bring an end to the Darkness Lilith has inflicted on my creation. You are the one to bring an end to the reason I created the Salem Witch. *That* is your gift, Hayden."

"But my darkness... doesn't it come from Lilith?"

"No, Hayden. Lilith's darkness comes from *Me*. I am the Eternal. There is nothing else. I form Light and create Darkness. I make Peace and create Evil. I am the infinite source of Light, and when I withdraw, Darkness is created. When the infinite source of Peace withdraws, Evil is created.

"Evil is the absence of the Creator. The rejection of Us time and time again. Lilith believes she is evil because it gives her independence from me, but that is her delusion. Her power and immortality originates from Us. But We give Our beloved creations the freedom of choice. Lilith chooses every day to betray the Creator, and that is what makes her evil. Everything exists because of me, even Darkness."

"If I beat Lilith, what will happen to my darkness? Will my demon blood go away?"

"Did I remove your demon blood when your mother beseeched me?"

"No."

"Then why would I do it now?" she asked gently. "The more you deny you have a dark side, the more power it has over you. If I took away your demon blood, you would still have darkness within. I would rather leave you with the darkness you have confronted and conquered and know how to fight than give you a new identity to grapple with, an identity your stubborn soul will likely deny, and you will go through your Fire Trial again."

"If you look for the dark, that is all you will ever see. But even in the darkest of night, we can find the Light, if we choose to," I said, repeating the lesson I had learned so long ago when I merged my holy flames and hellfire.

"Even on the darkest days, the moon is whole. People fear the night, believing it is evil." Goddess gestured to her skin darker than the night sky but glittering with stars. "Yet they forget the night is when we can see the moon and the stars. Magic is neither good nor evil." Goddess placed a hand on each of my cheeks, her silver eyes glowing like the moon. "The same is true of you, my child. You will always walk the line between good and a little wicked. It is your nature, as it is for all my children, whether they are demons or not. You simply understand your darkness better than most. Like the moon, part of humanity will always crave the dark. But the thing about Darkness... It has never overcome My purifying Light."

Goddess's silver eyes peered into me, and my breath hitched at the beauty and wonder staring back at me.

"Many witches, including the Salem Witches, think the Trials are meant to make you physically and magically stronger, more powerful, which is true to an extent, but I had another purpose for the Trials. The Trials teach you different lessons to bring you closer to the essence of My Spirit. To Me.

"Air teaches you sacrifice, intelligence, and seeing life in a different light and hones a cunning, sharp mind. It teaches you to challenge your perceptions and see beyond the obvious. But it also teaches selflessness and humility, traits that are difficult for mortals to learn." She tapped a dark finger against the tip of my nose and smiled.

"Fire teaches you passion, self-acceptance, and self-worth, which comes from the Divine who chose you and loves you. It creates and destroys. Two halves of a coin, like you and me." She pressed a dark hand to the center of my chest and the other to her own heart.

"Water teaches forgiveness and healing, and that you cannot have one without the other. Water comes after Fire because knowing your own darkness is the only way of healing the darkness in others. Your darkness has never stopped you from finding the light within." She pointed a finger at my stomach, where I found that silver sliver of light where my soul and body bridged together.

"Earth teaches you that at your weakest, when you hit rock bottom, I am the rock on which you will rise again, with renewed strength that comes from above. It is knowing yourself and knowing your Creator and knowing We will not let you fail, even when all seems lost and when your life crumbles around you. But in the wreckage, you find that you are unshakeable." Both of her hands landed lightly on my shoulders.

"And Spirit... Spirit is inexorable. It is part of the Holy Trinity, divine in its entire essence. And the Spirit of the divine lives within you, thriving and alive. Spirit knows all the secrets of the Universe and will teach you all things. It is the giver of life to mortal bodies and to those who become immortal.

"You received the power of the Spirit when it came upon you, and your magic will continue to magnify as you walk in the presence of the Spirit of wisdom and understanding, the Spirit of counsel and might, the Spirit of knowledge. The fruit of the Spirit is joy, peace, patience, kindness, goodness, faithfulness, and above all else, *love*. This is the fruit you have produced as the Salem Witch and will continue to produce as a soul. You are not perfect, but Spirit will transform you as you live within its loving Grace for eternity. It is not always pleasant, and life is often painful, the Trials more painful and grueling than the lives that other mortals lead. Pain shapes a woman into a warrior. *My* warrior. But Spirit... Spirit will always guide you."

"If I wasn't Nephilim..." I began, asking the question whose answer I wasn't sure I wanted to know. "If I weren't Nephilim, would I be able to resurrect?"

"You laid down your life, Hayden. No one took it from you, but you did it of your own accord. You had the authority to lay it down, but *I* give you the authority to take it up again. This is the charge you have received from your Creator. Every Salem Witch is given the choice to resurrect, but not all do. It is a selfless decision to return to so much pain and destruction, but the Universe is My creation, and I never abandon My creation, especially My children who have obeyed My commands with so much love."

"Am I making the right decision?"

"All will be well with your soul." Goddess smiled, her silver eyes shining brighter as she swept open her arms. "Merry meet, merry part, and merry meet again, my dearest Davina."

As I stepped into her embrace, silver and gold light erupted from where our bodies met. Heavenly light surrounded me in a blinding display, and I felt holy, unconditional love flood my soul.

CHAPTER FIFTEEN

THE WEIGHT OF A SOUL

I didn't dare open my eyes, afraid to twitch a muscle as my throat stitched itself back together and air forced itself into my lungs. I didn't move, didn't make a sound, just listened.

Darkness covered the earth, but Light was coming.

"The Salem Witch is dead," Elliot roared, eliciting a deafening cheer from Lilith's demons and agonized screams from the Asylum witches.

Time worked differently in Hell.... It worked differently in Heaven, too. Time was eternal up there. But barely any time had passed in the mortal realm.

My magic sang to me, sensing the energy around me to map my surroundings. My body hadn't been moved—why would it have been? As far as Lilith was concerned, it was a corpse.

Only Nephilim had the power to resurrect, and thanks to my mother's brilliant planning, Lilith did not suspect the identity of my sire.

Leyla hung from her cross behind me, while Elliot and Lilith stood in front of the witches who had fallen into a somber silence as watch their last hope died.

Lilith cackled madly, and her demons laughed in guttural tones as the Mother of Demons jeered mockingly.

"Give in, witches. Your champion, the Salem Witch, the supposedly great and powerful Hayden Black, is a coward who chose to take her own life rather than face me. ME, the Mother of Demons, the Queen of this Realm, and your new *goddess*."

Not if I had anything to say about it.

My eyes fluttered open a fraction.

Elliot pumped a fist in the air, displaying my amulet athame like a trophy. That vile serpent had pried the dagger—the weapon completely attuned to all my being—from my cold, dead fingers.

And I wanted it back.

"Bow before your Goddess, pathetic mortals. Hayden Black, your last hope, has *died.* Heaven's champion is gone, and so is your connection to the Creator. Now you put your faith in Lilith." Lilith spoke in the third person like a lunatic.

"No," shouted a young woman. Dani Sanchez stepped forward, and I forced down the panic rising my throat.

Damien reached for her with terror-stricken eyes. But his hand on her elbow did nothing to budge her from where she rooted herself.

"No?" Elliot scoffed with indignation. "You dare to stand against the goddess?"

"She's not our goddess," Dani argued defiantly.

Raising a hand to strike her, Elliot growled, "Why you little—"

"Hayden may be dead, but I'm not," Dani raised her voice as she spoke to the witches rather than to Elliot. "And until I am, I will keep fighting."

My heart swelled at the ferocity of fight alive in Dani.

Thea's ethereal, melodic voice rang out. "Hayden transferred her blessing of impenetrable free will to me last year. She died so Lilith could not harness the power of the Maiden through her."

"Hayden sacrificed herself so you couldn't channel her." Kelsey spoke directly to Lilith, all fear set aside. Leave it to the former witch of terror to be fearless in the face of the Mother of Demons. "Without her, you can't claim the power of the Maiden, and without that, you don't have the Power of Three. You know it, Hayden knew it, and we know it. You're nothing more than a pathetic, petulant child pissed off at her mommy for wanting you to grow up and act like a woman. Pfft." Kelsey flipped her platinum hair with black streaks over her shoulder and hiked her hands on her hips.

"I should have killed you when I had the chance," Elliot marched toward Kelsey, my dagger gripped in his hand, poised to strike her down.

Kelsey faced him without fear, neon yellow magic billowing around her as she placed herself between him and Dani, who held her blade at the ready.

Shadows gathered at my command, converging on my body, wrapping around me like a cocoon and hurtling me through space until I materialized before Elliot, my shirt blood-soaked and my neck stained with a line of crimson.

I had finally spooked.

"Boo."

Lunging forward, I head-butted Elliot in the nose, the bone shattering under my forehead. Simultaneously, I ripped my amulet athame from his hand, then spun in a circle and cracked the pommel against his temple.

Kelsey didn't miss a beat, jumping forward and thrusting out her arms as she glared at Elliot. He froze where he kneeled, ensnared by Kelsey's mind control.

Lilith, overcoming her shock, rushed me with my longsword as she hissed like a serpent. Black lightning shot from my hands, electrocuting Lilith until she collapsed to the ground, smoke wafting off her convulsing body.

"Form the circle," I shouted at my friends, who were already leaping into action.

Jamie shouted, "But we don't have a water elemental."

"Yes, we do," I yelled back, not stopping to explain.

I called upon the power of Spirit, and as a master, the element heralded my call. My hair and eyes turned silver as I rushed my mother. Silver, black, and white light flooded out of my hand, turning my athame into a weapon of Spirit and Light. Black lightning crackled in my hair as the holy power of Spirit infused every cell of my immortal body.

Without slowing, I leapt into the air, sailing toward Leyla with my hand outstretched, and slammed the athame of Spirit and Light into her heart. The light sank into her chest. Power erupted from the tool, sinking into my mother's body.

Black lightning ricocheted through her body, and she glowed with the light of the Heavens. Sheer power threw me back. Slamming into the ground, I rolled over gravel in a knot of flailing limbs, black hair tangling around my face and obstructing my vision. Skidding to a halt, I groaned from the road burn. I might be immortal, but it still hurt.

Flopping to my back and spitting out my black hair, I opened my blue eyes to a blade sailing toward me, aimed at my heart.

Lilith's dark purple eyes blazed with the intensity of Hell and murderous resolve.

A pale hand appeared from thin air, catching Lilith by the wrist and stopping her from sinking Nightmare into my heart. Not that it would kill me, but I did *not* want to have to resurrect a second time.

Shock and fear replaced the rage in Lilith's purple eyes.

"Hello, *mother*." My mother growled at Lilith. Leyla turned, twisting her body to throw Lilith over her shoulder. Lilith's back slammed into the ground, knocking the air from her lungs. Leyla stood above the Mother of Demons, my Nightmare clutched in her hands. "You will never lay another hand on my daughter, because Davina Michaelson is about to put an end to your days."

Understanding blossomed on Lilith's face at the mention of my last name, but Leyla had turned her back to her mother and swept toward Kova, who stood at the front of the watching crowd.

With a wicked grin, I shot another bolt of black lightning into Lilith, incapacitating her while I spooked to the eastern point of my circle. Materializing before Apalla, I had never been so happy to see her smiling face.

"Ready?" she asked.

"Let's end this war."

We didn't need to speak an invocation, not this time. Apalla gripped my hands, and together, we summoned air to our fingertips. Thrusting our arms out, a tornado of wind swirled around our circle.

Lilith's tased body was ripped off the ground to be flung through the fierce currents. I might have smirked a bit too smugly at her shriek.

With a wink, I spooked. Apalla disappeared and was replaced with my Jamie. He stared at me with wonder, awe, and pure joy on his face.

"You get the holy flames?" I asked.

"Only if you get the hellfire."

Without a word, but in complete sync, we swept our arms to our respective rights, our hands curled into fists. Black hellfire sparked from my fists and white holy flames surged out of Jamie's. Our fires rapidly spread, forming a protective ring around our circle. My black flames danced happily with his white ones, like the two always belonged to each other.

Spooking, I re-materialized at the western-most point of my circle.

"Hello, sister," Harbor's silvery-blue spirit form appeared before me.

"Welcome back, Harbor."

Jamie choked in surprise from where he stood on the south side of the circle.

"It is my pleasure." She grinned wickedly at Lilith's form spinning in the whirlwind above us.

Harbor offered her open palms, and I took them in mine without hesitation. Despite being a spirit, she felt like a solid body.

At our command, storm clouds brewed in the sky. A torrential downpour flooded our circle, the holy water sizzling against Lilith's skin, burning her demon flesh and the flesh of the demons aligned with her. The demons that chose me as their princess stood untouched by the waters of salvations.

Harbor winked, and I spooked to Thea.

Thea smirked, then said, "Welcome home, Daughter of Heaven."

With laughter in my voice, I asked, "Did you know all along?"

"What do you think?" She winked an emerald green eye, but it wasn't much of a question.

She lifted her staff between us, and with both hands, she slammed the butt of it into the earth. I placed my hands over hers, merging our powers. The ground trembled into a massive earthquake. But my circle stood unaffected.

Spooking into the middle of the tornado high above the ground, I grabbed a stunned Lilith by the throat and spooked to the ground. Lilith's knees slammed into the earth as I released the hand around her neck.

Heavenly Spirit flooded my body, transforming my hair and eyes to metallic silver as the mark of the Goddess kissed my features. Silver angel wings, made from wisps of light and Spirit, protruded from my back in a holy display of the might of the Salem Witch. Angel choirs sounded the call, the melodious tune a haunting music to the Mother of Demons as Heaven trumpeted their impending victory.

With the powers of Heaven and Hell in perfect balance within me, I summoned Isleen and the spirits who had accompanied her when I stood before the Gates of Heaven, unearthly whispering filling the air as they chanted in an unknown language—one my soul recognized even when my mortal ears did not. Enochian—the language of angels.

But it wasn't just the witches who died in this Salem War. Every soul slain by Lilith appeared in my circle, their hands joined.

Lilith's purple eyes widened with undiluted fear. We were a fearsome sight to behold. Isleen laid a hand on my left shoulder as the man who raised me rested his hand on the other.

The sensation of a call echoed through me, a call that demanded an answer. And my magic eagerly responded to the Creator. The power was intoxicating, and the sheer amount of Spirit coursing through me was simultaneously frightening and exhilarating as I channeled it with absolute certainty.

With Spirit in my soul, I placed my right hand on Lilith's heart and pressed the left hand to the crown of her head. Feeling the power rage through me, I urged Spirit to its zenith.

The earth began to shake, and the veil was torn, allowing me to reach my right hand into the depths of Hell, where a sliver of purple light glowed dimly at the bottom of the Pit, writhing in agony from the fire around it.

The white light of Heaven flowed from my hands and into Lilith. Light that pushed back the Darkness.

As only the Master of Spirit and Death—a Princess of Hell and Daughter of Heaven—could do with the powers gifted by the Creator, I pushed the Light of Grace into her body.

White light flashed, and when it faded, the souls who had joined me departed, returning to their Home in the Garden of Eden where they could rest in eternal peace.

Lilith lay prostrate on the ground, her limbs weak and black locks of hair covering her face as she laid before Heaven, finally humbled after countless millennia of sin.

White light shined from the sky above, and bolts of black lightning shot to the earth, obliterating the demons aligned with the Dark Mother until the army of demons that had infiltrated my home was ash on the wind.

The magic left my loyal demons untouched. Spirit knew. It knew everything, and It rewarded those who were obedient, even if my demons lacked a soul. But it wouldn't be long.

Thanking Spirit, I released my hold on the magic, letting it fade from my body, and with it, my hair returned to its normal shade of black and my eyes sparkled their normal blue. Thanking each element, I closed the circle. As the magic released, my friends rushed toward me, joining me where I stood over Lilith.

Lilith groaned and rolled to her back, her once alabaster skin now a luscious tan, like it was before she fell and became the Mother of Demons.

"What did you do to me?" she rasped out the words like it was a struggle to speak.

"What the—" Kelsey jumped back. "You didn't kill her."

"Nope." I popped the 'p' as I placed my hands on my hips.

"Then what was the point of summoning the circle?" Jamie waved a hand. "All of those souls?"

"Because killing the Mother of Demons was impossible. Even if I could bring myself to drive a sword through her heart, it wouldn't kill her. Lilith fell from Grace to gain immortality, so I turned her into the thing she despises most."

"Which is?"

Staring Lilith directly in her dark purple eyes, I said a single word, the power of the Salem Witch reverberating in my voice. "Human."

She gasped, horror tearing through her features.

"No!" Her infernal scream reverberated through the field around the cathedral.

Squatting, I held her gaze. "You are no longer immortal, for I reached into Hell and placed my right hand upon your soul and pulled it from the depths of Hell to reunite your Darkness with your Light. You can never again separate from the soul bestowed upon you by Heaven. You will live the rest of your days as a human, devoid of magic, and when your mortal body turns to dust, you will meet your Maker, but you will not be allowed into the Garden of Eden until you have atoned for your sins.

"Instead, you will reincarnate into another mortal body—human, not witch—and when that one dies, the cycle will repeat itself until you redeem yourself in the eyes of the One True Redeemer. Then, and only then, will you be welcomed Home with open arms.

"So long as you freely choose to reject the Creator's love, eternity will be nothing less than torment, because the Creator will continue to love you. All you managed to achieve in these sinful millennia is to create your own personal Hell.

"Here's the thing, Lilith." I grabbed her chin, forcing her to look me in the eye. "You have to learn how to be good. Want a hint? Temptation will be laid in front of you, like the Devil did with the golden apple in the Garden, but being good isn't about being pure and perfect. It's knowing there is something more important and choosing to overcome temptation instead of giving into it. Until you learn that lesson, you will be stuck in this cycle of reincarnation."

Snatching her left wrist, I lifted her hand so she could stare at the band of ink wrapping around her left ring finger—black filigree edging a colorful image of a serpent biting into a golden apple.

"And it will be torture for you, being separated from your soulmate who rests in the Garden. Yes, Adam was flawed, but he found his redemption in the millennia since the Fall. Imagine the pain he suffered being isolated from his soulmate while you felt nothing. Now, you will pay the price you inflicted on him. And it will be what drives you to save your immortal soul. Even Evil needs the Light. The Creator is eternal... They will wait until you are ready."

"No," Lilith screamed, pounding her fist against the ground. "No. No. No. No. No." She thrashed against the ground, throwing a temper tantrum like the petulant child Kelsey had called her earlier. She gasped. "This cannot be! You cannot do this!"

A swirling red portal burst to life mere feet from where Lilith lay screaming into the grass.

From the Devil's portal emerged an alluring woman with thick, curled black hair dyed red at the ends, creamy mocha skin, and supernatural red eyes with snake-like slits instead of round pupils. Her nails were immaculate, and her makeup was perfection, but it was the way she walked, like a wild mountain cat on the prowl, that made every witch draw their swords and all my demons hiss in warning.

The Red Demon sauntered toward Lilith, sneering at her mother in disgust. Ignoring everyone else, she addressed me. "I've come to collect the payment you promised Lucifer in your Bargain."

Witches and demons gasped. Kova looked to me in alarm. But Leyla rocked back on her heels, unphased by the revelation of my Devil's Bargain.

Apalla muttered, "Hayden, do you have any idea who that is?"

I nodded, a wicked grin twisting my lips. "How could I not know Lucifiana Nightfall? She is family, right Auntie?"

Lucifiana scowled, but I could see the mischievous humor alight in her eyes that was probably lost on the rest of the world.

Always poised, Lucifiana inclined her head toward my mom. "Hello, Sister. Glad to see you free again."

"Hello, Lucifiana," Mom spoke without malice, but with blatant curiosity as to why her sister—a greater demon—was here to collect on a deal I made with the Devil. "It feels good to have my free will back. I hope life is good for you..."—she furrowed her brow as she said the next words—in Hell."

Lucifiana gestured to Elliot immobilized by Kelsey's neon yellow magic. "You upheld your end of the Bargain?"

"No fatal wounds or permanent maiming." I held my hands up placatingly. Elliot's arm had regrown.

Nodding, she started toward Lilith, but I shot a stream of silver flames in front of her, forcing her to halt. "Just so we are clear, the moment you take her through your portal, I have upheld my end of the deal. I require nothing from Lucifer, and I owe him nothing."

Lucifiana gave me a cheeky smile. "You're as cunning as the Devil, mutt. I'll give you that."

The Red Demon used one hand to scoop up a screaming, thrashing Lilith and toss her over a red leather-clad shoulder. With the other hand, she snagged Elliot by the scruff and, dragging him behind her like a rag doll, marched through the swirling red portal. The portal slammed shut behind her, as though the entrance to Hell had never existed.

Silence descended on us. Not a word was uttered. Like we had been fighting for so long that we didn't know what to do with ourselves now.

"Hold on..." Leave it to Kelsey to break the silence. "You died." She poked my chest with her finger, as if checking I was truly made of flesh and bone. "But here you are."

I snorted. "Yeah, it didn't stick."

"Why is everything with you so weird?" Kelsey scrunched her nose at me, eliciting an eye roll from Apalla.

A distinct voice floated through my mind. A voice I knew intimately, for I had met one half of the Divine face to face outside the Garden. It was ethereal and melodic, masculine and feminine, earthly and otherworldly.

When light shines in the east, your mark shall be complete.

Silently, I thanked my Creator for the extra time.

"Haywire..." Jamie choked on my name as he approached me. Raising a hand, he reached to grab my shoulder, then hesitated, like I was a ghost and his hand would pass through me.

My bottom lip trembled. Tears stung my eyes, threatening to overflow, but I wouldn't cry. If I did, I wouldn't be able to stop.

"I promised I would come back to you, Angel Boy," I said, my voice quivering as I fought the tears.

Jamie made a strangled, choking sound, and I threw myself at him. His arms flew open, catching me and pulling me into his warm, muscular chest. Strong arms embraced me, and a hand stroked my hair. I nearly purred at the touch but grimaced as his hand snagged on the tangles.

I didn't want to think about how nasty my hair was after going to Hell and back, fighting a war, and then dying and resurrecting. But none of it mattered while he held me in his arms. I never knew I could feel this way with someone, but I should have known it was Jamie. It was always Jamie.

"I recall you never actually said the words, 'I promise'," Jamie murmured into my hair.

Laughter bubbled out of me, and a strangled choke escaped my lips as I reluctantly extracted myself from his embrace, but kept my hands in his. Neither of us wanted to let go of the other.

Someone coughed, and another person cleared their throat, but Kelsey loudly said, "Oh Goddess, they're nauseatingly cute."

But for once, I didn't care. I had lived through too much and died through too much. I couldn't wait for sunrise.

Rolling my eyes, I pulled my hands from Jamie's, but winked at him, and this time, I saw his heart melt in his chest.

"Weird it out, Kels," I said to the air witch. I didn't care how weird it made her feel—she could endure the weirdness of our PDA. They all could.

"Weird it out?" She rolled her pale blue eyes. "There's something seriously unhinged about you."

I grinned wickedly. "Oh, most definitely. But life is so much more interesting when you're a little crazy."

"It's even more fun to make things weird in the afterlife." Kova nodded in agreement. "I'm sure Gabriel never wants to see me on the other side of the veil again. I drove him nuts."

"Speaking of which..." I turned to her, my head cocking. "How did you do that? I know when we die a mortal death, our souls temporarily cross the veil, but I swear, like no time passed here on Earth. So, how did you keep yourself dead for seven months?"

"I used Spirit to expand the length of time I spent on the other side of the veil. Time doesn't work the same in Heaven as it does for the mortal world. Nephilim can choose to return immediately if we want, but we always have the option of hanging around for a while. But eventually, our immortal bodies pull our souls back to this side of the veil." She shrugged. "At least I got to spend quality time with my mother for the first time in over three centuries."

"But the pain of killing yourself repeatedly..."

"It wasn't the pain of death. It was the pain of separating my soul and immortal body, which are eternally tied, that was unbearable...." Kova grimaced as she recalled the pain. "Killing myself with Spirit while Lilith tried to use black magic to tie my soul to the mortal plane was pain like nothing I had ever felt before. It was being struck with a hundred fists as invisible hands ripped open my chest and wrenched my soul from its bodily shell. As soon as my soul snapped back into my body, I killed myself again, so Lilith's magic couldn't seize my soul and channel the power of Spirit."

"I hate to be the one to ruin the moment," Thea began. Gesturing to the meandering witches and demons, she asked, "But... what are we to do next?"

Kova released a haggard sigh. But it was my turn to be the leader. She had shouldered the burden for over three hundred years, and this war belonged to me, and I was going to see it through, no matter how grim.

"Everyone, go home," I announced, causing whispered murmurs to break out among the people. "Get cleaned up, rest, eat something. Tend to your wounds. Those of you who need medical attention, seek it. Anyone who is able-bodied and won't drop dead of exhaustion, we could use your help."

"To do what?" a random witch shouted.

I stared at my people. "Many of our own have fallen in this war, sacrificing their lives so we may live. It is only right that we honor their sacrifices with the Rites of the Warrior. We will gather the dead and give them a proper burial. My demons," I called, earning shuffling of feet and looks of uncertainty from many of the witches. But I didn't care as I smiled at my beautiful, dark, demon army.

"My demons, you have fought bravely and valiantly. You, beings without souls, chose to align with a Daughter of Heaven. You stood defiantly against Lilith and for that, you will always have my thanks. But it is only fair that I give my warriors something in return."

Demons muttered amongst themselves. My eyes found Jackal's amber orbs as I spoke my next words. "I can bestow upon you the power of Light. I can merge your essence with the power of Heaven to turn your consciousness into a soul. This is different than what I did to Lilith. She can never separate her Darkness from her Light, but you who did not previously have a choice as you were born exclusively from Darkness will be able to fall from Grace as she once did. But, as a soul, you will have the free will to make the decision for yourself."

Silence blanketed the crowd.

And then somewhere, a hellhound howled, then another and another, and the demons broke out into cheers and applause. There might have even been a few sobs.

"All hail Hayden Black," Jackal shouted, his panther tail swishing wildly as he leaped in the air. "The Warrior Witch has saved us all." The crowd of demons went wild.

Demons and witches cheered, though some witches broke away from the crowd, most of them limping or helping others to seek medical attention.

"Kelsey." I beckoned her over. "How are you holding up?"

She casually shrugged a shoulder. "Better than most. What do you need me to do?" she asked, already knowing what was on my mind.

I gestured to the demons. "It's going to take me a while to give souls to seventeen thousand demons."

"You need me to organize the people into shifts so they can rest but also help us gathered our dead."

"Yes."

Apalla appeared beside me. One look at her face had me asking, "What's the problem?"

Her face was grim, and her eyes flashed gold as she relayed her warning, "The Supreme Council will be arriving by portal just before dawn. We only have a few hours to prepare."

Kelsey rolled her eyes and groaned. "Oh joy, I get to explain to Regalia why I didn't abandon the war effort and come home when she commanded me to. This should be good."

I placed a hand on her shoulder. "You don't have to explain a thing to them. They can go through me if they want to get to you or any of my people." A wicked smile pulled at my lips. "What can they do to a fully realized Salem Witch?"

Apalla snickered as Kelsey cracked a smile.

"Thank you," she said sincerely, causing Apalla's jaws to drop. Apalla still had a hard time accepting Kelsey's genuine goodness. Kels frowned. "What? I'm not always mean and scornful."

"Just most of the time," Apalla pointed out.

"Exactly," Kelsey agreed. "I'll get started on those things." Turning on her heel, she marched off, barking out orders.

Apalla and I stared after her, in awe of the force of her command.

"She's going to make a man very happy someday," Apalla remarked.

I snorted. "No, she's going to ruin his life."

We grinned at each other.

Apalla sobered as she asked me, "What do you need me to do?"

"Get Harlan and have him build three pyres to place our fallen. We need white cotton linens to wrap them in. Kelsey will get the air elementals to move the bodies." Apalla flinched at my last word. "Hey," I spoke softly, placing my hands on her shoulders. "Death is not the end. I saw Isleen and your dad. My dad has reincarnated in an endless cycle for the last three centuries to be with Kova. Maybe we can't all resurrect, but they are at peace."

Tears welled in her eyes. "I-I know," she sniffled. "But... Mom and I didn't always get along." She laughed hoarsely. "Actually, we never got along, but I love her."

Wrapping my arms around my bestie, I pulled her into an embrace, probably squeezing a little too tight. "And she loves you with all her heart. And so does your father. I'm sorry for your loss, Apalla. But they are watching over you. I know it."

Apalla sobbed into my shoulder, and I held her amidst the chaos, giving ourselves a temporary reprieve before we had to be brave and face the world.

Apalla pulled away, wiping at her eyes with her sleeve, "O-okay, I'm good now." And with one last hug, she turned and sprinted into the crowd, disappearing into the swarm of witches and demons.

When she was gone, I searched for the rest of my circle, but they were nowhere to be found.

"Kelsey dragged Jamie off, and Thea is returning the remaining soldiers from the Terracotta Army to their underground vault," Kova said, running a hand through her spiky red hair.

"Ugh," I let out the groan. "Crap, add returning my army of the dead to their final resting places to my ridiculously long and growing to-do list."

Kova raised an eyebrow at me. "Aren't you forgetting something?"

"Oh no, what else?" I sighed, closing my eyes with a grimace. "Just hit me with it."

Kova chuckled. "You have another Salem Witch at your disposal."

My eyes flew open. "Oh wow, I totally forgot." I cocked my head at her. "You know, I'm not sure it's ever going to sink in that you're Alice Parker."

"Oh, no? And why is that?"

"Because you'll always be the mentor who is like a big sister to me." I scrunched my brow. "And the woman who dated my dad for the last three centuries. That one will take some getting used to."

Kova tossed her head back and roared with laughter. "Ah kid, never change."

"So," I braced my hands on my hips, "as my predecessor, tell me—how did I do in the Trials?"

"Incredible, kid." The Salem Witch winked a hunter green eye at me. "The Trials taught you well. You are the most powerful witch to walk the earth, and we will need that power for what is to come," Kova warned gravely, placing a hand on my shoulder. "My Salem War ended when I killed a demon. Yours ended when you saved one. Even with Lilith gone, Evil is not. Evil does not die. It bides its time."

She cupped my cheek with a hand. "But love is stronger than death. You showed mercy when I had none, and now Elliot holds the power of a Prince, which will be a problem, yet I can't bring myself to regret killing Asmodeus. But the Trials are about choices we make with our own free will, and your actions have proven why you are the greatest Salem Witch." She patted me on the shoulder. "I'll take care of the army of the dead. You get these demons their souls. After eternity, they've waited long enough."

She spooked in a flash of brilliant green light.

And for the first time in my entire life, I was granted a moment alone with my mother, the woman who had sacrificed her freedom so I might live. I just stared, drinking her in.

She was short, no taller than her mother, who stood at five foot three. She had the same long wild locks as Lilith, the same midnight black pigment she had passed on to me. The shape of her face, the curve of her chin, her high cheekbones, even her sharp nose, which had a slight bump like it had been broken and healed, were exactly the same as mine. Everything except the eyes. While I inherited the eyes of my father, hers were a beautiful lavender.

"Mom," I didn't mean for the word to come out as a whisper, but she heard me, her eyes snapping to mine in an instant. Tears filled our eyes, and I said it again, this time louder, "Mom."

Lunging forward, I pulled the woman, who was so much shorter than me, into a bone-crushing hug. She dropped Nightmare, leaving it to sink into the mud so she could hug me as hard as I hugged her.

Together, we sobbed, not out of frustration, not because of the years we spent apart, not because of the life stolen from us, but because despite all of that, after all these years, we were finally embracing as mother and daughter should. I didn't know how much time passed. All I knew was it didn't feel like enough when we finally pulled away.

Mom placed both her hands on my cheeks and stared into my eyes. "I owe you my life, Davina."

I couldn't help but laugh, my voice hoarse from the crying. Half laughing, half crying, I said, "I'm pretty sure you saving my life is what got you into this mess. I owe my life to *you*, Mom."

She smiled so broadly, her jaw popped. "You have no idea how good it is to hear you call me that."

"You've always been my mother. I just didn't always know it. I'm sorry," I choked on a sob. "I'm sorry for all those years I harbored anger for you. I didn't know… I didn't understand it at the time, but now I do, and I'm… I'm just really sorry."

"Shh, shh, shh. It's not your fault, Davina."

All I could do was nod, because I was afraid if I tried to speak, I would be hit with another wave of the waterworks.

"Now, what do you need me to do?"

I choked. "Mom, you can't be serious?"

"What?" Her face twisted in confusion.

I stared at her with wide eyes. "Dude, I just freed you from seventeen years of slavery, and you're ready to jump in and clean up? You need to rest, Mom."

I would never get sick of saying that word.

"No, no." She shook her head fervently. "I have been resting for seventeen years. I want to do something useful."

My lips twisted into a grin. "Then I have just the thing."

CHAPTER SIXTEEN

AFTER ALL THESE YEARS...

If demons could get drunk, I would have sworn several were hiding flasks. They were drunk on the life and freedom denied to them for an eternity.

Even with my mom's help to contain my demons while I blessed all seventeen thousand with a soul—one by one—it was a grueling task. But it was a task I willingly completed for my demons. And my beloved Jackal was the first to receive his soul, followed by Buddy.

My first, most loyal demons finally had their souls and their freedom. I couldn't help but smile as the green-eyed cat nuzzled his face against my neck as he perched on my shoulder. Green-eyed, because the moment I created and imbued a soul in my demons, their eyes changed from amber colored or balls of hellfire to an array of colors, each unique to reflect their soul.

Despite the amount of magic I extolled, I didn't feel drowsy. Magic sang in my veins—barely a drop gone from using Spirit to create souls—begging to be used. It was *more* than it had been before my resurrection.

Was this how Kova always felt? Was this the power of a fully realized Salem Witch or the intoxicating power of an immortal? If it was the latter, I understood how easy it was for Lilith to give into her temptation, but part of me longed for the Garden, which is how I knew I was nothing like my ancestor.

My blood-stained combat boots slammed into the ground as shadows deposited me next to Kelsey, startling her so fiercely that she jumped five feet in the air. Literally—air witch.

Pressing her hand to her heart, she scolded, "You scared the hell out of me."

"Seems like it's becoming a regular thing for me." I smirked at her, eliciting an eye roll. I nodded to the witches gathering the bodies of our fallen brothers and sisters in the field outside the cathedral. "How are things going?"

"Progressing since Kova and Thea returned the Terracotta Army and your creepy army of skeletons." A shudder wracked her body. "For the love of the Goddess, please never bring those things to life again."

I snorted and held up my palms. "No promises. You can blame Kova for that army. She's the one who stashed them in the tomb under the Spellery and my house."

Kelsey rolled her eyes and muttered something about insufferable Salem Witches. "Apalla said we have two hours before the Supreme Council arrives via portal. We won't finish in time, which is fine, but—"

"No," I cut her off, my expression darkening with fierce resolve. "We will finish, and we will give our people the burial they deserve before the Council arrives. I won't allow them to taint this ceremony."

Kelsey nodded, doubt and determination mixed in her pale eyes. "The infirmary is overflowing with wounded patients. The people with lesser injuries are toughing it out, but after three days of battle, the healers are low on magic."

Magic sang in my veins, ready to do my bidding. "How can I help?"

Kelsey pursed her lips, thinking for a minute before saying, "Kova has been spooking between here and the hospital. We should tell her to stay there, because no offense, but you don't exactly have the healing touch."

I snorted. "None taken. Master of Death and healing don't exactly go hand in hand."

She frowned. "Can't you heal yourself now?"

I opened my mouth, then closed it, shaking my head. "Yeah, but it's different. I don't know how to explain it. It's like Spirit resurrects my body without me asking. But I'm still a trash healer," I grumbled.

You would think my healing abilities would have improved after I passed my Water Trial, but I had a sneaking suspicion the angels were laughing at my pathetic abilities.

"Have Kova stay at the hospital and transfer Spirit into the healers."

Closing her eyes to send a telepathic message to Kova. "Done."

"How can I help?" I asked Kelsey, my eyes scanning the field filled with witches working to pile bodies on the three pyres.

Air witches used their element to lift and move the bodies. Earth elementals rolled the earth under the bodies, and water witches summoned their element from the lake to freeze the bodies in an icicle, then passed the ice cube from witch to witch until it reached the pyre, where another witch melted the ice. But fire elementals… fire wasn't exactly helpful until we were ready to burn the pyres, so they carried the fallen by hand, my mother working alongside them with her petite stature of five-foot-two.

"Can you detect the dead?" Kelsey asked, tearing my focus from the working Asylumnites as she summoned a gust of wind to lift the body of a fallen Knight. A twinge of guilt ripped through me. "We need someone to find and transport the fallen bodies scattered throughout Asylum."

Solemnly, I nodded. "I can do that."

And I disappeared in a flash of black to reappear where Spirit told me lay a dead witch.

"Hello, Kane," I said sadly, staring at the mountain of a man lying in a mountain of black demon dust. He must have taken out thousands of demons before they killed him.

Crouching next to his head, I swiped my hand over his face to close his eyes. "Thank you for all the years of training, and thank you for protecting my home when I could not." I placed a hand, fingers spread wide, on his barrel chest and spooked, bringing his body to rest alongside his brother and sister Knights on the center pyre.

Disappearing in another flash of black, I located the next body and brought it to the pyre. Then again and again, until I lost count of the number of bodies I recovered.

Seven pyres were a heartbreaking sight, stacked far too high with the bodies of our fallen brothers and sisters. Demons and witches had gathered at Kelsey's call, and I stood at the forefront of the crowd.

My mother stood beside me, her calming presence soothing and comfortable, like a mother should be in times of grief. Kova stood on Mom's left, waiting to invoke the Rites of the Warrior for our comrades.

Red light flashed in my peripheral, and Jamie's warm hand enveloped my own. He didn't say a word, and neither did I. We just took comfort in knowing the other was there. We hadn't gotten the opportunity to speak since right after I resurrected. The moment wasn't right. Not until sunrise.

"Davina," Mom spoke my name softly. "It is time."

I nodded and released Jamie's hand, stepping forward. A heartbeat later, he and Kova followed me as I strode to the middle of the circle of witches gathered around the pyres.

Kova's green eyes scrutinized me. "Are you ready for this?"

I blew out a haggard breath. "How did you do it?"

"I didn't," she spoke quietly, only loud enough so I could hear. "I was among the last eight to die in the trials, and they were buried in shallow graves next to mine. When all of Salem assumed I was dead, I reburied them in the dead of night. I didn't have an audience or loved ones to bring solace to. The Creator is always with you. And your father. Ask him, and he will answer."

I didn't respond as I closed my eyes and bowed my head, humbling myself before my people and Heaven as I asked my father for guidance.

I think about you always, my Davina. Do not speak to them as a warrior, nor as the Salem Witch. Do not speak to them as an immortal. Telling them of the Garden will not ease their grief, for finding the Garden within ourselves is a trial of faith we all must face as individuals, even angels. Speak to them as one of their own, as one who shares in their grief.

A single tear welled in my eye, and I let it roll down my cheek and drop to the dry dirt below. Thanking my father and my Creator, I lifted my face to the sea of witches to share the words that came from a power greater than me.

Raising my silver wand to press against my throat, I muttered the words to the spell to magnify my voice.

"Brothers and sisters, it is with a heavy heart I stand before you. Today, we won a great victory, but at an immeasurable expense. We defeated Lilith—no, do not be afraid to say her name," I insisted as they erupted in hushed mutterings. "But we lost our loved ones, never again to live among us on this side of the veil."

"But you did," someone shouted from the crowd. "You returned from the dead."

Mutterings erupted among as they speculated the vastness of my power.

"You can bring them back," someone half demanded, half asked, grief and desperation ripping through their voice.

Pain panged through my chest. They didn't understand the ways of Spirit. Not like I did. Not like Kova did.

"I had to answer the same questions," Kova muttered. "Although, all of Salem knew who my mother was and why I could resurrect."

"The power of resurrection is not one I can bestow on others." Sympathy laced my voice. "It is not my power, but I am a vessel for Spirit. And while the Creator is unlimited, I am not. But if I could restore souls to this world, I would not." Roars of rage rang out in response to my words, but a blast of magic had them quieting. "Not without their permission. When a soul enters the Garden, the most painful thing you can do is rip them from their eternal home and force them back here... like it is for those of us who become immortal."

"That's a load of crap," someone argued, hatred and rage brimming in their voice. "Immortality is a privilege, and you act like it's a punishment."

"Explain why Harbor Bishop, Nephilim daughter of Gabriel, didn't return?" I countered gently.

Silence.

"Why did you?" a small voice asked. A girl, no older than thirteen.

My eyes flickered to Jamie for the briefest fraction of a second, but the child caught the movement. Her shrewd eyes, which had seen too much death and destruction for her age, cut to Jamie, as though she knew the depths of my feelings for him.

"Because," I started, kneeling before the child. "I had a duty to this world. A duty only my soul could fulfill. And because the Creator asked it of me. The Creator's path is not always easy, but no servant of God and Goddess can enact Their will and build Their kingdom without enduring suffering and trials and pain."

Satisfied, the little girl nodded, then rejoined her family.

"Now, I ask that we honor the sacrifice of our loved ones, and all those who died because of Lilith, with a moment of silence and stillness."

Asylum followed my example in folding their hands and bowing their heads. I'm not sure how much time passed, and I was kind of freaking out that I either let it go too long or cut it too short, but when I raised my head and thanked those gathered, they looked to me once more, waiting for me to continue.

"Every life lost is a tragedy—a tragedy that cannot be undone. We are free because of the brave. Every person here died with the honor of a true soldier, and for their sacrifices, they have earned the Rites of the Warrior, a small thing compared to what they have given us, but it is all we have to offer them."

Lifting my hands, palms facing out, holy flames flew from my palms to spark a perfectly white fire underneath the pyres. Pouring power into my holy flames—the gift I now knew came from my father—I fueled the fire until it crawled up the pyres, licking over the wood until it reached the bodies wrapped in white cotton cloths.

Lowering my arms, I stared at the flames and chanted the Rites of the Warrior.

The Spirit of the Warrior Archangel resides within you.
You honored yourself, your ancestors,
And your loved ones as you alone stood for your Creator,
No matter the odds, no matter the consequences.
When the world quaked and rose against you,
You did not move, but planted yourself as a tree

Beside the river of truth
And stood with the stance of a warrior.

Though you fell with the courage of a thousand armies,
May you one day rise with the innocence of the Maiden,
The love of the Mother,
And the wisdom of the Crone.
We commit these bodies to the ground
From whence we all came,
Earth to earth, ash to ash, dust to dust,
In sure and certain hope of the eternal life
Awaiting us in the Garden.
Rejoice in knowing they are at peace
And know one day we will reunite through our Creator.
Merry meet, merry part, and merry meet again.

"Merry meet, merry part, and merry meet again," the swarm of witches repeated before slowly dispersing.

Ending the spell amplifying my voice, I released a heavy sigh.

As the crow thinned, Apalla approached. With a grimace, she said, "Hayden... the Supreme Council has arrived. They're waiting in the cathedral."

With a sigh, I closed my eyes, paying tribute to my fallen soldiers one last time and collecting myself for what came next. Opening my eyes, I turned to face my friends, their faces full of sorrow.

"The sooner this is done, the better," Kova muttered. "Hayden, are you prepared to deal with Regalia and Elizabeth?"

"I am."

She studied me intently, her ancient green eyes seeing more than I realized. "They will use everything in their arsenal to force you to submit to them. Regalia will blame the deaths of these people on you to tarnish your reputation in the witching world. Do not let your rage get the better of you."

"If she can discredit you, she will be the ultimate power in the world." Mom said sagely. "With Lilith gone, Regalia fears one witch—*you*. You are the only thing standing between her and the power she craves—dominion over the witching world."

"And Elizabeth hates you," Kova added with a smirk. "Don't worry, she always hated me, too. She still doesn't know Hunter is my soulmate."

"Oh, this is going to be fun," I chuckled with a wicked grin, provoking groans from my circle. "How do I look?" I held my arms wide to show off my blood-soaked shirt.

"Frightful."

"Excellent." I grinned mischievously. Regalia had no idea what was coming for her.

Power rushed through my body, my magic singing as it flowed through my veins to command the shadows. Black shadows eagerly obeyed, rushing to wrap around me, Kova, Mom, Apalla, Jamie, Thea, and Kelsey and submerge us in darkness. We melted into the shadows, and the soles of my combat boots slammed into the elegant cathedral floor.

Funny. Since I resurrected, my stomach no longer rolled with nausea when I spooked compared with the sickness I experienced with spooking for the last five years. I rolled my eyes at the angels.

Gasps rang out from the crowd gathered in the hall, profound shock at the display of power. Even the Supreme Council members looked startled that I spooked myself and six others. Clearly, they didn't know much about Kova's abilities, but something told me that was how she wanted it.

Composing herself, Regalia Kensington cleared her throat. "Ahem, Miss Black, I didn't realize you were capable of spooking. The last reports we received said your previous attempts were pathetic failures."

Brushing off the slight, I replied curtly, "Things change." I hooked my thumbs through my belt loops and rocked back on my heels.

"I see," Regalia said icily, narrowing her eyes at me. "Yet you continue to keep the company of demons," Regalia ridiculed, gesturing to the soul-blessed demons crammed into the cathedral alongside the Asylum witches and Mareena's Blairsville reinforcements.

"I am a demon."

She carried on as if I didn't speak. "After you disposed of the First Eve, I thought you would rid the world of their blight."

"I did." A smug smirk playing on my lips. The power of the Salem Witch reverberated in my voice. "I gave them souls."

There were sharp intakes of breath from the Supreme Council as their eyes widened in surprise.

I continued, pretending as though nothing had happened. "Look, it's been a long night. I'd like to hurry this along. Resurrection can really take the life out of a girl, ya know?"

Jamie snorted, but covered it with an obviously forced cough, earning him glares from the Supreme Council. Their scowls were nothing compared to the murderous look on my paternal grandmother's face.

Indignant, she abruptly rose from her seat, sending her heavy chair toppling over. "Why you little—"

"Hush, Elizabeth," Regalia scolded.

"But—"

Another glare from Regalia silenced my dad's mother.

Regalia turned back to me, a calculated look on her face rather than the fear-struck expressions of the other Council members. Pressing the tips of her fingers together, she peered over her hands at me. Her eyes flicked to Kelsey before scrutinizing my mother and returning to me. She finally asked, "You resurrected?"

"Yup," I popped the "p." "If I didn't, then I'm dead, and this is Heaven, which would really suck."

Regalia's eyes flickered to Leyla briefly, a touch of worry in them. "I didn't realize this is an ability of higher demons."

"Because it's not."

Understanding struck Regalia's face long before the rest of the Council. Her jaw dropped as she glanced between me and my mother.

"But then..." she started, unable to finish her sentence. I watched as she struggled to put it together, frantically searching for a way to rationalize how I could be the daughter of Leyla and Hunter, yet resurrect as an immortal.

Finally, she closed her mouth and asked, "Hunter isn't your father?"

"Oh, he is, but I think you meant to say *biological* father. Yeahhhh, nope." With an evil grin, I looked Elizabeth Black in the eye. "He's my uncle—well, half uncle. You see, his dad had a second child—a beautiful demoness who gave birth to me."

You would have thought I slapped Elizabeth from her horrified expression.

Mom intertwined her fingers with mine.

Regalia accepted the information in stride. "Hunter raised you in lieu of his younger sister, but he did not sire you. So, if you truly died and resurrected—"

Motioning to my neck, my voice dripped with sarcasm as I said, "Nah, I didn't die. I drenched my clothes in my own blood and painted my neck red for the effect."

"Hayden," Kova muttered a low warning.

Regalia ignored my comments and concluded, "You have a Divine parent."

"Ding, ding, ding. We have a winner," I mocked.

"Who?" she asked, ice lacing her tone.

Mom gave my hand a squeeze. I squeezed back, knowing this was her story to tell.

"Eighteen years ago, when I was barely into my adult years as a witch, the Creator approached me and asked me to conceive and birth a special child—a soul specifically chosen to undertake the task of ending my mother's reign of evil. I did not know who the father of my child would be, but I wanted Lilith to face the consequences of her sins.

And here the Creator was, choosing me to be the mother of Its Champion. So, I accepted.

"The Archangel Michael appeared to me, and we conceived a child. This child was part Heaven, part Hell. When she was born, the Heavens thundered their agreement, and the demons of the underworld trembled with fear. It was the same night Davina Michaelson was born that I placed her in my beloved brother's care and forfeited my freedom."

Every eye in the room was either on me or my mother, staring in amazement. All at once, the witches standing in the hall dropped to their knees and bowed their heads, each with a fist placed firmly over their heart. The Supreme Council didn't move, but Regalia Kensington inclined her head.

I addressed the room, "Rise, my fellow witches, and never bow to me again. I am one of you, now and forever. I am not an angel, nor am I the Creator, who is the only being to whom you should bow before. But never me."

The Council balked, steam unfurling from their ears as their faces heated with flushed rage.

Mumbling, the crowd clamored to their feet. The whispers of the witches intensified as Regalia turned to her fellow Council members, convening on the spot to discuss this revelation. Timid, uncertain looks stained the faces of some, while others wore masks of stone. But Regalia, for all her vileness, appeared pensive as the Council muttered uneasily to one another. And it was that very expression that told me she was formulating a vindictive power play.

The Council resumed their positions facing the hall of crowded witches.

Regalia cleared her throat, earning a quick silence from the witches eager to watch the aftermath of the Salem War unfold.

"Due to the revelation of recent events, the Council has agreed to keep our deliberations minimal, choosing instead to pursue swift action in the consequences of the war on the First Eve."

"Lilith," I corrected her, causing each Council member to flinch.

Regalia continued as if I hadn't spoken. "Although we suffered many casualties in the battle—"

I opened my mouth to snap at Regalia. Had she and the Council rallied the other witching communities and assembled the army of Knights we needed, we wouldn't have suffered as much. Before the words could escape my mouth, Kova's hand clamped around my forearm, stopping me.

From my peripheral, I saw her give the slightest shake of her head, a motion so slight I doubt anyone else could have seen it. But I got the message. Attacking the Council, even for a purpose so noble, wouldn't earn me, or Asylum, any favors. I would have to usurp them all at once.

Stick to the plan, Kelsey spoke telepathically. *This is our only opportunity to put Regalia in her place. If we mess this up, we lose more than just political power.*

"We are blessed that our powerfully gifted young witches were spared." Regalia swept her arms wide, gesturing to my circle. "Therefore, the Council hereby decrees that upon proof of her parentage, Hayden Black will no longer be known as such, but will be presented to the witching world as Davina Michaelson, daughter of the Warrior Archangel. Furthermore, it has come to the attention of the Supreme Council that the Asylum High Priestess has passed to the Garden, and so we elect to appoint Davina to this role. What say you, Salem Witch?"

Every eye in the room locked on me, eagerly awaiting my answer. Tension hung in the air, nervousness wafting off the Asylum witches as the Supreme Council oozed greed.

"No."

Regalia choked. "What?"

"No," I repeated.

"But the Council decided—"

"The Supreme Council doesn't decide anything for me," I roared in a thunderous tone. "I am Hayden Davina Huntleigh Nightfall Michaelson Black, and that is something the Supreme Council does *not* get to decide," I raised my voice and spoke to not just the Council, not just the Asylum witches filling the hall, but to the entire world as Apalla and Thea combined their magic to broadcast me to every witching community throughout the world.

Whirling around, I faced the green and gold magic screen that transmitted me to the rest of the witching world. "Witches of the world. I speak to you now as your Reigning Salem Witch and as the Daughter of the Warrior Archangel Michael, leader of Heaven's armies, fighter of demons, and holy force against evil, and as the daughter of the Princess of Hell, Leyla Nightfall. I am both demon and Nephilim, and today, through the Grace of the Spirit alone, I resurrected.

"The Supreme Council wishes to use the fallout of the battle against Lilith—and no, I am not afraid to say her name and neither should you, for she is human now—they wish to use our pain against us in our time of grief. They want to control me by offering me the name Davina Michaelson—a name that belongs to me by birthright. By accepting, I would become a dog to the Council. They seek to elevate me to High Priestess of Asylum—a title they cannot, by law, bestow upon me. But they've tried because they wish to control Asylum by taking away the people's right to choose their own leader."

I stood strong and tall, my shoulders thrown back and black hair blowing on an unseen breeze as magic wafted off my immortal body.

"I refuse. I refuse because I will not become a tool for the Council to rule the witching world. The choice belongs to you, and no one, not even the Supreme Council, has the right to take away your freedom.

"As the Salem Witch, I promise to be your shield against evil. I will be the guardian of humans and witches—and my demons whom I have blessed with a soul—and I will fight to defend your freedom. Because the Creator loves us, we have the gift of free will. Let no man or witch stand in the way of that."

Curling my hand into a fist, I placed it over my heart and bowed to the people I was broadcasting to, sealing my promise.

Roars of victory erupted from the Asylum witches, their cheers drowning out whatever the Supreme Council shouted at me, their faces flushed with anger as they glowered at me. But their anger was nothing compared to the joy I sparked in my people, and that joy was infectious.

I beamed at my mother and friends, all of them cheering together, hugging one another. Witches cried with a mix of grief and relief.

Turning back to the Council, I magnified my voice with the power of the Salem Witch. "I think it is time you leave."

"Go to Hell," Regalia snarled.

"Been there. Done that." I smirked. "The Devil asked me not to come back."

Snapping my fingers, my magic gathered the shadows in the hall and shaped them into a swirling portal of black, white, and silver, like the night sky filled with shining stars.

"You can go now."

Regalia and the others opened their mouths to balk.

"Unless you'd prefer I forcibly remove you?" I raised an eyebrow, daring them to argue.

Snapping their mouths closed, the Council rose from their seats to approach my portal. Hesitantly, the defeated Council took their leave, one by one, until only Regalia and Elizabeth remained.

Elizabeth glowered, but Regalia addressed Kelsey, "Granddaughter. Come, we will return to the family estate."

My head whipped around to Kelsey, concerned she would falter beneath the horror of her family, but I was proud to find the defiant courage on her face.

"No," she refused adamantly.

Regalia's jaw dropped, her nostrils flaring. "Kelsey, it was disgraceful enough that you threw yourself into battle for these ridiculous people, but this is absolutely absurd. You cannot betray your family. We are the Kensingtons. Kensingtons do not associate with—"

"With who?" Kelsey sneered, taking a forceful step forward. "People who throw themselves in front of swords for one another? People who sacrifice their lives to save billions of mortals? There is a certain person I strive to be, and if you don't like it... that's not on me."

Regalia's face remained icy, not so much as a flicker of emotion passed over it as she turned on her heel and walked through my portal, which slammed shut behind her.

We hadn't seen the last of the Supreme Council—particularly Regalia—and I would have to deal with the political minutia eventually, because Regalia would be out for my blood. But for now, I discredited the Council in the eyes of the entire witching worlds and expelled them from Asylum, and I had time to figure out how I would end Regalia's reign.

"So," Kova crossed her arms—less muscular than before Lilith captured her—over her chest, "now that they are gone, what are we doing about our Athenian Council? You know, the one in ruins."

"The Supreme Council was right about one thing—we need a new Athenian High Priestess," Apalla said, her lip quivering with emotion, but Maddox Fenske had come over while I faced the Council, and he wrapped a comforting arm around my bestie's shoulders, pulling her into him.

"And a General."

"And a new Water Representative," Naida said, appearing from nowhere, Zola gripping her arm and leaning on his cane.

Everyone's eyebrows flew into their hairlines.

"You're willingly defecting your position?" I asked in surprise, my jaw hanging open.

"Besides the fact that you stripped me of my title," Naida explained with a pained expression, "I have made many mistakes in my lifetime, none so bad as helping *her*." Remorse, like actual regret, filled her face as it fell. "I am not fit to serve as a leader of Asylum, but I want to help."

Everyone, even Kova, stared at her in shock. But my mother surprised us all by wrapping the normally ice-cold water witch in a warm, motherly hug. Tears streaked down their faces, and that's when I finally understood.

Lilith had ripped away my mom's freedom, but she did the same to Naida. If Lucifer was a master manipulator, then Lilith was unequivocally excellent in the craft. Naida, although free, had been manipulated to walk away from the Light of Grace. Perhaps for the first time, I understood Naida, because there was a time when I almost gave into my darkness.

A raspy cough rattled out of Zola as he cleared his throat. "It will soon be time to elect a new Earth Representative to the Council. I do not plan on resigning anytime soon, however, I am 'older than dirt,' as

Hayden likes to say." My face turned the color of a tomato. "Thought I didn't know, eh?" He winked. "So, Thea, any recommendations for apprentices?"

She smiled sagely as she twirled her wooden staff. "I have a few ideas growing in the soil."

"Excellent, excellent. Let us go for a stroll outside and discuss these ideas."

"Do not linger outside for too long, Grandson," Kova patted Zola on the arm. "You and I have much to discuss, too."

It was strange for a thirty-three-year-old woman to call an old man "grandson", yet it felt more natural than all the years I believed she was his granddaughter. Like my soul always knew the truth.

Soon, a familiar voice floated through my mind.

Spinning in a circle, I searched for Jamie, but he had vanished. When did that happen? And how did I not notice? My magic range extended beyond what it was before. Magnified by the full power of Spirit, stretched to every corner of the wards and found nothing.

"Go to him."

Loving lavender eyes found my own. Mom bobbed her head. "Go to him," she repeated. "You know where he is waiting for you."

Swallowing the lump in my throat, I said, "How did you—"

"A mother always knows." Her smile was bittersweet. "Even one who was kept from her daughter for nearly two decades. Call it Mother's intuition—a gift from the Goddess."

Smiling, I wrapped my mom in a hug, holding her tightly to my body, soaking in the warmth and love only a mother could give. Finally, I let her go, and she swatted my shoulder.

"Go." She shooed me with her hands. "Hurry."

Grinning, I melted into the shadows, letting my magic spirit me away.

In a flash, I re-materialized on the rocky shore of the secret lagoon—a secret lagoon that I now realized Kova knew about all along because she had created it.

Jamie stood at the edge of the shore, skipping pebbles across the surface of the water, his back to me.

CHAPTER SEVENTEEN

THE WARRIOR WITCH

Silently, I approached, not needing to alert him to my presence—I knew his magic would sense mine as surely as I sensed his. He whirled around to squint at me in the faint morning rays of sunlight.

"James," I whispered his name as I closed the space between us.

"Hayden, I—" He choked, cleared his throat, and tried again. "I miss her. Despite the victory, I miss her so much it aches. She didn't get her happy ending. I came here because I wanted to feel close to her, but... something is missing."

"Jamie." I swallowed my nerves, focusing on the love budding inside me. "Jamie, there's something I need to tell you."

"Me first."

"No," I said, placing my hands on either of his cheeks, forcing him to look me in the eye. "James Gabrielson Bishop... I love you."

He stared at me, his ocean blue eyes hooded, and then his hands were on my hips and his lips crashed into mine, and I was consumed with everlasting love. Like our first kiss, everything clicked into place, and all I could think was how we fit perfectly together... exactly as the Creator intended. And I knew with pure and piercing certainty that he and I were meant to be forever.

Only when my lungs burned from lack of oxygen did I pull back, prying myself away from him. Breathing heavily, we stared at each other, speechless, as we struggled to catch our breaths.

"I love you too, Hayden. I always have, my beautiful, breathtaking, crazy Haywire."

A smile split my face as he pressed his forehead to mine. "Since the first moment I looked into your blue eyes, I was yours, Angel Boy. Even if I didn't always know it."

The sun rose completely above the horizon, washing us in golden light.

Explosive pain ripped through the ring finger on my left hand, but it barely registered as the man before me completely consumed me. My equal in every way. Since the day we met, he challenged me to be better, pushed me beyond my limits, and he was the truest, loyalist friend I had ever known. Somewhere in my mind, I registered silver light shining from my hand and golden rays glimmering around his finger.

The pain disappeared as the light faded.

Keeping his royal blue eyes locked with my crystal blues, Jamie took my hand and raised it to his mouth. He kissed my finger, right over our soulmate glyph. Entwining our left hands, he positioned our glyphs side by side.

I gasped, awe-struck by the sight.

Our glyphs were spectacular. Silver and gold wings adorned the tops of our fingers. Neither was a single color, but a shining mixture of both, a representation of both of us. Nestled between the wings was a tiny flame of red and gold that appeared as if it were a burning fire. The element we shared. Outside the wings, a silver band wrapped around our fingers in intricate, glittering swirls.

Beaming, I looked into Jamie's eyes, dancing with love and happiness, and pulled him in for another kiss.

"Told you they'd be all lovey-dovey," said a familiar voice, startling both of us. "Look at them. We could have easily taken them both."

Jamie's eyes widened in surprise. "Harbor," he shouted his sister's name, leaping toward her. Despite her being a spirit, he wrapped her in a bear hug, nearly toppling them both.

Ethan stood beside Harbor, smiling as his soulmate embraced her twin, until I pulled him into a hug of my own. Overcoming his surprise, he squeezed me tightly.

"Thank you," I whispered so only he could hear. He squeezed harder in response, and I understood. Sometimes you don't have the words to explain.

As I released Ethan, Harbor pulled me into a bone-crushing hug. When she finally released me, I was surprised to see my mom and friends had joined us in the lagoon.

"I am not sure how I feel about our children being together," Gabriel's deep timbre boomed as he and Michael materialized next to Harbor and Ethan.

I wrinkled my nose. "Ugh, when you put it that way—aren't you two brothers?"

"Angel genetics and lineages don't work like that. Brother is a term to recognize another son of the Creator. We are completely unrelated." Harbor answered with a devious smirk.

"Thank the Creator," I exclaimed, letting out a breath.

Jamie snorted from beside me. "You did *not* think we were cousins and soulmates, did you?"

I shrugged. "Hey, there was some weird stuff back in ancient times. I didn't want to be counted amongst them."

"You're crazy, Haywire."

"I know," I said, grinning maniacally.

Michael clapped Gabriel on the shoulder. "I am not worried about Jamie's influence on my daughter, however, I am concerned for your son. Davina is a bit..."

"Sarcastic," my dad chimed in, appearing in spirit form next to Kova. "Sassy. Mischievous. Stubborn. Arrogant."

"Hey, I prefer willful."

"Temperamental," Dad continued.

Mom sauntered up, chastising Dad, "Now, now brother, I think temperamental isn't strong enough of a word. Something more like hot-headed or—"

"Right here, guys. Right here." I rolled my eyes at the siblings. "And careful, Mom, whatever word he uses to describe me, describes you, too. My temper comes from your side of the family."

Mom threw back her head and laughed, really laughed. It was the first time I had heard the sound, and it was nothing short of magical.

Michael smirked. "I was going to say you're trouble."

My friends burst out in laughter. Kova cried from how hard she laughed while Dani and Damien leaned on each other for support, and Palla doubled over at her waist as Maddow held her upright. Thea laughed in the melodious tune only the Heart of Earth could make. Harlan just wagged his eyebrows at Jamie like the surfer boy he was.

My grin broadened, and I shrugged my shoulders. "I still say trouble finds me."

Jamie beamed at me like rays of sunshine, and I couldn't help the smile splitting my face as I stared into his ocean blue eyes. His arm snaked around my hips and pulled me into him. Our bodies fit perfectly together.

"I love you, Haywire," he whispered, then pressed a kiss to my forehead.

"I love you, Angel Boy," I whispered back.

"Ugh, Dad, they're doing it again. Make them stop," Harbor mock complained, but couldn't keep her face straight as she smiled and sashayed to her father.

Gabriel rolled his uncanny blue eyes with the white pupil. "I seem to recall you were the one face-palming as you watched their first kiss from beyond the grave, dear Daughter."

"You watched that?" Jamie shouted accusingly at his sister as I snorted.

"Oh, totally." Harbor grinned wickedly, making me laugh harder as Jamie's face reddened. "Way to fumble, twin. If I were Hayden, I'd refuse to date you, even if you are soulmates."

"What happened with their first kiss?" Harlan asked, his eyebrows knitting together in confusion.

"Oh, he kissed me, then spooked away." I bumped my hip into Angel Boy, sharing a smug grin with Harbor.

Harlan stared at his cousin for a heartbeat, then threw his hands in the air as he shouted, "You ghosted her? You finally kissed the girl you've been in love with since you laid eyes on her, and you GHOSTED her?"

Harbor and I could barely contain our laughter as Jamie hung his face in shame while his cousin berated him for being... well, a dumb boy.

Kelsey flickered her platinum blonde hair over her shoulder, hiking out a hip. "Now that you're caught up on drama from, like, a year ago, Harlan, I have more questions."

My eye caught Apalla's as we suppressed our grins. Leave it to Kelsey to have a list of demands.

"Is it just me, or is anybody else confused as to how two angels and three dead people—no offense—are just chilling here?"

Murmured agreements filled the air as the others echoed Kelsey's question, except the immortals, who always knew more than they shared.

Although I was one of those immortals now. Thank the Creator that I was in the know for once.

Gabriel's mighty laughter filled the air. "Ah, yes, Alice has yet to explain."

Kova groaned. "Gabe, how many times do I have to tell you? Call me Kova. Nobody has called me Alice in over three hundred years."

Dad, who had wrapped both arms around Kova, frowned at her. "Oh, I didn't know I had changed my name to 'Nobody'."

"No, I didn't mean you, I—ugh... know what, forget it." She threw her arms in the air in exasperation, then leaned into his embrace despite standing five inches taller than him.

Gabriel chuckled. "You will always be known as Alice to the angels, Little Bull. Uriel would be most upset if you denied the name given to you at birth. She is rather fond of her mortal daughter."

Kova smiled sheepishly at the mention of her mother, a slight pink tinge to her cheeks.

Little Bull. I laughed to myself. Lucifer had called me Little Warrior. It seemed Luci still thought like an angel sometimes.

"Lucifer was not the first to call you Little Warrior, Hayden. Your father called you that from the moment you were conceived."

"Hold up." I raised a flat palm, glancing between Michael and Gabriel. "Michael, I love the nickname. But Gabriel, how is it you always seem to read my mind?"

Gabriel smiled a dazzling smile as he crossed his arms over his chest smugly. "As the Messenger, I am the only telepathic archangel."

I gawked at him. All those times it seemed like he could read my mind... because he literally did.

Harbor bumped her arm against her father's. "Why do you think Jamie and I had twin telepathy? Special powers courtesy of our sire."

"Now that's just sneaky," I accused, eliciting an eye roll from Gabriel.

"As I was saying," Gabriel continued. "As the daughter of Michael, Hayden can summon him whenever she pleases. Granted, he may not appear right away, but we will always use the excuse to see our children."

Jamie choked. "Wait, we can do that?" He turned to Harbor. "Why didn't we ever do that?"

"Because you do not have this power until you turn seventeen," Gabriel explained. "Being exposed to too much angelic energy would alter your development and you would find yourself longing for the Garden. But, at seventeen, the age of maturity for witches, you are accustomed to your life in the mortal realm and do not desire the Garden any more than any other witch or human."

"Actually, you will," Kova sighed. "But Nephilim always long for Home more than any other being. But after seventeen, you won't be tempted to follow the angels to the Garden."

"Oh, but now that I'm seventeen..." he trailed off, looking to his father.

Gabriel smiled brightly. "You may call on me whenever you wish."

Jamie beamed at his father.

"Especially since you are a Resurrected Nephilim."

Jamie looked like the angel had slapped him. "What?" he said the word breathlessly look, a mix of horror and disbelief on his face. He glanced at me before asking his father, "Did you just say I'm a Resurrected Nephilim?"

Gabriel pressed his lips into a tight line and nodded once. "You are."

"But how? When? I mean... I don't remember."

Harbor glided over to wrap an arm around her twin.

"When you were a year old, Lilith killed you in your sleep. She was going to kill Harbor, too"—Gabriel cast a regretful stare at his daughter—"which is why Harbor had to be the one to use her Glory.

When you resurrected, Lilith realized killing Harbor would be futile and would cause another immortal Nephilim to roam the realm."

"But I... I came back?"

"Your soulmate was here," Michael rumbled, his eyes glancing between me and Jamie. "As a soul, you chose to return, knowing she would do the same for you. And while Davina had many reasons for returning, I believe knowing her soulmate was waiting to spend eternity helped her leave the Garden behind. You had my blessing from that day forward."

"Oh my goodness," I said as the realization hit me. "You blessed Jamie... because you knew he is my soulmate..." I trailed off, staring at my sire with wide eyes.

Michael grunted. "It is a man's highest calling to protect his woman. While you are plenty capable, Davina, I blessed Jamie so he could be your match—an equal consort to the Warrior Witch."

Jamie leaned against me, letting me support his body weight. "I died... I died and came back to life..." His gaze landed on me, the strife in his ocean blue eyes settling as he drank me in. "Because of you, Haywire. I chose you." He pressed his forehead to mine, inhaling deeply, like he was trying to memorize my scent.

"And I came back for you. Salem Witch or not, I will *always* choose you, Angel Boy."

"It is ironic that Jamie has my blessing and may call upon me, just as Hayden, like Alice, can call upon Gabriel."

"Wait, what?" Jamie and I asked at the same time.

"As fully realized Salem Witches, regardless of your birthrights, you and Alice have the power to call upon the Messenger Archangel," Hunter explained.

Gabriel glared at Kova, shaking his finger at her. "But I swear to the Creator, the next time you summon me seventeen times in a row, I will *smite* you." He spun, jabbing an aggressive finger at me. "That warning goes for you as well, young lady."

I threw my hands up in surrender. "Whoa, hey now, I didn't summon you seventeen times. And I don't think anyone in the history of the world has called me a lady." I smirked at Gabriel, earning an eye roll for my sass. I raised an eyebrow at Kova. "When did you summon him seventeen times?"

She shrugged, shoving her hands into her jean pockets. "When you first arrived in Asylum, I begged him to let me tell you my true identity. Clearly, it did not go well."

"Okay, but can someone answer my question?" Kelsey snapped her fingers to get our attention.

My piercing blue gaze caught Apalla's, and I smashed my lips together to keep from laughing as we shared another look.

"That would be my doing," Michael announced, crossing his arms over his chest. "Angels can help spirits cross the veil at times other than Samhain. It is also a gift bestowed on the Salem Witch after they master Spirit."

"Yes, but it's a power I do not want to abuse, so I rarely mess with it," Kova added, shooting me a warning look.

For once, I agreed with Kova on something without feeling the need to rebel because it sounded fun.

"Just because I can, doesn't mean I should," I said, meeting Kova's ancient green gaze. "Summoning the dead doesn't help us to move forward with our lives and coming to Earth disrupts their peace. Using this power lends us to the delusion that we control Death."

"You don't?" Damien asked.

"No, I can't raise anyone from the dead."

"Uh, am I the only one who thinks that's a load of crap, considering you just resurrected?" Kelsey pointed a finger at me.

"Davina resurrected, but the power does not belong to her," Michael's deep voice rumbled, and I knew I would never get sick of hearing my sire's voice, because I would never have enough time with him since we were immortals doomed to different realms.

Agreeing with my sire, I explained, "Resurrection belongs solely to the Creator. It is only through the Spirit that I returned to Earth. But it came at a cost."

Kelsey's jaw dropped open, and she squeaked, "Oh."

"Immortal life comes at a price," Kova agreed solemnly. "We can never die because we are cursed to wander the mortal realm for eternity, and so, our souls can't return Home to rest. Fair warning, kid, it's lonely being more powerful than anyone you know."

"Conquered death but can never die."

Harlan stared at me inquisitively. "But then, how did you create a soul for Lilith and your demons?"

"That was a clever idea of the Goddess when She made Davina's soul." Mom grinned wickedly, fire dancing in her eyes. "The Creator asked me to carry and bear a child with a dual nature, a soul in complete harmony with Heaven and Hell. When I agreed, the Creator used part of my soul and merged it with part of Michael's to form Davina. Davina's soul was then placed inside my womb."

"Lilith may be a wicked, manipulative genius, but for all her gifts, she can never overcome the Throne of Grace. The Creator is wise beyond our comprehension," Gabriel remarked. "Davina was created specifically for the purpose of defeating Lilith, with the intent for her to reach into Hell and grab hold of Lilith's soul to reunite it with her body."

Hayden Davina Huntleigh Nightfall Michaelson Black—boy, all six names would take some getting used to.

"But the Creator, with infinite wisdom and love, gave Davina the choice. She was not forced to come to Earth either time, but she chose to follow the path the Creator laid before her. Without her choices, none of this would have come to pass." Michael added, pride infusing his tone as he patted me on the shoulder.

"This is what I was created for. And I chose it for myself," I said, meeting my father's piercing blue eyes with my matching ones. "We always have a choice. And it is the decisions we make with our free will that matter more than our abilities." I turned to Gabriel. "I didn't understand it at the time—well, maybe somewhere deep within my soul, I did—but I do now. My Trials weren't about how adept I was with magic."

Gabriel shook his head, a sly smile pulling at his lips.

"It was about the decisions I was confronted with, and my choices decided which path I walked. All those decisions led to my resurrection, and only then did the Creator grant me the power to create souls." I turned to my friends, splaying my hands and summoning the power of Spirit as black lightning to crackle between my palms. "The power isn't mine. I'm merely a vessel through which Spirit flows."

Michael rested both hands on my shoulders, towering over me with his massive frame, and it finally hit me why I was so much taller than my mother. "My dearest Davina, I could not have asked the Creator for a better daughter."

"Even when I make mistakes? Because I'm definitely going to make a lot more mistakes in my life." I grimaced. An endless life. Full of endless mistakes. Yeesh.

"Especially when you make mistakes," Michael emphasized, brushing a lock of black hair behind my ear, then cupping my cheek. "The Creator uses the seemingly weak and unexpected to build Its Kingdom. You, a lonely child raised in the human world, a world to which you never belonged, were thrust into a world that you were supposed to fit into. And from your first day here, you were different because you were destined for greatness. And then you discovered the truth of your demonic heritage, which makes you altogether unique from any other witch.

"The Creator took the most unexpected being, and turned her into the Salem Witch, the most powerful Salem Witch in the history of mortals, to raise the Kingdom of the Creator here on Earth. Who would have thought to do such a thing other than our Divine Mother and Father?"

Tears burned my eyes as I threw myself at my sire, wrapping my arms tightly around his middle and squeezing as my feet lifted off the ground. "I love you, Dad."

"I love you too, my Little Warrior." He hugged me back with the ferocity of the Warrior Archangel in the best hug I had ever received from him. Not that there were many, but as he squeezed me back, I sensed how proud he was of his daughter and the sacrifice she made to save humanity. As he pulled away, his piercing blue eyes simultaneously filled with joy and sorrow, and I knew.

"You have to go, don't you?"

"We do. But I am always with you, Davina, even when you cannot see me or hear me. You might not feel me, but like the Creator, I will never leave you."

"I know," I choked out through the thickness clogging my throat. "I just wish I had known it was your voice sooner. It wouldn't have changed anything, but it would have been nice to know it was your voice."

"You will know me for all of eternity." Michael patted my cheek and stepped away so I could face the man who raised me as he stepped away from his soulmate. Closing the space between us, I embraced him like I never had before. He hugged me back tightly, the hug of a father saying goodbye to his daughter for the last time.

"I love you, Dad," I sobbed into his shoulder.

"I love you too, Hayden." He kissed the top of my head. "Raising you was the gift of a lifetime, and I cannot wait to come back and see everything you will have accomplished."

Pulling away from him, I stared. My face broke into a grin as I asked, "You're being reincarnated?"

"I am." His smile was bittersweet. Glancing at Kova over his shoulder, he said, "Maybe this time we can get it right."

Kova's smile was bittersweet as she said, "And if we don't, I will wait for you time and time again until we do." Dad strode back to her and, grabbing both of her cheeks, dragged her lips to his and kissed her like he was dying.

Jamie pressed his chest into my back as his arms wrapped around me, and he whispered in my ear, "Is it just me, or is it a little weird to see your dad making out with Kova?"

Leaning into him, I whispered, "Mega weird."

Dad finally released Kova, whose face looked like a tomato. But the rest of us grinned so broadly our cheeks hurt. They didn't have their happy ending. Yet. We weren't going to deny them what little time they had together.

They whispered something to each other, but we couldn't hear, or maybe we chose not to for the sake of their privacy, letting them have one more moment of this lifetime together.

Tears rolled down Kova's cheeks as Dad pulled away from her, reluctantly releasing his soulmate so he could wrap Leyla in a brotherly hug. They exchanged a few words, and tears streamed down their cheeks as they embraced.

"Even though we won't be related by blood, you will always be my baby sister."

"And you will always be my big brother. I cannot thank you enough for what you sacrificed for me and my daughter."

"I would do it all again. And when I regain my memories in my next life, we will be a family again."

Turning his back on his baby sister, Dad approached Jamie. He offered his left hand to Jamie in the traditional witch handshake. "Look after my daughter."

Jamie slipped his hand past Dad's to grip his wrist. "Yes, sir," he said, ever the dutiful soldier.

Smiling, my dad shook his head. "Who knew all those years I spent training you and you would end up as my son-in-law?" He shook his head again. "The Creator certainly has a sense of humor. But I couldn't have picked a better man to be my daughter's soulmate."

"Thank you, Dad. For everything, but especially for loving me like your own. You'll always be my dad. Even seventeen years from now, I don't think anything will change."

He kissed me on the forehead. "You'll be my daughter, now and forever."

Hunter turned to the angels, who stood on either side of a gorgeous woman with blood red eyes and translucent skin. Amara opened her arms as Dad walked into her embrace without hesitation. There was a blinding flash of white light, and they both disappeared.

Harbor's hand fell on my shoulder, a mix of joy and sorrow twisting her beautiful face. "It's time for us to go as well." She gestured to herself and Ethan, who smiled contently as he held her hand in his own.

Jamie sighed, and I felt his pain echo in my heart.

"I miss you so much, Harbor."

"And I miss you, James, the way an Ocean misses waves."

"Will we see you again?" I asked, knowing my soulmate struggled to get out the words.

"Oh, we will reincarnate. Just not right away." Harbor smiled wickedly as she winked at us. "I know who I want to be reborn as, though, not until you two are ready."

The blood drained from Jamie's face. I threw my head back and roared with laughter.

"It better be a while before that happens," Michael growled in warning from where he stood next to Gabriel, his arms crossed as he glowered at Jamie.

Jamie jumped away from me, throwing his hands up. "I didn't touch her."

Harbor and I burst into manic laughter, and Kova fell to the ground from laughing so hard. Apalla shot me a conspiratory grin, waggling her eyebrows. Poor Jamie, having to put up with our psycho butts for the rest of eternity.

Michael glared at Jamie as Gabriel grimaced. Shaking his head, the Messenger Archangel said, "You two are a match made in Hell."

I grinned wickedly. "That's the irony. It would be so much worse if Angel Boy was part demon, too."

Harbor pulled me into one last embrace, and as she pulled away, she said, "Summon us on Samhain. It will be less painful for us to leave the Garden when the veil is thin."

"I guess we can consider it a family holiday."

Harbor smiled, then embraced her brother. "Goodbye, brother. I love you with all my heart and my soul. I will always watch over you."

Smiling, Ethan took Harbor's hand and approached Gabriel. As Harbor walked into her father's arms, a brilliant white light flashed, and they disappeared.

"It is time for us to be on our way," Michael announced. Inclining his head toward my mom, he said, "Leyla, thank you for the sacrifices you've made for our daughter. I could not have asked the Creator to choose a more worthy mother for my child. You will forever have my gratitude."

Mom beamed at his praise. "I think we made a spectacular daughter, Michael."

With a smirk, my father warned me, "Stay out of trouble, Davina."

"Oh, I most definitely won't," I said, earning a strained groan from the angel.

Gabriel frowned at me. "I am more worried about your antics than I am about my own son's behavior."

Jamie rolled his eyes. "Because I'm a straight-laced guy. It's her who pulls me into trouble."

I shrugged. "I plead the fifth."

"Are you not worried about that?" Gabriel asked Michael.

"Since the day she was created." Laughter rumbled in Michael's chest. "But my daughter is more than capable of holding her own. Especially when she has a certain familiar to guide her."

"What?" I asked, confusion twisting my face.

White light flashed from his palm, and the most heart melting little Yellow Labrador puppy appeared in his hand, sound asleep. Salem, reborn as a tiny puppy, was curled up in my father's massive palm. He gently tipped her into my arms, and I cradled her like a baby.

"An immortal familiar for an immortal witch," my warrior father said softly.

I gasped. "Really?" Tears of joy stung my eyes.

He winked at me and in a flash of white light, the two angels vanished.

"You know," Kova started, studying the spot where the angels disappeared. "Sometimes I wonder if you get your wildness from Michael instead of Leyla."

Mom smiled cheekily as she popped out a hip. "Oh, I know she does."

"And that's who I get my sass from."

Snorting, Kova shook her head and ran a hand through her spiky red hair. "In other news," Kova said. "We have a new High Priestess."

My head snapped up. "We do? Who?"

Apalla beamed a golden smile brighter than the sun. "Me."

My jaw dropped. "You're kidding me." I squealed and jumped forward, pulling her into a hug with one arm while I cradled Salem in the other.

"The whole town voted, except you two, and it was unanimous." Kelsey smugly declared, "I was the one who nominated her."

"Okay, now you guys are just messing with us," Jamie said.

"Nope, she actually did, much to the surprise of everyone in Asylum," Damien confirmed.

"And she nominated Damien as our new Air Representative." Harlan threw his arm around Damien's shoulders. "And he's already been sworn in."

"Yeah." Damien laughed uncomfortably, wiping fake tears from his eyes. "This town is soooo screwed. Why on earth people think I would be a good leader, I'll never know."

"Maybe because I forced you to be in charge during the war." I pulled him into a hug. "You'll make a great leader on the Council."

"This is the youngest Athenian Council in the history of Asylum. There's a lot of work ahead of you." Kova ran a hand through her spiky red hair and blew out a haggard breath. "Meaning there's a lot of work for *me*. Ugh, the joys of being immortal in this town."

"Especially since Harlan is Zola's new apprentice. It won't be long before he assumes the position," Thea added, causing Harlan to blush.

"Because of your recommendation." He gently elbowed Thea, smiling at the child goddess.

"I recommend the worthy," she stated matter-of-factly.

"Congrats, man." Jamie offered his left hand to Harlan, then they did one of those weird bro hugs and slapped each other on the back.

"Congrats, Harlan. I couldn't think of a better guy to sit on the Council." I smiled at him. "But what about the Water Representative?"

"Aunt Bridget." Harlan smiled conspiratorially.

"Wait, what?" Jamie asked, incredulous.

"Yeah, she was sick of the ambassador role, so when someone nominated her and she was elected, she accepted the gig. But now we need a new ambassador."

"What about you, Hayden?" Apalla asked. "Who better than the Salem Witch to be the ambassador between Asylum and the rest of the witching world?"

I shared a look with Jamie, communicating almost telepathically, or as close to it as soulmates could get. After all, the connection between our souls was eternal.

"Honestly, I don't think I'm right for the job. Not right now. The last five years have been enough of a whirlwind. I don't want any leadership responsibility for a long time."

"Traveling the world will keep you too busy to be a leader," Jamie added. "Don't forget, we made a pact."

I beamed at my soulmate for remembering the deal we made all those years ago at my house in the human town of Salem. "How could I forget that you promised to travel the world with me and show me every fire festival?"

Kelsey yacked. "Ew, the two of you are kinda nauseating."

All I could do was laugh. The weight of the world was off my shoulders, and for the first time in five years, I could plan a future with the love of my life.

"How about you, Kelsey? I think you'd make an excellent ambassador."

Kelsey's eyes bugged out. "You think so?" she asked, her eyes sparkling with pride.

I nodded.

"I mean, yeah," she tripped over her words. "I'd love to. It's not like I have a home or a family to go back to."

"That's not true," I countered with a smile. "You have us. We're your family now."

Kelsey gulped and looked at Apalla. "Even you?"

Apalla smiled. "Even me."

With a kind smile, she said, "I'd love to, but I need to make it work with my class schedule."

"Uh, Kels, didn't you graduate the Spellery?" Damien pointed out.

"Yeah, but I'm enrolled at the University of Carthage in the human city for the fall semester."

I choked as I laughed at the look on everyone's faces.

"*You*," Dani, who had been standing silently next to Damien, emphasized the word by flamboyantly thrusting her finger at Kelsey, "are going to a *human* university to learn *human* subjects?"

Kelsey sneered. "Yes. Why is that so hard for everyone to believe?"

"Um, maybe because it is widely known that you despise humans," Dani pointed out.

"I do not," Kelsey snapped, then her anger deflated. "Yeah, okay, I did at one point, but hello, people. I'm good now."

She rolled her eyes as she slapped her hands on her hips, and I had to cough to cover my laugh.

"Mom," I turned toward her. "Now that you're free, do you have any plans?"

She smiled up at me. It was strange to tower over my mom. "My plans are to get to know my daughter. I have seventeen years to make up for."

"Good, because I have a room waiting for you in the home you and Dad built for me," I said, fighting the tears welling in my eyes at the thought of living with my mom for the first time in our lives.

Tears welled in her lavender eyes as Mom choked on a sob. "You have no idea how good it is to hear that I am free to live with my daughter."

"Oh, I think I have an idea." I knew exactly how it felt, knowing I could finally get to know the mother who had given everything to me.

"Kova, this is the second Salem War you've lived through. What are you going to do now?"

Kova massaged her jaw with a hand. "Oh, I don't have any plans, at least not for another seventeen years. I'll keep serving on the Council and do what I've always done."

Jamie and I shared a look.

"Well, if you want to join us in our travels, you're always welcome." Jamie said.

"All of you are," I announced. "Thea, will you join us?"

"I like the sound of that," she admitted. "Though I will return to Africa with Silas for a while to say hello to my family. Perhaps I will join you on your travels or return to Asylum."

"So, that's it?" Dani asked in dismay. "The most epic circle in history is breaking up and going your separate ways?" She sounded disappointed.

"Not at all," Apalla said, her eyes flashing gold. "This is a temporary vacation."

"I was about to say that." I frowned at her. "But since your eyes flashed gold, I'm concerned why you said it."

She smirked at me. "You know I can't tell you about my vision. Some prophecies are better left untold."

"Great," Jamie muttered. "That definitely means it involves us."

With a fake exasperated sigh, I smiled. "At the very least, we have another adventure to look forward to."

"But we're missing a water elemental," Jamie reminded me. "And I sincerely hope Harbor doesn't come along anytime soon, because can you imagine her as part demon? My life is going to be absolute chaos between the two of you."

"You love it, and you know it," I grinned wickedly at him before turning to Dani, giving her a once over. "But I was thinking you might want the position after you graduate the Spellery."

Dani gasped excitedly, her brown eyes growing wide as saucers. "Really?"

Damien gawked. "Girl, you can't be serious."

"As a heart attack."

"But she's just a kid," he argued. "She's not Nephilim or a Prophetess or anything special."

"Hey," Dani whined, shooting him a nasty glare.

"And that's exactly why I've picked her." I placed my free hand on Dani's shoulder, stained with black blood. "Dani, you stood up to Elliot when nobody else would. At fifteen years old, you had the courage to stand against the evilest being in the world—something grown adults have failed to do. If the Trials have taught me anything, it's that it doesn't matter what you were born as because it is your choices that show who you truly are. It's not about power, it's about who you are as a person, and you are exactly the kind of person I want in my circle."

Dani lit up like a firework at my praise. "Two years? You can wait that long?"

Apalla nodded her head, a small smile on her lips even as Spirit whispered Its knowledge in my head.

"Absolutely."

"Aw, heck to the no," Damien said, shaking his head. "What is it that you two know that we don't know?" He wagged a finger at us.

"Some prophecies are better left untold," Apalla said cryptically.

"What?" Damien's voice escalated several octaves. "That's not concerning at all."

Apalla shrugged, unconcerned. "I wouldn't worry."

"What about Elliot?" Kelsey asked. "The Red Demon took him after the battle. Are you going to track him down?"

Jamie and I shared a smile.

"No. As much as we would like to, it's not our path," Jamie added with a grumble, "Plus, someone made a Devil's Bargain with Lucifer to not kill Elliot."

I told him and my circle about the Bargain before I faced Lilith, since I had to explain why I didn't kill Elliot after he killed Isleen.

"I promised I wouldn't personally kill him. Doesn't mean I can't help. Sins of the flesh seem trivial to the virtues of the soul, don't they?" I winked at Dani. "You'd be amazed by the things Spirit whispers to me. Air blows, fire glows, water flows, earth grows, but Spirit knows all things, for it is the keeper of the mysteries of the Universe. The Apokalypsis war isn't for another three years, so I have three years of freedom."

"The WHAT?" Damien, Dani, Harlan, and Kelsey shouted simultaneously.

"Oh, nothing major. You'll find out soon enough." I winked mischievously at them.

"Oh, sure, I can't share my visions with people, but Hayden can just go around telling people whatever she wants." Apalla threw her hands in the air as she shouted at the sky, probably at Apollo. But she winked a hazel eye at me. "I'm not sure how I feel about you always being in the know."

Oh, it was *so* dangerous for Heaven to pair us together now that I heard the whispers of Spirit.

"For the first time in a long time, I don't have a path to follow. Heaven hasn't given me a course to set out on." I couldn't help my smile, especially when I looked into Jamie's ocean blue eyes. "After we gallivant across the world, I want to come home and study practical magic at the Spellery."

"Girl," Damien said sassily. "What is wrong with you? You're the Salem Witch. You have all the magic in the world. Why do you need to learn practical magic?"

I grinned at him as I stroked Salem's tiny head. "Need and want are two very different things, my friend."

"What about after that?" Jamie asked me.

"I don't know, but then again, do I have to?" He smiled like an angel, and my heart melted. "But until we're needed in the next war, I want us to decide what we do next, together."

He pressed his forehead to mine. "You and me, we're a forever kind of thing. When comes to soulmates, even death can't do us part."

"Ugh," Harlan groaned. "After years of us trying to get you two together, I'm kinda disgusted that you two are together."

"Even for me, this is a little too in love." Damien fake flipped his hair over his shoulder. "Seriously, how long is the honeymoon stage going to last?"

"For as long as it annoys you guys."

"Consider it payback for the years of embarrassment you caused us," Jamie said, shooting me a conspiratorial grin.

Creator, I loved my soulmate.

Apalla's eyes flashed gold as she turned on her heel to leave the lagoon. "Hey, I called it years ago. I knew it would happen."

"Girl, I didn't need to be a Prophetess to see that. It was a matter of *when*, not *if*."

Dani frowned, skipping after her brother. "Wait, I didn't see it. How did I miss it?"

Harland ruffled Dani's hair as he escorted Thea out of the lagoon. "Probably because you were too busy idolizing Hayden, kid."

"Do not worry, Dani. I did not pay much attention to their love lives either. But yes, I knew they were in love," Thea said in her regally melodious voice.

Kelsey snorted and flared her hands in front of her. "A blind person could see they were in love. They were the only idiots who refused to admit it."

That brought a smile to Kova's lips. "And yet, love always finds a way to reveal itself, even to those who try so adamantly to deny it."

"Did you and my dad deny it? In his first lifetime, I mean."

"No." Kova ran a hand through her spiky red hair and down her shoulder, as if she could feel the long locks she once had. "Even as children, we felt the bond, and we did not resist the pull. But each love story is unique, and sometimes you just have to let the soulmates work it out for themselves, because look at you two now... in love for eternity."

"What about you?" I asked, my voice straining with emotion. "What about your love story?" I didn't vocalize it, but Kova knew I was referring to the endless cycle of reincarnation my father was doomed to repeat.

Kova smiled bitterly as two butterflies danced around her head. "True love stories have no endings," she said with a wink, then disappeared in a flash of dark green light, leaving me and Jamie alone in the lagoon.

He let out an exasperated sigh and ran his fingers through his golden blond hair. "Are we really going to live forever?" he asked. "We can never enter the Garden?"

"Oh, I don't know about that." I smiled knowingly, earning a confused look from my Angel Boy. "Death happens to be an old friend. I think when we are good and ready and no longer have a purpose to serve here, she might just make an exception."

Jamie took me by the hand and pulled me into him. His blue eyes sparkled as he stared into my own. "As long as we go together."

"Not a chance in Heaven I would go without you. You're my home, Angel Boy. Without you, the Garden wouldn't be Heaven."

Leaning into me, Jamie grabbed my chin and tilted it up for my lips to press against his. It was a simple, chaste kiss, not full of passion and strife like the others, but full of unconditional, everlasting love. It was the kiss of a soulmate, and as we pulled away, eternal joy settled in my heart because I knew I would feel his love every day for the rest of my immortal life.

"You hungry, Angel Boy?"

"Starving, Haywire."

"Good, because I could go for some waffles and a breakfast burrito."

Jamie snorted, shaking his head. "I'm going to have to put up with your disgusting eating habits for the rest of eternity, aren't I?"

"Hmm," I hummed. I pushed to my tiptoes and brushed a quick kiss to his lips. "Probably. But you have an eternity to try to change that."

Grinning my signature wicked smirk, I summoned the power of Spirit to spook us to the Spellery's dining hall.

And all was as the Creator intended.

Read Alice Parker's Historical Fantasy in the Prequel Novella: The Salem Witch

Read it on Amazon today!

Prequel Novella: The Salem Witch

Magic is forbidden.

Ten-year-old Alice Corey is the Nephilim daughter of Uriel, the Archangel of Earth. The blood of angels runs through her veins, making her the strongest witch in the world. But in 1692 Salem, Massachusetts, being a witch is a death sentence.

As mortals are burned at the stake in Europe, paranoia heightens in the New World. But in a time when magic is a curse, Alice is chosen by Heaven as the next Salem Witch, destined to protect the world from evil... if she can survive the deadly Salem Witch Trials.

If she doesn't master all five elements—air, fire, water, earth, and Spirit—before her seventeenth birthday, she forfeits her life. To make matters more complicated, Alice falls for John Parker, the only person who knows her secret identity.

As Salem falls victim to the witch hunts, Alice discovers Judge Hathorne is hiding a treacherous secret. When Alice is accused of witchcraft, she must choose between her life and the fate of the world.

Will Alice master her magic and save her town? Or will she perish in the Salem Witch Trials?

The Salem Witch is the prequel novella to an urban fantasy series, Hayden Black and the Salem Witch Trials, intended for readers ages ten and above who love Percy Jackson and Avatar: The Last Airbender.

Help Me Out

Thank you for reading Hayden Black and the Salem Witch Trials: Book Five! Before you continue read the companion novels to Hayden's series, please consider leaving a review for The Warrior Witch.

Scan this QR code to leave a review:

Sign Up For My Author Newsletter

Subscribe to my newsletter to receive book updates and exclusive bonus content, including a free short story from Jamie's perspective of Hayden's disastrous arrival.

Jamie Bishop is bored. Bored with school.
Bored with training. Bored with Asylum.

But adventure is coming...

Or scan the QR code to read on Amazon today!

About The Author
B. C. Taylor

Click here to view a full list of B. C. Taylor's published and upcoming novels.

Visit her on the web at:

Website: https://www.brooklynctaylor.com
Instagram: https://www.instagram.com/brooklyn_tay
Goodreads:
https://www.goodreads.com/user/show/155122248-brooklyn-taylor
Pinterest: https://www.pinterest.com/brooklyn_tay7/
Facebook Page:
https://www.facebook.com/profile.php?id=100084524515084

B. C. Taylor grew up in small town Salem, Wisconsin, alongside her loyal yellow Labrador, Salem. Her passion for witches and magic sparked at a young age, as did her love for reading and world mythology. Since the fifth grade, B. C. Taylor wanted to be a writer, but being a total nerd, her equal passions for science and math drove her to study engineering at the University of Wisconsin—Madison. Soon after graduating, she began writing stories again, and Hayden Black consumed every spare moment of her time. When she's not writing or designing cars at her day job, B. C. Taylor can be found swimming, paddle boarding, or keeping her boxing skills sharp.

She invites readers to get first looks, exclusive content, and more by subscribing to her newsletter:

Acknowledgements

Wow, has it been a journey! After two years of writing and publishing nonstop, and several other years dedicated to writing the first book of this series, the finale is here! Hayden's story has been an absolute joy for me to write, and as much as Hayden grew up throughout the books, so did I. Hayden Black changed my life in so many ways, and I am forever grateful to the Lord, who blessed me with the desire and drive to write.

To fans of the Hayden Black series—thank you! Thank you for loving these characters as much as I do and for being so excited for the next installment every time you finish a book. It is such a joy to hear from fans who tell me how much they love the books, and I am so proud to have such an impact on the lives of children and adults. I pray that Hayden Black will continue to inspire people of all ages to continue to read and even to write their own books someday!

Thank you to the friends and family who have supported me along the way and were on the receiving end of a million texts about how many words I had written each day. Thank you for putting up with me—I love you guys.

To my Lord and Savior, Jesus Christ—thank you for choosing me time and time again, and for changing my life irrevocably. I wouldn't be the woman of God that I am today without your love, and I am eternally grateful to be a Daughter of Heaven.

To Michael—thank you for bringing me to God... even if you never even intended to. But the greatest act of love and bringing someone closer to the Lord.

To my mom—I love you. This one's for you.

www.ingramcontent.com/pod-product-compliance
Lightning Source LLC
Chambersburg PA
CBHW020459310726
48979CB00016B/2722/J
9781959090311